THE WESTERN REACH

GLACIAL SEA

THE MORTAL COAST

FROZEN FJORDS

NORTH PLAIN

CASTILE

ARTERA RIVER

GRIM SEA

CHALK CLIFFS

CALSA FLATS

CALSA RIVER

LAKE CASPIA

THE CATACO...

SOUTH PLAIN

SQUALL COVE

SKELAT FORMATIONS

BALKAN BADLANDS

SOUTH CASPIA

THE CITADEL

SIN... BAS...

CHADRON

SHALE SETTLEMENT

SALTED SHOR...

JIDANA

GLEAMING SEA

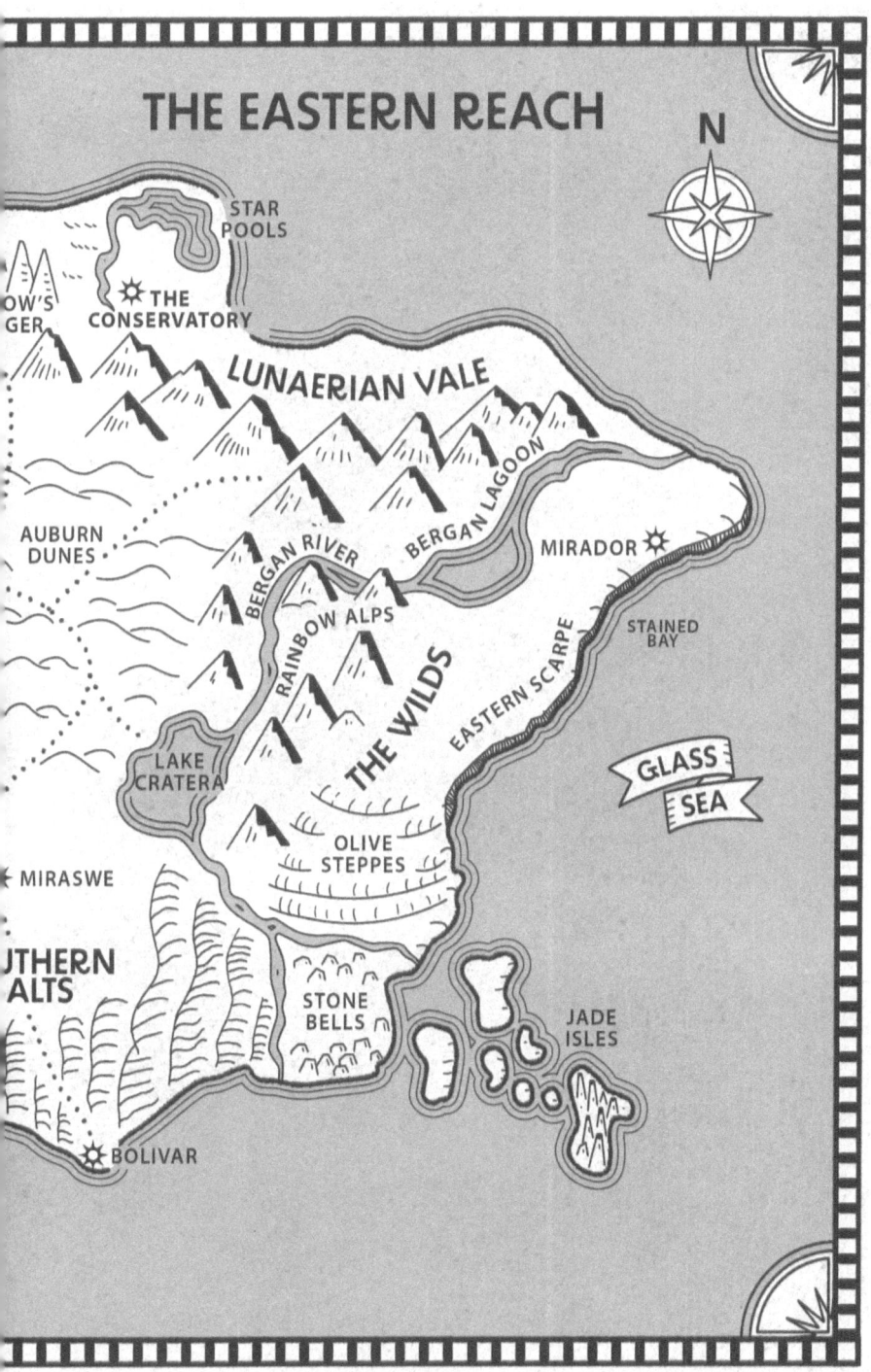

KINGDOM OF TIME

An Heir of Ever Novel

LUZ EVAN
KANIN

Cover design by INKfluence
Cover copyright © 2025 by Dark Star Books
Map creation by Yopi Kwb
End page design by Amy Frerichs
Interior Artwork and typesetting by Niokoba
Author photograph by Bella Photography

ISBN: 979-8-9933199-0-2 (trade paperback)

First Edition: November 2025

Printed in the United States of America

For all the tight-lipped girlies and their mouths
full of fangs.

THE CURSE

In our eternities, our monotonous, never-ending eternities, we are permitted only one true Parallel. It is not a rule set by our Elders or The Senate, neither have any authority in matters so sacred. No, this particular rule was written by The Everstar. And the sniveling prick seated behind the table before me—*he* murdered mine.

Well, he murdered the spectraline I had hoped to be worthy of the honor, at least.

"Yes, sir. I'm positive. That is who I saw."

As it turned out, though, he was not.

I wish I could say hushed murmurs rolled through the pews of the little courtroom, but they did not. Though, it was not a huge surprise. We had just moved to this town. Every fifteen-ish or so solar cycles, we took turns letting fate choose our next move in the world. And wherever it decided, we packed and shipped the boxes of our eternity.

"No further questions, Your Honor."

The gavel banged, binders were closed, and the gallery stood. I was escorted from the witness stand and told to return when the jury had rendered their verdict. And I would.

If I could not exact the punishment myself, I might as well relax and watch as the humans do it for me.

That was a rule of The Senate. Our kind are not allowed to harm humans—not unless they attack first. And any retaliation upon a mortal has to then be deemed an act of self-defense, of course. Because to damage them—to hurt any of the mortal beings—goes against everything that we are.

We are protectors. Defenders.

That is, and forever has been, the sole onus of The Spectraline—to protect Lesserkind by defending the borders, Known and Not. It is not a choice, but a birthright.

I have long suspected that my one true Parallel gave their life in honor of that sacred duty centuries ago.

Honestly, why else would I be doomed to suffer Priyatel upon Priyatel incapable of defending so much as their own hide? I mean truly, how inept must a spectral be to lose their eternity to the very beings we are born to protect?

But, more curious still, what would entice a mortal to slay their fiercest guardian? A guardian, I might add, Mortalkind should not know to exist?

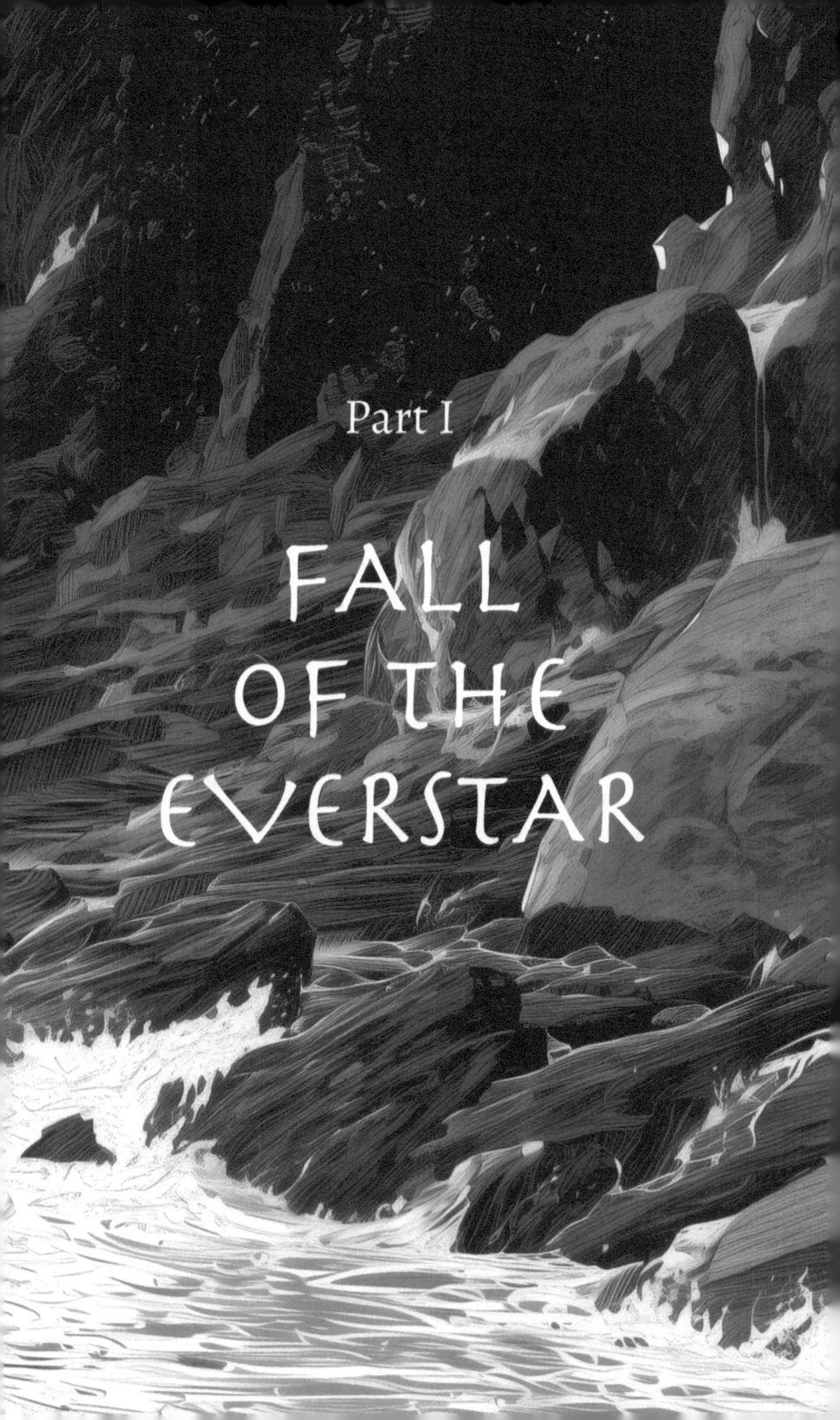

Part I

FALL OF THE EVERSTAR

Chapter 1

THE CONSERVATORY

"Again, Nora."

Nora Everstar's hot, choking breaths clouded the frozen air of the sparring arena. Snowcapped mountains and flurries of flakes surrounded her on every side. It was unbearable, all of it. There was not a thing she liked about this place. The Elder crouched before her, though—this was his heaven.

Or as close as he would ever get.

"I heard that, spec." The sharp-eyed General sank lower into his fighting stance. "Again. But this time, do remember that the threat will come from above."

Nora knew better than to remind the stick-wielding codger that the very last Beast of Old, and its vsadnik, had plummeted to the earth long before she had ever even been thought into existence.

So, instead, she dropped her short swords and picked up an oaken staff, twin to the one clutched in her mentor's hand.

"You know, Shi," she said, sinking deeper into her own heels as she readied the spear, "the humans merely send their young to be married off or to work in the fields."

Faster than she could think, The Shihan of Shields struck with his own—angling to send her useless legs soaring out from under her. Luckily for them, the decades of ruthless training—and countless concussions—had forged her body into a weapon her mind could only dream of becoming.

Shooting into the night sky like a comet, she leapt from the stones. Somersaulting through the air, spear shaft spinning as a deflector, her target blurred into focus. Before he had a chance to raise his dented shield—or roll out of the strike zone—she released.

Sailing true as she knew it would, her lance struck the backs of the shihan's knees—the backs, where she knew his armor was the weakest.

The battle-seasoned spectral crumpled like a novice as Nora landed on the ice-slick stones with her eyes locked upon the stars, her body pitched to defend them.

"And their young might just live to see adulthood, if you keep that up," her shihan coughed.

Claps and hoots sounded from the darkness outside the chalk circle.

"It is about time," sang a lilting, female voice. "We are all famished beyond reason, Nora."

Replacing the long spear to its rightful place on the weapons rack, Nora waited for Shi to grant her leave before strolling over to the gallery. Her plummeting heart rate paired with the subzero temperatures had her bones stiff and her muscles aching by the time she reached the fair-haired female.

"Do not blame me for your voyeuristic fetishes," she chided happily, linking a sore arm through the onlooker's. "Your drills ended hours ago."

"You know very well that I have to keep tabs on you." They headed for the warm halls of The Conservatory. "I simply cannot allow you to run around and surpass me. Now can I, little sister?"

"You speak as if you have some choice in the matter. But, alas"—Nora's sharpened canines flashed in the dim candlelight—"I was simply born better."

And Stassie—the spoiled sorceress—lunged.

Her linked shoulder dipped low and threw power while her other fist slammed into Nora's clavicle. The vertebrae of her spine cracked, one by one, against the rough, carved wall of the corridor.

"She told you she was hungry."

Smiling at the newcomer, Nora smashed her forehead into her sister's unguarded skull.

Stassie rocked, blinked, and it was too late. Nora's kneecaps crushed her biceps into the unyielding floor as she sat on her belly, pinning her in place like the preening land lizard she was.

"And I told her not to stalk me from the shadows like some kind of perverted deviant."

Giving the elder degenerate a big, wet kiss on the cheek, Nora allowed Dima, a spec one series behind her and Stass, to help her to her feet. Laughing, Stassie the Stubborn declined his other outstretched hand, instead opting to heft her sorry carcass up off the dirty floor herself.

"I will save you a seat in The Atrium," she said as she dusted her sleeves and made for the stairs. "No promises on dinner, though."

It is a mystery how that vast ass still fits in her—

"This *vast ass* can still hear you," she tossed over a shoulder as she disappeared to the upper levels.

Thought-Tellers, as her kind were known, really got under Nora's skin.

"Will you ever be able to do that?" Dima asked from beside her.

Their people, The Spectraline, grew into either mind-readers or mind-benders. However, until they graduated from The Conservatory, a fortress-like battle academy built where the earth meets the stars, they were not full spectral and thus could not use the title.

For all the solars they lived here, from the first series until the first shield, they were referred to only as specling or, more commonly, as specs.

The burden of Lumin, however—the gift of clairvoyance bestowed upon the spectraline—was meant to be forever shared. Forever shared between two beings, that is. Alas, a spectral was always one or the other, but never both. And for a spectral to gain access to their sacred gift, they must first find the one willing to share in their burden—they must first find their one true Parallel.

A Parallel is a warrior of equal heart and equal spirit who, once sworn, would give their very eternity to save the other's. The only caveat being, if one dies, the other soon follows. So, justly, The Senate and The Conservatory both recommend that each specling give the matter some serious consideration before they decide on who it will be they forever anchor themselves to.

Nora's sister, however—lovestruck and senseless—did the *exact* opposite. She and her mutton-brained betrothed completed The Rite without telling a soul. Hence, her premature—super irritating—ability to eavesdrop on inner monologues.

"Maybe," Nora answered the younger spec. "If ever the day comes I decide that a Parallel would be more of a boon than it is a burden."

Dima winced, his dark curls falling just below his brow line.

It was a shame, Nora thought to herself as she studied the younger warrior. A shame, indeed, to cover those eyes of liquid gold.

"You best hurry, though. I do not need to be a Thought-Teller to know Stassie is going to try and eat all the food The Atrium has to offer."

And it was as if someone turned up the flame beneath the molten metal in his stare.

"Do not worry." Straightening his back, Dima smiled softly. "There will be a plate saved for you. Mark my words."

And he did not give her a chance to thank him before sprinting up the staircase after her troll of a sister.

Chapter 2

THE CATACOMBS

Savallin Prim did not particularly care for surprises. She especially did not care for them when they arrived at this hour. And she definitely did not care for them when the fate of The Living was involved.

The raven-haired sahira cloaked herself in the fine, silken dressing robe she had discarded, with some haste, in the warmth of the hearth's fire only hours before. Then, with a wave of her slender finger, the handsome maiden nestled amongst the fur coverlets rose from the bed, dressed, and promptly fled the private cavern.

Half a chalice of goldspice later, Savallin followed the travel-worn emissary and her two most-trusted sentinels through the lambent, snaking corridors of the capital citadel.

As they walked, the heavily-lashed eyes of the newly-roused covenary reread the smeared script, word by word. She translated each one, over and over, in every tongue she had ever been taught.

It is likely a simple disconnect, she thought. Some forgotten crevasse between The Ever Language and her own.

Though, that would be... well, it would be rather uncharacteristic.

Their differences aside, The Lasting Scribes were the very best in existence, their vast wisdom unrivaled in all the Known realms. It would be unlike them to dispatch a missive with such an error.

The lofty, stained-glass doors standing guard outside The Cavern of Council groaned awake as their party rounded the final bend. Without having to see them, Savallin already knew who waited patiently within. And, who did not.

Situated most strategically, The Cavern of Council sat five leagues beneath the dangers of the Surface. And it was by no accident that the blessed, starry space was the last livable chamber left amongst the deepest depths of the covenary stronghold.

For thousands upon thousands of years, far longer than any living sahira can recall, The Five Majlis of Covenarykind have convened in this cosmic cavern at the heart of their subterranean citadel, at the heart of The Catacombs.

And flowing from the cavern's truest center, a gift from a goddess who sees all—the untouched waters of The Infinite Spring. Ringed by a sparkling, black-sand shoreline, the prophetic Tellings of Her depthless well were once worshipped above all else.

In the ever-changing hues of Her streams, so swift as to eclipse their black shore, the greatest Diadets of Covenarykind were oft able to glimpse The Yet—the outcomes of unending war, the remedies to devastating plagues, the malicious intent of allies and the mistaken intent of enemies.

But, in the last five centuries, there had been not a single Diadet born with the gift of reading the Tellings of Her streams.

And before Savallin Prim could get anywhere near those streams, before she had even made it through the star-lined archway that led to them, the covenary responsible for her mid-slumber awakening rasped from the shadows, "Tell me it is true."

Perched on two of the six cushions arranged in the glittering sand along the bank of The Infinite Spring, Euclid Istra, Keeper of Warriors, and Amira Vasser, Keeper of Wealth, sat together in silent anticipation.

And like the guards of the other three Majlis present, Savallin's two sentinels took up their post along the rear crystalline wall of the sweeping cavern.

"Is the claim *true?*" Phaedra Halla, Keeper of Whispers— and Keeper of Monumental Pains in Savallin's backside— chafed again. "Have the covenary, at long last, been vindicated?"

Savallin did not turn towards the petulant voice calling out from the darkness. No, the no-nonsense sorceress instead lifted two fingers, gently tapping them upon her forehead, before drawing them downwards in a crescent-moon shape towards the center of her chest.

"Have you gone deaf, Keeper of Wis—"

"I have not," the Keeper of Wisdom tore the words from Phaedra's lips. "But I have grown tired of your impatience. Of your insistence. Of your insolence."

At the foot of the cavern's largest crystal column, what had appeared as no more than just another shadow cast upon the charcoal stones rippled away to reveal a fine-boned female with a creamy-white mane, alabastrine skin, and a face honed by a lifetime of hate.

"Well, then. Maybe you should not have kept us wai—"

At once, both Majlis sitting cross-legged on their cushions raised their left arms level with the ground. And at once, the poinsettia-red lips of the self-proclaimed Shade of Snow sealed tight as she toppled backwards and began to tumble through the starry twilight that was The Cavern of Council.

"She is young," reminded the slight, narrow-eyed Keeper of Warriors. "She must learn her place in this hallowed cavern."

Savallin watched the covenary somersault through the air.

Phaedra was two and thirty, she recalled. Three years older than she herself was.

"She is not *that* young," frowned Amira, the stoic and steady Lady of Summer. "If she keeps that up, we will be forced to Raise another."

That gave Savallin pause.

Such a tremendous measure had only been taken a handful of times throughout their history. For a covenary to become a Majlis, for a sahira to be elevated to the status of esteem and sworn to the duties that came along with it—it was a lifelong servitude.

The sole path for a Majlis to forgo her responsibilities, her blessed burden—or, to have them stripped away—was by fading. *By death.*

The Keepers of Warriors and Wealth could not mean to... to...

Could they?

Covenarykind was many things, but a flippant people they were not. For reasons only Her was privy, the sisters of the covenary were born every bit as stunning as they were cunning. A Divine deception to best exploit their fleeting time in this life.

Were they lovely? *Goddess-like.* Were they frivolous? *No.* Were they petty? *Blessedly.*

The two elder sahira *were* right, though. Phaedra *was* young. Even if her body might have been born before Savallin's, her heart had surely not. Its beating felt wilder, louder, and more eager than her own.

She understood why the sahira, why her sister, so badly wanted answers. They all wanted answers. But unlike Phaedra, the rest of The Five were well too aware of what rushing could cost them, of what all it had cost them.

Savallin regarded the two covenary seated before her for a moment more before raising her own arm parallel with the shimmering black floor.

With half a thought, and not a word, the Keeper of Whispers ceased her spinning. And, as Savallin drew her arm towards the glistening pool, Phaedra Halla found herself righted and kneeling upon a hand-stitched cushion atop the midnight sands.

Now the last one standing, the Keeper of Wisdom strode for her own seat at the water's edge. And the icy stares of her sisters did not unnerve Savallin, not in the least, as she settled onto her knees and prepared to address the council.

She knew it had been ageless curiosity, laced with near-feral bloodlust, that had dragged the three Majlis to this cavern at such an hour. She also knew precisely how much of a strain it was for them to uphold those cool façades. So, instead of doing them the favor of lessening their tension, Savallin looked to the furious face of Phaedra.

"Do try and speak in turn, sister." Nearly imperceptibly, the Keeper of Wisdom lowered her own façade—the elaborate, mist-sewn veil she forever wore to mask herself from the many wandering eyes around her. "Or, the Himalayan Huntress and Lady of Summer are going to rather relish tossing your limp figure into The Infinite Spring."

"The Infini"—her pale eyebrows arched up in horror as Phaedra gasped—"it is pure bane."

"We know," the two covenary crooned in unison.

The Keeper of Whispers shifted fretfully.

Her veil again securely in place, Savallin proceeded onward. "Has word yet arrived from Cora?"

Cora, or Coralis Carveil as she was more widely recognized, had been inexplicably absent of late. The Keeper of Wisdom would not be so dishonest as to claim the prolonged absence did not trouble her.

"There has been no news from the Keeper of Wonder," reported Amira, *not* Phaedra.

The latter looked as if she wanted to say more, but Euclid forged ahead, cutting her off. "What of the letter, Savallin?"

The Keeper of Wisdom, after making a quick mental note to follow up on that, translated the parchment's perfectly-scrawled text one final time before opening her mouth to answer.

"I cannot yet authenticate its content, but I can attest to the source."

The earthen head of Amira and the inky-basalt head of Euclid whipped towards one another in utter disbelief.

Phaedra Halla, her light eyes wide, breathed, "The Malqatil."

We have been misguided.
We have *all* been misguided.
Summon The Skapahni.

Chapter 3

THE CITY

No more coastal woods, no more going months without sunshine. Everly Castile was swapping that dreary eternity she never wanted for the skyscraper forests and rivers of concrete better known as The Empire City.

In all her centuries, she'd only ever visited this place. For as many darts—and daggers—as she'd thrown at the map, none had ever stuck in the island at the heart of the estuary. And, with as many humans as there were calling The Mortal City home, it would be little problem for her to blend in.

Additionally, this city was somewhat of a mecca for the particular faction of mankind growing more and more eager to inject paralytic neurotoxins beneath their mortal skin. So, the likelihood of Everly's never-changing appearance being noted as strange was significantly lesser among this lot.

By design, her new apartment overlooked the largest of The City's famed parks. And while most of the other residents in her building, she assumed, were likely to take one of the elevators in the lush, marble lobby to reach the tower's highest floors, she—she preferred the stairs.

The unit had come with a small balcony. It was just wide enough to fit a single chair and a side table, possibly a few potted plants. The interior of the apartment was a bit bigger. It had floor-to-ceiling windows in every room, a footed soaking tub, and ample space for calisthenics. All her furniture, clothes, and loose ends had been unpacked and put away before she had ever walked off the plane.

So, the only thing left for her to do now was to explore her new neighborhood and try to make herself feel at home... for the fifty-fourth time in her eternity.

She knew she shouldn't be such a snot about being rehomed. Not with as few of her kind as there were left in this world. Nowadays, it was unlikely for any spectral to casually bump into another of their kind. She had stopped looking forward to that chance decades ago.

It was the phase of the solar cycle when the chill began to creep in earlier every day. The leaves on the trees in the sprawling park were a mix of fiery and dead. There was no in-between.

Canvas pop-up stalls had been set up on one of the lawns as part of a seasonal, weekend market. The wares in the various booths ranged from holiday ornaments to confections to handmade soaps.

She didn't need any of it, not really. But... it wouldn't hurt anything if she just had a quick peek. For the first twenty, or so, solars of her eternity, all things without purpose were discouraged. If you couldn't carry it on your back or if it didn't serve to aid you in an unforeseen attack, it wasn't considered a wise possession to tote.

And even now, almost a millennium later, that old habit still held sway.

The stall on the end, closest to the last pink rays of sun as it set over the duck pond, was stocked with shelf upon shelf of beautiful artisan breads. There were circular, oak-colored loaves, pale and twisty baguettes, and even individually wrapped slices of holy sourdough.

The smell was phenomenal.

She couldn't help but wander closer. Her stomach was outright growling its request by the time the shopkeeper looked up. Actually, its howling was probably why she looked up at all. And when she began to speak, Everly drifted to a time and a place far, far away from that peaceful park in the center of The Mortal City.

Even though their bodies are stronger, faster, and more resilient than most other races on Earth, that does not mean spectral are without harm. No, the dangers they were built to face—or used to be—were unlike anything the modern era has ever known.

When a spectral is wounded so gravely that even they fall from the field, nothing—save time or a proper healing bath or... or maybe an Illicit Offering—can get them back on their feet and conditioned for combat. And while the spectraline body does heal quicker than those of the mortal, they do not heal as quickly as all.

In the first winter of what the people of today know as The Second Ice Age, The Spectraline's forward-most outpost along the rocky, western coast of Jidana had been ambushed in the thick of night. Many warriors—many spectral—were lost to that darkness.

Everly's first Priyatel was nearly one of them. The foolish worm had forgotten himself, forgotten his purpose, forgotten his eternity of training. His limp form had plummeted from atop the Chalk Cliffs only to disappear beneath the howling, black waves.

By the time the bloodshed had ended and the threat had been dealt with, Everly had hunted that imbecile down. She had found his pathetic, unconscious body laid up in the bed of a mortal.

A mortal woman—more girl, really—who was prepared to protect her new charge with all the might a cast-iron skillet would afford her. And it just so happened, that woman's cottage had also smelled of freshly baked bread.

Everly had felt a thousand stones lighter as she walked away from that girl, as she'd walked away with nothing more than a sack of her rye thrown over a shoulder.

And so, without another thought, Everly traded one plastic tap for a warm slice of the buxom woman's sourdough. Before handing it over, though, she smeared one side with a healthy slather of honey butter and then gave that a light sprinkling of cinnamon dust.

Everly was not upset about it.

With a mouthful of her brilliance, she thanked the woman again before meandering towards the white, twinkling string lights hung over the pathway leading towards the park's exit. The loss of the sun had brought a cold she did not care for. Nothing good ever happens in the cold.

Time to get inside.

Humans in heavy coats and boots trudged past her as she crossed underneath the stone arch and onto the busy sidewalk. Horns and hollers, laughs and cries, and the shrill screech of birds flying overhead helped to dull the rising thrum in her ears. But, as usual, the darker it got, the louder it became.

The thrum is a natural reaction, a sort of call to arms, that The Spectraline experience in the presence of peril. The more severe the threat, the more severe the thrum. The only problem is that as the population of humans skyrocketed, so did the number of things wishing to do them harm.

So, nowadays, it is almost impossible for a spectral to have any peace or quiet. That is, unless their apartment is on one of the highest floors of one of the tallest skyscrapers in one of the most vertical cities in the world.

Polishing off the snack and tucking her hands into her pockets, she hurried across the street before the blinking stick figure on the flashing signal morphed into a stop sign. Three steps up onto the crowded curb and the thrumming began jabbing at her eardrums.

Where is it?

Scanning the passing faces, she checked for the telltale signs. Bugging eyes, throbbing veins, unnecessary perspiration, and—

There.

Down a dingy alley, between two mid-rise buildings, a pair of feet—small ones, facing the wrong direction—disappeared behind a dumpster. With the awkward angle of the little toes and the pitch of the heels, the *child* those feet belonged to had not been moving of their own accord.

And it was the thoughtfully arranged circlets of rainbows and glitter beads on those dirty shoelaces that had Everly Castile slipping into the alleyway after them.

Chapter 4

THE CONSERVATORY

The tall, stone archways lining the far side of the airy lecture hall did little to protect the occupants from the harsh, unforgiving elements beyond. And it was not just The Hall of Ages, either. Each of the twelve high-vaulted galleries making up The Conservatory's Lessons Ell were indistinguishable in their torment.

The cruel design of the academic wing was neither mishap nor oversight. No, every last facet of the cliff-hewn Conservatory—even those outwardly insignificant in nature—had been scrupulously contrived to either impart wisdom, instill fear, or imperially madden each of the specling dwelling within its walls.

According to the supreme sagacity of the all-knowing shihan, the never-ending draft that howled through Lessons Ell was meant to be a ceaseless reminder of the most crucial lesson specling are taught during their final six series.

Icy be thy mind, or death you shall find.

As tenderly dictated by The Spectraline Senate, if a specling cannot conquer meek, weaponless academia amidst the elements, no hope would they have at surviving the windswept scourge coming to conquer them.

Nora Everstar was perched atop a polished-stone stool in the farthest corner of The Hall of Ages. No other specling in the vast gallery dared approach it. For each one of them knew, they all knew, this seat belonged to her.

Every new morning, Nora awoke well before first light. She rose in that darkness to don her warmest leathers. Then, on silent feet, she climbed those steep, ice-covered mountain steps to the highest ring of the sparring terrace. And it was there, under the watchful, unwavering eyes of the stars, that Nora honed her craft until every last shred of muscle in her body begged her to stop.

With the final Canons looming ever nearer, Nora would not allow herself the luxury of rest.

And yet, even with her rigorous, predawn exercises, the misty-haired specling somehow managed to stride beneath the opulent, mosaiced ceiling denoting The Lessons Ell before any other spec in the sixth series.

And every new morning, as she quietly studied the images depicted in the colorful, glass tiles above her, Nora claimed this same seat in the back corner of the hall.

The specling preferred this seat for its proximity— farthest from the preachy shihan at the head of the gallery, and closest to the third of the mammoth archways peering out over the frosty vale.

The cold was sinister, yes. And the wind, it was far worse. But the two in tandem kept Nora awake, kept her keen as the heavily-framed shihan paced back and forth behind her pulpit and droned on about the happenings of the past. Happenings that Nora knew like the slice of her favorite blade.

This morning, Shihan Halor commenced her lecture with a rather lackluster account of the opening battle in the last great war of old.

The Mortal War.

The Mortal War had been a century-spanning conflict so unequivocally merciless in its devastation that The Spectraline—that the world in its totality—would never again know its like.

"The enemy host had been lying in wait with the patience of a thousand ages, drifting in the frozen bite of the creeping shadow, for the might of The Everstar to fade from the sky."

With startling ease, the stout Elder at the front of the hall turned on her toe and indicated to a winding line carved through the easternmost third of the continent.

"War had been on the horizon for some time. And thus, the outward Shield fortresses had swelled well beyond their troop capacity. The Sempiterne Scholars postulate, tenfold."

Halor paused her pacing long enough to let that visual of the horrifically cramped living conditions settle in. While she lingered, a square-headed male at the end of the second row of tables ripped a monstrous snore.

Muffled sniggers echoed through the sky-lit chamber.

"*That*"—square-bodied Halor barked from her righteous pedestal—"will be ten summits. *For all of you.*"

Nora glared her contempt through the skulls of every boar seated in the five rows ahead of her.

"And it was this fateful nightfall," not a single gripe, nor a sigh, rebounded off the opalescent gallery walls as the shihan stepped from behind her podium. "*This* ill-fated night when the moon was brightest in its sky, that The Israsensore struck."

A black-haired sixth-series two rows up winced as the shihan kicked the stool out from underneath the drowsing spec. The male's dense, flaccid form thudded to the stone like a sack of catapult fodder.

34

Shihan Halor's omnipresent promise of bare-bodied alpine ascents had the rest of the assembly dutifully upholding her silence.

And if Nora did not think the female averse to the mere mention of it, she would have been certain it was the faintest of joys she glimpsed on Halor's hard mouth as the Elder resumed her retelling.

"Their Screaming Sky Legion, The Isransensore Iclara, led the midnight attack—both the vsadnik and their legendary mounts shattering through The Shield's strongholds as if they were built of nothing more than futility and glass."

Oh, Shi Hal had certainly rehearsed that one in the looking glass.

"Because the outward posts were not outfitted to shelter near the number of shields that had been ordered to march, many and more spectral—warriors, commanders, and naturopaths alike—perished that first, moonlit night."

Embarrassing, Nora purred to herself.

"The Israsensore, the vsadnik of the Iclara, they, like us, were long-lived. They, like us, wielded momentous strength, speed, and stamina."

A lone snicker reverberated from the back row, on the end opposite Nora.

Your eternity is mine, Wolf—

"Wolfton," the Elder's voice cracked through the brisk air like the iron whip that it was. "*Thirty* summits."

Oh. Nora could not help but smile to herself as Wolf banged his head upon the pearly stone. *My regards to you, Madame Shi Hal.*

"But what was it"—the squatty governess asked, gesturing to a strapping male in the front row—"that the Isra forces ultimately lacked?"

The ginger-crowned sixth-series with the pallor of The Fallen looked to his left, then to his right. The lecturer raised her thin brows, the expectancy plain. But the slack-jawed male, he did nothing. Nothing, save gawk.

"Fallon O'Hara," the old spectral intoned, her exacting words becoming unnervingly slow. "Before you so much as consider dragging that rotting face and festering carcass into my hall tomorrow, I strongly suggest that you complete the assigned self-study."

The specling bowed his rotting face in shame.

Ever bless, Nora thought. *Why, in all the wisdom of the stars, would he choose to sit in the first row?*

Shihan Halor was still trying her damnedest to elicit fear from the assembled sixth-series when Nora's own tablemate elbowed her in the side.

Had it been anyone else's elbow in her side, that someone would have very promptly found themselves locked in quite the impassioned embrace with the moonstone floor.

But, as Nora drew her sparkling gaze from the lip of the stone archway and the treacherous chasm just beyond, her posture remained calm. Even as the alpine chill gusting through the gallery's three wide openings blew several strands loose from the tight plait down the center of her scalp, Nora only glanced to the female beside her.

Although she made her disdain known every time she glided into the hall, although she berated Nora's absurd selection for the entirety of each lecture, her sister, Stassie, never once failed to take the stool on her right.

"Did you check The Vitoska this morning?" her sister whispered when the shihan did her next routine spin.

The Vitoska? No... Nora rarely ever even remembered The Vitoska existed, let alone squandered valuable time checking it. But her meddlesome sister, she knew that. And she would not have bothered to bring it up, not unless...

Not unless another sixth-series had... had somehow... by some miracle... accrued the adequate Scars to rival the reigning Premier.

To rival her.

From the relentless murmurs in The Conservatory corridors, Nora Everstar was believed to be so far ahead of every other specling in her series that not one of them, nor any amount of Canon victories, gave them even a fool's chance at catching her.

No. In her six solars upon the mountain, Nora had never once lost a sparring match, never once scored second-best on an assessment, never once finished a Canon in any place other than first. So... how could it be that another specling closed that kind of gap?

The tresses of Stassie's long hair—locks that shone as if washed in nothing but the purest gleams of The Everstar—danced riotously at her back as she awaited an answer. But Nora, she refused to do her sister the honor of narrowing her gaze.

So, instead, the specling simply shrugged her shoulders and shook her head, side to side.

"Which of you lot will spare your seriesmate from his summits?" the shihan crowed from her pulpit.

The whistle of the bitter wind roaring through the mountainside gallery was jarring, but the clamor ringing through Nora's mind was ever worse. And as the lecturer feverishly prodded her contemporaries, Nora began working through the drills she had selected for after the midday meal.

Incendiary catapults, advanced forward shielding, suspended archery.

None of which Nora was particularly weak. She was not weak in anything. Could she stand to improve? *Always.* But was anyone better? *Never.*

"Wipe that dismal look off your divine face." Her tablemate bit. "The killjoy has no chance, and he knows it."

The expression painted on her sister's own divine face was near feral.

"And if by some cryptic wonder, he *does* find himself within reach"—a savage grin pulled Stassie's pout taut—"I will happily aid you in pitching his pompous corpse over The Frozen Fall."

Despite herself, Nora wrinkled her nose at the inane notion.

"Everstar," the abrasive voice commanding The Hall of Ages called. "How about *you?*"

"Which one?" Stassie, Ever bless her, taunted in reply.

The shihan crossed her short arms.

"Whichever one of you possesses the intellect to answer the question." The older female angled her head to one side. And the smirk that spread across her stiff face could be seen from every last corner of The Conservatory as she said, "So, presumedly, not you."

Not even the risk of glacial summits could keep the swell of cackles at bay.

And Nora, she savored the searing heat as it rolled off her sister's body in vicious waves. And then, with each of the eyes in The Hall of Ages trained upon her, Nora answered Shi Hal's burning question.

"Discipline." Her voice was steady as ever. "The Israsensore forces, perhaps the superior host, were wild and unruly. They lacked discipline, order. That is why they ultimately fell."

At the head of the gallery, Shi Hal almost looked pleased until—

Soledad Adaleya furthered, "That, and they were far too engrossed with the savory flavors of Lesserkind."

"Forty—"

But just then, right as the thunderous laughter surged over the shihan's screech, the ancient iron bell in the central corridor tolled its faithful fury, sparing them all.

Chapter 5

THE CRYPTS

"Start at the very beginning," the baby-faced investigator seated across from her began. "Tell me, Ava, what all do you remember from last night?"

Ava's tongue dried out.

And the investigator, in his crisp navy suit, watched her way too closely. He... well, truthfully, it felt as if he couldn't take his eyes off of her. He stared at her—at her throat as it worked, at her gaze as it rose, and... and even at her wet hair as it fluttered in the A/C's breeze.

She felt out of place here.

Here, in this cold, windowless room with its buzzing, fluorescent lamps and stiff, metal chairs. But, even so, the soft fabric of her sweater and the familiar hug of her blue jeans kept Ava grounded and put her restless mind at ease.

"There's no need to be nervous," the young officer with the aggravating smirk added.

On second thought, it might've been his entire face that she found so aggravating.

With the cocky twang that did nothing to help his case, the officer continued, "Unless, that is, you have something to hide, Ava."

Yes, indeed. It was his entire face *and* entire persona.

To accuse her of being nervous? Ava?

Where had this man found the audacity?

Ava was not nervous.

The last thing she felt was nervous.

Was she pissed off? *Sure.*

Was she confused and a bit bewildered? *Double sure.*

Was she dog-tired and hungry enough to eat a horse? *Absofuckinglutely.*

But, was she nervous? *Not one damn bit.*

But... what did she remember, though? Did she remember anything? Could she recall anything at all that would be useful? Helpful?

Everything had... it had all gone bad... all gone to shit so, so fast. Everything had happened so, so fast.

Ava studied the interviewer looking down his nose at her. She stared, unblinking, at the rookie officer who had probably bet the farm that volunteering for this route, this detested post, doubled as a clever little shortcut to one day making detective.

Dick-headed clown.

Clearly, critical thinking was not one of the most promising skills in his repertoire.

What did he know? What could he even begin to understand about what she had just been through? About what she had just survived?

The cologne-sour sleaze licked his bottom lip.

Ava grimaced. On the inside, of course.

Nothing.

This man knew nothing.

Not too unlike the rest of them.

This try-hard wannabe likely could not see anything through the gleam off his own boots. He did not yet understand grief or sorrow; he did not yet know what true loss felt like.

And for the briefest of moments, Ava envied the man.

The man who was still sneering at her as if he couldn't decide whether he wanted to strip her down or handcuff her to the table or, maybe, try and test out some enhanced interrogation techniques he'd only ever seen in the movies.

Probably, all of the above.

Ava closed her eyes, took a deep breath, and shut the creep—and his sickening fantasies—out of her mind. She slowed her thoughts, steeled her heart, and tried to see into the past, tried to carry herself back in time just a few hours before.

It had been life as usual.

Her alarm had roared awake on the bedside table at five. And, as normal, she'd been too sluggish to silence it before the anti-snooze feature had it vibrating so hard that it tumbled right off the nightstand.

After a good bout of tossing, grumbling, and cursing her choices in life, she'd gotten up, gotten dressed, and shoveled burnt bacon and brown sugar oatmeal down her gullet as she hopped into her favorite pair of boots. By some miracle, she'd found her keys in the first spot she checked and even remembered to lock the door on her way out.

The subway station had been packed, nearly bursting really, but that definitely wasn't newsworthy. Though... her train had been perfectly on time, and that in itself was deserving of a headline.

As it had rattled along the tracks in the darkness of the train tunnels, Ava had placed her pick-up coffee order. It had been her turn, that much she remembered.

She'd climbed the long staircase leading out of the mess that was the subway station and walked out, straight into the chaos of the city's streets. The sun was low in the sky when she shouldered open the door to her usual coffee shop.

Her order was ready and waiting on the counter, both cups steaming their glory to the heavens. Smiling at the fierce team of baristas manning the brew machines, Ava offered her many thanks as she scooped up the two paper cups.

The old clock, hung high on the marble wall, read seventeen 'til as she pushed through the glass doors and headed for the basement stairs. The much newer, and cheaper, clock on her arm struck forty-five after as she sat and scooted her assigned seat up to the folding table.

From beside her, a giant—who could barely fit his legs beneath the table—fidgeted and coughed as if to say, *Seriously, could you have cut it any closer?*

Without acknowledging the pestering ogre, or his heartfelt concern, Ava slid the second coffee cup—the one that didn't have the tinted-Chapstick lip print—over in front of him.

It was her version of Monday—the first shift back after her days off. And it had all been... well, business as usual. Business as usual, until Ava had awoken on a filth-blanketed gurney in the back of an ambulance.

"Ava, are my questions boring you?" the dull-eyed infant with the snotty expression droned.

And the recollection of her morning vanished just that quickly.

"Well, I surely cannot answer for her, but they're boring the shit out of me."

Was that a—

"My sincerest apologies for being tardy."

It was. It was a—

"I got rather tied up on another case, but I'm here now."

A woman's voice. But when had she... who is she?

"Officer Gilcrest, would you be so kind as to excuse us?"

Wow, Officer? Not Investigator?

Whoever she was, she wasn't one to pull punches. Ava's kind of woman.

The stranger in the tasteful, charcoal pantsuit and red-bottom stilettos adjusted her not-so-tasteful, purple, plastic-rimmed glasses and admitted, "I've heard good things about you, Officer. How willing—no, *eager*—you are to assist with high-profile cases and heavy workloads."

At her kind words, unseasoned Officer Gilcrest appeared as if he might very well blush.

"Both are rare and extraordinary virtues we greatly prize in our best investigators."

Ironic... seeing as you've addressed him as Officer tw—

"With such a generously stacked plate, I can easily understand how you accidentally overlooked a matter as mundane as Ava's P.T.I.C."

Ava cleared her vision. Then, her throat.

"Her P.T.I.C.?" His arrogant shade of blush began to fade.

"Her Post-Traumatic Incident Counseling?" The woman tilted her head to the side with worry.

Post-Traumatic Incident what?

"Oh, of course. Her... I was going to schedule it... um, after," the officer stammered as he stood from his chair.

"After?" she questioned, resting a hand on her hip in anticipation. "Officer, do remind me, you have been excelling in this division for the better part of a year, right?"

The woman delivered the blow so deftly, so politely and professionally, that even Ava had to play it back to be sure. And by the time *Officer* Gilcrest had realized it, he was already halfway to the door. The pompous prick whirled so abruptly that he nearly toppled himself.

Ava rolled her lips to keep from laughing.

The mystery pantsuit-woman merely stepped aside and raised an eyebrow as the now seething—and probably mortified—rookie opened and closed his mouth. Unable to locate the words, he huffed once before storming out of the interrogation room.

When the stuffy air cooled and the door once again clicked closed, the woman floated towards his vacated chair and gracefully took a seat. She'd brought no files... no bag at all.

Ava assessed the woman's face, noted the lack of fine lines, the lack of a single blemish. She was impressive, Ava thought, in a vogue sort of way. Her ash-blonde bob, too-long bangs, and finely manicured brows seemed unduly posh for the bland, gray room around them.

It was then that an eerie feeling settled over Ava. An eerie feeling deep in her gut that she somehow knew this perfect stranger.

And then, the stranger's violet-painted lips quirked to one side.

Ava's stomach knotted as the woman's smirk grew.

"You would hope that an ass-kissing imbecile with such lofty career goals would have at least been wise enough to ask for some sort of identification, would you not?"

Chapter 6

THE CONSERVATORY

On the twelfth morning since Stassie had ridiculed her standing on The Vitoska, Nora Everstar found herself lined up before it. The jagged, black stone and its many silver etchings, rose more than twenty heads high at her back.

To her left side, two male specs from her series waited with their shoulders held proud. And on her other, vulture-haired Soledad Adaleya was vigorously batting her long lashes toward her Priyatel seated in the first row of onlookers.

The cold was particularly blistering this dawn as it thrashed across the barren terrace. Beyond the balustrade, the sea of white-capped peaks rose and fell like waves of earth. The bleary-eyed spectators, all bundled in their thickest furs, were no more than woolly dew in the mountains' shadowy wake.

And then, after what felt like an eternity of idling, Shi, The Shihan of Shields, strode out from the dark archway and onto the pale stone.

Nora let the pulsing in her veins slow.

But, before turning to address the gathered crowd, the battle-hardened Elder first met the frosty stares of each one of the sixth-series standing shoulder to shoulder in the center of the forward terrace.

And as the weight of his full attention passed along the line, each specling dipped their head in deference. When the master of weapons and warriors at last reached the end of their line, he bowed his own head, just once. And then, The Shihan of Shields faced the vale.

"Welcome, and be witness, to the dawn of this solar's Twenty-Second Canon."

The Canons of The Conservatory.

The sole motivation for any giver to pack their beloved specling off to this combat academy amongst the stars—to discover if their prized progeny possesses the tenacity it takes to undergo, and to hopefully survive, the twenty-four Canons of The Conservatory.

Even though attendance is not required until the final six solars, most specling arrive beneath The Conservatory's arches moments after they first learn to climb. While it is not yet a mandatory custom, the practice is highly recommended.

In fact, among The Spectraline, the forfeiture of one's young descendants is in no way considered cruel. On the contrary, doing so is widely recognized as an act of selflessness without compare. For the sooner a giver entrusts their offspring to the teachings of The Conservatory, the greater the advantage the instruction affords them.

It is well believed that the earlier a specling embarks on their study, the better their chances will be at becoming Premier—the very best of the very best. An illustrious and formidable feat, only attainable by claiming sufficient Scars—points earned through blood, sweat, and treachery—to top The Vitoska.

Yet, even though Premier is wholly out of reach for almost all who summit The Alpine Steps, the higher a specling's name is etched upon The Vitoska, the more prestigious their first posting within The Shield will be. A low etching, though, nearly guarantees a lowly posting. And, more often than not, a lowly posting ends in a modest demise.

A gloomy outcome both Nora and Stassie Everstar had been ruthlessly reminded of since the day they had arrived. Because unlike every other whimpering specling in their series, the sisters had not come to The Conservatory until the day they were summoned, a little over five-and-a-half solars ago.

The two specling had ascended The Alpine just in time for the final stretch of The Conservatory's curriculum.

Compulsory Combat.

Six solars chock-full of physical drills, mental stratagem, and veritable torture. Each solar, designated as a series, is structured into a set of four rotating Canons.

No two series see the same Canons, no two Canons are alike, and every Canon, regardless of the solar or the series it falls, is specifically designed to assess a specling's competence in combat.

Even with the substantial head start her seriesmates had over her, Nora Everstar had not yet lost a Canon. And the cool-tempered female with the stare of burnished steel, she did not intend on breaking that streak today.

"Before you this morning, upon this frozen terrace," the old warrior boomed, "are the only four specling of this solar's sixth series to successfully outmaneuver the qualifying rounds of the prior three days."

Nora could not see her, but somewhere in that dense, huddled crowd, she heard her sister scoff her scorn.

"In their last three dayrises, these four talented spectral-in-the-making have survived fogs of fire-kissed arrows, harrowing black caves of razor-tipped maces, and"—the grizzled shihan cracked a smile—"even the slew of snarling nightmares we sicced upon them, *thrice*."

That familiar tingle of excitement sparked at Nora's fingertips as Shi again faced their grouping.

"Specling, while the qualifiers were indeed dire, I believe you will find this solar's Twenty-Second Canon to be anything but."

There was a gleam in the shihan's spirit as he gestured to the second of three tapering, earthstone spires half a league beyond the terrace balustrade.

At its zenith, the pitted and crumbling spire at the center of the cluster stretched almost as high as The Conservatory itself. While the one in front of it was somewhat shorter, the one behind it loomed much taller.

The tingling in Nora's fingertips spread to her palms.

Because the specling knew, that even stranger still, the entire heights of each one of those steep rock chimneys was full of rippling, lilac water.

When Shi resumed his commencement, it was with the General's voice he had used to direct many a Brigadier, and their commanders, out amongst those storied battlefields.

"Soledad, Eleanora, Lattice, and Dalon, today, you shall summit Widow's Finger, you shall grasp the limit of her Sorrow, and then, if you still breathe, you shall wipe The Immortal Tear straight from Eternity's Eye."

Lattice, his unruly taupe strands ruffling in the wind, leaned forward only to sneer at Nora.

"Whoever amongst you first ascends The Alpine Steps and again walks upon this terrace, with The Immortal Tear in hand, will claim the Twenty-Second Canon."

With an unsettlingly lengthy stretch of rather intense eye contact, Soledad and Lattice forged a silent pact.

The same pact her seriesmates always forged.

Regardless the fall, fell the Everstar.

The latter only studied the stone spire where it rose before the waking horizon. Without giving anything away, she measured the distance from the mouth to the base.

Shi with the infinite wisdom, indeed.

The chute was too tall, even for an immortal. Even for her. If any of them somehow reached the bottom, by the time they swam that deep, their mighty lungs would be of no use. They would be completely out of air.

"Sixth-series," The Shihan of Shields continued. "There is but one rule in this Canon." The Elder's stern jaw softened. "Barring your strength, your wit, and your stamina, you are permitted no tools to aid in your ascent."

At that, Soledad, Lattice, and now Dalon shared another one of their looks. But the shihan, her shihan, his knowing look fell only upon her. And then, after a beat, the General turned to the crowd.

"And now, without further ado, will you all please join me in the commencement of this Twenty-Second Canon."

And while the fur-swathed spectators roared and howled and cheered with delight, Nora Everstar whispered to herself.

Icy be thy mind, or second place you shall find.

And then, the angry groan and crack of the battlement catapult set her feet to flying.

THE CITY

Strained yogurt, she pouted, *sure does taste a lot better on hillside verandas in the bright of spring.*

Scowling at the striped ceramic bowl on the little table before her, Everly heaped a healthy dollop of honey and a dash of cinnamon into the shoddy attempt at a Balkan breakfast.

The cozy neighborhood coffee shop on the corner was more crowded than she'd hoped it would be at this early hour of the morning. As she nursed her latte and mixed the lackluster yogurt, the shop's front door chimed open—*yet again.*

Two police officers, both with wind-rosied cheeks and purple bags beneath their eyes, shuffled up to the counter lined with miniature holiday trees.

It wasn't that their uniforms looked sloppy, per se... no, it was more that they looked... worn. And the manner in which the taller one on the right slouched and rolled his neck, together with the slow, pained gait of his partner, suggested that the pair had had a long, long night.

Nearly nine centuries ago, Everly was a little over twenty-five solars of age. That was the very last time she herself had been assigned to the night watch. Her version had been a bit... different... than these humans in their contemporary cities, but still, she did not envy these two in their duty.

Hot coffees in hand, the partners in blue made themselves at home on a pair of colorful wooden stools along the painted-brick wall behind her windowfront table.

Giving up on the sad breakfast, she pushed her bowl aside and cracked open the book she'd started in the bathtub the night before. The sultry, sweet song of sleep had summoned her under before she'd even reached the end of the first chapter.

The doe-eyed maiden had just sacrificed herself in a gloriously pitiful attempt at saving the obviously duplicitous—yet pointy-eared—love interest when the slouchy officer at Everly's back murmured, "I've never seen anything like that."

"No one has," his partner replied. "I mean, for Christ's sake, the goddamned Medical Examiner retched. *The Medical Examiner*..."

The words on her page suddenly became much less interesting.

"How did he even get up there in the first place?"

"Well," the slouchy one swallowed. "The witness said—"

"The witness is unreliable," snapped the second officer. "She doesn't know what she saw."

Ah, yes. What good is a female's recollection?

"His..." She heard a too-large gulp of black coffee fight its way down the policeman's bobbing throat. "His bowels were strewn across an entire city block."

Jaw on the floor, Everly whipped her head toward the two gossipers. Upon seeing her horrified face, one man blushed while the other snickered.

"This is a dangerous place," the shorter and portlier of the two sniveled. "Get used to it, sweetheart."

Rainbow beads on tiny white sneakers jingled into Everly's memory. *Where were you, prick, when she was having to find that out the hard way?*

Rolling her eyes, she spun back around in her seat. This was neither the time nor place for a dick-measuring contest. And then, a tad more quietly than they had been, the two officers continued on.

"The detectives think he might've jumped from the upper floors of a building."

She took a sip of her frothy goodness. While the café might royally blow at yogurt, she had to hand it to them on the coffee. Coffee, they had figured out. That was probably why it was not called the Yogurt Corner.

"Riiight." She sensed the slouchee straighten before speaking his mind. "So, the victim jumped to his death? But mid-fall, he found the time to wring his own guts from *here* to 97th?"

Lovely.

"And he did so all after punching a fist-sized hole through *his own* chest, ripping out his heart, and then hiding it someplace we—the largest police force in the world—cannot find?"

She had to drain her latte to mask her chuckle.

"I didn't say the detectives were right," the asshat chided, borderline embarrassed.

Do they not have a cruiser they can sit in and stink up and hash this out in?

Dropping his voice so low that she knew she was the only soul in this café capable of hearing him, the taller policeman muttered, "The girl said her attacker was torn into the stars by shadows."

"The girl is six."

Anyone attacking a girl, the spectraline thought, *was well worthy of a grisly end. More than deserving of having their wasted destiny damned into nothingness. Or sprayed across a few city blocks.*

The first policeman, after being emboldened by another slurp of joe, protested, "Why would she make something like that up, Carver?"

"Trauma," Carver spat as if he held a degree in the subject. "That girl was probably so traumatized her brain couldn't process what was happening. What she saw." The wooden stool beneath him creaked as a repulsive snorting noise worked its way up his nasal cavities. "That shit happens all the time."

Everly did not even try to hide the bunching of her face.

"Well," Anti-Carver sighed, "whoever—or whatever—it was that did come calling for him, I have a few more numbers in need of dialing."

If she hadn't seen the pair of mortals as they walked in, Everly would've thought it was a horse whinnying behind her.

"And tell me, Altano," his partner crowed. "Whose numbers would those be?"

And Officer Altano—he must have been itching for the ask. Because the catalog he began spouting off, he had given it some thought.

There was a clink of ceramic on glass, an intake of air, and then:

"Well, for starters, whoever owns that rusted-out freighter at the docks. The one rumored to be packed full of scared, starving children. And after them, how about every single judge who has stood in the way and denied Human Trafficking access to it?"

His loser of a partner tried to say something, but Altano did not stop to listen.

"Actually, while we're at it, let's tack on the list of judges that refused to sign off on Narcotics' warrant for 1200 Satander."

"Why would—"

"Because it was in The Tenements. Their investigators had been scoping it out for months. *Months.* But then, the night before they were finally to get their warrant signed, someone—they still aren't sure if it was an inside job, or out—but someone let it slip."

Mortals and their beloved, fucking paperwork.

"Who do—"

"They haven't said. But that night, that very night, the entire goddamned building went up in flames. The whole fuck's-forsaken building."

Everly, abandoning her dream of a peaceful morning, closed the cover of her book.

"There were bad things going on in that building, but most of its tenants were just that. Tenants. Tenants who couldn't afford to live anywhere else. Tenants who were not bad people, not criminals. Tenants—parents and their children, families—who were completely blameless. Innocent."

Sore silence was the only response Altano received.

Even the other patrons had quieted at their respective tables, their pastries, cutlery, and cups all forgotten.

But then, only after the hush had dragged on a hair too long, the rotund policeman blew out a breath.

"Damn," Carver admitted reluctantly. "Fucking damn."

Eloquent.

Scooting her chair out from underneath the round table, Everly stood. The spectraline did not care to hear another word about how rotten and ruined this world had become. Scooping up her bowl and the empty mug, she headed for the bussing cabinet near the door.

As she scraped the remnants of her breakfast into the compost, Stumpy-Grumpy whispered something concerning.

"That gets me thinking—did you ever see the crime scene photos of the bodies they found Upstate last fall?"

The spectraline paused her scraping.

"They looked just like—"

But then, a force like a maelstrom caught Everly by storm.

The bowl toppled from her hands, clanking loudly against the metal clearing station as she fell backwards toward the floor. One blink, though, and she had flipped her facing midair—the speckled concrete now racing up to meet her. She flattened her palms, readying to absorb the impact—but she—she never did reach the ground.

For in a flash, in the same flash it had taken her to rotate, the Maelstrom himself had caught her by the biceps, breaking her fall before she could cause an even bigger spectacle.

His laugh was deep and his apology profuse as he set Everly safely back upon her feet. Along the back wall, the two prattling officers had fallen silent and risen to attention.

As had everyone else in the café.

Her expression hardened to stone as she glared up into the eye of the storm.

"Are you all right?!" A shadowy stare, wide with alarm, searched her up and down. "Honestly, I'm impressed you didn't—"

"Do that again," the spectraline hissed, jerking out of his grip. "And you won't be."

And as he opened his mouth to—she really didn't care what—Everly Castile shouldered the glass door and stepped into the day.

Chapter 8

THE CATACOMBS

Diadet Nirvana, the Sovereign Supreme of Covenarykind, was not like the many sahira rulers that came before her. She was not warm. She was not kind. She was not gracious or merciful, at all.

And as far as she was concerned, the second-worst mistake any covenary could make—a mistake she saw as graver than murder, as greater than treason, as grander than even genocide—was to waste her precious time.

It was because of that notion that Savallin Prim, Keeper of Wisdom, knew that neither she nor any of the Five Majlis of Covenarykind could stand before Diadet Nirvana without first being positively, absolutely, deathly certain of the legitimacy of what they were calling The Midnight Message.

And as it—and she—stood, certain was nowhere in the vicinity. While she could confidently confirm the steady hand with which the fraught message was written, Savallin Prim had many questions in need of answering before she could ethically testify to the message itself.

She had said as much to her fellow Keepers as they sat together in the black sands beneath the twinkling stars of The Cavern of Council.

Three days.

That is what they had agreed upon. Savallin had three days to unveil the secrets behind five centuries of masked truths and bared lies. She had three days to unravel all that she thought she knew—three days to unravel all that everyone thought they knew.

As her lifetime of Keeper Tutelage had taught, Savallin recognized the steep costs associated with clarity on matters so controversial in nature. Alas, wisdom was the burden she had been chosen to bear.

So, with her head held high, the sahira had accepted the duty of navigating all the way to the murkiest depths beneath the storied history of her people. But she did not, however, accept the ludicrous time constraint.

Three days...

This task... this pursuit... it demanded three months, three years—or decades even, Savallin thought. To sort it out in under a week's time?

Impossible.

Wise as she was, she knew that to pull off a miracle of this magnitude, she was going to need help. She was going to need a lot of help.

Thus, upon her departure from the black sands surrounding the quietly burbling waters of The Infinite Spring, Savallin Prim had begun the hunt for the missing sahira—the hunt for the Keeper of Wonder and what she might know of the Shamed Sisters. What she might know of the sisters who were sentenced to fade.

The last time Sav had laid eyes on the fiery-red tresses of the Domina Diem, the two Keepers had been swaying, arm in arm, at the shadowy edge of the ethereal and monstrous Cael Ostium.

All around them, dizzyingly high in the carved stone crenellations and dazzlingly hidden among the immense falls of moonlit flora, a battalion of Euclid's finest and fiercest Sombers observed the world beyond the gate. Frighteningly still, and even more soundless, they monitored each and every coming and going at the main entrance to Covenarykind's capital citadel.

In the silky, fawn hand farthest from Savallin, Coralis Carveil clutched a small travel case with the meager provisions she had deemed necessary for her next journey into the unknown. As it was, her role as Keeper of Wonder oft sent her to some of the most exotic—albeit dangerous— settlements the Realm of the Living had to offer.

On many occasions, Cora's whimsical yet savage retellings of the barbaric and unjust nature of the realm's most populous people—humankind—left Savallin speechless and reeling, left her sincerely questioning why The Everlast were so dead-set on defending the brutal folk.

How her friend—her sister—survived excursion upon excursion into their vast, punishing lands, into The Surface, must have been thanks to one of Her's strongest blessings.

Now, as Savallin toed the cold stones on the corridor-side of Coralis' private chambers, she strained to recall precisely where the absent sahira had said she was off to that day. But, as she replayed that memory again and again, the destination continued to elude her.

Savallin huffed her frustration.

Entering the quarters of another covenary without her express permission was a crime punishable by whatever clever charm a sahira might have left in place to defend her home. And the covenary—well, the sahira of Covenarykind were crafty, creative, and divinely spiteful.

That alone was usually enough to dissuade any potential wrongdoers from their wrongdoing.

Yet, there stood Savallin.

With a heavy sigh, she pressed the palms of her honey-brown hands against the painted oak of Coralis' door. Centering herself—her breathing, her heartbeat—she listened to the melody of her friend's charm. And as the subtle, sultry song weaved from the wood, through her fingers, and into her soul, Savallin heard the hidden keys.

One by one, she collected them. One by one, she lined them up. And then, one by one, her own charm strummed them back—but in reverse.

The sturdy metal latch on the other side of Cora's door clicked free at once.

Savallin did not dare a step forward, though. Nor did she reach for the pearl knob. No, her eyes remained shut while she remained frozen. Her gentle breathing quieted further still as she focused even more intently—as she honed in on the surreptitious, on the scourge she had slipped her own sentinels to face.

Seraphic.

The other tune of covenary charm, of covenary power. A vengeful contortion of the serene Soul that coursed the veins of all sisters. A corruption so unnatural, so corrosive, that the mere mention of it was forbidden in The Catacombs.

There were but a handful of living covenary reckless enough to even dream of wielding Seraphic. Because, to outlive a dance with the deadly, deathly, barred tune, a sister must carry a symphony of Soul louder than even Hadi's Winds. She must possess a will so iron that all others break against it. And she, too, must harbor a steadiness in herself that never knows waver.

If a covenary lacks but one of those qualities, the illicitly summoned wave of unnatural power—of Seraphic charm—

would crush their mortal bodies before their soul knew to escape.

Savallin had always suspected, though, that if anyone were bold enough—capable enough, to dance with the dark charm and live, it would be Coralis.

But, as she stood there in the corridor, pressing her palms into her dearest friend's lavender door, she sensed... nothing.

Eerie, she thought. *It is eerie.*

For she had been confident—sure—she would hear traces of the forbidden tune.

Had her sister left in some manner of haste she had not before realized? She had seemed so calm that evening at the gate. Could it have been... could Cora have anticipated a prolonged absence? Had the Keeper expected that someone might need to enter?

Neither alternative helped to appease the twisting and knotting in Savallin's stomach. Nevertheless, the Keeper of Wisdom pushed the door wide and walked across the threshold.

The front chamber appeared as if the Winds of Hadi themselves had been trapped inside and had tried—tirelessly and valiantly—to whip themselves free of the unfamiliar, subterranean cage.

Wax-and-mineral-swirled candles, bronze trinkets, and stitched coverlets covered the floor. Colorful tapestries and abstract oil works hung slanted along most of the walls. And a low table, piled high with yawning tomes and ancient volumes, languished in disarray at the center of all of it.

Cora's belongings, it seemed, were left precisely the way she liked them to be.

In utter chaos.

Why her sister—whose position as a Majlis granted her any amenity she wished—lived in such a state, Savallin could not comprehend.

Shaking her head, she swallowed her displeasure and began the formidable task of inspecting the cluttered quarters one mess at a time.

Methodically, and not at all gladly, the Keeper of Wisdom rifled through stack upon stack. Some consisted of yellowing scrolls in languages that tickled the back of Savallin's mind; others were built of fancy gaming boards and what endured of their play pieces.

It was not until she made her way into the dining chamber that her breath caught.

For on the table against the back wall—just next to the place setting for one—a carefully arranged tower of books waited to greet her.

How did she know they were for her, and her alone?

Because... how many times had Savallin berated Cora for her shambolic ways?

How many times had Cora laughed in her face and told her that *if something was meant to be found, it would be found?*

How many times had Savallin scrunched her brow in exasperation at the outlandishness of that claim?

How many times...

The kneading in her gut intensified.

Coralis would not make it that easy, though. Yes, there was something in that mound for Sav—but she had no doubt that there were also things in that mound best not disturbed.

If it is meant to be found...

Easing toward the table, Savallin read the titles of each tome in the teetering stack.

Oblitus Monstrorum

Vltra

The Listing Isles of Lost

Cora was known to be a bit eclectic, but this assortment... this assortment had little to do with the mystical stories and enchanted creatures she was so fond of. No, this selection, in fact, was much more down Savallin's corridor.

After dusting the cover of the volume on top, Savallin set the book aside. She then scooped up the second and did the same. For Coralis, she knew, could not read The Ever Language. Few covenary could, and as such, most would have no use for these particular texts.

The final tome was different, though.

Savallin traced her fingers over each of the golden, embossed letters on the book's worn leather cover. It had been ages since she had laid eyes on a copy herself. *The Listing Isles of Lost* was well known—and well loved—among her people.

The beloved text—a vibrant fable of an ill-fated people and their doomed paradise—had once been housed within the sweeping marble shelves of The Catacomb's Markaziun Library. There it had lived for centuries, until the day Diadet Nirvana ascended the Obsidian Throne and banned all mention of it.

Savallin had been no more than seven years old when it happened. The thought of that day, and of the orders it had brought, still made her sad. Still made her grit her teeth and fist her hands.

The sahira, the hardened shell that seven-year-old covelette had matured into, peeled back the soft cover of the—

Savallin's mind cleared of all memories—of all thoughts.

For a note—a hand-scribbled note on a shimmering page marker—fluttered out from between the thick pages.

Plucking the delicate placeholder out of the air before it could float to the dusty ground, Savallin read, and then reread, the careful words swooped atop it.

Seems if you are reading this, the worst has come to pass. Absolutely do not squander sacred time fretting over my wellbeing, but do understand that your days are now numbered as well.

Venture above and find what has been lost. if it is meant to be found, it will be found. Reader, it is without any doubt that two of the five are not to be trusted. Unless it is three.

Now, go. my strength will soon be yours.
CC

"I knew you would find whatever that loon left in this swine-sty," a voice, like talons on whet stone, scraped from behind the bed chamber door.

And before she could reason, before she could stop herself, Savallin Prim sent the page marker and the treasured pages themselves up into a plume of brilliant, purple flame.

"*That*," the voice grated as it stepped out from the far archway, "was a mistake."

Chapter 9

THE CITY

Because she was not one to tire easily, and also because her pace far surpassed that of all the mortals dwelling within this city of towers and lights, Everly Castile had crossed off most of the tourist attractions within her first week of arriving here. She had fulfilled the collection in its entirety by the end of her second.

And now, at the close of her first full month living in The Mortal City, Everly was circling back to revisit a few of her favorites.

This morning, the spectraline had sipped her frosty, frothy coffee while strolling in the growing shadows of this world's first—and only—true titan of the land. She had wondered, as she sampled and strode, what it must have been like to exist amongst them. To live and breathe in the day when these beasts were more than just fossilized relics of a greater age.

For unlike the other females who had been perusing the intricate-ceilinged exhibits—the ones with the drooling offspring skreiching at their hems—Everly had been alive in the time of a different giant. She knew very well what it was to live amongst them. The giants of the sky.

In fact, it was their time, perhaps, when Everly Castile was last truly alive.

Now, zipped tightly into her heavy down coat, the cold railing beneath her arms didn't so much as nibble at her as she leaned against it at the edge of the brown river. The ever-famished spectraline, after a quick stop at her nutriment truck of choice, chewed on mutton wrapped in pita and greens while she stared into the clouds over the waterway.

This sleepy, modest park on the riverbank, while not technically a tourist attraction, was where the immortal female best liked to come to watch the sky giants of today as they descended from the mists to skid along the runways at the airport across the water.

Even with her extensive compendium of solars and centuries, Everly still marveled at the mortalmade crafts as they landed and leapt into the air.

As any Ever being does, the spectral understood the mechanics of flight. Throughout some of her most recent solars, she had even spiraled into the minutiae behind lift, weight, drag, and thrust. The Laws of Motion and the Principle of Differential Pressure were both well-ingrained into her psyche—likely because the female had spent an inordinate amount of her time bickering with Sir Isaac and the menace of mathematics, Bernoulli.

And yet, all these decades later, Everly still could not grasp precisely which essence of elemental charm was hard at work behind the scenes keeping these mortal concoctions of metal and conjecture from plummeting out of the sky.

Taking another healthy bite of the warm, tzatziki-drenched gyro, the spectral narrowed her eyes at the large passenger plane now aiming for the airstrip. Just past it, a little further across the murky water, the double-lined, barbed-top barrier at Everly's other reason for coming yawned wide.

The prison island.

This morning, while their nests of babes had been scream-crying and crumb-spewing and categorically spoiling the museum for every other visitor, Everly had overheard a flock of the women gossiping about the bust at the shipping dock that that incensed policeman had mentioned in the café a few weeks back.

According to the human women, the yowling bodies of nearly twenty alleged human traffickers had been spotted swaying from the monster offloading crane positioned above one of the dock's many cargo ships. The jarring scene had prompted a swift police and federal task force rescue response that ultimately led to a breach and sweep of the decaying vessel below.

In every one of the corrugated-steel containers they opened, they found children. Human children—battered, freezing, starved, and cowering in their own filth.

So then, since the sliced and diced corpses swinging from the lattice boom had clung to just enough life to stand trial for their evils, they were not-so-hastily cut down, crudely checked out and bandaged, and then were rumored to be awaiting transportation to their forever home.

From the looks of the armored vehicle now slow-rolling through the stone gates of the prison island, the ladies' daybreak gossip appeared to have been whispered straight from the puckered lips of reality.

Good, Everly thought as she trailed the prisoner transport until she could no longer see it. *Good for the mortal enforcers.*

The spectraline had once, very long ago, been in their boots.

Well... she sort of had.

The kind of boots she had worn—well, they had no like.

For once upon a time, Everly Castile had been one of the most dreaded, feared, and esteemed members of a ruthlessly trained and unforgivingly disciplined force of immortal warriors.

The Spectraline Shield.

The spectral soldiers eternally sworn to protect Lesserkind from the ever-rising parade of evils preying upon this world. Courageous guardians forever willing to yield their eternities to defend the borders—both Known and Not.

Everly had served passionately among their bravest ranks. It was never a question for her—she had always known what her eternity meant. Always known what she was destined for.

Until the dawn she didn't, that is.

Until the dawn her whole world fell before her eyes.

Until the dawn she had been *ordered* to sever her swear of eternity.

And these days, with the vast distance and myriads of ages separating Everly from that blindly obedient spectraline soldier she had once been, there wasn't one Ever-blessed thing in this vile world that could ever persuade her to return.

The immortal warrior simply did not give a single fuck.

Polishing off her delicious and much-needed snack, Everly crumpled the foil into a little ball before tossing it into the waste receptacle near the row of shaded wooden benches.

And she—she almost missed it. Almost.

As a large figure about two-hundred paces across the greenery of the park ducked into a boarded-up concession stand that surely hadn't seen patrons since the turn of the century.

She might have ignored it. Might have—if she hadn't seen another strangely sizeable form prowling amidst the darkest of the predator exhibits at the museum this morning.

And so, with the prison transport gone and in need of something new to occupy her attention, the female stuffed her chilled hands into her pockets and casually meandered toward where the figure had faded.

But after jostling the rusted handle a few times, she found the dilapidated stall to be locked. Locked up tight. A peek through the peeling boards told her nobody hid inside either. She even made a lap around the stand's humble perimeter just for grins.

Nothing. Not a trace.

Classic, Everly Castile hummed to herself, sure she had just firmly unsettled any onlookers. *Classic*.

Chapter 10

THE CONSERVATORY

The Promise of The Canons

I vow to thee, hopeful defenders of less.
Present to me thy all, thy intrinsic best.
If the fight thou vie strikes fiercer than the test,
The might of the sky, I swear at thy behest.

The might of the sky coursed strong through Nora Everstar as she watched another sixth-series—Dalon—disappear off the brisk terrace first on the morning of the Twenty-Second Canon.

His close-cropped, light-brown hair vanished around the bend of the cliffside staircase as the other two specling on the promenade—scavenger-haired Soledad and her rodent-nosed abettor, Lattice—whirled on the silver Everstar.

But Nora—though—she saw only the task at hand.

You shall summit Widow's Finger, you shall grasp the limit of her Sorrow, and then, if you still breathe, you shall wipe The Immortal Tear straight from Eternity's Eye.

Simple, she exhaled derisively. *Could not be any simpler.*

The challengers struck as one, the female's furious punches landing at the very same time the male's kicks rattled against Nora's shins.

Have it your way, she breathed.

And on the next swing, Nora caught the female's balled knuckles and drove them into the stone. Soledad's forehead was still cracking into the frigid terrace as Nora's rising back foot stomped Lattice in the mortal-soft throat.

From the gathered crowd, the golden Everstar applauded the loudest as the two sixth-series sagged upon the stones and her sister raced to catch the broad-shouldered male already on the staircase.

But Nora—she did not follow in Dalon's footsteps. While he had undoubtedly sprinted for the valley landing at the bottom of the blind staircase that serpentined down the cliffside, she descended only one flight before banking a hard right and climbing.

Nora reached the top of the tenth flight when she at last heard the huffing of her two aggressors as they began their sluggish scramble down The Alpine Steps. There was no way either one of them would catch up to Dalon, though. His long strides would make easy work of the uneven, cratered terrain he would need to cross upon reaching the valley landing.

When the wet heaves of Lattice and Soledad faded into the frost, the silver-haired specling hurried from where she hid crouched atop the landing in the clouds. The uppermost skywalk of The Conservatory's battlements stretched on before her—and the world, as Nora knew it, simply fell away to nothing at its pale, moonstone edge.

Her footsteps were quick but sure as she made her way from the stairs to what waited just before the battlement's wind-ravaged brink.

A mammoth, mountain-mounted crossbow.

As she hefted a heavy, iron bolt from the stockpile at the shooter seat's side and loaded it into the groove of the ancient wood, Nora strained her eyes to scan the valley floor thousands of paces below.

No sign of Dalon. Perhaps the large male was not as surefooted as she had thought.

With several glances down to monitor the progress of the other specling, Nora knotted a healthy length of rope through the tail of the iron bolt. Unless they were still in the shadow of the cliff, none of them had advanced very far into the slick boulders of the river basin.

Even so, just to cover all her bases, the specling spun to the sharp staircase behind her.

Empty.

That settled it. She would not sacrifice another heartbeat. And just before she leapt up into the crossbow's wide, weather-worn chair, Nora tethered the free end of her rope to the shooter seat itself.

The Shihan of Shields had forbidden all tools of any kind to assist with her ascent of Widow's Finger? Fine. She did not need them anyway—not even on her worst day. And this day? It would be far from her worst.

For she had no intention of ascending Widow's Finger at all.

Fine. It is fine, she thought as she stepped up onto the platform and slid into the wooden seat.

For Nora, she was not going to ascend the Widow—she was going to descend upon that dowager like a storm in the night, spearing for her watery heart of Sorrow with the unmatched swiftness of a loosed arrow.

Fine. Fine. Fine.

Tilting the butt of the crossbow high enough required the slender spec to lift with her entire body. But then, after a few soft grunts, the tallest of the three stone spires appeared squarely within the weapon's sights. She kept it centered while angling the rail of the massive crossbow so that the bolt would *just* clear the middle chimney.

From the forward terrace ten stories below, a surge of excitement echoed into the vale. Dalon must have finished his descent at last.

Truly, the female sighed. *Why not take your precious time?*

And then, with one deep breath in, Nora fired.

The iron bolt soared true, striking the third spire dead center. Nora had not even bothered to watch it fly. No—she had merely slipped a dagger from her thigh and clenched it between her teeth before pulling a second bolt from the store.

The moment the first had cleaved the stone, she had raised the second across the taut rope and gripped it on each end. And then, the specling did not spare a heartbeat to reconsider her plan before diving from the uppermost battlement amongst the clouds.

Her body plunged through open air until the bolt between her hands caught and the remaining slack was forced from the line. The muscles of her shoulders, of her back, tensed against the sudden tug. And the world beneath her feet, it whooshed by. The stepped levels of The Conservatory, the pale, frozen stones, the might of the mountain itself blurring into a stream of color until it all became one.

Faintly—ever so faintly—through the roar of the wind dominating her senses, Nora could hear the elated screams and shocked cries of the crowd gathered atop the widest terrace. But she was sailing down her line so swiftly she could hardly make out their faces as she blew past them.

And it was just then—just then as The Conservatory and the safety of the cliffside fell away beneath her—that her body rocked and rioted against an unforeseen force. An immense force that erupted from the shadows to jerk Nora out of the sky and back towards the earth.

Her arms shrieked their horror. Her top and bottom teeth clacked together so hard she tasted blood. The callouses on her palms tore and twisted up at the abrupt impact. But still, she did not slip. And both she and the spectators alike knew that it was by no amount of luck that she still clung onto that bolt—that she still held fast and had not yet fallen to a horrific death.

Nora blinked once, then gaped below at her feet—gaped below to spy what she had miscalculated. To spy what she had hit.

Rage rose in her chest. Rage at herself. For it was not what she had hit, but *who.*

Who she had hit. Better yet—who had hit her.

Because wrapped around her lower legs like his very eternity depended on it was Dalon. The male must have been lying in wait—hiding near the top of The Alpine Steps just paces below the forward terrace. Hiding there. Waiting for her. Waiting for her to pass over.

But the jump—that kind of distance—it would have been virtually impossible. Even with a sprinting start, it would have been mad.

Truly, mad.

So mad, in fact, that not even she would have risked it. She never would have even considered it.

But—

But he had. And his mindless wager had paid off. Because now—now he and Nora were shooting through the air a thousand paces above the valley floor.

And with both of her hands locked to the bolt, he knew she could not pry him loose. She could neither stab, nor strike, nor shake the brawny sixth-series.

The bastard was along for the ride, whether she consented or not.

The oversized horse's ass even had the mettle to smirk up at her.

To smirk up at the female literally holding his eternity in her bleeding hands.

Somewhere far, far underneath them, Soledad and Lattice gawked up in utter disgust. But ahead of them, the cluster of stone spires grew larger.

Grew larger, fast.

And as the dangling duo picked up speed, Nora smirked right back down at Dalon.

Icy be thy mind, or second place you shall find.

The specling stilled her heart and began counting. She counted down until they were five beats shy of the first chimney—the shortest chimney. And then, when the dimmest smudge of gray rock edged her vision, Nora willed her muscles to obey.

Wager this, Dalon.

With a gulp, the silver-haired sixth-series thrust her lower body forward and propelled herself up toward the horizontal bolt, gritting her teeth against the male's great weight as she did so.

Their sudden shift had even stoic Dalon reweighing her willingness to risk it all. Her willingness to sabotage herself and her claiming of the Twenty-Second Canon purely to stop it from becoming his.

It would be no different than the perpetual pettiness of her seriesmates.

Nora felt the racing of his heart as it quickened in his chest.

Felt it, until the next instant, when Dalon made his chanciest bet yet.

And then, Nora made hers.

Wager this.

She let go of the bolt.

The fiery bellow that ripped from the male's throat seared the cold sky as his body rushed toward the earth. For his second bet—the rash, nonsensical gamble against her—it was a losing one.

Forever, a losing one.

Wager. This.

He should have known better.

But alas, that lone heartbeat of uncertainty—that brief flicker of doubt in the stone-cold resolve of Nora Everstar—that was all it had taken.

The male's steadfast hold faltered right alongside his conviction, his traitorous soul tumbling through the air trapped within the confines of a not-so-stalwart mind.

Meanwhile, that very same—very ludicrous—moment Dalon had questioned her resolve and lost his grip on her legs, Nora doubled-down on it. She shot her cocked arms high— every bit as high above her as she could muster. Her silver-soaked fingertips had grazed the heavy bolt that by some miracle—that by her gamble—still teetered atop the rope.

Wager this.

And as her foe splashed into the misty, swirling waters of the wrong spire below, Nora regained her purchase on the bolt and sailed down the line toward the second chimney.

Toward Widow's Finger.

Toward sure victory.

THE CESSPOOL

"I'll take the wheel, Samurai."

"Um, bullshit," Sergeant Carlisle shot back at her new, unwanted responsibility. "You'll take shotgun. You will always take shotgun."

Snorting his amusement, Officer Vasquez stopped short of the police cruiser.

"Do you kiss your momma with that mouth, Ava?"

"No," his unamused babysitter answered tersely. "I kiss *your* momma with it. And it's Sergeant Carlisle, to you."

In the graying light of the parking lot, the young Sergeant fought to hide her smile as the thick brows of her ride-along arched to the rising moon.

Pulling on the passenger-side handle, he chuckled, "This is going to be a shift for the tabloids, *Sergeant* Samurai."

With one boot on the SUV's running board, the Sergeant tugged her own door open. Discriminatory nicknames and familial digs aside, she wasn't sure what their night held. It had been more than a year since she and Vasquez had worked the same shift. They'd gone through the Police Academy together, graduated. and then endured field training together, too.

And then, just two years later, it had been of little surprise to the Sergeant when her friend—her averagely intelligent, overly brawny, underwhelmingly male friend—had been the first from their group of lieutenant candidates to see promotion.

The Sergeant had scored higher on the written exam. She'd also completed the S.W.A.T. course faster. It had made no difference, though. She'd known it wouldn't. And after the Oral Board—after the lone subjective portion of the testing process—the Sergeant had been ranked last.

That, though, was neither here nor now. What was here and now was her freshly demoted friend and her ever-growing list of questions. Like, for instance, why he had gotten demoted and placed under her supervision in the first place?

Sliding into her seat, she hit the ignition with one hand and pulled the bar beneath her seat with the other. As her chair moved as far forward as its rails would allow, the Sergeant noted that Vasquez had also—somewhat miraculously—managed to stuff himself into the vehicle's front cabin.

With both their doors closed, and both their seatbelts buckled behind them, Sergeant Carlisle shifted the SUV into drive. They hadn't yet made it to the exit gate before the radios strapped to their shoulders buzzed to life.

"Queen One, copy call."

The Sergeant did not much enjoy this dispatcher's whiny voice. It reminded her of the children she often ran into in public. The children who wailed and screamed and threw fits when they didn't get their way. The children whose parents she desperately wished would keep them at home.

Lost in her revulsion, she missed the drop and her chance to be the first to key up.

"Queen One to Central," Vasquez answered, the call sign unfamiliar on his tongue. "Go ahead."

The Sergeant's mouth twisted to one side as she watched her passenger squirm at the feminine designation.

"Queen One, burglary in progress at the corner of Second and Main. Single actor is White, male, and approximately twenty-five years of age. Caller advises no weapons, possible intox, unknown drugs."

The radio waves fell silent.

"The corner of Second and Main?" the passenger repeated, bunching his forehead. "Isn't that a—"

"Queen One, copy. Show us en route," the Sergeant responded. But then, after a thought, she clicked her radio once more. "Did the caller give a clothing description?"

The dispatcher keyed the mic to reply, but her snivelly voice did not fill the airwaves. Instead, she let the transmitter go. A moment of silence stretched by, and then their radios again crackled.

"Central to Queen One, no clothing description." The dispatcher took an uncharacteristic, audible breath. "Caller advises there are no clothes to describe. The actor is wearing a thin layer of... of grease, though."

Rubbing her temples, the Sergeant pressed her head against the seat.

Vasquez had been howling to the dusky sky before the dispatcher could even finish her sentence. With his head thrown back against the rest in laughter, a fresh, silvery-pale scar was just barely visible along the taut, olive skin of his throat.

Hmm. Maybe his downward spiral had been worse than she first suspected. *What flavor of degenerate activity had he gotten himself into?*

Through his full-body cackling, he retorted, "Queen One, copy. Actor unarmed, but slippery."

The Sergeant cut him a glare.

"That is *not* how you'll get your bars back, dumbass."

"It's *Officer* Dumbass, to you."

The Sergeant's nostrils flared.

It took the pair just under eight minutes to make it to the caller's location near Second and Main. As their cruiser pulled up along the curb outside the darkened business on the northeast corner of the intersection, the caller—a gangly, string bean of an assistant manager—ran out to flag them down.

Vasquez rolled down his window as the Sergeant busily swore under her breath.

A fucking trampoline park? A man covered in grease, at a fucking trampoline park? Honest to The Mother.

What had she done to deserve this? Who had she pissed off in the heavens above? Was it a neglected ancestor? A guardian angel in dire need of new hobbies?

"Evening, Miss. You don't look old enough to work in a topless club, let alone a fully nude establishment."

Jesus Christ.

Sergeant Carlisle had had it. Not yet one call in, and she had had it. Clearly, Vasquez was no longer the friend she remembered. Clearly, something had rotted deep within him. Because that—that was no way to speak to a frightened caller. That was no way to speak to a woman, let alone a girl. That was unacceptable.

Slamming the SUV into park, she jumped for the street below as Vasquez's face had an intimate meet-cute with the dashboard.

How's that for Samurai?

The uniformed prick was still cradling his nose as she rounded the front bumper and approached the shaking girl.

"You do not have to excuse him," the small Sergeant glared up at the massive sack of shit sitting in the front seat. "He was totally out of line."

And then, ignoring the blubbering buffoon, Sergeant Carlisle patiently listened as the girl—Chrissy—recounted the events of the evening.

Chrissy had ushered the last of the day's guests toward the exit. She had followed them to the front, waited with a smile on her face for them to leave, waved a few final goodbyes, and then locked each of the three sets of glass doors behind them.

It was when Chrissy turned away to begin the closing procedures that a loud crash sounded at her back. The shocked teen had been thrown to the floor before she knew what had happened. When the weight crushing her back at last relented, she was too terrified to move.

So, Chrissy had lain there frozen—her stinging knees tucked into her chest and her trembling arms the only shield between her and whatever had barreled through the front entrance.

After what she said felt like hours, she could no longer hear the intruder. That's when she bolted for the safety of her office and dialed 9-1-1. She admitted, though—her words wobbly—that she had neither seen nor heard the intruder leave.

The Sergeant gave Chrissy's arms a light, reassuring squeeze and kindly asked the wide-eyed assistant manager to wait there, outside.

Then, walking along each of the street-facing walls, she peered through every one of the dark windows she came to.

Nothing.

With whatever tinting the owners had coated them in, the Sergeant couldn't see a damned thing inside.

Walking back around to the front of the building, she jumped into the police cruiser. Then, squeezing the button on the car's PA, she announced, "THIS IS THE POLICE. IF YOU ARE INSIDE, MAKE YOURSELF KNOWN NOW."

Still nothing.

She tried again.

"THIS IS THE POLICE. IF YOU ARE INSIDE, MAKE YOURSELF KNOWN NOW. LAST CHANCE."

And once more, she got nothing. No signs of movement. No sounds. Nothing.

Well. Shit, the Sergeant huffed.

And then, she climbed down onto the SUV's running board and again advanced on the corner. After instructing Chrissy to go and wait behind the cruiser, she glared at the simp still nursing his face. Then, drawing her duty weapon and toggling the light on, the smoky-haired Sergeant stalked up to the shattered doors.

And when she at last heard the unmistakably heavy footsteps of her asinine assist—and then felt his shoulder tap half a second later—Sergeant Carlisle and her partner made entry.

Chapter 12

THE CONSERVATORY

Although stained lilac, Nora Everstar's chilled skin was nearly dry when she ascended the final step leading to the forward terrace. Amidst the wild cheering of the gathered specling and shihan, the words of one steady voice carried above all others:

"Respect be yours, Eleanora Everstar, for you alone have claimed this solar's Twenty-Second Canon."

The Shihan of Shields parted the lively crowd as he made to meet her halfway, in the center of the Everstar-lit promenade. Taking her split, scraped, and bloodied hand in his, he raised it high as he repeated his words once more, a little louder this time:

"Respect be yours, Eleanora Everstar, for you alone have claimed this solar's Twenty-Second Canon."

Not one of the three other competitors had yet returned. And as she heaved that pearlescent, tear-shaped jewel—a stone that easily dwarfed a newborn babe—up into the midday sky, Nora smiled to herself. For she was well aware of what her three despicable peers were currently up to:

Earnestly trying to clamber out of that deep, deep crater she had shoved them all into.

"The enemy will forever fight—that is the given. But the fight they will give, it will never be honest." Shi clapped Nora on the back. "At The Conservatory, each one of you must learn to wield your discipline against them. Not only the discipline of your bodies, but also of your minds."

Nora, at last, found Stassie's beautiful, beaming face in the throng. Her ever-dull Parallel stuck to her side, as usual.

"You see, while it might at first appear so, our Eleanora here—she did not break the one rule of this Canon. No, perversely, she followed it to the letter. Instead of using tools to aid in her ascent, she used her strength, her wit, and her stamina to aid in her *descent*."

The zealous horde applauded louder than Nora even thought achievable.

"For there is but one way a specling can reach the bottom of any of those three spires with enough air to swim back up and live to tell about it."

The taller shihan then regarded her expectantly, patiently awaiting the answer to the overt conundrum she had figured out before that first crack of the catapult.

The memory of her perfectly executed, backward dive from the crossbow rope played in her mind.

A pair of golden eyes elbowed their way to the front of the pack as Nora straightened her shoulders and said, "Downward momentum."

"Lavendar is a nice change," Dima smiled, his rich curls bounding with each new stride as he walked alongside Nora toward her private quarters. "The all black, all the time—it is somewhat tired."

The sixth-series cut the plucky male a look.

"*I* am somewhat tired."

"Of dressing like a reaper or being glazed like a Widow nectar pastry?"

Nora snorted.

"Of you!" she laughed. "And Canon syrup."

The fifth-series had promised his menacing, gilded glower was more than up to the task of keeping the manic fans—and the even more manic misanthropes—at bay. The glare, though, had deterred exactly no one. Likely because it was in no way menacing, at all.

"Well, with that one out of the way, the solitary hope Dalon has at surpassing *you*," the younger male alleged as they rounded the last corner before the dormitories, "is if you throw in the linen and opt not to rejoin us after the Twenty-Third Canon."

And even though Dima's reassuring sentiment did soothe the worry blooming in the center of her chest, the female laughed it off.

"If only we had that option, Fifth."

The worn rugs of Res Ell softened the corridor beneath their feet.

"Well, I hold no doubts," the male's toothy grin was moon-bright in the dusky hallway. "You will be the next Taiso of The Conservatory."

"Oh?" Nora socked the fifth-series in his unsuspecting bicep. "Is that all?"

He cradled and rubbed his arm as if it had been a grave strike.

"Wow, somebody sure is famished," Dima grumbled in mock outrage. "Do you think, in *this* state, you will venture back up to The Atrium, or—"

He ducked her blow and came to a halt before the door to her bedchamber.

"—or should I bring your plate to you down here... like the cave-dweller you are?"

The haughty male was not swift enough to dodge her punch a second time. He threw his palms up in surrender as she grabbed for the polished knob.

"I am going to soak first," Nora tutted, giving the handle a twist before pushing. "I am going to soak for a long, long while. Until this lilac glaze of Sorrow dissolves like sugar."

The old wooden door groaned open.

"Then, and only then, will I come up and join you all for the evening festivities."

True to her words, after retrieving a fresh set of leathers and her favorite soaps, Nora padded through the damp archway at the end of the keep's lowest level.

The cavernous bathing chamber was all smooth stone, white steam, and tiered pools. Piping-hot, mineral water the color of ice crystals seeped in from the depths of the mountain.

With her lilac leathers and matching breastplate in a heap by the steps, Nora leaned against the cool lip of the pool and closed her eyes. As the water did its work, she relived each mistake she had made during this morning's Canon.

Not verifying Dalon's location for herself one last time after hearing the chaos ensue on the terrace. Not anticipating the male might pause when the front-runner did not descend The Alpine Steps as expected. Not giving proper weight to his willingness to risk it all—his willingness to risk *everything*.

And as the healing waters soaked away her tension, Nora vowed that she would never again allow anyone to come that close. Then, she gave herself over to the practice wholly, to her tried and true decompression exercise of remembering then rewriting and rehearsing her missteps. She became lost so deeply, in fact, that she did not hear the approach until—

Broad hands wrapped around her naked waist. Her eyes flew open to see a bare-chested man tugging her body into his. She hardly got a breath down before his mouth met hers and his fingers were fisted in her purple-streaked hair. His movements were urgent—and in no manner gentle—as he flipped her onto her stomach and pressed her body forward into the cold stone of the bathing pool's edge.

With a powerful thrust and one weapons-calloused hand clamped over her mouth, Nora knew that she would *not* make it to the evening festivities.

Chapter 13

THE CATACOMBS

Her mouth was so, so painfully dry. With every inhale she managed, it felt as if barbed rakes scraped across the length of her tongue and down the back of her throat. The unpleasant sensation had the shackled sahira envisioning the barren, cracked wastelands of the Southern Salts she had once visited.

Savallin Prim did not know how long she had been unconscious. She did not know who had given the command that rendered her so. She did not even know why the order had been issued at all. She had her inclinations, yes—but she did not yet know for certain.

Though, she did suspect that she was alone down here.

All alone, in total darkness.

For down here, in these putrid, primordial hollows— down here in the blackest cells of The Klekta Mortem—down here, there was not a living being on Earth that could reach their intrinsic power.

In fact, no sahira had ever survived more than a few days locked down here in these choking, sulfuric depths. That was precisely why, Savallin recalled, these levels of The Catacombs—the deepest in existence—had been abandoned and sealed off ages ago.

Or... or at least...

Savallin steeled her core and tried to swallow.

At least... that is what our people have long been led to believe.

She would worry about that later.

Being confined to the bowels of the caverns was not ideal. Imprisonment, while unfortunate as it was, did not free one of their responsibilities. Yes, the circumstances might be dire, but, no—they did not, they would not—prevent Savallin Prim, Keeper of Wisdom, from carrying out her sworn duty. From fulfilling her sacred obligation to her people.

So, mindful of the deadline steadily approaching, aware of the time still ticking away, the sahira beckoned the memories of the last two letters she had received. One: the desperate plea of a grim stranger. The other: a grim plea from a desperate friend.

We have been misguided.
We have all been misguided.
Summon The Skapahni.

Back when she was just a sahiralette—back when she was a young covenary, not yet bestowed Her burden—Savallin had attended conventional schooling. It was back in those days, back when the Tutors of Time taught history as history had happened, that the sahira most enjoyed learning.

But then, as each covenary one day would, the peaceful and adored Diadet Granada heard the Hail of Hadi. And in her place, a new sahira ascended the Obsidian Throne.

The youthful and beautiful Nirvana had been confirmed—without challenge—as the next Diadet of Covenarykind, thanks to her charismatic campaign centered on restoring the covenary to former glory.

What former glory she meant?

Nobody thought to ask.

The moment the stone crown touched down upon her bone-hued hair, a tyrannic rule—so restrictive, so bitter and hateful it scorched—whooshed through every last league of corridor in The Catacombs.

With the rise of Nirvana came the fall of truth.

Under her rule, no longer could the Tutors of Time recount history in its entirety. No longer could they study or teach from the books of old. No longer could they be objective in their lesson plans.

And beyond those limitations, there was still one offense Diadet Nirvana declared more unforgivable than all others:

Any breath of, or any reference to, the Shamed Sisters of Covenarykind became punishable by immediate execution.

It was the second fading of The Skapahni.

The Skapahni that Savallin was now somehow supposed to summon.

The Skapahni she was supposed to summon... on behalf of those responsible for sentencing every last one of them to their fading.

The torrent of her raging thoughts broke against the stones of her skull again and again. Spine aching in answer, she adjusted her shackles and bent to rest her head upon her bony knees.

It is absurd, she thought.

Absurd that as Keeper of Wisdom, as the collector of knowledge and understanding, she did not even know the truth of why The Skapahni were shamed to begin with.

Within hours of Diadet Nirvana's crowning, Savallin had been abruptly removed from the traditional schooling she loved. And then, after a few teary and rushed goodbyes, she had been packed up and sent off to begin her Keeper Tutelage.

To this very day—even shackled all the way down here in this smothering, rotting cell—the sahira could still remember that first starlight flight. She could still feel the night, still feel the kiss of the cool breeze as it tickled her face.

Still... that was not what she remembered best.

No.

It was the sinking—the lonely plummet in the pit of her stomach—that she would never forget.

The all-encompassing heartbreak of a covelette being forced from her home.

Forced to leave her family behind.

Forced to forget all that she loved and held dear in the world.

That was the feeling ever compelling Savallin Prim.

As if it were a goose-feathered coverlet, she wrapped that feeling tightly around herself and squeezed her eyes shut.

In the bleakness, she pictured the second note—the one that had sparkled. The warning.

Seems if you are reading this, the worst has come to pass. Absolutely do not squander sacred time fretting over my wellbeing, but do understand that your days are now numbered as well.

Venture above and find what has been lost. If it is meant to be found, it will be found. Reader, it is without any doubt that two of the five are not to be trusted. Unless it is three.

Now, go. my strength will soon be yours.

CC

The sahira had no qualms as to whether the letter had been meant for her. Her friend, Coralis Carveil, was many a thing. Subtle, though, was not ordinarily one of them.

What good is it, Cora had ranted upon countless returns, *what good is it to unmuddy the answers if only to muddy their meanings?*

Such tirades were common in the wake of Cora reading her own discoveries. It was her impassioned belief that if a scribe lacked the skill to rightly translate her findings, then maybe—just maybe—the art of linguistics was not their select medium. She would nitpick each sentence, every word choice, and each thought stop.

That was the key to her warning. The key to the message within the message.

Coralis Carveil, Keeper of Wonder, would never neglect proper grammar. She would never allow a lowercase letter to begin the first word of a written thought.

if it is meant to be found, it will be found.
my strength will soon be yours.

If read without the two erroneous sentences, the first letter of every sentence spelled out the command, spelled out her last gift.

Sav, run.

What Sav had yet to gain clarity on was whether the two flawed sentences were meant to be trusted as true—or if the two claims were intended only as fodder.

"If they were meant as fodder, would she have sacrificed the time in writing them at all?"

A wave of icy prickles crashed up the vertebrae of Savallin's spine.

That was not... it could not be...

She was... she was alone down here. She had to be alone down here, down in this forgotten prison of earth.

Who else would—*what* else would—

"You need not be frightened, covenary."

The voice—*that voice*—it guttered as if crafted from the last light of a dying star. It was so... so sad. So cold. But it—it sounded as if it were right behind her. Behind her... locked in the cell *with* her.

The crooked Majlis... they would not dare to... to... would they?

No. Not without first parading my disgrace through the entirety of the corridors.

Was it in her head? Had she already begun the steep descent into madness? How much longer did... how much time did she have left?

"Time?" the voice trailed off. "Well, I have existed here for hundreds of years."

Hundreds of... no. No... that is not—

"You think that because your leader banned the truth, that truth ceases to be?"

The sahira leapt to her feet, her eyes feverishly searching the darkness for what was not there. Finding nothing did not settle her—not in the least. No, she sprinted toward the mists of the black archway as swiftly as her feet would allow.

"She is not what you think, that clever Nirvana."

The heels of her slippers ground to a halt when she sensed it—when she neared that invisible drapery trapping her within. Hands shaking, Savallin sucked down a breath and opened her mouth to scream to the skies, but then—

"Coralis promised that she would introduce us," the unhurried voice whispered into the void.

All of the thoughts—each racing, conflicting thought—vanished from the sahira's mind.

"Who are you?" the trapped covenary bit into the dimness.

"I hail from a distant age," the other prisoner, the strange female, answered. "You would not know my name even if I voiced it."

Savallin felt the softness of her own lips as they again met. She turned toward where she thought the voice was coming from. Willing her heart to slow, to calm, she took a step in the darkness.

"And what is it, then, that you could know of Covenarykind?"

And the Keeper—she did not hear any echo off the moistened walls of her cage. Rather, she felt it. That low, unmistakably warm rumble of laughter.

How had... how had she...

The voice of coldest ice—the voice haunting the abyss—crooned, "I know that you, Savallin Prim, are the kind of covenary the world came to fear."

Chapter 14

THE CONSERVATORY

The chamber door very nearly flew off the ancient hinges as a booted heel smashed into the carved, polished wood.

Outside the delicately frosted window, the sky slumbered on—still peacefully shrouded in a thick blanket of stars—refusing to be woken by the symphony of crashes, splintering wood, and panicked howls of unsuspecting sixth-series rattling the walls of the dormitory corridor.

In the darkness of Nora's bedchamber, however, no screams or yells or cries for help threatened to disturb the Forbidden Hours of the sky. The only sound in this room—a sharp inhale—came from the towering intruder as he realized his fatal error a beat too late.

For in her room, it was not the sixth-series who had been caught unaware.

From the shadows of the corner opposite the modest bed, Nora moved like the night. As the masked ogre lunged for the bare mattress, she struck.

In a single, silent breath, she was upon his back, her legs wrapped tightly around his waist like a vice as her left hand ripped at his hair—yanking his head backward—exposing his throat. As the attacker panted, the blade angled in her right hand pressed up into the soft spot beneath his chin.

"You will not—"

Nora kicked her foot hard into the back of the intruder's knee and threw the full weight of her body to the low side. They were toppling toward the rug before the masked assailant—before Decard Battleson—could finish the insulting insinuation.

Pinning the foolish and bull-headed shield—who was now, by ways unbeknownst to her, a full spectral—to the floor, she taunted, "You know *nothing* about what I will and will not do."

As he bucked in protest, her dagger drew glittering, graphite-gray blood.

For Decard's unannounced appearance in the bathing chamber that evening had tipped her off to what this night would truly entail. And it was for that alone, she had let him have his way.

Gritting his teeth against the icy sting of her steel, the muscle-roped warrior gave a deep, guttural chuckle. Her skin prickled—and not in a good way.

Gripping a thigh and the length of her braid, the giant heaved to his feet as if her added weight were nothing more than imaginary.

Willing her body to twist out of his crushing grasp, Nora—

Tearing backward with the braid hand, Decard growled against her ear, "You know *nothing* about what I will and will not do to ensure that you become my Parallel."

It was her turn to gasp.

Nora's head swam, and ever-bright stars flooded the midnight chamber as the frosted window shattered with the violent impact of her body against the stone wall.

Her knife clattered to the ground.

The merciless, emerald eyes of the spectral staring down at her shimmered with delight as the breath was forced from her lungs.

"Say the words, Nora," the first-shield groaned, shoving harder—his *excitement* more than evident along her leg. "Say them, and I will stop."

It is not so uncommon for the unbonded spectral to be courted. What is uncommon is the understanding as to why.

Even though The Rite of Parallel forges two lives into one eternity for the rest of time, there is but one stipulation: for the ritual to be completed, the will must be in the hearts of both bodies. Thus, the sacred bond cannot be forced upon another.

And so, oftentimes, the milder of courtships—full of kind gestures and plenty of wooing—are misinterpreted by outsiders as acts of love. When in reality, they are nothing more than polite acts of selfish survival.

The Conservatory goes so far as to condone the depraved behavior by making The Vitoska standings known to not only the specling upon the mountain, but also the spectraline conscripted to The Shield's outposts. And as a specling's standing elevates, so does the volatility of their inevitable courting.

"Enough with the games, castress." The unrelenting asshole cracked her spine against the wall a second time for emphasis. "You know as well as I do—there is not an immortal on this earth more suitable for you than I."

By rankings, he was correct.

By everything that mattered, he could not be more wrong.

For since The Conservatory's founding two-hundred millennia ago, there had been only one specling who remained undefeated through the entirety of their Canons. But that spectral's name had long ago been stricken from time, their great achievement all but forgotten.

Until five solar cycles ago, that is. Five solar cycles ago, when another star specling seemed destined to claim that esteemed title of Taiso—a strapping, golden-haired standout from a noble bloodline who *would have* claimed the title, if not for the low-born first-series who absolutely wrecked him in his final Canon as a spec.

"I want to hear you say it," he ground out.

Stretching her arm as far as her shoulder allowed, Nora's fingernails just barely reached the window ledge to her left. Desperately, painfully, she raked at the breezy sill and spat, "Not in this li—"

A shriek she did not recognize ripped from her throat as Decard's pointed canines tore through the sensitive fibers of her bicep.

As her vision fogged, his *thrill* pressed harder into her inner thigh.

"Say it, Nora, and I will stop."

"Stop," her chest ached at the next words. "Stop, and I will say it."

"If you are fucking with me, specling—"

A broad hand clasped over her mouth so swiftly her skull snapped backward. White-hot pain bloomed in her belly as Decard's teeth sank into the crook of her neck.

"—the next few days will be your last."

Swallowing her fury, she smiled.

And then slowly—so slowly, as if he might change his mind at any moment—he loosened his grip. After a few more tense beats, his green eyes softened. And then, at last, he took a step back, away from the wall.

Nora laid a soft hand on his clenched jawline. And Decard Battleson, the youngest spectral ever to be named a Commander of The Shield, breathed in the chill air.

Rising to her tiptoes, she wrapped her arms around his neck and leaned in close. And with her lips all but grazing his skin, Nora whispered the words Decard needed to hear.

Chapter 15

THE CITY

Two weeks and thirteen subpar coffees had passed since Everly Castile first moved to this city in the North. The furious, unending melody of aggravated motorists and overzealous street vendors had become a somewhat relaxing tune.

Although Everly had promised her eternity to The Shield more than nine-hundred solar cycles before, the nature of her abrupt ousting all but guaranteed that the likelihood of her being called upon, in this day and age, was nonexistent.

So, as a highly skilled and decorated warrior stripped of her eternity's purpose—and fresh out of mortal tourist attractions to patronize—so oft does, she resigned herself to day upon day of aimless wandering. Day upon day of trying to outpace the old ways through the packed and bustling streets of The Mortal City's five boroughs.

But no matter how devoted she was to forgetting her past, no matter how much distance she put between it and herself, one watchful eye remained ever tilted toward the sky.

On this day, Everly found herself sitting in the middle of a wooden bench at the end of a long pier that jutted out into the green-brown waves. The thick layer of clouds overhead seemed to be getting grayer and hanging a bit lower than they had when she'd first arrived.

Way, way back during the height of The Shield's guard, overcast skies such as these were known to be rather tense. Today, though, there was not an ounce of tension thrumming through her body. Hunger, maybe. But tension? No.

This morning, after almost an hour of mindless waiting, Everly had been only three spots away from the front of the line that wrapped around an entire city block. The ridiculous wait was for the neighborhood's newest and trendiest internet-famous bakery.

She had been seriously contemplating how someone could live at the mercy of baked goods for almost a full millennium when a man—so extraordinarily generic that he actually drew the eye—stumbled by.

It wasn't the man's brazen act of thievery that had sparked Everly's curiosity. No, it wasn't even that the scumbag had chosen to steal from a heavily pregnant woman who pushed another baby in a stroller. No, that hadn't been it either.

Everly's focus had been snagged by the item at the heart of the theft:

A small, plastic cellular device. A relic, really.

Humans had forgone their humble, folding telephones in favor of sleek, glass super-computers decades ago. So... what would prompt someone to dispatch a novice to swipe an antique?

Everly had forfeited her place in line to find out.

The snooping that ensued had led her into the morning rush of the subway station, then onto an eastbound train headed for the boarded-up barrier island, and, finally, down the creaky length of this salt-kissed boardwalk.

The subject of her intrigue seemed to have an appointment with the four lowlifes standing on the adjacent dock.

Everly did not bother acting natural, nor did she care to fly under the radar. The men in the muscle tees would not see her—not as long as the sun stayed in the sky.

It was relatively clear that the quartet did not consist of law enforcement personnel. No, the men were neither beat cops, nor feds. That, the amateur thief whose ediness not even the cheap trench coat could disguise, and the lonely locale of the meet-up all screamed semi-organized crime.

The lady in line, one hand on the small of her back and the other rubbing gentle circles onto her belly, was likely a protected witness. The untraceable, low-tech phone she'd been carrying backed up the assumption.

Whatever she had seen—whatever secret the woman threatened to expose—it must have been juicy. Juicy enough to, at the very least, warrant the three bodyguards Everly had counted.

The pitiful filth who pass as protectors in this era.

Everly wondered what it was the woman knew—wondered at the damning truth it must be to frighten men too dumb to know fear.

She presumed that instead of killing the young mother, an act which would raise too much unwanted attention, the bastards on the neighboring pier had lifted her phone to steal its contact information. Contact information they could now use to silently threaten and extort her.

Cowards.

Everly smiled to herself when a light scuffle broke out on the wharf opposite her own. Her smile grew when a quiet pop wafted across the wind. And Everly's smile beamed when a body-sized thud sounded from the floorboards of the dinghy tied to the pylon.

May the journey suit the jester.

There was nothing more she could do for the mortal woman. Human-on-human affairs were not truly in her purview. All the spectraline could do now was wish the lady well.

So, she waited there on her dock until the last of the men's footsteps faded into the ocean breeze. Then, with her skin aptly chilled, Everly rose to make her way back home. Tucking the dark strays firmly behind her ears, she dropped her Brightbreak—her cloak of masked daylight—and turned for the subway station.

If anyone had been watching the empty bench at the end of the pier, the slim silhouette now stomping off, seemingly out of thin air, might've come as quite the start.

Even all these solars separated from The Shield, Everly Castile had not yet gotten used to wearing her hair unbound. She did not like the constant upkeep, nor did she care for how the long tresses waved about wildly in the wind. But more than that—above all else—Everly loathed having to occupy her hands in keeping the locks at bay.

Such frivolity is not worth an eternity.

She could practically hear her shihan's reproach.

And so, pulling an elastic band from her wrist, Everly wrestled her lengthy mane into a modest, chestnut bun at the nape of her neck. And as she walked on, away from the sounds of the sea, she sheepishly hoped that if she hurried, she might be met with a shorter bakery queue upon her return.

Her stomach was angrily growling its assent when, suddenly, her chest forgot how to rise and fall. For not one-hundred strides before her stood the impossible.

The midnight curls... the eyes of molten gold... a true one-of-a-kind pairing that to this very day stilled the beating within Everly's body. Her whole being—her immortal soul—felt as if wound in a chain of liquid misery, felt as if bound in barbs and then thrown from the highest peak of the snowcapped vale.

"It can't be," her wounded disbelief sighed to no one.

But then, at her words—at her quiet claim—the long-felled warrior she saw only in nightmares was lost once again.

Her feet flew, eating up the distance atop the peeling planks, before her mind could work it all out. She sprinted toward that memory—toward him—paying no heed to The Oath of Obscurity.

If the humans took notice of her, that was on them.

In an instant, the pier was dwindling away behind her, and the past—her past—beckoned from just beyond. She pumped her arms harder, pushed her legs even faster because he had been there—he was there.

Sucking in a deep, shaky breath, Everly filled her lungs and tried—really tried—to steady herself for the final turn, for the final corner where the midnight and molten had flickered one moment ago.

Even if she had second thoughts, even if her heart wasn't ripping out of her chest, Everly rounded the turn so quickly it would've been impossible to—

The muscle-thick forearm that shot from the shadows—the battle-seasoned bludgeon that crushed into her windpipe—it did not belong here. It did not belong in this time. It did not belong to the warrior who had left a hole in her soul.

No. No. No.

It belonged in the deepest, fieriest pits of Sempenihil.

No.

And as that evil cracked her bones against the concrete, over and over—as that evil stripped the air from her lungs and tunneled her vision—Everly Castile heard the *spectral* growl:

"Oh, how the Everstar has fallen."

Chapter 16

THE CONSERVATORY

Eighty-six specs from the sixth and final series of The Conservatory formed two straight lines down the candlelit corridor of the Res Ell. From the looks of them, her contemporaries had been dragged from their beds in all states of disarray. Some stood bleary-eyed, while others watched, alert as any midnight guard.

All of them knew what this night was. All of them knew what this night meant. All of them had endured six very long, very exhausting series, unsure of when it would finally arise.

The Twenty-Third Canon.

Tonight was the commencement of the Twenty-Third Canon.

Positioned between the mirrored rows, pacing atop the carpeted runner, the band of first-shields itched for their next fight. Down the lines, the fine assortment of black eyes and crooked noses implied exactly how much these soldiers enjoyed inflicting pain. It was not entirely surprising, considering the man they called Commander was a sadist at best—a war criminal at worst.

By the time they had come searching for said Commander, the blood spilling from Nora's nose and a gash above her eye had been soaking through his polished uniform. Their mighty Commander, it seemed, had quite the propensity for winding up pinned beneath lesser, little sixth-series females.

Now standing next to Nora, stiff as a spear, Stassie assessed the threat before her—no doubt searching the unguarded minds of the first-shields. Like the majority of the eighty-six specling waiting for orders, she was still wearing her nightclothes. The thin fabric would not do her a shred of good if her Canon ground was chosen to be somewhere high in the surrounding mountains.

Nora's crafty sister, however—unlike the rest of their peers—had managed to pull on a pair of battle boots. And even better, the hilts of her twin daggers could be seen peeking just out the top of them. If her busted lip and ravaged hair were any indication, those meager provisions had cost her.

From the very end of the hall, almost to the spiral stair leading to the lower levels, the olive-skinned spec with wide-set shoulders and light-brown hair cropped close to his scalp glared lazily in Nora's direction.

Someone is still upset about the Twenty-Second, I see.

But it was more than that—she knew. For his expression said exactly what everybody else was surely thinking as they stared at her in her full set of blacks.

Of course Decard's stuck-up whore would have been tipped off.

The only difference between that spec—the very same male who nearly plucked Nora out of the sky during this morning's Canon—and everyone else in the hall, was that Dalon was keen enough to see through the swine shit.

Much to her detriment, of course.

For that was how he knew something was amiss when she did not descend The Alpine Steps right on his heels. For that was how he pieced together her plan of attack. For that was how he came so close to besting her, once and for all.

For that was why the sting still lingered.

Because he had nearly earned that victory. He had nearly merited the win.

At the admission, a new wave of anger rose within the pit of Nora's belly as her dawn of missteps again played through her mind. Her vision began to darken.

But then she found herself biting back her thrill—and her every last thought—as Dalon's scorching lazuline gaze burned into a simmer.

Heavy footfalls—angry footfalls—stemming from her bedchamber echoed through the hushed hall.

Nora straightened her posture and looked to the door.

For just then, after being helped to his feet and having the blood wiped away from where she had held the shard of windowpane to his throat, Commander Decard Battleson sauntered into the hallway.

It is truly a miracle his arrogance fit through that door arch.

Stassie's giggle ricocheted off the stone walls before Nora remembered to reinforce her inner guard.

Shit. Her inhale was edged. *Shit.*

For her sister had risked herself—risked her own hide—for Nora. She had laughed as a veiled warning. Because Stass knew as well as she did that roughly half the first-shields under Decard's command possessed the very same gifts as her.

Thought-Tellers.

At the disruption—the perceived slight—Decard whirled. But Nora was faster. Much faster.

Before he could wrap his repulsive hands around her sister's neck and begin the slow, torturous process of choking the eternity from her body, Nora was in front of her with her blades drawn.

As the threat-in-charge towered over her, as dark thoughts that were not her own clawed at her conscience, that ordinarily distant spec at the far end of the dim corridor started.

Perhaps, Nora swore under her breath, *the brute is not as wise as I suspected.*

Decard, veritable steam spilling from his pores, made to storm toward the male who had recoiled.

Still, Nora told herself as she remembered the events of the dawn, *a warrior as cunning as he does not deserve to be skinned alive.*

And so, before the Commander could stomp down the corridor and order that auspicious specling thrown off the keep's uppermost turret, Nora hooked a forearm behind his head and pulled him in close.

His soldiers froze in place as her lips locked onto their leader's.

Decard flinched. And for a moment, Nora thought he might not fall for the ploy. But then—his good sense no match for wanton desire—he gave in, shoving so passionately that she and her sister both slammed into the painting mounted on the wall between their chamber doors. Nora's boot stomped down into the still-full plate of food that had been left for her some time earlier in the evening.

She tried to push him forward, tried to break the embrace, but he was not having it. And praise her wicked, golden soul, Stassie shoved off the wall and helped wrench Nora free from the Commander's iron grip. Not a spec, nor a shield, dared to even breathe too loudly—except for her elder sister, that is.

"For fuck's sake," from behind her, Stassie grumbled on. "Did you seriously awaken us—have your cowardly men grope us—just so you could suck my sister's face for all to see?"

Nora choked.

Dalon choked.

The entire Ever-blessed hall choked.

The shadowy gleam storming Decard's jewel-hued eyes made Nora's blood run icy, icy cold.

He has killed for less, Nora breathed. *For much less.*

But Stassie, so as not to be detected, pinched the underside of Nora's arm—her subtle way of saying, *He is welcome to fucking try.* And then, after studying Stassie for far too long, Commander Battleson turned on a heel and strode for his rightful place at the center of the hall.

Crossing his arms behind his back, his posture excruciatingly stiff, Decard began reciting The Promise of the Canons. It was pure vanity, for every single soul lined up in this dormitory hall against their will knew the words of The Promise of the Canons by heart. Plus, they were customarily saved for only the first and the last Canon.

Preening prick.

From the primary, each subsequent Canon increases in its level of difficulty. Each Canon until the second-to-last, that is. For the second-to-last, *it* is rumored to be all but unbeatable. The sole objective: return alive.

The Twenty-Third Canon was originally designed to find both a specling's mental and physical limits. It is a real-life, real-stakes test intended to locate a warrior's ultimate breaking point. But, in recent solars, the Twenty-Third seemed not only to find limits, but to tear right past them— often mincing the sixth series into pieces in the process.

In fact, last solar was the first time in The Conservatory's history that more specling returned home in burial white than in battle black.

But if a spec does successfully navigate this third Canon of their sixth series, it all but guarantees that they will live to see graduation. For the Twenty-Fourth and final Canon is essentially a performance—a ballet of battle meant to encourage the younger specs at the end of their all-daunting first series to continue on with their studies.

And it is because of that Canon that Nora was already slated to graduate. On a technicality that nobody—not a specling, nor a shihan, nor an Elder—could have fathomed, Nora was no longer required to participate in any Canon. Not since fulfilling her Fourth.

"Die," the former specling who was on the losing side of *that* Fourth Canon concluded his extraordinarily ominous words of inspiration, "or do not."

And as one, the flock of brutish warriors cramping the hall turned to face the archway at the lip of the stairs. Without a word, they gripped the arm of the spec closest to them. Nobody fought it.

Nobody—until Commander Decard Battleson snapped his fingers and the red-haired soldier holding Stassie spun, thrusting his broadsword straight into her heart.

The world-ending scream that ripped from Nora's throat was met with a steel fist to the windpipe. Hitting her knees, she gasped for air—for her sister.

Through the uncontrollable wave of tears welling in her eyes, Nora saw a pair of bare feet barreling toward her before her head cracked again and the world around her started to fade.

The taste of her earlier vow soured on her tongue as everything she knew went black.

Not in this eternity, or the next, will you live to be my Parallel.

Chapter 17

THE CRYPTS

"Let us begin at the beginning," the lady in the pale purple glasses began. "Tell me, Ava, what is it you remember of your mother?"

Ava snorted.

The woman seated across from her only pursed her lips and clicked a red heel against the yellowing linoleum.

"I assume you would like to leave this dungeon?"

Ava closed her eyes and pressed a thumb into the throbbing of her temple.

"Have you always been so hardheaded?" She could hear the ends of the blonde strands sway as the lady shifted in her seat. "Or, rather, did some life event lead you to this stubbornness?"

Peeling her eyelids open with theatric intention, Ava crossed her arms and leaned back in her chair. In the taut silence, the buzzing of the overhead lights grew louder and louder.

How long would they keep her here? How long could they keep her here? Her union rep should have arrived by now—her union rep, and probably her lawyer, too. After what had gone down, Ava fully expected there to be an investigation into what had happened, but she had not expected that investigation to center on her.

Another factor giving her pause was the interrogation room in which she had been placed. For only this room—this one room out of the twenty or so that lined the halls of The Crypts—did not yet have interior cameras or two-way glass.

This room was the last relic of a different day. A day when an accusation meant the forfeiture of rights. A day when an accusation was as good as a guilty verdict. None of which had been lost on Ava. She knew there were no accidents—knew this room had been selected strategically.

That was why she had changed into her warmest sweater. A thick, trusty cable-knit, well worthy of blocking the creeping chill of this room.

Familiar fabric to bundle foreign skin, she thought to herself.

The lady—the therapist... or whatever it was she called herself—scrunched her forehead.

"You don't happen to be"—the shrink arched a single ashen brow as she settled on her first prognosis—"cuisine-compelled? Now, do you?"

And before she could scowl at the nosy do-gooder on the other side of the metal table, Ava's no-good, dirty, rotten, traitorous stomach grumbled in answer.

"Ah, I see."

So pleased with herself that Ava pondered whether her ego now posed a threat of bodily harm, the shrink rose and clacked toward the door.

"Don't you go anywhere now," she winked as she slipped freely through the room's only exit.

Ava's eyes about rolled out her ears.

Why did the lady want to know about her mother? What help could that possibly be to this investigation? All the relevant details of her childhood—shit, even the irrelevant ones—were documented extensively in her Personal History Statement. If the shrink wished to know about her past, all she had to do was pull that PHS from her file and crack it open.

Ava tugged the ends of her sleeves around her fingers.

It had been a long time since anyone had asked about her mom. A very, very long time. So long, in fact, that she had almost forgotten how badly it hurt.

Almost.

Ava had been just a girl when her mother died. Even thinking about it now, all these years later, she lost her appetite. For that day... well. Well, it was not something she cared to relive.

Ever.

Ava had been old enough that she still remembered what it was like to be loved, to be held by a mother. But at the same time, Ava had been *so* young that she could no longer remember the face of the one who had loved her so—the face of the one who had held her so.

And there, alone in the cold room, alone with no ally save her sweater, Ava sank into that cloudy pool of her memory and tried to paint her portrait.

Her mother had been tall, Ava remembered. Tall with unruly, auburn curls that hung halfway down her back. She could remember running her little fingers through them, laughing as they caught on tangle after tangle.

She also knew that she had been beautiful. She knew it because, even to this day, she could still sense the awe that had radiated off all who had known her. Her mother, with her warm islander coloring and those sharpened, cunning eyes that had been stolen straight from the heart of the sea herself. They were the only remnants of her that Ava had left—the pieces she had passed down. The traces forever etched onto her own body, into her own stare.

But try as she might—try as she had for twenty godsdamned years—Ava still could not picture those features, her own features, upon her mother's face. Not through the mists of her mind.

She could feel her, though. Feel her skin as soft as warm silk, feel her strong arms as they enveloped her tightly. She could sense that tickle of cinnamon and vanilla in her nose— that hint of her mother's signature, spiced scent. A smell that, even after her death, had forever soothed Ava's restless spirit.

It was enough—the mere memory of it—to dissipate her tension now, to calm her rising worry. But just then, as quickly as the peace had come, it vanished altogether when the interrogation room's steel door again swung wide.

"I hope you didn't miss me too much," the flittering, jovial voice of the psychiatrist breezed. "I also hope you like waffles."

Waffles?

Ava pushed up her sleeve and looked down to the watch on her wrist.

Fuck me.

The cheap piece of shit must've been fried in the—

"I know, *I know.*" The lady pulled out her chair and retook her seat. "Where did I manage to find waffles at a time like this?"

The greasy white bag in her hand did not have a label.

"A time like this?"

"Oh!" The paper bag dropped from her hand. "She speaks!"

Ava, arms crossed and already reclined as far as she could be without toppling backward, sighed loudly.

"Stubborn *and* ill-mannered."

"Look, lady, I—"

"Alice," the lady cut in as she pulled two cardboard containers from her bag. "You may call me Alice."

Ali—

Ava took a steadying breath.

"Okay," she blew quietly before sitting up a bit straighter. "Alice, I appreciate you getting food. I do, truly. But is it really necessary?"

Alice slid a hot carton and a plastic fork across the table but did not meet Ava's gaze.

The ultra-reinforced, triple-locked lid on her dwindling patience was dangerously close to blowing sky-high, but she tried once more.

"What I mean is, how long do you pl—"

"You are asking the wrong questions, Ava."

The celadon starbursts in Ava's eyes pulsed brightly as she bit down on the rage rushing for the surface.

"I beg your pardon, ma'am?"

"Alice."

The lid shattered.

"For fuck's sake, *Alice*," Ava spewed. "What, *in your god's glorious name*, is it that you want me to ask?"

Alice, cocking her head to one side with an amused look, cut into her breakfast.

"Seriously?!"

The glue binding what was left of Ava began to boil.

"What's your fucking problem, lady?"

Alice stabbed a syrupy bite of waffle fluff onto her fork.

"Alice."

The plastic fork was clenched in Ava's hand and angled toward Alice's throat before the young Sergeant could see clearly.

Alice, though, simply glanced up at Ava—who was now stretched across the table like an absolute crazy—and popped the forkful into her mouth. Ava's jaw plunged so low she was sure it would never again close right.

"You stuck-up who—"

"You"—Alice said after swallowing her bite—"beckoned me, Ava."

The fork in Ava's hand began to hum.

"So, the question you should be asking is," Alice smiled knowingly, "How long do *you* plan on keeping us down here?"

Chapter 18

THE CITADEL

Nora Everstar knew pain better than she knew her closest peers, better than she knew her personal quarters, better than she knew herself.

The scars and callouses marring her body had long memorized the ins, the outs—each and every possible path a new agony might dare to weasel. Even so, if ever there came a hurt so great as to breach the impenetrable fortress she had honed herself into, then her mind—the cruel, cunning mind of a warrior—would shut that shit down.

But this pain... this crushing, aching pain in the pit of her heart... in the hollow of her soul... this pain was like nothing Nora had trained for.

Stassie.

"Open your eyes, castress," demanded the merciless, doomed spectral now topping her kill list.

Nora did not hear him, though. Not really. No, her focus was elsewhere as she lay there—wherever there was—on the rough, unforgiving stones.

Not her. Not—

The spiked toe of a climbing boot slammed into her side.

"You cannot feign death forever, Eleanora," his harsh voice warned into the wind.

She might have grunted. Might have tasted the bitter tang of acid... might have... but her eyes—her eyes remained closed.

Not her. Anyone but her. Stass—

With one swift motion, a foot's worth of filed steel cleats stomped down onto her unguarded abdomen. The air whooshed from her body as she jerked upward off the ground. Whooshed, as she jolted and—and caught.

Her eyes shuddered open at last. And then, as her mind tried to process what it saw, all the extraneous thoughts emptied from her head. For Nora was not on the ground. She was not within the familiar confines of The Conservatory either.

No.

The young sixth-series was far, far from the safety of those walls.

The stones she had felt beneath her, the stones she had mistaken for the ground—these stones belonged to something much, much worse.

The Pillars of the Sky.

The Pillars of the Sky at the heart of The Citadel.

How long was I out?

Thousands and thousands of solar cycles before Nora Everstar was born, these Pillars—narrow columns of earthstone carved straight out of the cliffs by the ruthless and ravenous fury of corequakes—were part of a grand and sprawling monastery. And resting atop each Pillar, quietly swaying in the gusts hundreds upon hundreds of paces off the earth's surface, had been either a dormitory, a worship house, or...

Or an Ever Step.

How did they... how had we... how did we make it all the way up here?

In the days of old, an Ever Step was the closest an Ever being might ever get to The Everstar herself. In truth, that was the sole reason the monastery had been built here in the first place. And it was also why a monstrous citadel was then erected around it in order to protect it.

Back in those days, though, there had been but one manner of reaching the zenith of a Pillar:

climbing.

To set foot upon an Ever Step meant scaling one of the many sheer rock faces adorning The Pillars of the Sky. The ascent alone would have been daunting. It could take hours— sometimes days if the season did not wish one to summit. And as if that were not strenuous enough, the substantial weight of the Illicit Offering one must carry with them on their climb was sure to be.

For an Ever Step was an altar among the stars. Altars lonely enough, isolated enough, as to avoid any mortal curiosity. Altars where young, untried spectraline warriors gathered to commit the most heinous of acts. Altars where ancient Shield battalions met to break through the boundaries of the Known. Altars where the very first of The Spectraline sacrificed their eternal souls to claim what did not belong to them.

Altars to the devils of the night.

Altars to the forgotten.

Altars... to the Beasts of Old.

"Are they, though? Beasts of *Old?*"

Nora's gaze whirled to Decard.

No. No, no, no. That is not possible!

"Oh, lover," he winked. "But it *is.*"

The very stones beneath her backside felt as if they would assuredly give way when the knot in Nora's stomach dropped like a lead weight.

He cannot. Decard cannot. He is not a Thought-Teller. So, how... how is this happen—

Decard's wicked smile worsened into the canine grin of Nora's nightmares.

What about The Canon... what about—

"The Twenty-Third? Oh, you need not trouble yourself worrying over that. *Besides*, you and I both know, you are not required to participate anyway." Decard crouched so low that his hot breath stung her frozen face. Then, he clamped his massive hand around her jaw and crushed inward. "*Remember?*"

"I mean, will anyone ever forget how I wiped the floor with your sorry ass *as a first-series?*"

So fast—too fast—Decard's canines ripped through her ear.

"You stole my shot at Taiso." A river of pearlescent charcoal rushed down her neck. "So, *I* will have yours."

Outwardly, she rolled her eyes in spectacular fashion, but inwardly—on the inside—Nora dug wildly, frantically, as she clawed to throw up her innermost shields, her mightiest defense. But that wall—her wall—it was not within her reach. It was... it was so far down she could hardly sense its presence.

Wrong. This is wrong. This is all wrong. I am... I am wro—

"Not entirely." In the flicker of the torchlight, Nora watched as her blood dripped from Decard's sharpest teeth. He rose to his knees. "On the contrary, Everstar, you are chasing the right thread. Or... shall I say, *chain?*"

Nora blinked.

And then she blinked once more, taking in all that she had missed.

The mesa—the tiny mesa—where the Commander had trapped her was less than forty paces across. Beyond it, absolute blackness. Absolute blackness like Nora had never seen. But also... also, stars like she had never seen.

Focusing harder, she strained to make out the neighboring Pillars. She knew they were out there, out there somewhere... somewhere within leaping distance... but she just... she just could not see them.

The higher she hauled herself from the stones, the gustier the icy, midnight air became. Silvery-white strands tore free from her braid and whipped against her face, but... but it was her hands... her arms... her—

"You like it?" Decard leaned in and cupped her chin, a bit more gently this time. "I had it commissioned especially for you."

And only then—only after hearing his words—did Nora feel the scorch against her skin. Against her bare skin.

Her clothes—the clothes she had raced from the bathing chambers to change into—were gone. Her armor, her knives, her throwing stars, her short swords—gone.

All gone.

Any advantage she had had after Decard greedily and recklessly outed himself in the healing pools—completely gone. Wasted.

And she was naked. Naked as the day she had been born. Naked in the frozen, wintry night.

He will die twice for this.

For where her warm leathers and battle black armor had been, only thin golden strips remained.

No. Not strips. It was not fabric at all.

Decard watched, pleasure painted plainly across his face, as Nora realized what truly bound her. As she stared at the horrific golden chains he had commissioned especially for her.

He admired—and nearly salivated over—the deceptively delicate restraints that spiraled down both of her arms and wrapped up each of her legs. His eyes darkened at the way the links bunched just below her waist, just above where her uppermost thighs met. The Commander had to shift on his knees to disguise what the crisscrossed chains, digging into her midsection and the swells of her chest, did to him.

But it was seeing that golden collar—the golden collar he had sized by imagining his hands squeezing tight around her throat—it was seeing that, and the manner in which it stole the breath from her lungs, that made Decard Battleson stand and turn away.

Nora lurched against her bindings—tried to rip them from their ancient posts—but as she did, as she fought to get free, the golden chains bore down with invisible teeth. They bore down and constricted.

Silvery-charcoal blood spilled from her skin. It was the sudden warmth—the momentary bloom of heat—that had Nora surveying herself once more. And when she did, when she glimpsed the carnage her thrashing had tolled on her body, the specling froze instantly.

For if she pulled again—if she even dreamt of it—the skimpy, metallic bodice would slice clean through her.

And it was then that Nora understood.

The heightened emotions... the dull senses... the lack of composure... of strength... the loss of my inner shield... my wall.

Her heart sank.

For there is but one peril that Nora—*that all spectraline*—know to fear. Only one, for nothing else still in existence poses such danger.

Born from the darkest ruin, it is the reckoning of reprehensible loss—the indomitable melding of sheer calamity and worldly righting. It is a soured, amber peril that seeps solely from the ashen orchards of failure. A soured, amber sap to fell those who failed. A sap tapped solely to devour starlight.

Starlight—the endless power of Ever beings, the life force of the immortal, the very blood of The Spectraline.

"Magnificent, is it not?" Decard chuckled from his place at the edge of the Ever Step.

Unable to swallow while locked in her golden collar, Nora only dared breathe its name. "Lastisap."

For this, you will die thrice.

Thrill rippled off Decard in waves.

A new sort of stillness settled over Nora. And faintly—so very faintly—she could feel it as her starlight struggled against the odious amber. Wriggling, *battling,* to reclaim its stolen shine. Her spirit would fight until the end, she knew. It would fight, but it would not win.

And it was but a matter of time before she succumbed to the overwhelming influence of the Lastisap-infused chains. For her immortal body was fully bound in the one peril with the power to render her powerless—the sole peril with the might to make her mortal.

She wondered how much time she had left up here, how much time she had left upon this stone altar in the stars, how much longer she had to live on this Ever Step.

Staring into the depthless black of the night sky around her, Nora made her peace with being brought to this forsaken citadel. She made her peace with why she had been carried up to this crumbling altar, after all. For it was not on behalf of any Canon that she had been packed across the plains and chained to this Sky Step of countless atrocities. Oh, no. Certainly not.

The Canon does serve as a rather fine ruse, though. I will give you that.

And there atop the Ever Step—bare save the delicate, golden chains snaking up and down her lithe form—Nora Everstar understood and accepted that she was to be a flawless vision of the past. That she, under the guise of the Twenty-Third Canon, had been brought to this Pillar of the Sky and swathed in the one thing that could reduce her to mortal—the one thing that could remake her into a flawless vision of the mortals of old. A flawless vision of the mortal *sacrifices* of old. A flawless vision of an Illicit Offering.

The very same Illicit Offering The Spectraline of the First Age surrendered their dignity and honor for, all in the vain hope of claiming The Night's Wings.

Chapter 19

THE CATACOMBS

"They approach on swift feet, Covelette."

Savallin Prim, Keeper of Wisdom, was not yet prepared to receive more news. She was still reeling—still struggling to process—the most recent upset The Mistress of the Dark had divulged.

"Can you tell who?"

The Lady of the Lair, one of the other titles Sav had come to know her companion by, floated through the darkened, subterranean walkways toward the sound of scraping steps.

No matter how diligently she had tried, not one of Savallin's niceties or pleas had cracked The Lady's resolve. She would not reveal her name. In truth, she did not share much of anything about herself at all.

With the ease with which she moved throughout the gloomy passages and invaded Sav's inner ones, Sav suspected her companion was some sort of lost, lingering sahira spirit.

"There are three Keepers. One, of huntresses and the Eastern Scarpe. Another, of angst and the palest bergs of the Glacial Sea. And the last"—a chilly whistle echoed through the void—"she is the Keeper of Keepers."

Marvelous, Savallin thought.

Euclid, Phaedra, and the Diadet herself.

They were coming to interrogate her, to torture the very knowledge from her bones. And yet, no matter how convincing their combined efforts might be, Savallin Prim had no answers to reveal—none, not even if she wished to.

"Of what is their aura, Lady?"

The voice of ice and longing sighed. "Truly, little covenary, do I strike you as an aura-reader?"

Savallin smiled despite herself.

"I can see lies and I can see truths, Covelette. I cannot see the trivial. I cannot see *auras*."

And wherever she hid amongst the mildewy shadows, Savallin believed The Lady of the Lair was smiling, too.

Since her internment began—however long ago that was—Sav had absorbed a great deal from The Mistress of the Dark. More even, she supposed, than she had throughout her extensive Tutelage.

The most startling truth she had learned was that The Klekta Mortem—this deserted and decrepit spiral of hollows now holding her hostage—had not begun as a prison at all.

No.

Back in the earliest days of The Catacombs, back when the capital citadel still smelled of the freshest earthen soil, back then, these ultra-deep stories housed dwellings without compare.

Every last suite had been hewn of purest obsidian stone, and each of its levels had been carved into a gently sloping ring that descended into the earth. At the core, an enormous upright tunnel had stretched the full distance, all the way from the deepest depths to The Surface.

Glistening within that channel, the shine of the sun, the moon, and the stars had illuminated the impermeable darkness.

Gorgeous species of flora—species Savallin could not even fathom—had grown wild and abundant, raining in kaleidoscopic waves from one level to the next. And there had been birds. So many birds, soaring and chirping and singing throughout every last nook and cavern.

And at the very heart of The Klekta Mortem, thundering down within that brilliant spillway of natural light, The Infinite Spring had raged into an infinite fall.

This place, she had learned—*her prison*—was once the home of Covenarykind's most privileged.

"Do you remember what you are to do, Keeper?"

And with that, Savallin focused back on the present—back on the doom striding toward her.

"I do."

She did remember.

But remembering and doing were two starkly different concepts. Alas, they were coming for her whether she liked it or not. So, as she saw it, there was really no choice to be had at all. And alone there in her cell, as she envisioned what she was soon to do, Savallin felt a brush of concern and pride run along her skin.

"You have nothing to fear, Covelette."

Sav inhaled sharply.

She could have sworn to Her herself that a pair of slender hands had reached out from the blackness. Reached out, and reached for her. Reached out for her to give her a squeeze—a tender squeeze of reassurance.

That soft laugh again rumbled through the pitch-dark chamber.

"You have nothing to fear from me, either, Savallin Prim."

And that voice was right, of course. Savallin felt ashamed. For throughout the entire time she had been a prisoner of The

Klekta, The Lady of the Lair had done nothing but provide insight.

Invaluable insight.

She had not tried, nor had she even threatened, to harm so much as a hair on her head.

"They will arrive in a few short moments, covenary."

Savallin swallowed, calming herself.

The Keeper of Wisdom still had so much she wanted to ask The Lady—so many secrets and mysteries she wished to know more about. But their time together... it was going to be cut short. So she shoved her curiosity as far inward as it would go. And in place of those endless questions, Savallin offered her deepest thanks.

"If I do not get the opportunity later, Lady, I hope that you know how grateful I am to have been gifted your counsel."

The formless female seemed, for once, caught by surprise. She stayed silent a beat before choosing her words.

"You shall have that opportunity, Savallin Prim."

And as she waited there, entombed amongst that heavy, choking, blinding air, Savallin found the thick frost coating each of The Lady's next words to be oddly warming.

"Consider it my promise to you, Keeper."

Then that comforting voice again paused to listen in on the corridor's secrets.

Unable to stomach the silence—or the rising wave of her fervent inquisitiveness—Sav finally loosed the one question that had been plaguing her thoughts the most relentlessly.

"How is it, Mistress, that you have access to your power down here? Is it..." She steadied her shaking voice. "Is it because you are... not alive?"

The Lady snorted. Actually snorted.

"*Alive?* That is an unbecoming mistranslation, Covelette." A disappointed hum rippled through the smothering cell. "Within The Klekta Mortem, no *mortal body* can access their innate power."

No mortal body...

Then, with a hint of amusement, her ethereal companion added, "The ancient curse does not begrudge *the living,* covenary. No—only those with *a mortal form.*"

An ancient curse?

Her amusement waning into impatience, The Lady of the Lair snipped, "Are you suddenly incapable of formulating original thoughts, Savallin Prim?"

Are you incapable of minding your own thoughts?

And although she could not see it—although she could see absolutely nothing at all—Sav got the sense that somewhere, unseen eyes were being narrowed.

"Your tutors, they truly teach you nothing of your own kind."

They... well, they were prohibited from—

"It brings me no joy to sever you short, especially within your own head, but they are nearly here."

They are close.

Savallin could hear them now—the quickening footsteps beyond the invisible curtain of bane guarding the cell's archway. And just then, just before those steps rounded the last curve in the dark path down, The Lady spoke again.

"My elemental power remains intact because *I* am no mortal. *I* am no caster of earth."

The Keeper of Wisdom could barely begin to comprehend what The Lady had said—what The Lady had revealed to her at last. Her mind was whirling, spinning, bursting with new queries, but—

But a blaze of brightest light exploded through her midnight cell. And as the sour scent of torch oil stuffed up Savallin's nose—as those noxious fumes made it even harder for her to breathe—that cryptic, comforting presence again whispered into her mind.

"Only *one* knows of your true Tutelage, Keeper. The others..." And then, as if in farewell, that gentle laugh caressed the lightless chamber one last time. "Well, I do not pity the ignorant."

Chapter 20

THE CITY

The old windows of the subway car rattled their protest as the train sped along the tracks. With a bump and then a rickety bank to the left, the thick blanket of shadows covering her eyes fell away. From outside, from all around her, the brightest light of the day poured in.

The Q train had cleared the tunnel, she thought. The Q, or maybe the F, had risen from the dirty shafts beneath The Mortal City, risen all the way to the surface, and now raced toward midtown.

Her muscles were stiff, sore as if she had just awoken from a deep, deep sleep. Her neck, though—her throat—it burned like she'd swallowed fire.

Burns like...

She commanded her eyes to open.

And it was then that Everly Castile felt the heavy arm draped around her shoulder. It was then that Everly felt the hard body that had hers tucked in close. It was then that the former spectraline warrior wished to be mortal.

Out the window across from her, she watched as the city of glass and steel towers disappeared from view.

Shit.

This was neither the Q nor the F.

This was the train out of town. The train out of town, packed full with mortals—mortals whose delicate lives would certainly be put in danger if she were to now cause a scene.

Fine. No weapons, then. If the male beside her even so much as listed toward wise, he would have disarmed her the moment she fell, anyhow.

And it could have been the displeasure seeping from her pores. It could have been her subtle shift in consciousness. Everly did not really care to know which, as the behemoth at her side cupped an enormous palm around her cheek and tugged.

She resisted his pull, resisted his demand, resisted him as she had for so long. She did not just resist, though. No. She fought it like the order to do so had been woven into her very being.

And he? He simply tugged harder.

"It is unlike you"—his rough fingers dug into her tender jaw—"to disobey."

She did not have to see it to know his mouth had quirked into a grin.

"Well, it is very much like you," she mocked, "to be a raging asshole."

And before the raging asshole could throttle her, Everly drove her fist across her body and buried it into his ball sac.

His teeny, tiny ball sac.

She had slipped his crushing hold and flown down the aisle before the brute had finished doubling over. She hit the rusted door at the end of the car, leapt the gap in the train, and had just shouldered into the next cabin when the male rose to his feet.

Everly could have scented the wrath rippling off him from the farthest corners of this world.

A monotonous array of mortal faces—some frightened, many bewildered, most annoyed—passed her by as she sprinted through the train cars. She made it to and through the last cabin, to the final door of the train. She strained and pulled at the handle, but... but...

Unreal.

Some motherfucking human had locked the godsdamned door from the outside.

Everly decided to rip it from its hinges when—when a sheet of warped steel shot past her head. As she twisted out of the way, the locked door before her clattered to the black tracks spilling from beneath the train.

Thank you.

She did not have to waste precious time turning around to see who had severed, crumpled, and then hurled the door from the adjoining car. No—instead, Everly gripped the top of the empty frame with both hands and swung herself up and onto the roof of the train.

Her feet were again moving—this time racing across the slick metal toward the front of the train—when the male exploded through the roof in front of her.

She flung her arms out wide to slow, to stop, to brace—but it was too late.

"I am going to savor this," the male growled as she skidded toward him. "I am going to savor sending you back to the black-fire pits you clawed out of."

And his sharpened canines gleamed in the sunlight as he launched for her.

Don't you da—

Alas, *he dared.*

Pain radiated through her as the spectral rammed his giant shoulder into her middle. The world—her world—pulsed, dimmed, and then tilted backward as he tore her feet out from under her. And then, then an onslaught of shrieks and screams clogged her ears—her mind—as she plunged from the roof.

The giant warrior wrapped his arms around her waist so tightly she could hardly breathe. But even helplessly pinned, Everly wriggled and thrashed against his grip until she at last managed a quick glance behind her.

Fuck.

That was why the humans were so fussy. The Ever-blessed train had rattled all the way to the river bridge. But just then, the arch of her spine struck something hard. Something unmoving. Something like a wide steel beam leaden with protruding bolts.

The male snickered when she winced, when the air vacated her body. His arms, though, tightened around her with every inch their tangled bodies fell. And they were falling fast, spinning toward the churning river below, until—

Until the sadistic asshole threw his locked arms right, sending Everly crashing into another bridge girder. A breathy gasp shuddered from her lips as her bones sang their misery.

It was too much. Too much for the male to bear.

He groaned low as they spun faster toward the river. And then, with another crushing squeeze and metallic clang, the warrior sank his greedy teeth into Everly's back—sank his dirty, diseased canines into her pristine flesh.

She roared, her blurry vision honing with anger. And at once, everything speeding past came into focus—braces, beams, gussets, anchors, columns, all of it. She stared at them, memorizing the patterns as she fell, memorizing them until she knew what came next—until she knew when to make her move.

And make her move she did. A diagonal brace—a pipe small enough that her fingers could wrap all the way around it—whizzed by on her left. And above her head, her hand was waiting.

Her palm hooked onto the pipe and her fingers did the rest. The muscles of her arm whined and strained as they snapped taut, as they stretched and struggled to support his significant weight as well as her own. But the spectraline— she had hold, and she would not let go.

Their plummeting bodies slammed to a halt, and Everly used every bit of that abrupt change in momentum when she sent her elbow swinging—when she sent her elbow soaring for the male's unprotected temple. The resounding crack was beautiful, beautiful music to her immortal ears.

And almost instantly, the vice-like grip around her waist faltered. So then, just for kicks, Everly drove her elbow home once more. The warrior grunted as his strength flagged again, as his death grip loosened further. And then—then it was Everly laughing when the spectral male, at last, lost his hold.

She watched his body the entire time it fell. Even after it splashed into the rushing, brown water, she watched the spot where it had gone under.

Her strikes had not killed him, she knew. The fall had not killed him either, it likely had not even hurt him. Nonetheless, Everly hung there below the bridge, hung there staring down at the river if only to gauge how much time she had left before the male found her again.

And only when she was satisfied that the spectral warrior would not erupt from the depths to resume the chase then and there, Everly scaled the lofty column of the river bridge without breaking so much as a sweat. Her heel had just tapped onto the concrete when she realized her mistake.

"That right there, young lady," the beat cop tsked, "that is a felony offense."

Everly had forgotten to raise her Brightbreak before vaulting back onto the bridge.

Careless.

She inhaled through her nose before turning to face the mewling man.

"Which part, Officer?" Sweeping her gaze from his dull boots to his unwashed hair, the once-spectral enforcer folded her arms over her chest. "The *civilian* having to climb beneath the tracks in search of the fallen woman because you took your sweet time getting here?"

She leaned back against the rail.

"Or was it my perfect landing?"

The mortal glowered at her. Everly did not bat an eye.

"That's quite a mouth you have, girl," the pretender grumbled, advancing a step in her direction. "I think it's going to be rather popular where you're headed."

"Yeah, you're probably right," she agreed before flashing her mouthful of teeth. "But I doubt even this mouth could dethrone your wife's."

An ugly vein bulged from the forehead sprouting out of the wrinkled, blue uniform.

"Talk about *popular*—your lady deserves sainthood," the spectral whistled. "I mean, truly, the woman does not discriminate. From what I've heard, everybody is welcome."

Strings of spittle spewed from the man's mouth as he sprang for her. The immortal took a casual step left to admire the water. Her eyes were still rolling when that reddening forehead tolled against the iron handrail.

And as that angry, little man lay there in a human heap upon the sidewalk, Everly untied and shook out her hair. She had just tucked the wavy strands behind her ears and turned for The Empire City when a set of hurrying footsteps thudded up behind her.

They were far too eager—far too loud—to belong to a spectraline. So, Everly Castile allowed them to catch up,

allowed them to fall into step beside her, allowed their bearer
to live long enough to state their—

"I'm sure you get this a lot," his voice, although breathless,
was steadier than she expected. "But—*damn*."

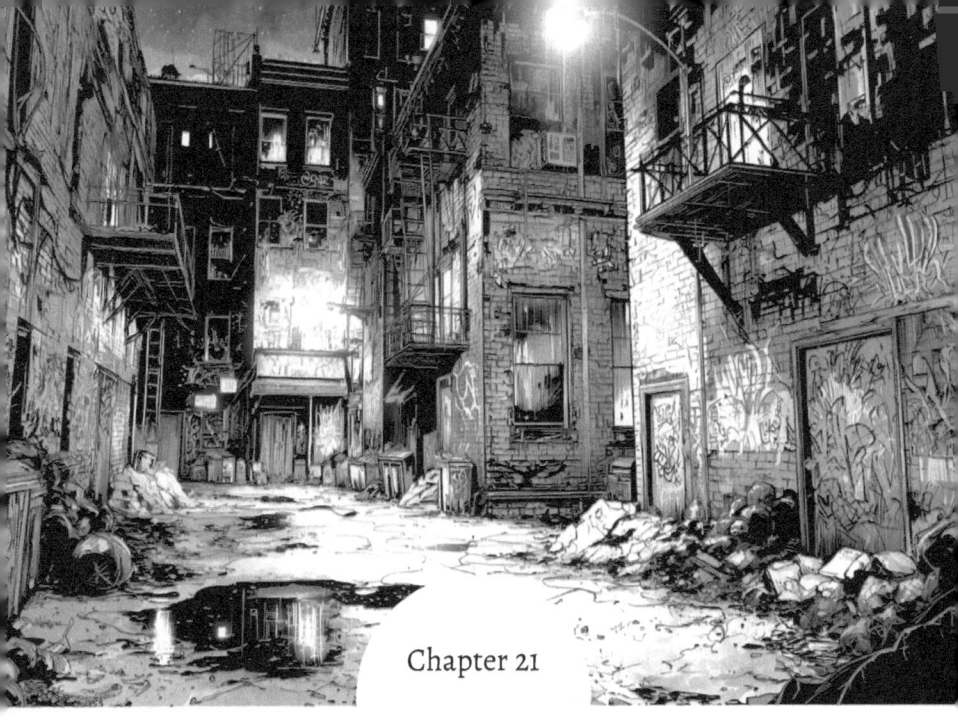

Chapter 21

THE CESSPOOL

The renovated ground level of the historic building housing the trampoline park was shaped like an arrowhead, its tip pointing toward the dusky street corner outside.

The portion projecting out to the left flickered with neon and nostalgia—the many-colored lights of the retro arcade games flashing and rolling into the shadows. The opposite section—the swanky, lamplit lounge area where soccer moms went to sip cocktails and slip secrets as their sweaty, sticky children screamed themselves silly—was devoid of both the gossips and their whispers.

"POLICE!" Sergeant Ava Carlisle yelled into the darkness before her. "IF ANYONE IS INSIDE, MAKE YOURSELF KNOWN!"

Without taking her eyes off the sunken main section ahead, the Sergeant signaled towards the blinking neons. Vasquez's heavy footfalls faded until they were one with the electric jingles of the eighties.

"POLICE!" he bellowed. "SHOW YOURSELF, ASSHOLE!"

Inhaling through her nose, the Sergeant bit down on her irritation and turned to the right—aiming the short bursts of light streaming from her weapon into the hushed cocktail bar. On quiet feet, she crept down the three carpeted steps, scanning each of the round, velvety booths as she passed.

"POLICE!" she screamed again. "POLICE! WE KNOW YOU ARE IN HERE! MAKE YOURSELF KNOWN *NOW!*"

Nothing.

After pausing to listen to the creaks and whines of the old building, she advanced toward the thick stone bartop at the rear of the lounge. Hitting her light again, she grazed the cushions of each of the golden, spinning barstools before raising the beam to shine over shelf upon shelf of premium liquor.

Nothing.

Across the building, in the far wing, she could hear Vasquez's thunderous voice busily asserting his dominance into the dark. And so, with only one more place to check in her area, she backed up a step, tucking her weapon in close to her chest.

I know you're in here somewhere.

Under the cover of darkness, she eased to the far side of the bar. Still, her ears picked up no suspicious sounds; her eyes tracked no subtle movements. So, with a slow breath in—and then a second—the Sergeant stepped wide, charging behind the chest-high counter and thrusting her weapon to the ready.

Her rush of light brushed across the checkered tile, swept the line of mini fridges and freezers, and then inventoried the stock of expensive glassware... and... and uncovered *nothing.* No intruder. No anything.

"CLEAR!" she shouted, cutting the light and spinning back toward the main section.

"CLEAR!" her partner echoed, his own footsteps growing louder in the deepening shadows.

The wash of their mounted lights met in the heart of the recessed pit that made up the largest portion of the building's ground floor. There was not a single square foot in the entire section that was not a godsdamned obstacle.

Closest to her, a plastic river of red, yellow, green, and blue spheres flowed steadily until crashing against the cubed-glass dam that was the Pizza Parlor partition wall. A sign fastened to the lip read, *5'-0" DEEP.*

Great, the Sergeant groaned to herself. Knowing full well that even *with* the added height of her boots, five feet was pushing it. *Awesome.*

She wasn't confident she could leap the river, either. And if she miffed it—if she tried and did not land on the other side—it would be mortification that killed her before anything else.

Opposite her, Vasquez was sizing up his first hurdle: a black-rope cargo net suspended atop larger-than-life piano keys that ran the entire length of the pit. She watched, through the dense forest of Velcro trees, as he leaned forward to test the netting. Lifting a boot, he hovered it just above a section of rope, and then—

Shit.

The whole run of cargo net swiveled on its anchors at the first hint of pressure. Like her river, his bridge was roughly ten or so feet wide—a distance not even he could jump.

Shit, she thought again. Vasquez was going to have to holster his weapon and use both hands to get across. Her partner would be hopelessly exposed—an easy target. An easy, enormous target. *No. Too risky.*

And... if they were somehow able to conquer their respective obstacles, an even sketchier hellscape awaited them within.

Shhhhit.

"Stand by, Vasquez. I'm coming to you."

A minute later, the two had devised a plan of attack. Officer Vasquez, using his considerably greater mass, would hold the cargo net in place and prevent it from rotating long enough for the Sergeant to safely cross. Then, once she was again firmly on solid ground, she would stand guard while he crawled through the piano pit beneath it.

Just a walk in the trampoline park.

"Ready?" her partner prodded, the heel of his boot steady on the edge of the pit. His shoulders were set, his weapon in position.

Sergeant Carlisle nodded, glancing to the toe of his boot, to the front half of his foot that extended out over the black ropes—the sole safeguard keeping her weight from flipping the net the heartbeat she stepped upon it.

Whoever shattered through the building's glass doors... whoever shoved that young assistant manager to the ground... whoever scared her half to death... they were still in here... somewhere. And so, the Sergeant had no choice but to cross the pit. No choice.

"If that giant foot so much as slips," she bit, easing both boots onto the braided ropes, "so help you, your gods."

And despite the circumstance, Vasquez snorted.

"I *curl* more than you weigh, honey. I think I can manage."

Honey kept her eyes forward, her steps light, as she hissed, "*Sergeant*. I curl more than you weigh, *Sergeant*."

The officer at her back did not trouble himself with a retort. No, the uniformed jackass with a superiority complex merely threw a bit of his own weight into the net—sending the whole fucking thing writhing upward beneath her unsteady feet.

The hell!

With a sharp gasp and a sudden jolt through her outstretched arms, she crouched lower, letting her knees absorb the brunt of the motion, the violent pitch of the net.

Fuck! she panted, dropping her center of gravity to stay level atop the roiling bridge. *Fucking fuck.*

Her new partner was out of his godsdamned mind. The Vasquez she had known during The Academy—the likable and driven officer-to-be—this was *not* him. Not even a distant cousin. No. Whatever had befallen him, whatever or whoever he had gotten tangled up with, whyever he had gotten demoted, it had altered him. Altered him for the worse.

She couldn't turn back to glare at him, though. Couldn't pivot to spew the profanities swamping her thoughts. She could only move forward—she could only remain focused, only maintain a clear head, only cross the black-rope bridge.

The Sergeant would write him up for that, though. For his inane recklessness—for his total disregard of her safety, of his safety, of the safety of whoever the fuck was still lurking alongside them in this gloomy jungle.

Not now.

She willed herself to settle. Commanded herself to take one step. Two more steps. Then three.

Deal with this first, she whispered calmly, scanning the bastion of shadowed obstructions lined up before her. *This first. He, and his bullshit, after.*

Another step, another shudder in the net. But she was almost there. Just two more strides. Two more, and—

A drowned choking noise burbled from the darkness behind her. A moist, rasping cough and then—then the whole run of braided net slackened at once. The Sergeant felt it before she saw it, before she saw the perimeter rope go limp and begin its plummet toward the piano keys below.

There was no time to think—no time to gauge distance or second guess. No time, at all. Pushing off her back foot with everything she had, she shot her body forward a fraction before the net gave way beneath her. Flattening herself as best she could, she stretched, reached—diving face-first for the pit wall.

The carpeted floor on the island side of the keyed trench did not rise to greet her gently. No, it sprinted and surged for her cheek, her shoulder blade, her hip bone. But she did not care, for she had made it. And she did not have the luxury of feeling the pain, of checking her body for signs of damage.

No—the Sergeant tucked her arms tight and rolled. Rolled onto her squared feet, her legs compelling her upright, her hand already moving for the weapon holstered at her side.

Her ragged breaths rattled in her chest as she thumbed the beam of light on once more. But then, the heaving swells and shaky swallows grew shallower and shallower with every strained effort as the Sergeant's brush of pale-yellow light painted the spot where her partner had just been standing.

The spot where he no longer stood. The spot now smeared in dark, shining blood.

Chapter 22

THE CITADEL

From her bed of frozen stones atop The Pillars of the Sky, Nora Everstar gazed up into the great expanse of the night. With the loss of her spectral senses—with the loss of her unique ability to see the dark as if day—mortality had gifted her something new. Something, she doubted she would ever be granted the opportunity to experience again.

Lying there upon her back, still as a corpse in her golden chains, Nora marveled at the unchallenged brightness of the stars—at the way they sliced through the crushing darkness as if without fear, as if it were no trouble at all.

The spectraline had never seen such a thing, such a humbling display of quiet might. Even if her senses returned, even if she tore free from her shackles, even if she liberated Commander Decard Battleson's thick head from his pompous body—even if—Nora Everstar knew she would not forget this.

And just then, the soon-to-be-expired soldier at the heart of her misery turned from his place at the precipice and strode toward her.

"I take it you now grasp why it is we have come here?"

"I take it"—Nora did her best to appear menacing from her... horizontal position—"you failed to attend even a single lesson in The Hall of Ages."

Decard sketched a mock bow.

"I consider reliving the past a colossal waste of valuable time."

How truly, truly dense one must be.

"Simmer down, specling," the fair-haired Commander lording over her growled.

Nora sighed. Loudly.

"Even with your astonishing scarcity of knowledge, did you not consider, *Commander*, that it might be somewhat difficult to sacrifice me to a beast that has been extinct for thousands upon *thousands* of solar cycles?"

Slipping one hand from his pocket, he smirked.

"I did not expect you to lose your taste for..." He traced his thumb along her lower lip. "Well... for fun. At least, not so suddenly."

The dimming glow of starlight that still flowed within her veins lurched at the insinuation.

"Oh?" Nora had to pause for a moment to fully comprehend the gravity of his words. "So, you simply have gone mad, then?"

"My apologies, Eleanora. I am having a somewhat difficult time hearing you from all the way down there."

Nora heard the pop before she registered what he had done. She whirled to see who he had signaled, but she—her limbs, her muscles, her mind—every part of her was too slow. *She* was—

Too slow.

One of the shields she had not noticed lurking behind her had already stepped forward, had already yanked viciously on the end of her golden chain. Nora barely had time to grit her teeth and steel her core for the slicing and searing and tearing she knew was coming.

She tensed and braced and—and as her chilled skin scraped across the rough stones, as her numb arms ripped taut over her head, as her frozen feet dangled helplessly beneath her—the burning of the poisoned chains worsened to the point that any lesser spectral would have undoubtedly lost all consciousness.

Decard took a careful step closer. Then, he smiled like a barbarian as he wrapped his grimy hands around Nora's bare waist, around the Lastisap chains digging into her flesh. Around the toxin, and... and...

Nothing. His skin did not react.

"Like I said, Everstar. These were commissioned *especially* for you."

And because her thoughts were no longer her own, Nora did not bother debating with herself about how exactly that insight might prove helpful. Instead, she centered her focus on the threat before her.

"So... what is your hope then? Do you think that if you string me up here... gift me bite of the frost... strip me of my chance at Taiso... *actually strip me* before your sad, little, second-rate squadron... that... that what? That I will give in and swear the vow... swear an eternal vow... *to you?* To a worthless, pitiful, pathetic excuse for a warrior *like you?*"

Red-hot wrath flashed in the deepest greens of his eyes a fraction of a moment before the Commander slammed the specling's body backward, straight into the waiting semicircle of his second-rate soldiers.

"I *will* bring you to your knees, spec," Decard spat when her body again swung forward. "I *will* bring you to your knees and I *will* make you beg me to swear The Rite of Parallel."

So swift to anger, you are.

His broad hand surged up and whacked her across the face, cracking into her cheekbone before her mortal reflexes even registered they had been struck. And it hurt like the mother of all mortal fuckers.

At her back—at her wholly exposed backside—a cacophony of snickers and howls erupted into the frigid night. Nora noted it, and she would not waste it. She would not think it for fear of Decard's inexplicable eavesdropping, but she would certainly make it count.

Six. She had heard six. That number would be of little worry if she had her strength, but in this state... in this fragile state she would have to improvise.

"Had you told me of your fondness for spectacle" —Nora bobbed her head at the soldiers she could not see, or as close as she could manage with the metal choker—"I would have extended invitations to your... to your buffoon battalion... much sooner."

A sickening twist of hate and envy contorted Decard's already vile features.

Nora took a shot in the dark.

"I have heard Mallard has the... *the skill* to make even our trysts last longer than thirty se—"

With a burst of air, a curved dagger spiraled past Nora's left ear.

A thud. A gasp. Two scraping steps backward. And then... and then there were five shields behind her upon the Ever Step.

Nora grinned. On the inside, of course. On the outside, she dropped her Ever-blessed jaw.

"Well, *that* was rather impolite," she squawked. "Now I will have to call on the next most *well-endowed*."

At her back, all at once, the squadron of hulking brutes erupted into roars and swears and affirmations of their laughable inadequacies. Nora had to roll her lips into a tight line to keep the corners of her mouth from twitching upward.

Commander Decard, though, was not laughing. No, he was outright fuming.

Good.

"Cavander."

Another blind guess, another snap of the wrist, another body knocked from the earthstone tower.

"This whore is toying with your mind, Dec," shouted a hoarse voice. "Snap out of it!"

Jericho.

First, Nora cursed herself. She most certainly should have recited his name first.

As if a tempestuous wood calming in the wake of the wind, the tumultuous forest writhing within Decard's eyes hardened to that unfeeling emerald once more.

"Clever," he whispered as his fist drove into her abdomen.

He repeated it, over and over, as he struck her again and again and again. Each blow was worse than the one preceding it. Each impact so forceful, so strong, her body choked on its own air. She tried to swallow against it, tried to gulp, tried to open her airways, but—but the unnatural, mortal weakness overtook her.

Racked with the undiluted pain of The Fleeting, Nora's head slumped and her body sagged. The Lastisap chains wasted no time. Where the gilded links burrowed into her body, her skin began to split. An inferno whose heat she could hardly fathom scorched along the chains.

And as Decard landed punch after punch, as Nora's tunneling vision began to spot and then darken, she saw it.

All along her outer arms, gushing from her caved chest, spilling from the splits in her hips, the gashes in her thighs— Nora watched her blood, her lavender blood, rain down upon the stones below.

Not yet red, but close enough.

Now was as grand a time as ever, she thought, to make the descent into madness. For if Decard could not have her, if he could not claim her as his Parallel, Nora knew full well, he would do everything within his power to ensure nobody else could have her either. And if nobody else was to have her, then Commander Decard Battleson would make damn sure he strode away with something for all his ill-spent solars.

And the something he had in mind—it was *the* something these Pillars, these Ever Steps, had been erected for. The something The Spectraline of the past had ascended them to claim. The something that drove their ancestors to commit unforgivable and unspeakable atrocities. The something that no spectral had been able to claim since the day the last living Beast of Old tumbled from the sky.

"If you allow me to die, Decard, if you allow me to bleed out all over these stones, your prize will not come."

The next fist hit half-heartedly.

"You know I will refuse you to the bitter end," Nora coughed, a mouthful of weakening blood spilling at her feet. The silvery-lavender had darkened into a shade of plum. "You knew long before coming here that I would not, *that I will never*, swear The Rite to you."

He swung again.

Her coughing grew worse.

"And so, you thought to use this Canon—my Canon—as a means to claim The Night's Wings."

Decard's mouth quirked to the side as his fists uncoiled and lowered.

"It seems you *did* taste it, after all."

Indeed, she had.

Prompted by his minor slip, Nora had scoured and scraped and clawed with what still remained of her guttering light force until she had found it—*tasted* it. That final, bitter answer she desperately needed.

The answer as to what had truly rendered her unconscious in the dormitory corridor. The answer as to how someone who was not a Thought-Teller could all of a sudden tell thoughts. The answer as to why so many specling before her had come home in burial white. And the answer as to why Decard Battleson believed he could now summon a beast that lived only in legend.

Unlike Lastisap, the amber kiss that all spectraline knew to fear, this peril—this essence of wicked—was one few had ever heard. An essence of wicked few outside the black caverns of the castress citadel had ever heard. A concoction of wicked so mighty that the natural world cowed in its wake. A corrupted concerto of Earth Song that was now Nora's soundest hope—*Seraphease.*

"If that is your hope, to claim your Lunae, you must keep me alive," the golden collar delighted in its ruin of her throat, but she had to keep trying. "And to do so, you must rid me of these chains."

The out-of-his-mind Commander took a cautious step toward her, studying every piece of her purpling, dangling body as if she might lunge at any moment. He brushed his finger in the now fuchsia cascade flowing from beneath her gilded choker and chuckled.

"The extraordinary strength of Eleanora Everstar..." Decard rotated that blood-coated finger in the flickering torchlight. "Soon to be extinguished into nothing."

And Nora—she said nothing. She did nothing. For she could not speak. She could not move. Not anymore.

"Hmm." Decard whipped his bloodied finger at the shields behind her. "I presume you shall have it your way then. Such a disappointment you are."

And then, Nora's gaze went misty as her arms slackened and her body crashed down onto the slick stones beneath her.

"Do it. Do it, now!" Decard barked as he ripped the golden chains free of her beyond-ravaged body.

Amidst the anguish and chaos, Nora heard the heavy steps of someone storming across the stones. And before her vision funneled and vanished altogether, she glimpsed the red hair of Jericho standing just in front of the large, tarnished disc suspended along the northern edge of the Step.

The large, tarnished disc suspended from the ornate jade frame. An ornate, jade frame that had been painstakingly carved in the image of two great, curving wings.

Liberated from the death collar, Nora swallowed.

Decard had actually done it. He had truly ordered the spectral to... to... to commence The Cry of Illicit Offering—to begin the drumming of The Night Song.

His second-in-command bent and then hefted the archaic mallet to his shoulder. He sampled its strange weight, flipped it once, and then took a few practice swings into the black air.

And as the final poisoned chain slipped from around her legs, Decard lifted her face and sneered, "Who is pathetic now, *Nora?*"

The spectraline took a slow, shaky breath. Then, she took one more. And then another. And then—and then Nora Everstar purred, "Who is premature as usual, *Decard?*"

And as Commander Decard Battleson staggered backward, as the male struggled to comprehend what it was he had just done, as that ancient mallet, over and over, struck the metal of old, as the crimson pool around her again shimmered silvery-gray—Eleanora Everstar smiled to the sky.

Chapter 23

THE CATACOMBS

Whitest light blackened her senses.

The onslaught of torches had burned straight through her coverlet of murk. They had burst in all at once, ripping away the darkness and devouring every last shadow. And as the blackness screamed out, as that heavy, weighty dark tore from the light—Savallin's very sight followed along behind it.

They had blinded her.

And the Keeper—she was not entirely stunned by it. No, for if the circumstance had been transposed, she, too, would have hindered herself in some manner or another. Not because she had survived in The Klekta longer than any covenary before her, but because of the power woven into her bones—a long-dormant melody of earth charm so pure, so vibrant, most of her energy was spent merely suppressing it.

And even with Savallin blinded, fading, and without access to her great charm, not one of her fellow Majlis—not the Shade of Snow nor the Himalayan Huntress—stood so much as a chance against her.

She did not fight back, though. Not when the two sets of hands lifted her from her feet. She did not struggle, not when the two sahira—Phaedra Halla and Euclid Istra—laid her body flat, laid her upon something rigid and hard that had not been there moments before. No, Savallin Prim did not fight her sisters.

Not yet.

"I sincerely hope, Savallin Prim"—a gentle rustling of skirts tickled the Keeper's ears as the sultry voice spoke— "that we did not disturb you down here."

Diadet Nirvana, Keeper of Keepers.

The Lady of the Lair had told Savallin much, and more, of Covenarykind's sitting sovereign. How The Lady had come to bear such knowledge, Sav was not privy. What she did know, however, was that if even one of the newly revealed truths somehow slipped into the wrong hands—the wrong ears— the ensuing fallout would be nothing short of catastrophic.

So, the Keeper of Wisdom played along.

"Diadet," she replied, her speech scratchy as if worn. "As always, my time is your time."

A light hand came to rest upon Savallin's forearm.

"Ah," the pale-haired Supreme chirped. "Very well, then."

And that fast, leather cuffs were tightened around her wrists.

Peculiar.

She did not recall feeling any bolts—no hooks or anchors either—as she had meticulously explored every corner of her cell, as she had fumbled around, upon her hands and knees, under the cover of darkness.

The cuffs must be attached to whatever table they had brought with them—whatever table she was now lying upon.

The soft hand pulsed just once before the Diadet began again. "Phaedra, Keeper of Whispers, came to my quarters this morning with a bit of startling news."

This morning...

Had she truly been locked away down here for less than a day? She felt... the toll—the toll that had been taken on her body—it felt far worse than a day's doing.

"She tells me, Savallin, that she caught you meddling in another Keeper's private chambers." The Diadet clicked her tongue. "Keeper of Wisdom, I now ask you: does Phaedra Halla speak the truth? Did that which she has accused you of indeed come to pass?"

Savallin pulled gently against her leather restraints, just enough to sample their strength but not so greatly as to excite Euclid. There was no point in lying to the sovereign. None at all.

Plus, she had only been conducting her sworn duty, diligently fulfilling her obligation to her people. None of what she had done was wrong.

"Yes, Diadet," the Keeper admitted, holding her head as high as she could while tethered to the table. "Yes, I did indeed let myself into Coralis Carveil's private chambers."

And even though she had been deprived of sleep and light and sight, even though she continued to wane amidst The Klekta's dark power, Savallin's body reacted—sending sharp prickles shooting along her skin—when Diadet Nirvana squeezed her forearm for a second time.

"And what, may I ask, was your purpose in entering the domicile of the Keeper of Wonder?"

The truth. Savallin would tell her the truth—the abridged version.

"Coralis has been inexplicably absent from the most recent Majlis councils. One day ago, an urgent missive was received. A missive that requires her expertise to validate." Her throat seared, but she forged on. "That is why, Diadet, I entered her domicile—to search for a clue as to where I might find her."

Hot breath blasted her cool face as Phaedra spewed, "Then why, Savallin Prim, did you incinerate whatever it was you found?"

Her help me, she swore. *Her help us all.*

Savallin's mind soared and swooped and spun, searching high and low, far and wide, for an explanation—any sort of justification—for what she had done, for what Phaedra had seen her do. She should have anticipated the question. She should have readied an answer long before this moment. And as the Keeper of Wisdom spiraled deeper in the silence, she sensed the growing sneer—the harshening slash of her sister's lips as her victory became apparent.

And it was then, then as Savallin stumbled blindly through a mental maze of ethics and reason and duty, that those heavy skirts swished again.

"Phaedra," the Diadet's tone was both tender and stern, "might I ask that you show a morsel of restraint toward your Majlis sister?"

The Keeper of Whispers said nothing, but Sav—pausing her soundless breakdown just long enough—picked up the hushed scraping of bitter slippers.

"Have faith, young sahira," soothed the covenary sovereign. And then, as if shedding an ill-fitting, false form, Diadet Nirvana whispered her next words with an edge so brutal, the rotting cell itself held its breath. "We will have this matter sorted out in no time."

This was the Diadet Nirvana she knew. This was the Diadet Nirvana Savallin had expected to face.

"Keeper Prim, what was it about the message, *specifically*, that you wished to discuss with Keeper Carveil?"

Sail me straight to Hadi.

The Sovereign Supreme yearned for her to say it, was all but begging her to say the word. Surrounded and emboldened by the impenetrable darkness of The Klekta Mortem, Diadet Nirvana yearned to hear the banned word as it slipped from Savallin's lips. The Keeper did not need sight to see how the ruler hungered for it, how she salivated for the sound it would make—the word, the name, *she* had forbidden.

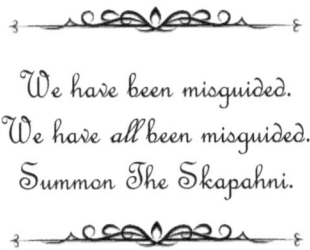

We have been misguided.
We have all been misguided.
Summon The Skapahni.

If Savallin told the truth now, if she said that word—that name—then, by Diadet Nirvana's own decree, she would be put to her fading. And with the unbridled ire flooding the black cell, that fading would likely be here and now.

But her sovereign had asked. Her Diadet had asked. Ignoring her demand, her request for an answer, that was also punishable by execution. And still, Sav reminded herself, there was little point in lying. So, the Keeper improvised.

"Your Supreme, The Midnight Message, penned in The Ever Language, advised that 'we have *all* been misguided' and ordered us to summon those... who have been lost."

And even though she had not openly voiced the name, Sav held her breath, listening quietly for the kill order—listening quietly for that easy whistle of a sword being swung high. Listening for any kind of movement at all.

And when none came, when not even the cloying prison air shifted, Sav pressed on.

"It was my intention, Diadet, to inquire from Keeper Coralis if she had come across any signs, during her many excursions of wonder, that might align with the lost... being... well, being *not so*."

That hand—the deceptively slight hand that had remained atop Savallin's arm—tightened one last time before releasing altogether. Air, both chilled and sticky, swarmed in to nestle the newly naked skin. And then, a low humming noise began reverberating through the cramped cell. The Diadet's heavy skirts swished as she paced the dying space, back and forth.

Savallin's stomach lurched and knotted. The back of her throat, the top of her mouth, her tongue dried out further than seemed possible. And she wished—so very badly—that she could see. She wished, so that maybe she might be able to brace for whatever torment came her way. For whoever tormentor came her way.

A muffled thud sounded from near the bane archway.

What was that—

"Keeper Prim," the sovereign's words were clipped, "how many years past is it that you concluded your Keeper Tutelage?"

Savallin would not let them see her flinch.

"Four years, Diadet."

"Ah, four years." A sharp inhale cut through the muggy but cold chamber. "And tell me, Keeper of Wisdom—in any of the nearly twenty years of your Tutelage, plus the four following—have you ever, even a solitary time, come upon *anything* that might lead you to believe The Skapahni live?"

At the forbade name, at the potency with which it had been spoken, both Phaedra and Euclid balked before quickly catching themselves. And the Diadet—she had begun speaking so rapidly that Savallin was afraid to interrupt.

"Well, Keeper?" An impatient foot tapped upon unseen stone. "Have you?"

Savallin, trying and failing to shirk the weight of the sovereign's scrutiny, let the rattling of her chest fill the prison chamber. And after the quiet had lingered too long, a cruel laugh bit into her bones, spurring the Keeper into speech.

"No, Diadet," she answered solemnly. "No, I have not."

"Ah, you have not?" The Supreme continued mockingly. "Not a trace in the Auburn Dunes? No goat path in the Rainbow Alps? What of footprints in the Olive Steppes? Or, Her tell, maybe a toll in the Stone Bells? No, still nothing? Not so much as a hint? Not even a trace or a lost gem in the Jade Isles?"

And Savallin—she did not even try to stop it when her mouth began to quiver.

The Diadet scoffed, ruthless as ever.

"Of course you did not," her seething grew worse by the heartbeat. "You could not because *they do not still live.*" And then, just when Savallin was sure the order for her life would be given, she heard the Diadet's skirts as she whirled. "And you? You witnessed this Keeper char illicit contraband into ash, did you not?"

The earthen cell was absolutely silent. Not one sister—not a sahira, not a covenary—dared breathe.

"*Did you not,* Phaedra Halla?" the Diadet shouted, fury limning each word.

The faintest rush of air breezed across Savallin's nose.

Youthful, she hummed. *Youthful mistake.*

For it had been Phaedra, she surmised. Phaedra—too petrified to speak—had nodded her guilt.

"Why were *you* in Coralis Carveil's private quarters, Keeper of Whispers?"

Her grating tone chafed against Savallin's skin, but she... but Diadet Nirvana was onto something. There was not a chance in Hollow that Phaedra Halla could have unwound Cora's dark charm alone. Cora's dark charm, her Seraphic that Sav knew had been there.

"I was there because the Keeper of—"

And Phaedra's desperate admission, her gasping flurry of fault, was viciously severed by the whirring of steel.

Euclid.

Sav had almost—almost—forgotten she was there. And she did not have a moment to spare. There was no time to wait for her vision to return.

Fine.

It would be fine. She did not need her sight anyway. In fact, she welcomed the challenge. Diving into her other senses, she saw exactly what she needed. And a fraction of a beat before Euclid could drive her sword straight down, before she could plunge it into the table she was bound to, Savallin snapped her thumbs inward, blocked out the burn, and ripped her wrists free.

She was rolling for the ground—rolling for where that thud had sounded—as Euclid's steel blade sang against metal and stone. The Keeper of Wisdom drove the heels of her hands into the floor and thrust her legs backward with all the might she had in reserve. Her feet made contact—a crash rumbled through the chamber—and the table, the one they had strapped her to, shot backward into the damp, stone wall of the cell. Shot backward, with Euclid Istra caught in the crossfire.

And as the Keeper grunted her pain and crumpled to the earthen stones, Savallin sprang to her feet and sprinted for the archway—the archway whose distance she had measured and memorized from each suffocating corner of her cell.

In half a beat she neared it, sniffing the air for that invisible bane curtain. The bane curtain that would boil her skin clean from her bones. But when she inhaled and smelled nothing but rotting, mildewy air, Savallin Prim picked up her pace.

And as she flew past the spot where she had heard that thud—that sack—hit the dirt, she reached out for it. Reached out for it, and darted through the archway. The heartbeat she stilled on the other side, the precious moment she stole to catch her breath, her sight came slamming back into her body—the tremendous force of which very nearly sent her to her knees.

But there was little time—no time—to process what greeted her. Phaedra, slumped in a pool of blood. And Euclid, her leg bent at a ghoulish angle, struggling to rise. And the Diadet—Diadet Nirvana—was gone.

Wholly vanished.

The Keeper's beating heart hammered in her chest. Her breaths were deep, audible. But her body—her body was primed, loose and ready to fight as she scanned the corridors spiraling above and below her. And just then, as if she had sensed precisely what Savallin might do, The Lady of the Lair laughed into the dark cavern of fading beyond.

"You have what you came for, Covelette. Go on, now. I will take care of this."

And before Savallin Prim, Keeper of Wisdom, could protest—before she could run back and scrape Phaedra from the dirty stones—the tangy scent of bane again flooded her nose.

Chapter 24

THE CITY

The human man in the canvas jacket and blue jeans had prattled on at her side the entire time it took to walk across the bridge. In their fifteen minutes together, Everly Castile had learned more about The Mortal City's sports teams than likely even their own coaches knew. And yet, the tall, dark-eyed mortal showed no signs of slowing as they stepped off the deck and back onto land.

She must have perished on that train, she thought. Somewhere on that lofty bridge. She must have slipped off that roof and shattered her skull. Shit, maybe she'd impaled herself somewhere on the way down. Or perhaps she had simply missed it when that brutish warrior severed her head from her worldly body.

Because this? This unique brand of unending torture—this was ordinarily reserved for the bleakest hollows of Sempenihil.

She did not wish to have to hurt him. She did not wish to have to crush his windpipe. She did not wish to, but she would.

And so, when the chatty man in the red ballcap made to turn right at the first crosswalk they neared, the spectraline female hurried left. She didn't make it three steps before he was beside her once more.

Enough.

"Excuse me," Everly—unsure of just how much more of this auditory assault she could stomach—cut in. "But, do I know you?"

The overly enthused mortal—he might have declared his name to be Jeff, or maybe John—ground to a halt mid-sentence.

"Seriously? You don't..." The suddenly speechless human turned a rich shade of rose.

Everly merely stared at him, stared at the embarrassment growing more and more visible on his face.

"I'm Jay." The man's wide-set shoulders shrugged in earnest. "Jay, from Coffee Corner? You don't remember me?"

Jay?

In the nearly thousand solars of her immortal existence, Everly Castile was absolutely certain she had never once known anyone by the name of *Jay*. Nonetheless, it was hurt that flashed across his fleeting features when the spectral female did not answer.

"I, uh"—a broad hand tousled the hickory tufts peeking out from beneath his backwards cap—"well, we sort of ran into one another."

We... ran into one another? Everly recoiled. *I do not—*

But then, then the spectraline warrior really looked into the human's face. Really looked, beyond the golden-tanned skin and into those rich, beckoning eyes. Eyes Everly had once seen wide with worry.

The Maelstrom.

"We did *not* run into one another," she chided, picking up her pace to lose him once and for all. "*You* ran into me."

But before she could storm off, before she had the chance to ditch the human, his hot, grimy hand clamped around her wrist. It would be the last thing that hand ever touched.

Everly spun, angling to pluck that entitled arm right off its incessant body, when—when the mortal spun *her* into the brick of the brownstone beside them.

The salty tang of anger tickled Everly's tongue, and Jay—his shadowy eyes were practically gleaming as she growled, "Remove your hands, or *I* will do it for you."

"Sweetheart," he groaned, leaning in so close his lips brushed her ear, "I would *love* to watch you try."

There were too many mortals meandering along the sidewalk for Everly to disembowel the man here. It would have to be an accident, something easily explaina—

"But"—Jay sang, craning his head backward—"before we jump into all of that, how about you join me for tonight's game?"

"*How about* I push you into traffic?"

He grinned. "Is that a *yes?*"

She bared her teeth. "Did it *sound* like a—"

Fuck.

Every inch of Everly's immortal body went rigid at once.

Fuuuuuuck.

For the salty tang she had tasted a moment ago—it had not been *her* anger. No, that taste was of a wrath much less forgiving than hers. That had been the unrivaled fury of a spectraline male—a spectraline male who had just watched a mortal man lay hands upon a spectraline female.

And it did not matter, not one bit, that *he* had just thrown her from the roof of a moving train. Nor did it matter that *she* had spent the greater part of the last millennium kicking his sorry ass. No, as far as The Spectraline customs were concerned, the only hands permitted to touch her were *his.*

And the cerulean flame simmering in Bristol's hard eyes said as much as the warrior glowered over the human's shoulder.

He would execute him. Right here. He would tear the mortal in half, right here on this very sidewalk. Right here, for the entire, Ever-blessed city to behold. And high-and-mighty Bristol wouldn't even think twice about violating The Oath of Obscurity. Not when she was involved. And why would he? The Senate had forever excused the depraved behavior of emotional males.

And so, Everly opted for the path of least resistance to keep the immortal killing-machine from ending the human where he stood. Looping her arms behind the man's neck, she pressed her body up and into his. The oh-so-smug face towering over hers fell utterly slack. Then, the mortal's dark stare doubled in size.

And it tripled, when she asked, "Do you have a home, *Jay?*"

Everly was just about to check the man for a pulse when he sputtered, "I, uh—"

Goddess, save me.

"I will need a sweater, Jay. To wear to the game."

And the saccharine-sweet smile that graced Everly's unearthly face was not *just* for the human.

"*Oh,*" Jay's murky gaze, at last, crackled back to life. "*Oh.* Yeah, yes! Yes, I do have a home!"

Everly Castile soon realized the question she should have asked was *do you have a home worthy of company?* And the answer? The answer would have been *no.*

The female had taken one step inside the door and known that she did not wish to continue further.

"Lochlan?" Jay yelled.

The apartment itself was not bad. Actually, the corner unit was well adorned with both natural light and timeworn character. Plus, here in the next hour or so, Everly guessed, the apartment's view of the cityscape would become quite lovely as the sun set behind it.

"Loch, are you here?"

What the unit did not have going for it were the two piglets that called it home.

Its historic walls were plastered with a suspect collection of crooked photos, torn movie posters, and framed sports memorabilia. And the original hardwood floor? Barely visible under the mildewing mounds of laundry and towels and pizza boxes.

"This is..." Everly grimaced at the coffee table built of Chinese takeout containers. "You live... in *this*?"

"No, not exactly." The half-mortal-half-swine led her, begrudgingly, through the pigsty that was the great room toward a hall at the rear of the space. "I tend to work a lot, but when I am here, I mostly keep to myself."

He pointed to a closed door at the end of the hall.

"I'm going to find my roommate, grab our tickets, and then maybe kill him." With his hand on her lower back, Jay guided her to the door. "My closet is in there. Pick anything you like."

The spectral must have forgotten to hide her cringe because the mortal laughed.

"It's clean, *I swear*."

And then, giving her one final push forward, he was off to find his chambermate.

"Loch! I love you, man, but I really need you to clean this shit up!"

Everly did not know why she waited there until he turned the corner. She did not know why she waited there amongst the peeling wallpaper and flickering overheads at all. But she did. And only when the human was gone, only when she heard his hasty steps moving across the living-sty floor, only then did she twist the brass knob on the bedchamber door.

And in doing so, the spectraline female who had bested eternity by forever expecting the worst—for once—found herself standing amidst a pleasant surprise. For the modest bedchamber surrounding her was immaculate.

Perhaps the Maelstrom, Jay is not.

Dissimilar to the rest of the dwelling, the air in this chamber was breathable. In here, the pungent scents of stale ale and mortal despair gave way to that of cedarwood and fresh linen. The quarter's large bed had been made with practiced precision, the matching oak bureau and desk were both devoid of dust, and the hardwood—perfectly visible—was polished.

Interesting.

The tension tightening Everly's spine eased as she neared the closet. And the neatness hiding within—it was something out of a catalog. For all of the closet's hangers were the exact same shade of plastic. Better still, every single one of them faced away from her and had been positioned to ensure equal spacing on both sides of each hook. And the clothing borne upon them had been arranged by season, and then by wavelength.

"Descending order," Everly hummed as she rifled through the dense blue of the winter section. "Correct."

The immortal was not shopping for style, though. No, with the evening of torment she was slated to suffer, comfort was her sole desire. Well, that—and sleeves. A high neckline wouldn't hurt either.

Settling on the finest of the meager, Everly tugged an oversized, ruby hoodie from its hanger. After a quick inspection, she lifted it to her nose.

"Oh."

It is indeed clean.

She had just slipped the sweatshirt over her head when something thumped against the floor. Stooping low, the spectral reached beneath the garments until she retrieved what had fallen from the shelf.

The skin of Everly's palm heated.

Why would the mortal still have one of—

"*That* doesn't belong to you," a voice croaked from the hallway.

The relic was out of her hand and back on the shelf before the stranger could blink.

"Chill, man. I told her she could wear it." With the necks of two amber bottles clutched in one hand, Jay used the other to clap the reedy voyeur on the shoulder. "And *dayyum* does she wear it well."

The paler mortal, Lochlan, did not once take his eyes off Everly as he strew a pair of tickets onto the bed's green coverlet and again skulked out of view.

And Jay, who was also busily gawking at her, did not seem to notice the weirdness at all.

"Is he... always like that?"

Rejoining reality at last, the golden-skinned man swigged from his bottle.

"Women... uh, well, they make Lochlan nervous." He extended the second bottle in Everly's direction. "And women like you make Lochlan *very* nervous."

Just wait until I formally introduce myself, then.

"Do you not—uh"—the mortal's arm was still outstretched—"you don't drink beer?"

The spectraline crinkled her nose at his offering.

"That is genuine poison."

"Well," the human considered, his smile broadening. "Genuine poison it may be, *Everly—*"

"How do you—"

But with one long stride toward her, Jay had a forearm hooked behind her waist. And then, pulling her in close, he whispered, "But without this poison, you won't last the first inning."

The spectral glared at him. At the nerve. The nerve to presume what she could and could not handle. She who had been the last warrior standing upon many, many a killing field before this rodent's eldest ancestors were ever even thoughts.

But then, as her sight listed toward red, the taste of salt again prickled her tongue. And she remembered why she was here in the first place.

And so, as that mortal man again drew the bottle to his lips, Everly Castile snatched it right out of his fingers. She had survived much and more. This baseball game would be no different.

Chapter 25

THE CRYPTS

"What do you mean, *I* beckoned you?"

"I do not casually toss words about, Ava." The large lavender glasses slid along the bridge of the shrink's nose as she dipped her chin low. "I said precisely what I intended. *You* summoned me."

Tugging the long sleeves of her sweater over her nearly numb fingers, Ava narrowed her glare at the woman in the gray pantsuit but did not speak again.

The lady seated across the metal table from her—the stranger who had introduced herself as Alice—doused her last bite of waffle into the little plastic container of maple syrup. And when Ava made it crystal clear she was more than happy to let their silence drag on, Alice plunged the sodden morsel into her mouth.

She chewed, leisurely. Politely. Then, gingerly patting her lips with a brown paper napkin, careful not to disturb her flawless lip stain, she crooked her ashen bob to one side. And then, placing the dirty napkin and the empty fork back into the cardboard carton, she waded into the tides of Ava's opaline frown once more.

"You summoned me here." Twirling a manicured hand lackadaisically, Alice the therapist furthered, "Here, to this lifeless crypt beneath the living city."

"How? How is it that you think I did that?" Ava broke. "How could I have possibly done that from down here? From down here? Down here, underground, in this—what did you call it before—a dungeon?"

The woman only observed her, only studied the twisting of her features, the escalation of her mannerisms, the untouched food before her. Softly clicking the heels of her stilettos against the old, yellowing floor, she examined Ava, listening to each of the words splattering freely atop the table between them.

"There is no Wi-Fi. Not a bar of cellular service. And—and I am fairly sure there are no godsdamned carrier pigeons familiar with the flight path into this tunnel."

The clicking paused.

"Have you ever dispatched a homing pigeon?" A knowing smile curved the lips of the woman in gray. "They are craftier beasts, I think, than you give them credit." After an unsettlingly lingering eye contact, Alice eased the purple frames back up her nose. "Intrepid little beasts, indeed."

Murder, Ava thought. *I am going to go to prison for murder.*

As if she had overheard her soundless epiphany, the counselor's face grew stern, professional, as she straightened in her chair.

"So," she posed, her voice like a calm brook in the stormy space. "Why is it, Ava, you so enjoy living in squalor?"

While Ava's dark brows shot skyward, her jaw came dangerously close to thunking against the metal table—against the yellowing floor, even.

"What…" She croaked, her throat suddenly dry with exasperation. "What does that have to do with—"

"Truly, Ava." She took a slow sip from one of the two bottles of water in the center of the table. "I thought it a simple enough question."

And even as her vision began to blur, even as a cloying, greenish sheen spread over the bone-chilling interrogation room, even then, Ava forced herself to breathe. Forced herself to remain unruffled, still. She commanded the muscles of her unnerved body to keep her seated, fixed atop her silver chair.

Was this—all of this—some kind of experimental new form of punishment? Some sort of unhinged reckoning set upon Ava for what she did… or, perhaps, for what she did not do? Was she being made to endure this—this strange woman and her prying, nonsensical questions—because she had failed so grievously in the line of duty? Because she had… had failed to protect her partner? Because she had failed to… to save him?

Are the powers that be demanding that I relive the worst of my life… as some… some foul form of justice? Some vulgar flavor of justice for what I failed to see sooner?

What else could it be? These questions… how did they pertain to the investigation at hand? How did they pertain to anything at all? How could their answers provide any sort of clarity in the slightest?

Across the table, the visitor—or the doctor, whatever she was—twisted her lips. "Shall I ask you again, then?"

The quickest path out of this dungeon, Ava knew, was not force. No; it was compliance. Answers. She swallowed against the drought in her mouth. Information—she could handle that. She could comply. She could listen. No, she would listen to the woman. She would listen and voice the requested, the expected, answers. And then, then she would get out of here. She would. Even if she had not been able to save her partner, she would save herself.

Fine, she conceded to no one. *Fine.*

And then, squaring her rounded shoulders and blinking the small room back into focus, Ava nodded to the lady—nodded to Alice.

"What compels a young woman, such as yourself, to choose a rundown studio apartment in a somewhat precarious part of the city instead of a serene, sprawling manor house with your family crest soldered prominently upon the gate?"

Ava, sculpting her features into a practiced mask of neutrality, vividly recalled her first day back in the city. The sinking sensation—that endless pit of despair low in her belly—was the most potent memory of that morning. The fluttering songbirds, the rustling whispers of the foliage, the deafening disquiet in her chest as she had paced along the perimeter sidewalk—all paled in comparison. All faded into nothingness as she stood before those soaring iron gates.

She did not remember how long she had stood there that first day, how long she had stood there, frozen in time, peering through those ornate, intertwining posts of the front gate, at the meticulous landscaping beyond. At the impeccable, remarkable groundskeeping that was exactly as it had been eleven years earlier.

In the dreamlike channels of her recollection, Ava again felt the warmth of sunrise upon her skin—just as she had that very morning when she wrapped her fingers around the jade-streaked bars of that golden gate.

She had clung there, held on for dearest life, as the unrestrained torrent of memory threatened to pull her under. And when she had, at last, surfaced—at last freed herself from the flood's mistiest depths—the sky overhead was bleak, the muted gray of windblown ash. And then, that kiss of warmth upon her skin, it was spent—swapped for a bitter chill.

"I did visit the manor," Ava admitted. "In truth, it was the very first thing I did upon my return to this city."

Absentmindedly kneading her fingers into, and through, one another, she gathered and sampled the taste of her next words.

"I did make the trip, yes. But, try as I might, all I could see as I looked upon that steady, elegant ironwork was heartache. Loss—the loss of a life I loved more than living itself."

And then, a shiver of heat shuddered Ava's eyesight. Her breath hitched... caught, at the gentle caress of light that began filling each of the dark, shadowy hollows she had just traversed. *Just relived.*

"Thank you, Ava, for sharing that with me. And for opening up. Truly, I fully recognize how difficult it can be."

Was it some gnarly side effect of the curious yet tender warmth now weaving its way through her past, or had the shrink always appeared so earnest when she spoke?

"But also, I trust that you understand my sole reason for being here is to help you."

Ava, unexpectedly unable to locate or lodge a proper dispute, found herself nodding along.

"Anyhow," Alice practically sang, folding her slim hands atop one another on the icy table, "how old were you, Ava, when you were whisked away to the Autumn Hills?"

"I was seven." And though her mind went hazy, she continued on, "Seven years old, when I was loaded into the backseat of a black car. It was the night of her wake."

And again, that comforting touch swept through the bottomless wells of her pain.

"I have heard that Upstate, that the Autumn Hills, are quite lovely. Exceptionally so, that special time of the season when the leaves overwhelm their confines and become whatever shade they wish. Whatever shade, save green."

Ava could picture it, the estate—its endless rolling hills, its fiery forest and rambling streams—like an ageless oil painting in a fine art gallery.

"I think... I think lovely does not really do it justice."

Nevertheless, a hint of a smile snuck across her cheeks as she remembered all of the times she had gorged herself ill in the orchards. As the neighing and braying of each mare she had spooked again bristled her hair. As the kind and nurturing and doting faces of the household—the family—who had raised her spun through the muddle of her mind, the chasm in her chest. As the exhaustive measures they had all—every one of them—tirelessly and devotedly taken to try and keep her mother's memory alive and well beat in her heart.

"What was it like, Ava, living amidst that level of isolation?" The therapist's posh exterior strengthened to something Ava could not quite name. "What was it like being thrust into that degree of seclusion at such a vulnerable age?"

Isolation? she puzzled. *Seclusion?*

The sundry sea of smiling faces—the pensive smirks of her academic tutors, the fierce grins of her equestrian and fencing and archery coaches, the weary half-snickers of her many dance and decorum instructors—flashed, one after the other, through the darkness in her mind. The parade of their likenesses followed closely by that inexplicable, soothing warmth.

No. No, Ava had never seen nor thought about it—thought about them, nor her upbringing—in that way.

"Did growing up alone, like you did... does it have anything to do, do you think, with your inability to trust others?" Alice, her glossy nutmeg hands still atop the table, leaned in closer. "Do you believe, Ava, that your unconventional rearing has anything to do with your inherent distrust in humanity?"

No. The shaking of her head became heated, the dampened ends of her hair skating across her shoulders. *No.*

No. How dare she—how dare she speak ill of any of those people. It was not their fault, not at all, never their fault. The way she turned out... no. No, it was not on them. She was the only one to blame for who, for what, she had become.

"I believe, Alice, that your insinuation is perfectly inverted," her voice was low, detached, as she bared the truth. "Despite their finest efforts, their years of assiduous work, *I* am the sole reason I cannot trust."

For she had deceived them. Every one of them, every one of those adoring faces that had looked after her, cared for her, when she had no one else in the world. Every ounce, every second, of labor and love and hope they had poured into her, she had squandered. For she had played along, played her part, only to deceive them in the end.

After everything they had done for her, given to her, gifted her, she had packed her bags in the heart of night and left them behind. Abandoned them there, without so much as a farewell or a thank you. Without ever once thanking them for everything they had done for her. Without ever once telling each one of them how much they truly meant to her.

Her stomach roiled at the thought of it.

"Hmm," the counselor hummed while tapping a slender finger atop the back of one hand. "Why is it, then, that you chose to return here? To this city?"

It was concern, Ava decided. It was concern weighing upon the woman's otherwise reserved features.

"What brought you back to this city that stole your whole world, Ava?"

Revenge? Retribution? Redemption? Obsession? Fascination? Intuition? An invisible string? A car? Who the hell knows?

She had asked herself that question hundreds, if not thousands, of times. And yet, it was still a mystery. Even though she had been here—here, in her squalor—for eight years, she had never been able to settle upon a single answer as to what had brought her here.

"I don't know," Ava sighed heavily, shoving her carton of food away before the smell made her sick. And then, then she told the lie she'd long been telling herself. "But my Personal History Statement refers to it as 'a calling.'"

Chapter 26

THE CATACOMBS

"I will not think less of you, Covelette, if you need to rest to regain composure."

Savallin Prim, Keeper of Wisdom, swore under her shaking breath.

"No," she gasped, gulping down darkest air. "I must hurry."

Her thighs burned and seared with every movement. And her shoulders, as well as her forearms and wrists, trembled so violently she was sure she would slip.

Slip... and tumble, Her only knows how far, to certain fading.

She had been climbing, hammering and hauling herself straight up the sheer tunnel at the heart of The Klekta Mortem for hours now.

Relent, she grumbled to herself, *is for the fallen, Savallin.*

If it had not been for the iron spikes and heavy mallet Sav discovered in the discarded sack of torture instruments, she did not truly know how she would have scaled the smooth, stone shaft leading to The Surface.

Even with the tools of encouragement, the ascent was taking its toll. Nonetheless, she much preferred this sort of torment over the alternative. Much preferred it.

But even so, her waning energy and glistening skin somehow did not go unnoticed in the black chute.

"There is a small nook less than three body-lengths above you—an alcove once home to birds of the night." The Lady of the Lair, it seemed, missed nothing. "It is ample for you to sit, rest."

Rest.

Straining her shoulders, she tugged her body upward.

There is no time for rest.

When her second hand latched firmly onto rock, Sav tightened her core and commanded her legs to follow.

The Majlis' deadline is still—

"The surest way to miss your deadline, Savallin, is to plunge yourself straight into the Winds of Hadi."

Her toes found purchase.

"You have quite the flair," Sav choked between her heavy heaves, "for the fussery, Lady."

A breathy titter tousled her fallen ringlets just as—just as the rock beneath Savallin's toes crumbled away into the blackness. Her stomach barreled into her throat as her first hand ripped clean from its hold at the sudden jolt downward. Shuddering breaths racked her body, hard and fast. The muscles in her arm—the single arm supporting her full weight—snarled and shrieked.

You will not, she huffed into her mind.

Five fingers, and a handful of shredded nails, was all that hung between Savallin and a bottomless freefall through the passageway of black stone.

You. Will. Not, she grumbled again, more forceful this time.

If the iron spike she clenched slipped from the wall—if it so much as loosened a fraction—her mortal body would plummet for leagues, for Her and Hadi and Hollow between.

You. Will. Not.

Her body would never be recovered. Her final whereabouts—her final resting place—would forever live in mystery. No one would know what befell Savallin Prim, Keeper of Wisdom.

You. Will. Not. Fall, her growl booming into a silent yell.

The Covenary of The Catacombs would forever wonder if she had just abandoned her duties. And the Keepers, the corrupt court of Majlis, would ensure that all of Covenarykind believed nothing else—believed that she had fled and forsaken her people.

Relent is for the fallen, the Keeper bit. *Only for the fallen.*

Savallin, the youngest covenary ever to be Raised to one of The Five, would not allow that to happen. She would never allow that to happen.

You. Will. Not. Fall.

Gritting her teeth, she clasped the spike harder. With one breath in, she called upon the strength of every last flagging muscle in her body. And without losing another moment to lethal doubt, Sav catapulted her bodyweight upward.

The momentum sent her spearing for that upper spike, spearing for the hold she had so carelessly slipped from. Her muscles screamed their agony. But with that single fluid motion, with that flawless surge upward, her strong hand—slick with sweat—locked onto the iron.

The weight instantly shifted back between both shoulders. Her heart slowed, and the shuddering of her ribs began to ease. Her slippers again hooked onto the sheer, stone face of the climb, this time checking the wall for slack patches.

"Do remind me, Savallin"—a delicate edge haunted the voice that glittered with ice—"*who* has a flair for the fussery?"

And despite herself, despite her brief brush with Hadi, a wide, brilliant smile cracked through the grime coating the Keeper's face. "Still you."

"Earth wielders," The Lady scoffed. "You will be the end of us all."

"See?" Sav puffed. "Nothing but fussery from you."

She could nearly feel the hot waves of ire as they rolled through the sweeping dark.

"If you somehow manage to make it to The Surface alive, Keeper, I will show you *fussery*."

When I make it to The Surface alive, she wordlessly corrected. For Savallin could not help herself—she was competitive by nature and by nurture. And her Tutelage had only made it worlds worse.

And with her throbbing legs still driving her body upward, Sav snipped, "Let us make a bargain, Lady."

"Oh?" A frosty sneer tickled her back. "You feel *now* is an appropriate time for a bargain?"

"Well, as suitable a time as ever, I suppose," her fingertips burned their fury into the iron she held. "Seeing as I might plunge into Hollow at any moment now."

If she had to stop and rest, she might as well make it worthwhile.

"Let us hear it then, this bargain."

And for whatever the reason, the sharpness of The Lady's tone calmed her nerves.

"I will rest," Sav puffed through her strain. "Rest, in the nook. But only"—the Keeper swallowed another large gulp of air—"only if you tell me all that you know of The Skapahni."

Two birds of night, one black stone.

"Ah," her formless companion sang into the void. "Is that all?"

And then, the lonely passageway went eerily silent as The Mistress considered.

"I know a great deal of the Shamed Sisters, Covelette. Sharing the sum of my insight would require... well, it would require a rather lengthy respite."

The Lady plays, it seems.

"Splendid," Sav said as she eyed the recess above. "Considering the rather lengthy ascent still ahead of me, the respite shall be welcomed."

Another hushed laugh warmed her chilled face as she pulled herself up the vertical pass.

"Then, you have yourself a bargain, Savallin Prim."

And a short time later, she and her sore backside rested upon the small, stone ledge carved into the wall. Her tunic, soaked in sweat, clung to every curve of her body. But as her feet dangled over the edge, swaying from side to side in the utter darkness, the covenary listened eagerly as The Lady of the Lair upheld her end of the deal.

"As you well know, Keeper of Wisdom, it is The Samaritan—our three great Saviors—who shelter the spinning of time," she began. "The first two, distant and everlasting, are the warriors of legend. Warriors forged to stand against any threat."

"The Sword and The Shield, "Sav chimed.

"Yes. And the third Savior, rooted and fleeting, are the ambassadors crafted to keep the balance between all."

"The Shepherd."

"The Shepherd, indeed," The Lady affirmed. "You, and your people."

Quiet upon her dark perch, Savallin nodded to herself as her shapeless companion continued on.

"Each Savior of The Samaritan draws their strength from a different space within our world. And the closer a Savior exists to said space within nature—to their elemental origin—the mightier the power they can command."

And then, before she had even thought to summon it, The Lady of the Lair's declaration from before, from when she had taunted her down in that rotting cell, roared into Savallin's mind.

My elemental power remains intact because I am no mortal. I am no caster of earth.

"Precisely, Covelette," The Mistress of the Dark missed nothing. "And that is why your capital citadel lies beneath The Surface—why your beloved Catacombs lie *within* the very Earth itself."

"Because we—because the covenary," Savallin charged forth. "Our charm, before it is ever ours, it sounds through the Earth. It is *of* the Earth, it is Her very song. We siphon our Soul directly from Hers."

A click of approval echoed down the bottomless shaft.

"Yes. You and your people, the Earth Casters."

And after allowing a short moment for the Keeper to fully absorb her words, The Lady started again.

"And, to further amplify the abilities of your strongest wielders—of your most elite casters—your kind cleaved their quarters, cleaved what is now this Klekta Mortem, straight through a primordial deposit of solid obsidian."

"Straight..." And the gasp—Sav hardly recognized it as her own. "Straight through a vein of pure *earthstone*."

"Vicinity," the voice of ice and shadows purred. "Nature's paramount balance."

Savallin blinked once. Twice, as the sense of where this was headed inundated her consciousness.

"Vicinity," her ethereal tutor again emphasized. "The very reason why—even though your bodies are fleeting, even though your bodies are *mortal*—the Shepherds, the beings charged with keeping the balance, vicinity is why you possess the fiercest might of them all."

The Keeper of Wisdom wished she could lie down, wished she could splash cool water upon her hot face, wished she could somehow just quench her belly's—no, her soul's—sudden, violent thirst.

But as Savallin teetered, as she became lightheaded on that little ledge, The Lady of the Lair kept right on, kept on drowning her in waves of fulfilled promise.

"And the fiercest among you, Savallin, your most elite wielders, they were not the subdued and spiteful sahira." Over the drought storming her body, she heard the sound of a smile as it brightened The Lady's tone. "The fiercest among you, Savallin, they had the supreme might to rip the elemental power from *any* being who dared threaten the balance."

The Keeper's mouth became desert parchment.

"The kind of covenary..." Yet again, she recited The Lady's earlier words. "That the world came to fear."

A thick silence settled over the pitch darkness—over the whole world as she had known it. But her mind was racing, spinning—spiraling—through all that she had ever known, through all that she had ever been taught. Through all that she had *not* been taught.

The elite... This was their home.

"It was," a soft sadness dimmed her companion's spirit. "Until it was not. Until the day the fiercest Shepherds this world has ever known were betrayed."

Newly heavy with understanding, the Keeper did not think it likely she would finish her climb. *This* was their home. Their home, until the day it became their tomb.

Their home, she whispered to herself, *until the day it became The Klekta Mortem... became their Klekta Mortem.*

"Indeed," The Lady of the Lair's calm voice simmered with fiery rage. "When your elite were sentenced to their fading, when they were sentenced to fade within this very cavern, they unleashed a collective curse so potent, so profoundly vengeful, that it would never be broken."

And at last, Savallin, Keeper of Wisdom, pieced it together.

"The Skapahni *were* the elite. The fiercest of the fierce. They cursed this place so that no other covenary—not one of the sahira who had been forced to carry out their sentence—could live in *their* beautiful, cherished home."

She had hoped to one day uncover the truth of The Skapahni's demise, but she had not planned for that truth—for the reality of her Shamed Sisters' desperate, defiant end—to hurt as much as it did.

"Their Death Promise," she rasped. "In The Ever Language, Klekta Mortem... it means Death Promise."

And as The Lady's knowledge sank deeper into her heart, a new sort of energy—a dusky, angry energy—blossomed like a moon bloom in Savallin's hollowed chest. And with that dark energy vibrant at her fingertips, the Keeper rose from the small, chilly cranny at the edge of escape. She reached inward, reached for that serene inner cosmos where thoughts and fears and dread quieted into nothing—for where the steadiest of all Premier had trained her to win wars.

"Thank you, Lady. For everything." Her gratitude ran deep as she hefted the canvas sack onto her shoulder. "I do hope to one day know your true name, to one day thank you properly, for all that you have shared."

And as she drew her mallet, The Lady of the Lair's voice brushed along her ears once more: "It will not be long now, Covelette."

One stinging strike after another, Savallin climbed through the darkness and despair. For every iron spike she drove into the wall of that stone shaft, she pulled and clawed and tore another free. And with each daunting thrust upward, each handhold and foothold a little higher than its predecessor, the dense tomb air began to lighten. As rushing trembles shook her arms and her back, as fresh blisters enveloped her already scarred hands, as the sharpest rocks split her skin and streamed her blood, the crushing blackness started to soften.

And then, at last, after what had felt like a lifetime's worth of days, Savallin Prim, Keeper of Wisdom, hoisted herself over the jagged, crumbling rim of the endless tunnel into the crisp, starry air of The Surface.

Chapter 27

THE CESSPOOL

A faint ringing whispered through the darkness to
Sergeant Ava Carlisle, tickling her innermost ear as it crept its
way in. She blinked once, then twice, the strobing of the
arcade neons casting the too-large smears of blood in a
sickening, cartoonish glow. Her breaths were shaky, loud—
too loud—as she scanned the colored shadows for... for... she
didn't know. Her partner? His body? Another's?

Over the rattling of her own respiration, above the wistful
tunes tingling the depths of her memories, beyond the faint,
hollow ringing in her eardrums, the Sergeant did not hear
anything. No more wet chokes... not a hint of scuffle... not so
much as a footstep... just nothing.

And now—now, while her partner was somewhere
incapacitated and bleeding—she was wholly useless...
trapped on an island for children. An island, home to nothing
but obstacle upon sticky obstacle, tucked precariously
between a river of plastic and a black-net bridge.

Fuck. Fuck. Fuck.

The Sergeant eased backward, silent and cautious steps carrying her through the swaying foliage of coarse, climbing ropes toward the dense forest of towering Velcro-vested trees just beyond. Only when her spine brushed against that rough, telling texture did she remove one hand from her weapon and depress the talk button on her shoulder radio.

Willing her voice level, willing it to be clear and precise, she said, "Queen One to Central, officer down. I repeat, officer down. Start all—"

In the stillness of the heavy gloom surrounding her on all sides like an ever-patient army, the very blood in Sergeant Carlisle's veins ceased its coursing all at once. At once, as a lone droplet of dark liquid splashed down atop the slight swoop in her delicate nose. At once, as she craned her head backward, the thick liquid trailing along the gentle bridge as she leaned. At once, as her pastel-bright irises settled upon what was perching atop the Velcro tree's lowest and broadest branch.

A pair of eyes. A pair of milky-white, unblinking eyes.

"Central to Queen One, welfare?"

But the young Sergeant did not hear the dispatcher's voice. She did not hear a word the woman had said—not a syllable. For the instant that radio had hissed into the darkness, the cloudy eyes above her had leapt—had sprung off their branch, straight for her.

The... the thing... didn't make a sound as it crashed into where she had been standing. It did not make a single noise— not as it caught itself on all fours, landing flat like a feline on both finger and toe pads. Flat like a rabid, ravaged, ruined feline.

For the creature's spine protruded from its colorless skin like the jagged peaks of sister mountains rising from a translucent sea—the bones bent sharply where they should have lain level. Its reedy arms... its squashed legs... they were still—somehow—limply tethered to the thing's torso, but not at the proper angles.

How it was even moving at all... how it was doing so... so effortlessly, so suddenly and silently... it should have been impossible. No, it *was* impossible. But the Sergeant had seen it with her own eyes—was still seeing it with her own eyes as she kicked herself backward, kicked herself away from the soundless snarls of the wrecked creature. The wrecked body. The wrecked human body.

Viscous, black blood dribbled from behind mangled lips. The corners of what had once been a mouth peeled up, pulled back, almost as if it were trying to... trying to smile.

The Sergeant's back collided with something hard. She grimaced, but dug into her heels—hoisting herself, step by step, into a low crouch. Her duty weapon was again at the ready, the muzzle aimed directly into the heart of the rubble that might have been a man.

The contortion of a smile on its face morphed into a soggy gnashing of bare gums against shattered molars. Where the thing's front teeth had gone, the Sergeant did not know.

Is this what the caller had reported? She thought of the shaken assistant manager—the shaken girl—still waiting out on the corner. *Is this what had sprinted through the glass doors? It is without clothes, just like the dispatcher said... but that's not... that's not grease... no, that's not grease slathered atop its skin, through its ruddy-blonde hair.*

Her heartbeat thundered within her chest. She remembered the smudges of dark sheen. The smears of her partner's blood. Her gigantic, muscle-roped partner who could have easily moonlighted as a professional wrestler. *Is this what... why... how did it... how is it so strong? How did it get over here without ruffling the plastic balls... without striking even a single piano key?*

The thing arched its broken, peaked spine, crawling forward a foot. The sloshy clacking of its jaw intensified.

Why is it here? Why is it coated in... in blood? In black blood? She did not dare take her eyes off the creature as the deluge of questions flooded her mind. *What could it possibly want with a trampoli—*

"Central to Quee—"

The breath whooshed from the Sergeant. She nearly jumped out of her skin, snapping a sweat-slick hand to her shoulder—jostling, thumbing, fighting frantically to silence the voice spilling from her radio.

But it was futile. Far too late. Her pale eyes widened as the decimated creature hunching before her became airborne once more.

And Sergeant Carlisle, alone in the dark, her back literally pinned against a wall, squeezed her trigger finger and unloaded her duty weapon. The barrel flared with blinding, white light. A series of deafening cracks whipped through the distant electric melody. A stream of lightning-laced bullets flew from just beyond her fingers, racing single file toward the attacker with her centered in its sights.

With every shot, every bang and flash, the tip of her gun rose. Her arms, her aim followed the creature on its arcing path through the air. She watched, her jaw falling slack, as bullet after bullet struck true.

But the... the thing... it was not dissuaded. No, it simply kept on coming. Kept on lunging for her. So the Sergeant kept on firing. Firing until the slide locked back and the trigger clicked empty. In half a breath, she released the first clip and pulled a second from her belt, shoving it into place.

She hit her mark every single time—each one of her bullets piercing the thing's thin, caved chest... but it... it did not slow. Not at all.

Its milky, glazed stare was just above her—barreling straight toward her—when she struck with her legs. Dropping her spine to the ground and digging the heels of her hands into the carpet, she drove her legs up and into the charging creature's brittle diaphragm. The grating sound of cleaving bone was unmistakable as the thing—the body—careened to the side.

But the... the monster... it did not seem to notice.

What in the actual—

Gnawing its teeth loudly, the thing sprang for her again. A new type of adrenaline plunged through her. And at once, the dull ringing chafing her ears quieted. The blurred edges of her periphery sharpened. The shadowed space, the aggressor before her, brightened as if kissed by an emerald sun.

The Sergeant tucked tight and rolled out of reach, a primordial instinct, a dust-riddled voice, a susurrant intuition guiding her hand to her hip.

The creature overshot, hissing and sliding across the carpet at her back. She whipped to face it. The thing's soured-cream glare pulsated, recoiled. Then, its fissured lips drew back ever farther.

"*Mudamira*," the warped scrap of body moaned, trails of murky gore leaking from its torn, mutilated mouth. "*Death... death... death. Death to the apostates.*"

You'll sure be wishing for death, she growled to herself as the monster charged her again. For the canister of OC spray had already been freed from her belt. It had already been freed, palmed, and was now eagerly awaiting its moment. *Death doesn't burn nearly so bad.*

The narrowed, milky eyes angling for her went wide with surprise. They stretched even larger when the shock of pain sank in. The Sergeant jumped to her feet as the stream of chili-pepper resin tore from the canister in her hands. The creature—*the blood-crusted man*—shrieked in anguish, his broken, battered form collapsing in a heap upon the scratchy carpet.

Sergeant Carlisle did not look back over her shoulder. She had not waited around for the thing to scramble to his feet. No, she was running—sprinting toward the plastic-ball river on the far side of the obstacle island. The forest of sticky trees thinned, transforming into a barren maze of winding, slouching mirrors.

Fuck, she panted. *Fucking fuck.*

For even though the isle had been designed with children in mind, she was small. Small enough that she could not see over the tops of the mirrors. No, she could not spy the path out. She would have to find it.

There was no room for error, no time for backtracking. Over the pounding of her own heart and the hoarse swallows of air, she could just hear the creature as it began to stir. When it did rise, though, its vision would be impaired, inflamed and watery—she knew from personal experience.

Good.

She moved on silent boots, testing path after path, turn upon turn, until, at last, the way out presented itself. She darted for it, pumping her arms and catching fleeting, misshapen glimpses of a woman she did not fully recognize in the curved mirrors that passed her by. Behind her, a guttural howl slashed the darkness.

Her chest shuddered, but her legs pushed off the ground harder, sending her traveling faster and faster toward the inner bank of the river. Five strides. Four. Three.

Another yowling bay split the stillness.

Two.

Thundering beats—a cadence of four feet, not two—drummed from where she'd just come.

One.

The Sergeant's legs never stopped moving—never stopped propelling her forward as she reached the bank and leapt—as she dove, headfirst, into the pit of plastic. Her outstretched arms sliced through the colored spheres until they smashed into something hard. Something—

Wall, she murmured, a flicker of relief prickling her fingers. *The outer wall.*

Grabbing the edge with both hands, she kicked off the river floor, pushed her body upward, and hooked a knee upon the lip. But the heartbeat she pressed herself up, the moment her submerged leg lifted from the river's bottom—that was the very same second that something cold and bony coiled around her ankle and yanked her back down.

Sergeant Ava Carlisle's scream—her promise of vengeance—drowned as the stagnant torrent of spheres sucked her under.

Chapter 28

THE CITY

"Did you enjoy yourself this evening?"

Everly Castile did not spare even a glance toward the velvet sofa with the newfound snark. She merely bolted the entry door and strode for the kitchen. Popping open the fridge, she let the bright, cool air kiss her face as she admired the many offerings.

"Did you enjoy the eleven meat wieners I counted you swallow?" The spectral plucked a pie pan from the middle shelf. "Did you even chew them?"

Stalker Bristol was off the sofa and lording over her before she could pull open the utensil drawer.

"I did a little counting, as well," the warrior fumed. "And would you care to guess just how many times that human man groped you?"

"Hmmm," she thought aloud as she reached around the massive meathead for a fork. "Probably more times than you have been bedded this mille—"

The pie dish clanged to the countertop as Bristol's monster hand crushed down on her windpipe.

"You reek of him." The male's turquoise scowl practically glowed in the darkness of the penthouse apartment. "After you bathe, you and I are leaving."

But the living metal churning in her eyes put Bristol's baby blues to shame. With one powerful sweep of her dangling legs, the spectraline female had the muscled warrior pinned beneath her, face-down, on the marble.

"Your wish is my command, Brigadier."

And then, instead of dismounting the prone male in a timely fashion, Everly let him serenade her in the vilest of profanities until she again had her cherry pie in hand. Bristol was on his feet the moment she released pressure. She didn't care. She had dessert. But the male, he wasn't finished yet.

"We are in agreement then?" His longer strides overtook her saunter at the end of the hallway. "You will leave here with me?"

Everly smiled up at the male sweetly.

"*Fuck* no."

Then slammed the door on his stupid face.

She had barely gotten the hot water running when it splintered into a thousand pieces.

Frowning, she slid her pie safely out of harm's way.

"What is this vendetta against doors?"

The male only thundered toward her.

"I am here on behalf of The Spectraline Senate."

"*No?*" The female feigned the deepest offense. "Here I was thinking you missed me."

A healthy pour of lavender crystals splashed into the burbling tub. The water swirled and hissed. Scents of spring began wafting through the chamber.

"I have been sent as your escort," he roared.

Past the tub, and the floor-to-ceiling windows beyond, the synthetic radiance of the tower city dimmed the sky.

"Look, Bris, I don't know how best to tell you this..." Using the mirrors to track the male's movements, Everly shoveled a forkful of cherry goodness into her mouth. "But... lumbering and lacking doesn't really do it for me anymore. Not in the way it once did, at least."

White-hot heat, a very different kind than that running from the faucet, flared through the bathing chamber. The immortal, it seemed, was not amused.

"You are going to Helavos." He stalked to where she stood, his battle-scarred hands pressed into the glittering, black countertop on either side of her. "How you choose to get there, though, is entirely up to you."

Helavos? she parroted. *The Crevasse Citadel? I think not.*

Rolling her eyes clear to the gates of Sempedormir, Everly scooped another bite of buttery crust and juice-sweet filling into her mouth. Though, she had not missed the subtle flickers of light illuminating the hems of Bristol's thick, charcoal sleeves.

"Well," the baggy sweatshirt she had been sporting all evening plopped to the tile, "perhaps if you share why it is that I am so abruptly needed in The Black Chasm—*without a formal summons*, I might add," her creamy v-neck and dark-washed denim joined the sweater pile, "well, then perhaps I will do you the service of sharing how it is that *I* would prefer to travel."

The ancient warrior, though, said nothing. Not a single word. He did not swear to the goddess, he did not curse Everly's wretched eternity, he didn't so much as strike for her. No. Actually, she wasn't even sure if he was breathing.

For Bristol—Ever help her—was gone, wholly lost to the red hoodie heaped upon the floor.

She sighed under her breath, letting her undergarments slip to the cool tiles at her feet. But her fork—her fork was spinning through the steamy haze before the frothy waters had welcomed her under.

The Shield Brigadier didn't waste energy turning. He simply reached up and caught the projectile the heartbeat before it skewered his brain.

And he still did not turn as he growled, "We are being hunted."

The lofty walls of the dark bathing chamber danced with gentle bursts of silver, gold, and lilac-blue light. Everly sank lower into the tub. The ballet swirled into a thing of dreams.

"That is not news, Bristol." She closed her eyes and pictured the faces of every friend she would not see again. "That is our fate."

"No, Ev"—the brooding soldier, at long last, peeled his focus from the laundry—"our *fate* is to protect Lesserkind from all that wish to prey upon them. To protect them by defending the borders, Known and Not."

You don't say?

The female dipped her head back into the water.

"But now"—Bristol's expression could have very well been chiseled from stone—"now, it is Lesserkind who wish to prey upon *us*."

Everly sat straight up. "What?"

The immortal warrior, hesitating a beat as he noticed the violety-metallic glimmers swirling along the walls, bent to turn off the faucet. And then, crouching so low they were nearly eye level, he asked, "Which part should I say slower?"

And it was her own tedious curiosity that kept that bastard's tongue attached to the rest of his worthless carcass. Her canines glistened through the steam.

"What is it, Brigadier Bristolwood, that leads you to believe, up in that insanely dense skull of yours, that there is any Lesser being out there capable of killing a trained spectraline warrior?"

The gratification in the male's smirk all but guaranteed blood would be shed. For there was only one thing Brigadier

Bristolwood would be that pleased about. Everly knew what was coming before the words ever left his mouth.

"The slaying of the latest embarrassment in your"—his mild simper stretched into a brilliant, wild dagger target—"in your extensive collection of *pathetic* Priyatel."

The wooden luffa stick was snapped in two and angling for his heart when the warrior seized her shoulders and slammed her to the bottom of the tub. Her spine cracked against porcelain. Bristol did not relent.

Water splashed to the ground, splashed everywhere. Glass jars and unlit candles went flying. Legs kicked, fists balled, and punches sailed, but Bristol did not relent. No. With that smug smile on his merciless face, he held Everly under that water until she stopped thrashing, until she stopped fighting—until she started bluing and losing consciousness altogether.

And he continued to shove her down, continued to hold her there under the water, until she did the one thing she hated most in this world, until she did the one thing she hated most in this eternity—until she gave up.

She could smell his thrill the moment he let her up for air. And while the coughing fit violently racked her body, while she convulsed and fought to gulp down air, while the male salivated over his victory, Everly plotted his death.

"He was *not* an embarrassment."

Still crouching beside her, the self-satisfied warrior brushed the sopping strands of hair out of her face.

"You are an embarrassment," he whispered. "If you truly believe that."

And instead of killing him right then and there, instead of ending his suffering quickly and decisively, Everly opted for something much worse. She pushed the soaked sleeves of his jacket up his forearms.

The flickering constellation of charcoal and silver sparks lit her face as she watched it glide across his golden skin. The

Valo markings, similar to true constellations, are only visible during the Forbidden Hours when The Everstar sleeps.

And The Valo stretching from Bristol's wrist to elbow was by far the most intricate and resplendent Everly had yet beheld on another. Even to this day, though, she could not look upon it without a profound sadness stilling her heart.

For each Valo mark, each tiny, shimmery burst of light, is the undying reminder of an eternity ended—the everlasting token of an Ever life taken.

The Valo is the bodily reflection of the soul's scars. And Bristol's soul, as so clearly illuminated by the galaxy upon his skin, was every bit as fucked as his mind if he thought he could insult her Priyatel and live.

You started this, she swore to only herself. *But I will drag it out for all eternity.*

"Well," she sang, turning his thick arm in her hand, "I did believe in you once, so I suppose you are ri—"

His calloused hands were ripping her from the bath before she could finish. She tried to brace with her feet, tried to dissuade him with her nails, but spite made him strong and senseless. And as his rage burned hotter, Everly's foot began to slip from the tub wall. But then—just as it finally did come free—the electricity in the building, the electricity to the entire block, groaned to a halt.

And suspended there in the steam above the bathtub, locked within Bristol's rage-fueled grip, Everly Castile could only watch as the penthouse apartment erupted into an inferno of glass and fire.

Chapter 29

THE CITADEL

Too soon.

The imbecile had cut her loose too soon.

For Decard Battleson could not have known that Nora Everstar had long trained her body for far worse things than lethal combat. He could not have known just how often she had swallowed Lastisap before stepping foot into the sparring circle. He could not have known the staggering resistance her immortal body had built up.

He had underestimated her—underestimated the great lengths she would go. The specling would be an imbecile herself if she did not think to fortify her body against the one weapon sure to bring it down.

And Seraphease? Well, Nora knew a bit about that one, too.

It is a colorless, odorless, tasteless tonic—save for the bitter, acidic prickle left at the base of one's tongue. It is simple, it is elegant, and it is very easy to overlook.

First brewed in the earthen caves of the covenary, Seraphease's origin was innocent. Its sole purpose was to aid in the healing of mortals—by easing time. The castresses thought, hoped, that by slowing time around the sick, their ailments might have a chance to mend on their own. And for that reason, the castresses spelled the tonic to alter time according to the afflicted—according to the severity of the affliction. Thus, the more grave the damage, the more powerful the alteration.

But what the castresses did not realize—what they did not fathom down in the darkness of their cavernous tunnels— was that by altering time, they were also altering space. That their honest, harmless, healing tonic possessed the power to alter the very fabric of nature.

Out of the goodness in their mortal hearts, the covenary had brewed a tonic so potent it suspended the laws of the natural world. By all recorded accounts, that lesson was not a particularly pleasant one to be had. As ordered by The Spectraline Senate, The Shield had stormed their capital citadel and seized both the tonic and those castresses skilled enough to craft it—by force.

And now, evidently, The Senate and The Shield were in the habit of plying it down the throats of unsuspecting sixth-series on the eves of their most brutal Canon. Unfortunately for every spectral soldier still stranded atop that desolate, frozen Pillar of the Sky, Nora was privy to Seraphease lore. And worse for them still was the final secret she knew of its workings.

For the silver-haired specling now crouched at the heart of the mesa, she knew that while Seraphease warped the world around the afflicted, the tonic also bestowed upon them the faintest note of castress charm. And not Lull—the gentle tune that sang through their mortal veins. No, it was the other tune. The dangerous tune. The tune that created and decimated worlds.

Seraphease gifted the afflicted the expelled tune of castress charm that The Spectraline called Lyric. Lyric—the power of incantation.

And though the faintest note it might have been, Nora had tasted it there at the back of her tongue and known. Known that the quiet note was more than she needed. Known that it was more than adequate to sway the color of her spectraline blood.

And so, she had spurred Decard on. Encouraged him to beat her senseless. Driven him to steal her lifeforce, drop by drop. She had urged him on so as to strengthen the potency of the Seraphease—one fist at a time. And when she had sensed the bow in the natural world was great enough, Nora had convinced him of his handiwork.

The moment that final golden link had been peeled from her broken body, the moment the last of the Lastisap had cleared her ruined skin—that was the moment the full force of her starlight came screaming down from the skies above.

And now, with the thrum of his fear loud in her eardrums, Nora Everstar was going to show that sniveling bastard what real pain felt like.

As Decard skittered for the safety of Jericho, she whirled on the three shields posted behind her. Blowing a sweet kiss at the spectral farthest to her right, Nora reached down and tore the ancient hanging post—the one they had watched her swing from—clean off its mortar base.

Before that soldier could realize what was to come, Nora broke the metal post in two and hurtled it for his heart. He had not yet disappeared from view when the towering, brassy-haired spectral stumbled backward after him, a makeshift spear square through his eye.

That left one.

The smallest of the hulking detachment. And he would not go over the edge just yet—not before Nora commandeered his blacks.

She took a step forward, one small step, and the quivering shield threw his hands up. It did him little good, in the end. With her gashes healed, her body anew, Nora smashed her bare heel into the mesa's stones. Rocks and earth and shattered shards flew into the air around her. Catching a solid, brownish stone in one hand, she lunged.

The spectral shouted obscenities and prayers—and then gurgled—as Nora drove him to the ground and brought that stone down upon his skull, over and over.

She had already donned his pants and boots when his chest at last ceased its rising. And it was a matter of heartbeats before she had pulled his thick tunic over her head, wrapped his cloak around her shoulders, and buckled his sword belt at her waist. Truth be told, she much preferred her scabbards worn across her back. It was easier, she had found, to cut, to spin, to duck low, when her swords were not dragging the ground like walking sticks. Nevertheless, she would choose irksome steel over no steel any night of the moon.

Jericho was still guarding the giant bronze disc, still hammering the center with that ancient mallet, still sounding The Cry of Illicit Offering, when Nora Everstar booted his naked comrade right off the side of the Ever Step.

After watching the spectral male fall for as far as she could see—for what had to have been more than four-thousand vertical paces—Nora turned to face the last two corpses.

And then, she surveyed the fevered duo from head to toe. She studied their trembling stances, their cowed posture, the poor manner in which they gripped their weapons. She searched the pair for anything that might hint at where they had located the outright nerve to believe that they—two dismal, wretched rejects—possessed even a drop of what it would take to stand against a Beast of Old. Of what it would take to stand against an *ísdreki.*

Nora looked and looked at the two males near the edge, but she came up blank. Just as they would.

Because to provoke a bout with a Beast of Old... to summon an authentic giant of the sky with the hope of overpowering it... to trust that two spectral—that even ten spectral, ten spectral warriors—could wrangle the creature to earth, kill it, and then sever the Lunae from its moonlit spine...

It is folly, she laughed to herself. *It is the sole manner by which a spectraline can earn their wings, but it is folly.*

"It is not!" Decard snarled from behind his fiery-haired friend.

"It is," Nora said coolly. "You will both die here for your ambition. And truly, and I mean this with my entire being, the world will be better for it."

The heat that rippled off the Commander's form nearly warmed Nora's bones.

"You know nothing," he fumed. "You know nothing of this world, specling. I will claim my wings. I will claim them here, tonight, and then I will no longer require your miserable hide as a Parallel."

She placed her hand atop her heart in a show of mock indignation.

Decard's gemstone eyes went wholly black. And as the icy winds continued their blustery dance beneath the stars, Jericho Dupree diligently bashed that tarnished gong. But Nora could have sworn his ghastly pallor faired further.

One hand with a death grip upon the carved, jade frame, Decard Battleson spun to observe the darkness beyond. He searched, she surmised, for a massive shadow with all-mighty, midnight wings—The Night's Wings.

He could stare his fill, though. He would not find it.

For Nora also knew that if Decard had even attended one lesson in The Hall of Ages—or, better yet, read a scroll on the trials of time every now and then—he would be well aware that The Night Song was not just an arbitrary tolling of the ageless gong. No, it was a complete piece of music. A blessing to the ears.

And Decard, while he had commenced The Cry of Illicit Offering, he had *not* yet begun The Night Song.

"Hmm." Nora rested one hand upon her hip and pursed her lips. "Seems a sound deal to me."

Decard and Jericho could not whip their attention fast enough. They could never have imagined the female would agree—that she would give in, permit them to dig their own graves, so readily.

But Nora... she was already singing. Singing to the darkness in the skies, to the absolute black between the glittering stars, singing in a language the males would not know.

With every word that slipped from her lips, with each lyric that rose into the night and sailed for the moon, the freezing winds around them hastened their starlit dance. And as they did, the thrumming in Nora's mind became louder and louder.

Silvery-white strands ripped free from the long braid between her shoulder blades. As she raised her voice, the rogue pieces blew up, blasted down, bit crossways, sliced in front of her face, lashed into her eyes—flew every which way possible.

Decard was screaming commands at his Lieutenant, at the only member of his squadron still breathing, when the torches sputtered out.

"What—what—what tongue is she—"

Nora smiled through her song.

"Is—is she actually trying to—"

"I—I do not—she is wicked!"

"How does she even—"

A heavy wingbeat tore into the night. Jericho dropped the mallet and hit the stones.

"Stop her!" Decard screamed, stumbling away from her. "Stop her now!"

"You stop her!"

Nora's grin stretched wider.

The soldiers did not approach. Her song rode upon the wind. Another boom sounded from the darkness—closer this time. And the two valiant shields—the same two shields who thought to slay a Beast of Old—scrambled for cover that was not there.

"You have proven your point, castress! Cut it out!"

"Nora!"

As another huge roar shuddered the very stones beneath their feet, she began the final verse of her song with joy in her heart.

"Damn the wings! Damn them! Is that what you need to hear?" Decard was wide-eyed, panting. "Okay, I said it! Now quit!"

"You heard him, Nora! You heard the Commander! Stop it, you traitorous whore!"

"Shut your godsdamned mouth, Ev!"

And Nora... she did not think she had ever heard Commander Decard Battleson's voice so high.

"We are sorry for bringing you up here! We are *sorry*, Nora! It was all part of the Twenty-Third, all part of the fucking Canon!" Jericho Dupree had been reduced to tears. "Please!"

"Go shut her up!" his superior screamed.

Jericho gave him a classic *go-boot-stones* look in return. She laughed, then. For neither of the panicked males atop that mesa had the pale, silvery eyes that she did. Not the shrieking Commander, whose eyes were deepest green. Nor his sobbing Lieutenant, who most unluckily had been born with eyes of dirt. She hummed the words, tickled by the knowledge that neither of the males atop that column possessed her extraordinary, Ever-blessed ability to see danger even in the darkest of nights.

She belted her ballad delighted to know that neither haughty bastard could see what was coming for them—that neither haughty bastard could see what she saw coming for them.

And then, once more grabbing ahold of the Seraphease she had so graciously been gifted, Nora whispered into the minds of the two males before her:

I wish you both the ends that you are worthy.

For she had realized, while bound in her coffin of chains, that the tonic had not made Decard Battleson a Thought-Teller. No—it had not had the chance, for he would never have ingested it. It would have only been the sixth-series. Only her.

No, the tonic had not made Decard a Thought-Teller. The tonic had made *her* a Thought-Twister. He had not been listening in on her thoughts. No—she had been whispering into, and then ripping what she sought, from his.

The patterned rocks, the patches of earth, even the tufts of grass trembled at her feet. The monster of the moon was nearly upon them now. And as she watched it, Nora took one last swallow of air.

As its powerful wings ripped the night in two, as those stunning Lunae soared over the abandoned citadel, as that legendary Beast of Old barreled into the new, as the unrivaled might of the ísdreki again shook the world, as the Pillar of the Sky began to sway like a flame in the wind, Nora finished her song.

And then, loosing the stolen twin daggers in her hands, Eleanora Everstar leapt from the Ever Step.

Once upon the starlight,
The gold of the brightest dawn,

Atop the icy wind, sail wings of the night,
Scales so bright, all hope is gone.

When they soar through the cliffs,
When they rise to the moon,

They will have, in their lifts,
The first blood and last rune.

Yet, still to come, there is far worse,
In the skin of a friend.

They will prey, it will curse,
Bare as the day, but fear not the end.

For they will clash, they will claw,
Up where the stones kiss the sky.

One shall live, most shall fall.
All save one, will soon die.

Be sly, be swift, best the fall.
For once it is done, one shall fly,
Higher than them all.

Part II

RISE OF THE NIGHT HEIR

Chapter 30

THE CONSERVATORY

Much to the bewilderment of all within The Conservatory, Dalon Bristolwood had been the first specling to ascend The Alpine Steps after surviving the Twenty-Third Canon. He had not only returned first in his solar—Dalon Bristolwood had returned faster than any specling in any solar.

Even with the new record, though, the ordinarily quick-footed male had rounded the final bend to the uppermost landing with heavy, dragging footsteps. His battle-broadened shoulders, too, had been hunched, his chest caved and heaving. The light brown hair he usually wore cropped short had grown longer than seemed possible for the time he had been gone—on one side, at least. On the other, charred, blistering skin was all that remained.

And as the gaunt-faced warrior had slowly limped his way into the warmth spilling out of the stone archway, Dima had seen the hollowness—the utter hollowness—that leached the very blue from his eyes.

The mountain fortress had been holding a collective breath for nearly half a fortnight awaiting the return of the eighty-six sixth-series who had been ripped from their beds. It was all anyone cared to speak about—what kinds of deadly battles and horrific nightmares their friends and siblings and mentors were giving their all to best.

Every day between lectures and drills, Dima found himself among the hushed congregation of specling sprawled across the wooden benches at the edge of the forward terrace. As his eyes traced the frosty, winding trails leading through the vale and up the jagged crags, he could not help the wandering of his mind.

Something had gone amiss.

For this solar's sixth-series was different from the ones who had come before them. They were swifter, stronger, more mindful and disciplined than the many series of brutes and rabble who had entered The Conservatory's gates in all solars prior.

And their notable prowess—well, their prowess was thanks to one specling above all others. The one spec, the one female, who refused to quit. The one female who never ceased training, who never ceased learning or honing her craft. The one female whose name they had all worked so persistently to try and knock from the top of The Vitoska.

It was because of her—because of their reigning Premier—that this solar's sixth-series had been anticipated to return in remarkable time. It was all because of her.

And yet, she still had not come.

Whispers and murmurs of what could have befallen Eleanora Everstar swept through the candlelit corridors day and night.

They grew worse when, three days following Dalon's homecoming, Lattice Spader—newly blind in one eye—had climbed The Alpine Steps on all fours. And then again, one day after that, when Marin Hollaway and Olin Faroe had helped haul each other's broken bodies up the never-ending, ice-slick stairs.

With their return, eighty-two specling remained unaccounted for.

The next evening, long after the light had fled the sky, long after all the other spec had filed off toward The Atrium for the late meal, Dima was at last preparing himself to yield the day's vigil and join them when a fuming torrent of white-yellow hair stormed up The Alpine, straight out of the darkness.

His breath caught in his chest. For they... they looked so much ali—

"Where is he?" the wild-eyed female ground out through clenched teeth.

Where is who? Dima blinked. *Her Priya—*

The deranged specling grabbed him by the tunic.

"Where. Is. He."

Her sharpened canines shone through the dark. The fifth-series swallowed.

Even with two arrows sticking out of her shoulder, even with one arm hanging limp and out of socket at her side, Stassie Everstar was not one to be trifled with.

"Your—uh—" She rattled him with her good arm. "Uh, Ta—Tabor?"

With her fistful of tunic, she drew him in close.

"Obviously, Tabor, specling." Her voice went eerily low. "Where is *he?*"

She did not know... No... How could she have known?

"Stassie, I—"

"No," she growled. "If he were dead, *I* would be dead."

"Right. No. That is not it. It is—" Dima was suddenly very glad he had not yet eaten. "It is not him, Stassie."

He stared down, right into her bright, starry eyes. Right into Nora's eyes.

The incensed sixth-series had fallen scarily silent. Her breathing slowed—might have stopped altogether. And there on the terrace, standing before him, Stassie was still as death.

Steadying his nerves, Dima spoke at last.

"It is your sister, Stassie. It is your sister who has not yet returned." He paused to keep the falter from his voice. "It is Nora who has not yet returned."

The golden Everstar did not respond. She did not say anything at all. She simply surrendered his tunic and turned back to the icy stairs.

"Where are you—"

But she was gone.

"Wait!" Dima yelled. "Stassie, wait!"

She was already down the first flight and heading for the second when he caught up to her.

"Stassie, you do not even know where they took her!"

Her long legs made easy work of the grueling descent.

"Stassie, stop! She could be anywhere! Anywhere!"

She did not stop.

"We must find out before we—"

Goddess-golden hair whirled through the night as Stassie spun. In a single breath, Dima's legs were swept out from underneath him as a dagger was pulled from a boot, as that dagger was jabbed in his direction—jabbed, and now pressed up and into his throat.

Her steel was shoving into him so forcefully that he could feel the chill of the stone steps seeping into his breaking soul.

"My sister is out there, Dima. My *sister*." The silver ringing Stassie's irises glowed like moonlight. "*Nora* is out there. *Nora* is in grave danger."

Bless the Ever, he swore inward.

"If the happenstance were flipped, specling, *Nora* would not hesitate."

He did not want to have to halt her. He did not want to hurt her any worse than he already had. But he could not let her charge out there—charge out into Everstar-knows-what—with two fucking arrows sticking out of her body—without some semblance of a heading.

"*Nora* is also ten times the fighter you are."

Stassie ducked low and rolled, but it was too late. Dalon Bristolwood had appeared out of thin air.

And as if she were not a highly lethal warrior-in-the-making, as if she was not throwing every hardened joint and bit of wrath she had left, Dalon hoisted Stassie from the steps and folded her into a sleephold.

"You cannot hope to stand against whatever it was that *she* could not."

And with that, Dalon Bristolwood carried the newly unconscious Everstar away.

And Dima... he remained where he had fallen on that cold, switchback stairway under the stars. He stayed there, gazing out into the immense blackness beyond as he wondered at what great evils his friend had bravely faced. At what unthinkable perils she must still be facing. And while he sat there and speculated, he, too, sent his silent gratitude to that hollow-eyed sixth-series who had spared him further guilt.

But it was not until he stood to follow the elder specling inside that Dima truly realized he had not been alone in his worry. That he had not been the only one within The Conservatory's walls to harbor such concern, after all. Nor had he been alone in his diligent vigil for the overdue warrior.

Dayrise upon dayrise, Dima returned to that wind-ravaged terrace. And dayrise upon dayrise, he caught glimpses of Dalon waiting there, too.

With every new light, each new rise of the Everstar, more and more battered sixth-series began to trickle up The Alpine stairway. More and more—but never her. Never the female whose name had lain etched in stone atop The Vitoska since her very first Canon.

And so, bound together in their grief, Dima and Dalon came. They came, and they watched—for the head of silvery-white hair who should have been first.

Chapter 31

THE CROSSING

When the merry, wafting songs of the morning birds roused Savallin Prim from the murky depths of restorative sleep, the sky overhead had just begun its blush for the rising sun.

Groaning gently, Sav twisted her torso and stretched her limbs. Slowly but surely working the soreness from her stiff muscles, she peered at her new surroundings.

Long years had passed since the young Keeper last beheld a shade as stunning as the rosy-citrus glow now warming her golden-brown skin. But even that paled in comparison to what encircled her.

Where Savallin Prim was certain—absolutely, positively certain—that she had clawed her fingertips, and what remained of her nails, into a wall of pure, unrelenting earthstone and then hefted and scraped her exhausted body across a lip of sharp, jagged rock teeth jutting out in all directions, the covenary found only an azure pool. An idyllic, crystalline, azure pool.

Outlining the peaceful loch like a circlet of life, towering juniper palms, shrubs spilling with vivid blooms, and slender shoots of knee-high grass swayed in the dawn breeze. And beyond the lush border, undulating from the small oasis like an ocean of fallen sunrise, pristine, sandy dunes rose and fell for as far as Savallin could see.

Out here, she supposed, at dawn and at dusk, the skies and the sands would transcend all Known bounds—the heavens and the earthly dominions blurring and swirling and melding together as one. And amidst those hours of extraordinary charm, it would be all but impossible to tell where this world ended and the beyond began.

The Keeper permitted herself one heartbeat to revel in the wonder—to appreciate the breathtaking spectacle swarming her from all sides. And then, she got to work.

Rifling through her canvas sack, she took inventory of her meager supplies: a single length of chain, two serrated blades, some sort of rusted clamp, half a flint stone, three glass vials, and her trusty mallet. The set of iron spikes she had used to tow herself up the vertical pass were... well, they were still in the passageway.

After neatly packing the stock back into her bag, the Keeper rose to her feet. Without squandering any more time, she padded around the oasis, searching the sparkling sands for the largest of the fallen tree fruits. In a matter of moments, Sav had plucked up two of the shaggy, hard-shell husks and added them to her satchel of supplies. And then, casting the waking sun over her left shoulder, Savallin started walking.

"I thought you were supposed to be the Keeper of *Wisdom*."

Sav whirled—crackling, jade heat spiraling from her fingertips, spiraling like spears—before the shock words had even landed. But the blast—her blast—rolled right off the assailant's shield. The assailant's invisible shield.

Drawing her arm back again, Savallin listened for the symphony of power thrumming just beneath her feet. As she reached toward it, reached for that rhythmic crescendo, she could *feel* the molten jade—jade, twin to her Soul—bubbling hot in her eyes.

"Impressive," the attacker whistled before—before stepping out of the morning light. "Impressive, indeed, Covelette."

Savallin's arms fell slack.

"It is... it is truly you..." The startled covenary surveyed the foreign female from head to toe. "You are... you are *real*."

The tall female arched a pale brow.

Her thick braid, tied nearly at her waist, was even fairer than Phaedra's... than Nirvana's. And her eyes—those sharp, predator's eyes—were so pale, so blue, that they must have been carved out of coldest ice.

Savallin had never seen anyone so striking. But the beautiful female—The Lady of the Lair—was looking at her like she had three heads.

"I am *real*, yes." The fem—the warrior—crossed her arms in front of her lithe form. "And you, you intend on *walking* across the entirety of Eastern Jidana?"

The baffled covenary could only blink, the astounding enormity of what she had missed settling atop her like a blizzard upon mountain peaks.

My elemental power remains intact because I am no mortal. I am no caster of earth.

"You are a..." Sav swallowed hard against her astonishment. "You are Everlast."

At that, both pale eyebrows raised.

"I"—the female laughed softly—"am your escort."

But she... but the warrior... she did not deny that she *was* an everlast. Though, she certainly was not dressed in their traditional garb. She donned no sleek black armor, no visible steel... only a loose, lavender tunic and flowing ivory bottoms. But she—why would *she* be escorting a covenary?

Why would she be escorting me?

The everlast cocked her head.

"You tell me, covenary."

Savallin's mouth snapped open in outrage.

"Stop that!"

A wide smile stretched across The Lady's face in answer. The prominent tips of her canines glinted pink in the dawn sun. If the Keeper had thought the female striking before, now—with that smile warming her impeccable features—what the covenary beheld was not of this world.

"Fair enough, Covelette," the husky, frost-lined voice chuckled again. "I will cease with the wake weaving, if you will recite something aloud."

Lines formed between Sav's dark brows as she considered the potential consequence of agreement.

The inner debate must have been plastered plainly on her face because the everlast said, "You now harbor Nirvana's map, do you not, little covenary?"

Right. The map.

"And because you are a covenary, and to be covenary is to be bound by mortality—"

Bound by a body that tires, you mean.

'That is why, I"—the knowing female placed a slender hand over her heart—"*I*, an untiring warrior with no such bindings, have been sent as an escort to protect you on your daunting journey."

Savallin's eyes must have doubled in size at the admission, for her escort rolled her own and sighed.

"Yes, Savallin Prim, *I am* Everlast," she winked a frosted eye. "Covenary do not often come in my stature, now do they?"

No... Sav gasped to herself. *No, we do not.*

It had been years since the Keeper was last among their kind. Many years... many enough that she had somehow forgotten how tall they were—how intimidating their mere presence could be.

"What is your name?" Savallin asked. "Seeing as we are no longer rotting in a prison of black and despair, what can I call you?"

The immortal's full lips quirked to the side.

"I promise, Keeper, to tell you all you wish to know. But we must get going. It is not wise to stay in one place too long."

Sav once more studied the female before her—the female who had done nothing, so far, but aid in her quest. The female who had listened, who had shared her own insight, who had steadied her, who had emboldened—and lightly threatened—her to continue pushing.

She had a growing catalog of questions for the stranger, yes. But, Savallin supposed, the shortest, quickest path to all those answers was the towering, impatient one currently staring into her earthly soul.

"Fine," she groused at last. "What is it you need to hear me say?"

Mocking a shallow bow, the haughty guardian purred, "Sajada Tapaté."

Savallin soared and raced and searched through the farthest cavities of her mind for the meaning, for the key to what had to be a riddle.

Sajada Tapaté, she echoed as her expedition inward came back bare. *Sand Tapestry?*

"Does Sajada Tapaté mean something diff—"

But it was too late. She had caught on too slowly.

The words had been said. The *incantation* had been said. The forbidden charm had been cast.

The sand glittering at her feet began to tremble. Waves of sunrise grains started to swell and swoop and slide away in every direction. A throaty rumble pulsed from the earth—

pulsed through the cerulean pool, through the circlet of greenery, through her every limb.

And right when she was certain the ground would split and swallow her to Hollow, right at that moment of sure demise, right before her very eyes—an elegant, fluid tapestry woven of auburn sparkles floated free from the desert floor.

Her, Hollow, and the Hail of Hadi, she swore. *An Aerie Arras.*

The sly, conniving immortal warrior had duped her— duped the Keeper of *Wisdom*—into summoning an Aerie Arras. Into summoning the barred tune.

Into summoning *Seraphic.*

And she... she did not fade. The unnatural charm, the illicit incantation, had not killed her. No... and the Keeper was not afraid of the torturous end. She was not frightened, nor upset, by the host of repercussions sure to come. No, because what glided before her now... it was gorgeous.

"No," her escort chuckled as she strode over and sat gracefully atop the Seraphic tapestry. "Sajada Tapaté means the same to me as it does to you."

But the covenary was still deep in the throes of bewilderment when the white-haired immortal patted the tapestry beside her—patted it, as if she had ridden through the skies a thousand times.

"Come along now, Covelette," the protector beckoned, in that frozen voice that soothed all worry.

And slowly, hazily, as if dragging herself through a river of deceit and sap, Savallin Prim rose to meet that glacial gaze.

"Audrian," the female grinned. "You may call me Audrian. Audrian Adivostov, Special Sentry of the Eastern Reach."

Chapter 32

THE CITY

It was the heady smell of roasting meat and frying eggs that finally enticed Everly Castile to crack open her eyes at last.

She and Bristol had been up all night. That explosion she'd watched in the foggy bathroom mirror—the explosion that had decimated the penthouse of the neighboring tower—had caused quite the mortal stir.

Even all the way up on the top floor of her building, the thrumming in her ears had been severe. And she had noticed, with no small satisfaction, that Bristol seemed especially overcome by it.

The archaic beast was not accustomed to living among mortals. He was not familiar with the sound of their fear. Not like she was.

Nevertheless, their birthright called. So, she and the Brigadier had tabled their quarrel to spend the night helping evacuate the lower floors of that flaming skyscraper. And, miraculously, not a single mortal life had been lost to the attack.

And attack it was. For the penthouse apartment at the heart of that blast—it was the publicly listed address of one Ms. Everly Castile. An address she had chosen for two reasons: the first being that its proximity made it simple to monitor, and the second being that the ten stories directly beneath it were still under construction and, thus, vacant.

Wrapping herself in a silky robe, she padded out into the kitchen toward the smell of breakfast.

Bristol had been busy, it appeared. Her white marble island was covered in flour. And dishes. Mixing bowls, cast-iron skillets, plates, aluminum baking sheets… just about every pan Everly owned lay strewn about.

She winced, her hands balling into fists.

But while most of the dishes were dirty and dripping, a few bore heaped offerings that forced her to take a breath, that forced her to calm—like the stack of lemon-vanilla griddlecakes piled chest-high.

Her stomach grumbled.

"Did you sleep?" the overbearing iron-chef asked as she climbed up on an emerald-cushioned barstool.

"Bris," she said, looking from the stack of griddlecakes to the mound of buttered biscuits, and the skillet of eggs and pans of bacon and sausage in between, "how many warriors are you planning to feed this morning?"

"One," he grumbled, inspecting her form for hints of proper rest. "But she eats like a full battalion."

The female cut the warrior a withering glance before her attention snagged upon the ceramic mug in his hand.

"Bristol," her nostrils flared wide. "Where is the coffee?"

The Brigadier's smile was a thing of wicked and vicious beauty as he raised the steaming mug to his lips and promptly drained it.

"You're fresh out."

Everly blinked at the male, just once.

"I *will* kill you. You know that, don't you?"

"You're more than welcome to try, Ev."

With a sharp inhale through her nose, Ev stood.

"Maybe when I get back."

But she had not even rounded the island when the warrior's massive body was before her, blocking the doorway.

"You aren't going anywhere dressed like a common courtesan." And then, with a dish towel thrown over one shoulder, Bristol scooped the female over the other. "Eat first, and then we will go."

Her stomach was growling its accord when he placed her back upon her cushioned stool.

Fuck it, she huffed. *Those vanilla cakes aren't going to eat themselves.*

And then, thrusting her palm towards the brute, and his buffet, she waited.

"So, Mr. Modest, do you plan on donning a shirt before our coffee run?" Everly's outstretched fingers wiggled in demand. "Or are you content with sending the mortal women to early graves?"

For Brigadier Bristolwood might be wholly unremarkable as far as spectraline males were concerned, but compared to mortal men—Bristol might as well have been Zeus. The slew of coronaries his half-naked presence would undoubtedly cause... insufferable, it would be insufferable.

The smirking male handed Everly a plate stacked generously with everything she had eyed. And it took the bulk of her power not to shove it right back in his smug little snout.

"And what is it, Everly," Bris asked, pouring two glasses of dusky-peach juice and sliding one her way, "that you would have me wear?"

Refusing to be the first to sever eye contact, the female stabbed a plump link of chicken-apple sausage onto her fork.

"Oh, I don't know," she shrugged, popping the forkful into her mouth. "How about a nice pair of black eye—"

The male lashed his dish towel for her face so fast it was nearly imperceptible. Nearly.

With her left hand, she caught the towel out of the air and ripped it forward. And when the male staggered toward her, she used the fork clutched in her other hand to spear the seafoam cloth straight into the stone countertop—straight between the male's first two fingers.

Once an imbecile, she smiled to herself as she let him go. *Forever an imbecile.*

The imbecile merely muscled the fork from the marble and tossed it in the trash.

"I am genuinely offended," Everly said, rolling a griddlecake as if it were a burrito before dunking it twice into the saucer of maple syrup, and taking a bite, "that The Senate, with their eras of wisdom, sent your lowly ass to chaperone *me.*"

"You and I both," the male said as he made to fix his own plate. "I have far better things to do with my time than safeguard your miserable excuse of an eternity. Like—I don't know—commanding The Spectraline Shield's entire Northern Legion."

Touché.

The warrior opened the drawer just below his hip and pulled out two clean forks. Keeping one for himself, he passed the other to Everly.

"Like I said, Ev, *we* are being hunted. That explosion last night is proof enough. And as much as it chafes me to say it, The Spectraline—*your people*—cannot afford to lose you."

My people? She chuckled silently. *The very same people that ordered my killing? Twice.*

"Well," the cyan river and teal streams intertwined within Bristol's eyes churned as he corrected himself, "we can't afford to lose you to something as excruciatingly mundane as execution by mortal."

There it is.

Neglecting the fork, she rolled another sweet cake.

"So, who exactly are these hunters anyway?" The rich, brown syrup sloshed onto the white island as the griddlecake plunged in yet again. "Why do they wish us harm?"

She took another bite.

"They are—"

"And, more importantly," Everly interrupted, her mouth full of lemon-vanilla cake, "how is it that Lesserkind knows of our existence at all?"

Bristol's sandy-brown eyebrows rose in a manner as if to say, *If you had but the slightest semblance of refinement, you would already possess the answers you seek.*

The female simply plucked the crispiest slice of sugared bacon off her dwindling plate and waved it at him.

He didn't bother trying to hide the dimple in his cheek as he waded into his explanation.

"What do you know of the demi-sensore?"

The spectral sipped her juice, narrowing her steely glare at the shirtless chef.

"Well, for starters..." Memories of a mountain-lined killing field littered with ice-charred bodies, both immortal and non, flashed like incendiaries through the darkness of her mind. "The demi-sensore are nothing more than rumor."

"Not even an exile as lengthy as yours could reduce the female I once knew to that degree of rash."

The spectraline warrior pushed her half-eaten plate away.

"How would they exist, Dalon?"

The keen-eyed Brigadier must have noted the hurt that flickered across her features, or perhaps softened at the name rare from her lips, because there was no menace in his words when he answered.

"They—" He took a deep, steadying breath. "After—" Rethinking what was sure to be an ill-laid path, he tried once more. "When the last war ended, when the Isra were all but wiped from the earth, the females of their kind were left with an unthinkable quandary: mate with the only race ignorant of their innate perversion, mate with the very beings they had vowed to eradicate, *or* disappear into time."

Countless eternities, her mind's voice whispered. *Countless eternities were lost, were sacrificed, to that war.*

Bristol, steady as the times were bleak, let Everly be as her temper soared free for the skies above.

And for what? the spectraline bit at herself, silver-soaked plains of ruined bodies and frozen wildflowers overwhelming her memory once more. *For what? For. What.*

For the surviving israsensore females to pivot and *mate* with their sworn prey—to mate with the mortals their kind was sempenihil-bent on ending? To mate with the mortals that great spectraline warriors gave their eternities, gave their Parallels, to defend?

Everly bowed her head.

The loss, the age-bridging ordeal—it was unthinkable.

"Ev, Everly," the male's throat worked. "I understand aversion for wars of the past. Trust me, I do." Bristol's face was nothing but earnest as he slid a bowl of honeyed yogurt topped with red, blue, and black berries in front of her. "But if you avert breakfast any longer, it is unlikely either one of us will survive the war of the present."

And that fast, the female had to roll her lips into a hard line to keep the laugh from slipping. That dry, uncaring humor had always slipped even her steeliest defenses. And though she still hated him—though she still despised and distrusted all that made the Brigadier who he was—she didn't wholly hate that.

"Fuck you," Everly swore nonetheless when he offered her a spoon. "You wrecked my appetite."

"Please. *You* without an appetite?" The spectral polished off his juice. "How dense do you think me to be?"

"I think you would sink in mercury," she deadpanned.

Spooning a healthy dollop of creamy yogurt into her mouth, Everly asked, "Am I correct to assume these *demi-sensore* are hunting spectral because they deem us responsible for..." She searched for the proper sentiment. "Well, it either has to be for annihilating their gutless ancestors *or* because they view us as being the cause of their creation."

Bristol waited in silence until she had eaten another bite from her bowl.

"Well?" Her loose waves fluttered with the violent shake of her head. "Do you suppose they abhor their existence that much?"

"No." The domineering kitchen giant glanced from her empty spoon to her yogurt and then back again. "I think the demi-sensore covet their being very much. In fact, I think they are willing to do whatever it takes to guarantee it endures."

"Are they long-lived?"

"No, we do not believe so. But... well, we never really let them stick around long enough to find out." His words took on a nostalgic sort of sternness. "Make no mistake, though, the ones we've encountered thus far, they were both exceedingly strong and swift."

In a forgotten corner of her memory, a dusted bulb flickered to life.

"Still, they are not like us—not in creation. Not only do their thoughts come slower, but they seem to fancy themselves divinely invincible." Straightening out those broad shoulders of his, Bristol admitted, "It can be irksome."

"Hmm," she tsked. "Who else do I know that's slow... and wannabe invincible... and irksome?"

Irksome galore, yet informed aplenty to know the ins of the ilk I stalk through the streets.

Bristol, goddess save him, choked on a golden, rosemary biscuit. Everly's head listed perilously to the side. Her mind, the beating in her diaphragm, quieting. The blundering male already had his hands thrown out before him.

"Everly, calm down." His speech was rushed. "It is not what you think."

"You," she fumed. "You are a *Thought-Teller?*"

"Everly," he tried. "Take a breath."

Something akin to pain sliced through her chest. She shouldn't care. She should not care. For what did it matter? What did it matter if this asshole had completed The Rite of Parallel? What did it matter that he had not had the courage to tell her?

"When?"

"Calm down."

"*Who?*"

"Everly, I—"

The glass bowl of yogurt and berries narrowly missed his Thought-Telling skull.

"I—"

He ducked to avoid the still-loaded plate that sailed after the bowl as she jumped to her feet.

"Everly!"

But while he cowered behind the kitchen island like the titanic coward he was, the female was already striding for the entry door. She had just palmed the knob, just twisted and pulled it toward herself, when Commander Coward roared from behind, "For goddess' sake, Everly, it's—"

Too little, too late.

For the heavy entry door had already swung wide open. And the mortal—the human man—standing there slack-jawed on the doormat with a coffee in each hand had *not* been expecting to see the half-naked male chasing Everly Castile through her penthouse apartment.

"Jay," she breathed.

Chapter 33

THE CRYPTS

"A calling?" Alice's simple question ricocheted through the coldest chamber of the police station crypt. "You find yourself called to... to what, exactly?"

Ava, the brisk chill in the air at last wearing its way through her thick, trusty sweater, could only be upset with herself. She should have known—should have seen the question coming.

"To..." She paused, searching, reaching for a string of words she had not yet tied.

To serve the city, to support the people... those were the answers she had given to her recruiter. And while they were true, they were not the full truth. No. Because what Ava felt— whatever force it was compelling her on this path—was rooted much, much deeper within.

But her recruiter, her subsequent interviewer—neither one of them had ever pressed her for more. Neither one had urged her to dive farther beneath that false surface. So Ava...

she hadn't. She had allowed herself to drift along on those shallows, never really giving her motivations a second thought.

Alice, promptly spotting the vacuum spreading behind Ava's pale eyes, suggested, "Perhaps you felt called to prevent others from experiencing the same sort of suffering you did as a girl?"

No. Her spontaneous dip inward froze to a practiced halt. *No.*

Kisses of a cloudless day. Wisps of untamed curls. Quiet flutters of a flowered sundress. Rushes of laughter that knew no bounds. All at once, the memories began to crackle through the black in Ava's mind.

No. She sealed her eyes tight—so tightly, in fact, that small lines formed, stemming from their outermost corners. *We will not be going there. Not today,* she breathed. *Not today.*

"I understand, Ava, that you do not wish to talk about that day. But if ever you do, know that I can help you. That I want to help you." The therapist's voice was not forceful, but it was not so pliable either. "I can help you to see that day, those memories, in a..." Ava heard it as a careful smile softened the counselor's stained lips. "I can help set your past to a happier soundtrack."

That strange warming sensation lapped toward the crackling embers of her memory. Maybe it was exhaustion, maybe dehydration, or possibly something as monotonous as mental strain. But whatever the cause, she could not staunch the flow of time through her mind's eye. No—the harder she tried, the tighter she squeezed her eyelids shut, the faster her inner defenses crumbled.

The kisses of a cloudless day sharpened into searing bites of lightning. Those wisps of untamed curls thickened into whips of untold agony. The quiet fluttering of that flowered sundress stilled to a screaming heap of flowery ash. And the rushes of that laughter... they found their bounds.

But then, just when Ava was positive she would slip from her chair only to tuck herself into a snug ball upon the yellowing floor, that soothing tingle coasted in. Like menthol upon a burn, the sensation snuffed out every flaring ember it touched. And Ava... she did not fight it. She did not understand it, not at all, but she welcomed it still. She was glad for it.

And when, at last, her mind was once more her own, she opened her eyes. Opened them, and stared at the odd, posh woman seated across the table.

"Who are you?" she asked, her voice tired, gravelly, and yet, sound. "Who are you, Alice—truthfully? And why have you not asked me, not one time, about what happened earlier tonight? About earlier during my shift? Anything about why it is I am sitting in this room?"

The large, lilac frames slid down her nose as the shrink lowered that inquisitive gaze.

"Prudent inquiries, Ava," she hummed, adjusting her glasses. "Prudent inquiries, indeed."

Ava schooled her features, refusing to take the bait. Refusing to be riled by the latest drop in the vast well of nonanswers.

"Why is it, Alice, that you are so focused on my upbringing and not the downfall of my career, of my life? Why is it, Alice, that you seemingly have no interest in the calamity that put me in this seat?"

A light titter escaped the professional façade.

"Oh, Ava." Her cool tone shifted abruptly to that of an arrogant governess. "Honey, I do not have to ask you what happened tonight because I already know."

Ava blanched, her trained features fracturing at the seams.

For... she couldn't know. There was no way. All the body-cam footage had been destroyed—incinerated. And... and because... well, because there had only been one survivor, and she had been locked in this room all night. All night... unsure if even she truly knew what had happened.

But the shrink only crossed her arms low in her lap. Ava watched her, waited for her to say more.

"Ava," Alice sighed her name almost as if she were... disappointed... or perhaps saddened? "Ava, I knew it the moment I walked through that door."

That fast? She pictured it, then—envisioned that moment when Alice's heels had clicked through the opening. She relived it, tried to remember anything she might have done, might have said to give it away. She had been irritated, yes. Shocked, surely... but had she... no. No, she hadn't even spoken, had still *barely* spoken. *So, how had Alice—*

"It was scrawled, plain as day, in the boldest of all hands across that lovely, weary little face. Anybody with even the slightest gift of perception would have been able to see it." The woman glanced to the side, wrinkling her nose ever so briefly. "Well, anybody but that infant-faced boy I spared you from. That one, I'm afraid, is certain of your guilt."

Of course he is, Ava huffed. *Everyone but you is.*

"So anyhow, while it might appear to you that I have no interest in the calamity that earned you this grilling in the hot seat, do not mistake me, Ava." A brilliant glow sparkled to life in the depths of the woman's lively eyes as she illuminated, "For I have immense interest in the circumstance that truly brought us together once more."

The circumstance that truly brought us together? Ava shook her head. *What circumstances?* Her back, forgetting its ache, stiffened. *Which one, pray tell, would that be?*

Alice, no doubt enjoying the scene now unraveling across her lovely, weary little face, inclined her head knowingly.

"Ava, I only began with these questions about your past because I am intrigued as to why you—a young woman with both endless potential and resource—elected a thankless life of dangerous work and meager reward."

Well, hell—me, too, Ava snarled to herself, fixing the mouth she hadn't felt fall open. *Me, frickin' too.*

The shrink again set her clasped hands atop the cold metal table separating them. Her rich, infuriatingly smooth skin looked wholly out of place resting atop such dull silver. She did not belong in this crypt, Ava thought. No, a woman like Alice belonged among finery... among other beautiful people... among... well, among anything that was not this.

And yet, Ava realized. *And yet, she had still come.*

And she was... waiting. Ever the patient counselor—or therapist, or psychiatrist, or behavioral analyst, whoever she was—she was waiting. Waiting for her to answer the questions. And had she not just sworn to supply the woman with answers anyway, so that she might soon get out of here?

Alice is here to help you, she snapped at her own stubbornness. *To. Help. You.*

And then, with several centering inhales, Ava reset her composure once more. She swallowed against the desert thriving in the back of her throat as she struggled to recall the woman's inquiry.

I am intrigued as to why you, a young woman with both endless potential and resource, elected a thankless life of dangerous work and meager reward.

"I..." But she hesitated, again scrounging for something she couldn't quite articulate. "I just... I..."

Drawing a slow, wobbly breath—and then another—Ava turned her attention inward. Inward, toward the gentle drumming in her chest. She concentrated on it, on its steady rhythm, on the sure beat, on the feeling of—

That... that's it.

"It's a feeling," she blurted, her words finally spilling over that internal dam. "It's not something outward that calls to me. It's a feeling—a sort of... song."

Ava quieted for a moment, listening in until she again heard it. Until she was sure.

"A song," she repeated. "A song, from deep within, that cries out."

Across from her, the subtle angling of Alice's ashen bob sent pangs of worry climbing up the vertebrae of her spine.

Oh, no.

The admission—her revelation—must have come off as crazy, disturbed... possessed, even. Because for a counselor, a shrink, to regard her like that... to judge her...

But then, Alice's lips parted, and Ava's rising fear—her mounting mortification—lulled altogether.

"What does this feeling, *this song,* sound like?"

The kneejerk exhale that followed was anything but unruffled. For it had been all Ava could do to even identify that it was a feeling—some sort of intrinsic song—compelling her on. Forever motivating her. And to now describe it... its cry... its sound... it was ludicrous.

Answer, her inner voice scolded. *Make it the fuck up, if you must.*

"It's... um," Ava tried and failed. "It's... like, uh—"

"Like the whistling roars of the wind as it spurs you forth into the heart of the looming storm? Like the beckoning toll of a bell unyielding, suspended within a tower ever stooping to time? Like the warmth of the laughs, of the flames, about a hearth you have never sat?"

And although Alice had not moved—had not leaned in any closer at all—Ava had the overwhelming sense that she was peering straight into the darkest caverns of her mind.

Her mouth quirked up in a disarming half-grin when she said, "It is an ageless melody you have forever hummed, yet never grown weary of."

"Yes," she was nodding wildly, her truth whispered before she had even thought it. "*Yes.*"

Ava understood then that the radiance blooming from that timeless face positioned opposite hers was genuine—that of an ally.

"I see," the ally mused. "While that—that sort of song—is a rarity amongst this time, I would have expected nothing less from the lost daughter of Cadence Carlisle."

Chapter 34

THE CITADEL

He would be executed for this, he knew. He would be stripped of his rank, paraded through the mountaintop stronghold, and then—then—he would be executed.

The order he had been given, the task he had volunteered for—he had known from the beginning it would be impossible. He had known it, but he had not refused it—he could not have refused it. For if not him, they would have commanded somebody else.

And the thought of somebody else... someone else... stealing and groping and hurting her... well, that was simply not a thought Decard Battleson could live with.

He had known the mission would fail, and yet, he had put his neck on the line for her anyway. As he always had. As he always would.

And while he had busily worried over her well-being, while he had carefully crafted a show even they would believe, while he had tried to fulfill his duty to test the specling's breaking point—she had summoned the monster spectraline nightmares were made of.

She had summoned the monster of Night itself. She had sicced it upon him. And then—as one final *curse-you*—she had lodged a dagger of wrath high into his thigh.

Maybe they were right... to fear her so. To fear the young spectraline who had forever kept her head down. To be wary of the quiet specling with a propensity to humble. To fret over the budding Premier who had no kin, no givers, no blood of note. To be frightened of the cunning female who had nothing but a warrior's heart and a bastard's name.

Maybe they were right.

But to order him—a Commander of The Shield—to ensure that a sixth-series did not return from her Twenty-Third Canon... what did they know that he did not? What great, terrible truths did they claim to know?

It did not matter, though. For what they had asked of him—demanded of him—was wholly unjust. He had never planned to follow through with it anyway. And Decard Battleson was not foolish enough to truthfully believe that choice had ever been his to decide.

Not even with six full spectral at his beck and call.

And he certainly did not, nor had he ever, wished for Lunae as she had accused him. It was all a show—a show for them, a show for when they peered into his mind, a show while his truth willed her survival.

That was why, had he known... had he known the chains he had been given were pure Lastisap, he never would have let them anywhere near her body, never let those godforsaken chains so much as touch her immortal skin. The same way he had not let a single member of his squadron close enough to even think of grazing her body during the days-long journey to The Citadel.

He had not cared how strongly his legs ached on that mountainous trek. He had not cared how badly his shoulders and arms burned and trembled on the climb into the sky. While she had lain unconscious, nobody was getting anywhere near her.

And the way his soldiers had stared at her... the way they had ogled and lusted over her naked, freezing body... well, if she had not killed them so swiftly, he would have dragged it out a bit.

But the worst part—the part the Commander would never forgive himself for—was doing nothing save watch in horror while those vile, golden chains—the chains that he had dressed her in—split and tore her taut, paling skin. And how, not only had he not moved to protect her, to save her, but instead he had been helpless—entirely unable—to halt his fists from striking her limp body over and over. It was that that had almost killed him.

And Decard... he had not fully understood his outburst upon the Ever Step—the wanton assault of a shackled, poisoned female—until she had fallen backward, into the night. Until he could no longer hear the ring of her steel against stone as she leapt between pillars. Not until she had cleared the distance did that misty haze within his mind give way. It was only then that the Commander discovered himself cowering like a rat atop the stony waste.

The Seraphease, it seemed, had gifted Eleanora Everstar the ability to twist thought. And she... she had harnessed it to drive him mad, to move him to attack, to use him to exacerbate the tonic's effects. A tonic she should not have known to exist, let alone command.

And yet, she had. She had commanded it—compelling him to wound her so gravely that the Seraphease would hear her true end calling. And the tonic... it had been listening. For the moment that end came, the castress charm had bowed both time and space to give Eleanora one final, fraught, fool's shot at life.

It was the immensity of the damage wreaked upon her body—the immensity of the damage he had wreaked upon her body—that drove the Seraphease to the brink. To the brink beyond healing. To the brink where the natural world was bowed so brutally that Eleanora Everstar had been able to reach into time itself and rip a Beast of Old straight out of history.

And even as the icy stones, even as the very pillar beneath him, rattled and rocked into the dark, Decard shook his head and smiled.

Maybe they were right.

And just then, a vicious, blood-curdling roar blasted up from deep in the canyons.

"Do you intend on regaining a bit of sense anytime soon?!" a scratchy voice shouted from beside him. "Preferably sometime *before* we end up in the belly of your Priyatel's new pet?!"

Decard's grin promptly faded.

Jericho was fortunate, he thought, that his Priyatel did not overhear that snide remark. Something told him she would not much care for the title—the title for one in a pair set to be two.

Looking to his friend, he grimaced.

For maybe it was he who was fortunate. Because where Eleanora aimed, Eleanora hit. And in the case of his Lieutenant, that happened to be his groin.

"Why are you sitting on your ass, Dupree?!" Decard fired back at the redhead. "This cannot be the first time a female has thrown a knife at—what did you claim it—your *meek* manhood?"

He paired the jab with a face that said, *oh yes, I do remember.* Jericho honed his hatred as he grabbed for the hilt of the dagger.

"We need to move," the shield half-yelled as he did the very same. "Right now!"

"Oh? Is that so, Commander?!"

But when the two soldiers yanked upon the knives, neither blade budged. No. Instead of coming free, searing pain sang from the blades, sang through their wounds and into their palms as the daggers burrowed deeper.

Convulsing, the Lieutenant snarled, "Your castress of a specling hexed the Ever-fucking steel!"

Right. He is right, the male fought to agree. *She had cast a hex, but... but how...*

And as Decard opened his mouth to defend her, the slender column of earthstone and hewn jewel vibrated so violently that the giant bronze gong and its heavy jade frame crumbled away into nothing.

"Run!"

It was all the Commander could get out before the world tilted and he began to slide. The beast, though, he still could not see it. Bless the Ever, he could see hardly anything at all. For in the darkness, without the light of the torches, he was as good as blind. His vision near mortal. Their vision near mortal.

Decard knew the nightmare was nearby nevertheless. He could feel the gushes of air as it circled them, as it preyed upon them. And with every new bellow that erupted from the monster's unseen maw, the mettle in his bones melted.

And he was sliding—skidding down the steep slope of the toppled mesa that had careened into the side of a neighboring Pillar of the Sky. A neighboring pillar that had exploded upon impact into groans and cracks and splinters, into a terrible medley of crushing rock. The dark, impenetrable air filled with dust. But still, even as he collided with the cloud of debris, even as the second ruined column neared, he could not slow himself.

It was not until the black cloud had swallowed him whole, though, that the male's alarm eased—that the male's alarm was silenced entirely. Because it was not until then—then, aided by the ebbing and swaying of the silty dust—that his eyes could see.

That was when he could see it—the danger that sought him. That was when the shield relieved his bladder. That was when Commander Decard Battleson realized he would not make it to his own execution. For what sailed hard and fast through the thick cloud of rubble—what sailed hard and fast straight for him—there was no known depiction, no oil painting, nor sacred scroll that did it a shred of justice.

The Beast of Old bearing down upon him—the ísdreki— was not of this world. It did not belong in this world. It was enormous, unfathomably massive. Its wingspan... no less than five-hundred paces from spiked tip to spiked tip. And its armor—the flowing yet unyielding armor that spanned its body—was made of... no... it *was* the night.

And what Decard had been able to glimpse, what he had mistaken for stars shooting across the vastness of the sky, were the glassy, sharp starbursts shimmering along its oscillating spine, shimmering the full length from the crown atop its head to the tip of its mighty tail.

They had the same ethereal spark about them as the axe-edged talons now cleaving chunks of earthen stone—larger than any catapult could launch—from the upset pillar he frantically clawed his nails into. The pitch was near vertical, but he fought it—fought it by plunging his fingers into hardest stone, by tearing each nail from its bed, in a desperate attempt to slow.

It was of little use, though. Not only was he still slipping, he was picking up speed. The lowest edge of the listing mesa loomed before him. He would be on it—over it—in a matter of heartbeats. And then... then there would be nothing. Nothing save a yawning freefall into Sempenihil.

Unless I am eaten fi—

"Roll over!" The heaving shout of his second-in-command thundered through the choking haze. "Roll and strike!"

Roll and—But that shriek... that shriek had not been waning, not been falling. Jericho was not falling. Not anymore. *Fuck!*

Decard threw his shoulder, spinning in the darkness to roll to his belly. The moment he did, his front—and the knife wedged in his leg—scraped and snagged on the wreckage of the collapsing mesa. He blocked it out, blocked everything out, as he drew a dagger from his belt and punched it into the fleeting stone.

That fast, his body ceased its scraping, ceased its skidding, its falling. He ceased falling. His friend sighed heavy. And when he dared a glance down at his dangling boots, the Commander was met with nothing but sheer cliff face and crushing darkness for as far as his straining eyes could see.

Lifting his gaze to where his Lieutenant clutched onto the blade he had driven into the mesa, Decard swallowed the sea of dread that had very nearly done him in.

"About fucking ti—"

But his friend did not finish the taunt. His friend would never finish the taunt. For at that very moment, a triple-headed spade gleaming of blackest ice slammed into the overturned mesa. The strike, the reverberation—it was not deafening, not devastating. No. It was cataclysmic.

And when its haze of obliteration cleared—when Decard Battleson's teeth, at last, stopped rattling amidst his skull—all that remained of Lieutenant Jericho Dupree was a crater of earthstone and glittering silver where he had clung on for his very life.

Chapter 35

THE CROSSING

They had been soaring through the cloudless sky since sunup. And still, no matter which way Savallin Prim turned her head, the endless sea of shimmering sand surged on. For hours she had watched, silently relishing each gentle kiss of the wind, as their shadow slowly stretched and skated across the rosy dunes below.

Audrian had not been particularly forthcoming as she rested a palm on the curl of the sparkling tapestry and steered them on their way—steered them closer to the distant Wilds of the East.

"I must warn you," Savallin's stoic escort began, as if noting her thoughts. "The farther we journey, the looser my influence on the Majlis minds."

The Keeper looked up at that, into those ageless eyes of solid ice.

"You..." But Sav paused to consider all that she knew of The Everlast—of The Spectraline—and their gifts, before continuing. "But you are a Thought-Teller?"

"I am, indeed," Audrian confirmed, her expression all but daring the covenary to challenge her. "What of it?"

"Spectral... they—you—are either one or the other, *never* both." Her nervous assertion tumbled out. "Never both a Thought-Teller and a Thought-Twister, I mean."

The immortal female smirked, the tips of her canines catching the sunlight.

"That is what you were taught? In your Tutelage?"

"I..." Savallin ventured back yet again, just to be sure. "Yes, that is what we were told."

"Hmm." Audrian pursed those dusky-rose lips. "Well, how tremendously fortunate is it for you, then, that I am somehow the sole exception to that teaching?"

The Keeper of Wisdom batted her lashes as she weighed the words, considering their implications over and over.

"Do not fret, though. Even if I were not as exceptional as I am, without knowing the true details of your Tutelage, it is unlikely either of the Majlis gleaned the map your Diadet laid bare."

And as the covenary relived those fateful moments in the bowels of The Klekta Mortem, her natural inclination was to agree.

And tell me, Keeper of Wisdom—in any of the nearly twenty years of your Tutelage, plus the four following—have you ever, even a solitary time, come upon anything that might lead you to believe The Skapahni live?

For Diadet Nirvana, in her skillfully feigned outburst, had led the other Majlis to believe that the gush—the enraged nonsense spewing from her lips—was just that: an enraged, nonsensical outing of the secrets of Savallin's Tutelage.

Not a trace in the Auburn Dunes? No goat path in the Rainbow Alps? What of footprints in the Olive Steppes? Or,

Her tell, maybe a toll in the Stone Bells? No, still nothing? Not so much as a hint? Not even a trace or a lost gem in the Jade Isles?

When, in all actuality, Diadet Nirvana was well aware that Savallin had never once left the Lunaerian Vale during the entire extent of her schooling. And the Keeper could not keep herself from smirking at the memory.

"However," the female kneeling at her side continued, wrenching Sav from the past, "once we breach the vast expanse of the Auburn Dunes, my tender, loving hold on your sisters' minds will begin to wane."

It was outright preposterous for the immortal to truly think her Lumin would cast this far—this far, let alone another half day's travel.

The Spectraline may be something to behold, she snickered. *But not even they are that stro—*

"And alas, my hold will continue to do so until the Keeper of Warriors comes to her senses. Or, at least, until she senses that the bane mist does not truly rain from the archway."

Until she senses she was never trapped at all.

"Yes, Euclid Istra will find herself free of The Klekta Mortem." Then, with a sly tilt of her head, Audrian happily added, "Heading or not, she will concoct quite the reckoning for the Keeper who fled free—for the Keeper who fled Her."

At that—at reckoning—Savallin's hollow gut roiled with unease. But she only lowered her gaze to the glistening peaks of rippling sand whooshing along beneath their Aerie Arras. The beauty with the skin of winter, though—she was all but salivating.

Insane, the Keeper shook her head at no one. *Spectraline are insane.*

"Do not fret, Covelette." The fair-haired warrior held her shoulders impossibly straight. "For not even five-hundred of Euclid's finest Sombers could wish to stand against *me*."

"You *cannot* truly believe that," the Keeper laughed before gawping at her escort—her escort who gave her a look worthy of inciting Hadi herself. "Can you..."

But the female did not need to reply.

Mad, Savallin thought as she stared into the lovely, unbothered face before her—searching it for fissure, for any splinter of veiled reservation. Salvaging nothing from it save unwavering poise, save supreme conviction in the words she had spoken.

Audrian is mad.

And as the sun danced its way across the heavens, the disbelief of the fleeting and the faith of the everlasting glided on as one.

It was a good while later, well after the Keeper's excited contemplations had tired even her body, when Audrian's chilly voice warmed the quiet once more.

"We will make our camp at the edge of the desert, in the shallowest of the daybreak sands. And then, when the freshest of light rises to greet the new day, then, and only then, will we begin the steep ascent into the Rainbow."

The light of this day, far from fresh, had deepened from a pale blue to a violet pastel.

"We cannot just... fly? Over the Alps?" Savallin tittered. "Over the Rainbow?"

"The Aerie Arras incantation," the everlast sighed, "does not so well agree with cumbersome thread."

Oh. She suddenly felt sheepish. *Right. Sajada Tapaté.* Sand Tapestry. Boulders, she guessed, would make for a rather unwieldy weave.

"Precisely," her meddlesome guardian agreed aloud. "And beyond that, my Stellae—the light breaker obscuring us from every eye that wishes wander—it can only be brandished when Bright rules the sky."

A light breaker... the covenary mulled. *A Sahira Sway for The Everlast.*

She was too engrossed, too dazed by the sudden reveal, to hear the hardening of Audrian's voice as the warrior reiterated, "The last place we wish to be exposed is in the Rainbow Alps."

Her Stellae... Sav gasped. *That is how she crept upon me at the oasis!*

The female scoffed. "If you sincerely believe that I need a Stellae to creep upon any being, it is *you* who is mad."

The Keeper scoffed right back. "Then why are *you,* an elite, unrivaled, immortal fighter of legend, so afraid of a few painted mountains?"

And the wide, wicked smile that spread like hoarfrost across that beautiful, ice-hewn face had Savallin regretting her words the moment she had speared them.

"Have patience, little covenary," the everlast purred, leveling those otherworldly eyes straight through her soul. "Evil takes many forms in the Crossing—She wears many skins."

And as the desert breeze drifted by, the Special Sentry leaned in close. Then, after tucking an errant ringlet behind Savallin's far ear, she whispered in that voice from the abyss, "I am not so foolish, nor novice, to believe that we shall be so blessed to skirt them all."

The Keeper did not need a reflective glass to know the rich, creamy color had soured and drained from her face altogether. Beside her, however, the everlasting terror listed back and admired her own doing.

"You should have beheld what I fended off last darkrise," Audrian's long, dark lashes dipped in the dying day. "While you savored a serene dark of splendorous slumber, I savored severing the spiral-fanged maws of every last dune dweller that swam to shred the Soul from your mortal body."

Blessed be, she inhaled. *Dune dwellers...*

For the Keeper had been so very asleep, so lost to dream, that she had not even felt the sand shift.

"And the thousands of spiraseris that did not dare surface last darkrise"—the band of muscle along her forearm flexed as the female angled the tapestry down toward the pink sands—"those slippery little devils still hunger for your very essence. Your very sound."

And Savallin, for once, her mouth hanging low in horror, had no words. No words as the luminous tapestry floated to rest atop a lull between the dunes. No words as it dissolved into nothing—as each grainy thread of the Aerie Arras knitted into the desert floor once more.

As her slippers nestled into the warm ripples of sand, the covenary beseeched her deepest reserves of resolve not to scramble atop Audrian. Audrian, who still sported that broad, terrifying grin.

"Do heed me, Covelette, when I say we *do not* wish to be exposed amidst the Rainbow Alps."

And through her haze of heightened focus, through her crush of concentration aimed upon the sand—the gleaming waves of sand harboring the sea of sound serpents—she nodded feverishly.

"Savallin," the sentry breathed through her nose, observing the rapid decline in composure, "what good will come of compelling yourself catatonic?"

Compel... myself... The covenary's jade eyes, her irises glowing brighter in the falling sun, darted across the sprawl of undulating slopes. *Compel... myself... catatonic?*

For it was not compelling of her own. In fact, it was not any compelling of Her at all. No—it was the scaled, serpent demons now swimming for her—for her very sound—that had swallowed her sangfroid whole.

Spiraseris... They are so incredibly swift that their movement, she fought to turn a small circle as she recounted the rumors, *cannot be marked by the naked eye.*

"Oh, Covelette, do not forget," the female's calm, chilly voice sliced through the distress, "you are not alone. And you are in luck," Audrian winked, "for my naked eyes have no trouble marking them whatsoever."

Imm... immortal, Sav shuddered. *She is... I am... I am with her. With Audrian. With an immortal. With a Special Sentry of The Spectraline.*

"Exactly," she sang. "So, do us both a favor and tone the fussery down a notch."

And before the stunned covenary could shirk that heavy fog of focus to glare up at her smug companion, the everlast crooned, "Besides, Keeper of Wisdom, you are about to learn something new."

There was something—something about the way she said the words—that had Savallin reeling anew, that had her bracing for an entirely different sort of evil. With novel urgency, she scoured the valleys and skimmed the slopes, searching, hunting, for roving eyes masked in shadow, masked in time. And only when she was certain they were alone—certain there was not another soul to be found for leagues—only then did she face the sentry.

"Audrian..." The covenary spoke so softly that no one but an immortal would hear her. "Need I remind you that I am a sahira. I cast Soul, nothing more. What happened with the Aerie Arras—with the forbidden tune—it cannot happen again."

For even if it had been one of the most breathtaking spectacles she had ever beheld, even if it had given her a thrill unlike anything before, even if she had not instantly faded upon its utterance—even still, it could not happen again. For the forbidden tune of incantation—for Seraphic—was expressly forbidden in The Catacombs, expressly forbidden by Diadet Nirvana herself. And Savallin... she could not, she would not, betray her sovereign, her people, by wielding it.

And as if she had paused just long enough to eavesdrop upon the silent scolding as it dragged on, Audrian's voice sounded once more.

"Today," she said, narrowing her icy stare until it was steel sharp, "you will raise a Skapahni Shasta."

No... The Keeper's head was shaking side to side as the declaration—*as the command*—settled in. *No... No, I will not.*

"There is a reason they are called *Skapahni* Shastas," she spat. "You must call upon unnatural charm, stolen charm, charm not of Soul, not of the soul." The covenary struggled to catch her breath. "You must call upon *Seraphic*—the charm of the Shamed Sisters."

The everlast female quirked her lips to the side.

"Tell me, *Keeper of Wisdom*, do you truly believe, in that Soul of yours, that a Special Sentry would be sent to escort a *sahira* out of The Catacombs?"

Chapter 36

THE CITY

"Jay," Everly breathed into the crisp air of the elevator lobby. "Jay, how did you—"

But the human man's attention was not on her. He cut her off cold.

"I have gone to that shitty café on the corner," he snarled, voice low, "every morning since the day I first ran into you."

The muscles of his upper body—his arms, his shoulders, his neck—were taut as bowstrings. She did not have to look behind her to know why.

Wipe that arrogant smirk off your Ever-cursed face right fucking now, Bristol, or I will take my time peeling it off your thick, moronic skull.

But then—beneath the salty spray and crushing swell of testosterone—the mortal's words settled in. The female blinked.

"You—*what?*"

Even though she stood between them, the human man had no trouble looking straight over her head—straight at the immortal warrior in the fuckboy sweatpants.

"That,"Bristol chimed in, "is predatory behavior."

Everstar save me.

For the human, his mouth curving upward into a brutal sneer, stepped closer to the apartment's threshold. His tense body was now less than half a pace from Everly's.

"How about"—his scowl was molten—"you quit hiding behind her?"

You will do no such thing, Dalon Bristolwood. Move even a hair on your head. I dare you.

And Bristol, for once in his dismal eternity, made a wise choice.

Thank the goddess, she exhaled, combing the foyer for the quickest route out of this nightmare. *Thank. The. Goddess.*

But when the warrior did not advance—when he stayed where he stood—the human cocked his head to the side, the flesh-and-blood portrait of the Maelstrom within.

Fuck, the female huffed inwardly. *This godsdamned mortal has a fucking death wi—*

"How about you come out here," he growled, "and say that to my face, needle dick?"

The blazing heat of immortal anger seared Everly's backside the heartbeat before she jerked the entry door closed.

The slam was still ringing through the lobby when the mortal staggered back—one step, then two. His eyelids fluttered rapidly, too rapidly, as the dark irises beneath darted without aim.

The spectraline studied him until the only sound in the pale foyer was the hum of passing cars.

And after several somber breaths, it was once more just her, him, and the two coffees still clenched in his hands. The Maelstrom was gone, all traces of the storm washed away.

Where wrath had been, warmth returned. Warmth—and shame.

Curious, she thought. *Curious, indeed.*

For a male—a man—to fathom his own fault... it was foreign. Strange. Stranger still for one to feel guilt over it. And it was for that, for the remorse worn plainly on his features, that Everly decided she would not allow the Brigadier to rip his prowling spine out through his teeth. Not yet, at least.

Though even with the heavy steel door between them, it was evident the spectraline male still lusted to try. Alas, Shield or Extori, preserving the likes of Mortal Jay would forever fall within her fealty. No matter how irritating that fealty was.

"Jay?" the female tried.

"I'm sorry," the rushed words were clipped, his gaze still fixed on the floor. "About... about that."

"I'm sorry," she lied, dulling her edge just a touch. "You shouldn't have had to meet him like that."

You shouldn't have had to meet him at all.

"Who is he?" The mortal was solemn when he finally looked at her.

"I promise," she sighed, "it's not what it appears."

As I wish, a salty film coated her tongue, *both of you had not appeared.*

"Then who is he?"

A sly smile skimmed across Everly's lips as she whispered to the immortal eavesdropper, *I doubt you'll enjoy this as much as I do.*

And then, the spectral peered up at the taller man through lowered lashes. "He's my cousin."

Jay's dark, candied glare flared, his surprise audible.

And his handsome, human face softened yet again when she nodded. "My very gay, very celibate cousin."

The front door flew wide.

Shortly after shuffling into the apartment behind her—shortly after slipping past the festering oaf in the gray sweatpants—Mortal Jay's sights had snagged on the absurd amount of food still resting atop the kitchen island. His stomach had all but rioted by the time she thought to offer a plate.

As the human piled it high with three slices of cold mushroom-spinach frittata and a sampling of every red meat left on the counter, Everly—and a royally pissed-off Bristol—began their subtle interrogation.

Why had the mortal come? How did he even know where she lived? Better yet, how had he reached her floor at all?

Between mouthfuls of egg and steak tips, Mortal Jay readily admitted to feeling somewhat guilty after plying Everly full of shitty beer for nine whole innings at the baseball game the night before. And so, to repent—and as a weak excuse to check on her after the fiery havoc across the street—he had nobly vowed to bring her a beverage he knew she actually enjoyed.

He'd used the same ruse that had earned him her name, he said—begging the barista. He'd gone to that quirky little café on the corner, waited his turn, and then asked the barista to craft him whatever coffee "the fearsome drop-dead with the slicing stare" had ordered that day he'd nearly swept her off her feet.

The young coffee-slinger with the spiked-indigo updo and floral neck tat had considered him with dead eyes, before clarifying, "You sure you don't mean that scary lady you nearly knocked to the ground?"

Bristol—the incessant bovine—had coughed, just once. Just once, as if to say, *Nearly toppled by Lesserkind?* Everly, while marking the dig, had opted to ignore it. Instead, she made a mental note to tip that young woman handsomely the next time she stopped in.

And after the cinnamon, quad-shot, whole-milk latte had been acquired from that young woman, Mortal Jay said he had headed for the nearby skyscraper he had only hoped was residential. The nearby skyscraper, he alleged, he'd watched Everly disappear into that very first dawn.

That was when the Brigadier's quiet disapproval had become a bellowing brute in its own right, billowing and blowing against the female's cool façade—right up until the moment she blew back. With a quick thought of her lips wrapped around what was certain to be the most pleasing part of the prattling human, Everly had the immortal dickhead choking on his own saliva.

The unsuspecting object of Bris' newly wild ire continued on, wholly oblivious to the soundless battle being fought before him. He recounted how he'd barely stepped foot into the lush, yawning atrium of a lobby when the slim, hawk-eyed concierge demanded the name of the tenant he had come to see. Said name, he smirked, was the only key he'd needed for the concierge to unlock the elevator bank.

And it was there, at the end of his tale, that the spectraline's questioning backfired. Brutally backfired. For the human, it turned out, had quite a few queries of his own.

How long had she lived in The Empire City? Did she like it? Did they like it? Where had they come from? What did they do for work to afford a place like this? Was it illegal? Were they hiring?

Full of answers and garlic-roasted potatoes, Mortal Jay was now busily stealing glances in Bristol's direction. Though they were cautious—innocent, even—what he obviously still sought was very, very dangerous. And while it was apparent the human possessed the good sense not to ask, Everly, on the other hand, had no qualms about it.

Bristol, aptly sensing a forthcoming spectacle, took up a seat on the barstool closest to the mortal.

Hiding her delight at his pathetic attempt to deter her, the female raised her cup to her lips and tutted. "You've been in town for what... like two, three days now?" She smiled, sipping the milky warmth. "Where's your coffee bringer, Bristol?"

The look that crept over the male's face all but begged her to forge ahead. And Everly, being the goddess-blessed female that she was, devotedly obliged.

"I've seen you perusing The City's premier," she said, swallowing another sip. "Surely they can point you to someone fuck-deficient enough to play hide the wiener even with—"

The mortal began choking on his link of jalapeño pork. He doubled over, the spectraline scowling in disgust as he hawked and hacked until the spicy sausage vacated his esophagus at last. Only when his skin again shone summer brown—in lieu of the grim blue—did the female resume her fun.

"Is that it?" she gasped, brightest stars flickering to life in the depths of her eyes. "Is that why you're so cross? Because of your fragility?"

Beneath his ballcap, Mortal Jay's features went rigid.

"Because you were born only to break the very moment things get hard?"

You have witnessed me fell dark kingdoms, the male groused into her thoughts as the lines of his face harshened to that of a statue.

Everly merely held up a slender finger. "In the home..."

You were there, at my side, as I slaughtered hosts so monstrous even The Fallen took notice.

The female lifted another. "In the workplace..."

You have watched as I rallied troops and as I ended them, all without breaking so much as a bead of sweat.

A third rose to meet the first two. "On the sporting fields."

The Brigadier's seethe was nearly spilling over when he growled, *I recommend, Everly Castile, that you think long and hard before making an accusation like that again.*

"Bristol," she tapped her chin. "Conceived to choke."

The butter knife he sent arcing through the kitchen lodged into the stone column a hair above her head. The mortal leapt to his feet, nearly toppling his stool in the process.

His fork was still clattering atop the tile below when he yelled, "What the fuck, man?!"

"It's fine. He's fine," Everly reassured from the opposite edge of the island. "He just—he throws hissies sometimes. But don't worry, he couldn't hurt an angel like me even if his life depended on it." She tossed her cousin a wink. "He just needs a good lay, that's all."

Or perhaps, a fall from the terrace.

But positioned behind his stool in some sort of human fighting stance, Mortal Jay did not look convinced.

"Bris, will you please apologize?" The spectraline rested a hand upon her hitched hip. "You spooked our guest."

"I would rather"—his expression was hewn of cruelest stone—"let our guest geld me."

"Gods," Everly exhaled, staring up at the ceiling, as the guest's jaw dropped to the countertop.

If you do not apologize right this second, Brigadier Bristolwood, I vow to you, I will drag that human into my bedchamber, lose this silk, and—

"I apologize," the male gritted through a clenched jaw. "Little man."

Really? she barked in silence, manicured fingertips massaging the sudden ache in her temples. *That's the best you could muster?*

The immortal warrior only smirked at her. And Mortal Jay, having stooped to pick up his fork, did not appear even the slightest bit relieved.

I will not soon forget that, she blew as she strode for the at-odds pair.

"Well, there you have it," she sang, her energy now meant solely to soothe. "As he just so kindly demonstrated for you, Bristol here lacks—well, he lacks almost everything."

The unease coursing through the mortal's body morphed into that of purest shock. Bris' charming little smirk, meanwhile, only grew. The female did not skip a beat before charging on.

"My sweet, sweet cousin... no, he is not swift, nor is he agile. He has little balance, even less stamina, zero skill *or* intellect of any kind, and—most detrimental of all—he is absolutely dreadful to be around."

Everly paused, tickled nearly to tears, as the human struggled to find words while her cousin dreamt up new and colorful ways of turning her body inside out.

"So," she shrugged, before cheerily answering the mortal's final, unspoken question at last, "the choice of chastity was never truly his own. It's more that nobody can stomach being around him."

And before you pipe up, your hand does not cou—

The bastard pinched her ass so hard she had to bite down on her own tongue to keep from bashing his skull into the marble.

"He has a way of making minutes feel like millennia."

"Damn," Mortal Jay—supremely unaware of the soundless skirmish—grimaced. "Have you tried the apps?"

"Your very gay, very celibate cousin?"

"Well, a female can dream," Everly cooed, sliding twin short blades into the leather scabbard at her back. "Just think how fantastic that would be—how fantastic you would be. And how stylish. How groomed."

After giving the sour-faced Brigadier plenty of unwelcome—yet astute—tips for getting his online dating profile up and running, the mortal had left them. Something or another about work. But, as he departed, he had very graciously offered to accompany Bristol to The City's liveliest gayborhood, to be an ally in the male's quest for love.

Everly had been elated.

"We do not have time to play with mortals," the blue-eyed brute roared, stepping into her path. "And we certainly do not have time for you to rile the half-breeds who are actively hunting our kind."

"Move," she ordered, tying her long, dark hair into a tight bun at the nape of her neck. "You know, if I didn't know better, Bristol, I would believe you to be scared."

"And if *I* didn't know better, *Everly*, I would believe you to be thoughtless."

"Well," the female's sharpened canines glinted in the dying light outside the windows as she stepped forward—so close her body pressed into his—"with your sparkly, new Thought-Telling gifts," she snarled, "you should be well aware of just how mistaken you are."

Bristol's cruel expression faltered. And the female did not care. Not one bit. For whatever long-lost memories and forgone feelings now stampeded their way through his twisted mind, they hailed from a different day. From a forgotten age. From a vanished people.

No—whatever Bris was remembering, whatever flurry of regrets he was having over his subpar choice in Parallels—it was for him alone. Reaching up behind the stormy swine, Everly grabbed her black coat off the hook and readied to let him suffer in peace.

She had just turned the knob on the entry door when the warrior's gravelly voice sent an army of spears shooting down her spine.

"Korol Qanun."

Her lethal form went deathly still.

It... cannot... The faces of her past—the brave, bright, fearless faces—threatened to bring the spectraline to her knees. *It cannot be...*

Bristol, the first to free himself from the asphyxiating hold of the bygone, padded over to where she stood. With a broad hand placed on either side of her face, the male leaned his weight into the door. The female was lost, though—pinned by a gone stare twin to her own.

"*Everly,*" the warrior snickered, his merciless breath hot on her ear as he whispered down to her, "the renowned... the revered... the forgotten redeemer of The Castile Plain."

He leaned into her until his amber-oaken scent permeated even the past.

"You do remember custom."

They were brave. They were bright. They were fearless.

An easy slip of the Brigadier's forearm and Everly's back was against the door, her nightmare-stained eyes locked upon his.

"Tell me, General, what goes into effect the moment The Spectraline Senate falls?"

An insurmountable barrier of silver-soaked ice smashed down onto that painful longing in her chest. The glowing images of her closest companions, her hopeful paramours, her only kin, evanesced as one. And then, the spectraline's immortal heart once again froze into the coldest stone known to the stars.

"Korol Qanun," the forgotten General fumed. "Raise the Kings."

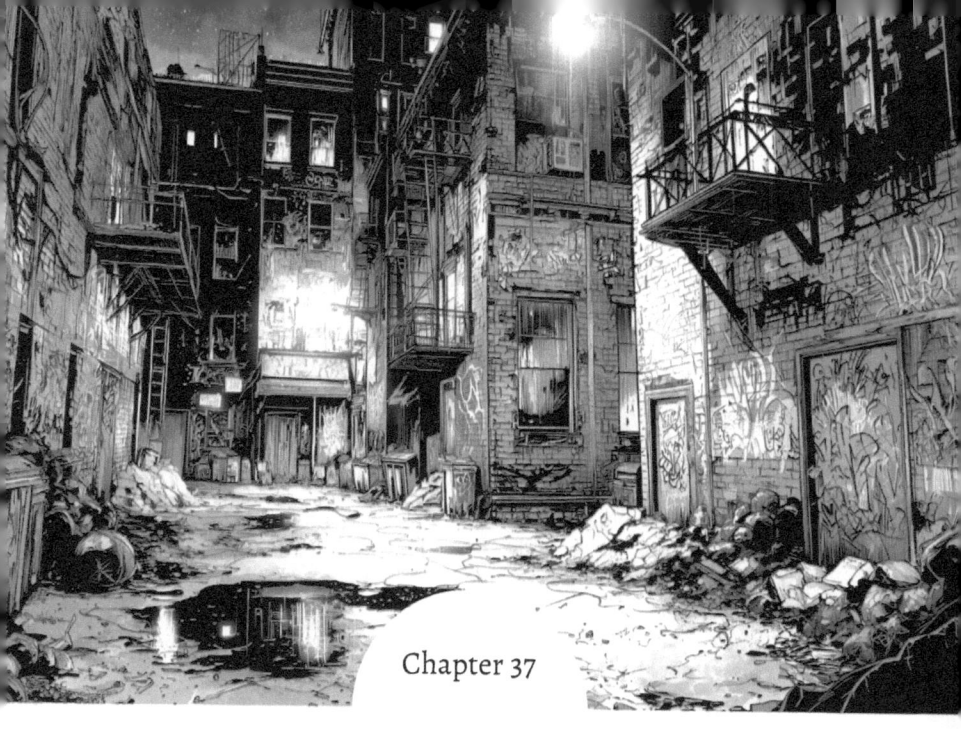

Chapter 37

THE CESSPOOL

The depths of the ball river were pitch black. The mass of plastic spheres above her was a continuous riptide of quicksand dragging her down deeper. But there was still breath in her lungs, still power coursing through her body, as the assailing creature clawed its broken nails into her calf.

She kicked against the burning in her flesh. She twisted and flailed beneath the surface, trying frantically to slip the thing's impossible hold. She loaded and emptied her last clip—the thud of each shot telling her they'd found their mark, they'd found her attacker.

A wet, fuming roar spewed from its jaws, but its strength did not flag. No, the monster heaved, thrashing her body so violently she might as well have been a ribbon in a hurricane. And it was then, when Sergeant Ava Carlisle's skull rang against the faux-stone river bottom, that she knew she was in trouble.

The feeling in her feet faded first. The movement—the control over her limbs—went next. And then, just as her consciousness readied for its turn into oblivion, the Sergeant's world upended yet again.

Something—something that felt as if made of iron—caught beneath the fabric strap running from her collar line to the tip of her shoulder. The very next moment, it heaved upward, jerking her limp body up from the black bowels of the ball pit river.

Her vision, quivering in the grainy darkness like a timeworn reel of film, shuddered at what it saw next—at what it captured holding her up at eye level, at what inspected her motionless form as if she were no more than his catch of the day.

"Vas," the young Sergeant exhaled, the cool mists of relief fluttering through her chest. "Vas, you're ali—"

The butt of his gun smashed into her temple before she had the chance to finish her thought.

"It seeps from her skin," a ruined voice hissed. "How did you fail to scent it?"

The slow, predatory drum of footfalls pulsed through the wooden floorboards beneath the Sergeant's cheek.

"You ignorant waste," a bawdy laugh rumbled into the darkness. "That scent"—the man's volume plunged eerily low, a paralytic venom dripping from each new word—"that scent is the only reason I didn't rip your worthless hide in half after the absolute shit-storm you set into motion."

Even though she could only feel the one set of steps—the heavy, familiar footsteps of her partner—Sergeant Carlisle knew that the other creature, the other monster, circled nearby. And that her partner... her partner was talking to it. He was conversing with it—speaking to that mangled mess of a monster—as if it were just any old person on the street.

"The shit-storm *I* set into motion?" it moaned. "The shit-storm I set into motion while I obediently cleaned up yet another of your fuck-ups."

Vasquez stopped his pacing.

"And what fuck-up would that be?"

The bare, blood-cloaked body—the disfigured corpse that had once been a man—scoffed.

"Oh, I don't know," the cadaver croaked. "How about grabbing your ankles for the most dangerous, goddamned drug lord in the whole fucking city?"

Drug lord? From where she lay unmoving upon the hardwood, the discarded and disregarded Sergeant strained to shake the thick clouds of fog from her mind. *What on the Mother's green earth has he gotten himself into?*

"Who else, do you suppose"—his voice was so brusque she hardly recognized it—"has both the moral depravity and the comprehensive means to source the very specialized, very expensive sort of armaments that we—very clearly—need?"

Armaments? the Sergeant repeated, disbelieving her ears.

When the human wreckage didn't offer an answer, Vasquez continued his tirade.

"Who else, do you reason, finds themselves constantly plagued by pesky operational problems that I am so uniquely positioned to solve?"

Shit. The soundless realization was so loud she could hear it even over the heavy drum of her own heart. *He's an informant.*

"Pesky operational problems you forced me to solve on your behalf, asswipe," the creature snarled back.

The distant click of a weapon being restored to its holster split the tension.

"I'll admit," Vasquez said. "I did ask far too much of you."

The corpse's muddled breaths speckled the calm as he waited for the officer to go on. And when he did, something lurking in his lighter, relaxed tone was deeply, deeply unsettling.

"Yes, I will admit it. I thought far too highly of you, pal. I expected far too much from that simple, simple mind of yours."

Pal? The Sergeant gagged. *What on the Mother's green earth have I gotten myself into?*

But the broken man had gone graveyard quiet, not even the phlegmy pulls of his labored breathing stirring the air.

"No, I didn't think it through. Not fully, anyway," Vasquez sniggered. "Maybe if I had, maybe if I had stopped and considered that you might not be suited for the very simple task of setting a fire unseen, maybe I wouldn't be in this predicament right now."

Kingpins... informant... fire... a discreet demotion...

And then, there in the darkness, it was as if a blazing torch had been shoved down the Sergeant's shadowed throat.

"Maybe if I would have taken the time to stop and consider your limited ability, maybe then I would have foreseen the goddamned witness you left behind." His feigned cheer detonated *that* fast. "*The witness* I had to hunt down and blackmail to keep your sorry ass off Death Row."

Witness tampering, she breathed. *The Department had disciplined him on suspicion of witness tampering.*

They must not have been able to prove it, though... No, because if they had evidence, if they had anything concrete, Vasquez would've been terminated or charged or arrested— something. But no... Narcotics couldn't prove it. Not beyond a reasonable doubt, not yet. That's why his demotion had been so hush-hush.

It's still being investigated.

But the Department—Narcotics—they didn't know. They couldn't have fathomed how much worse the truth really was. They hadn't dreamed that Vasquez, that one of their own, might have not only threatened a witness, might not just be knee-deep in the fire cover-up... but that he might have orchestrated the whole fucking inferno himself. That *he* had orchestrated the whole fucking inferno himself.

The Tenement Fire.

"And now," Vasquez's voice soared, "now, you have left me with yet another witness to deal with."

"*She* is a—"

"I don't care what she is," he shouted, severing the monster's throaty hiss. "*She* is now a loose end in need of tying."

Backup. Her woozy memory was like a golden bolt of lightning hurled into the starkest face of darkness. *I called for backup.*

And even though she had not gotten all the words out— even though she had been cut off before she could tell the dispatcher exactly what she needed—the unanswered welfare checks, the sudden radio silence, would be response enough.

The quiet would speak for her.

Her fellow officers would respond. They would arrive, any moment now, and then—then they could hear the confession, the uninterrupted admission recorded by her body cam, for themselves.

"Why the fuck"—Vasquez roared, at last resuming his pacing—"did you skulk here anyway?"

The once-human started, then stuttered, then retched something both liquid and not. And only after the gagging ceased did the man crack his jaws open once more.

"I could not so easily go home," he growled. "Not with your *friends* out there hunting for us."

The Sergeant was frozen where she lay. The feeling in her toes, the sensation in her fingertips, had not yet returned— not fully. But her mind, her wits, they had come back for her. And as her partner's steps turned to stomps, as each of his footfalls thundered louder than the one before, Sergeant Ava Carlisle raced to mount an attack.

Officer Vasquez's angry howl was the last thing she heard before his marching came to rest at her side.

"Get lost. Now, before I have a change of heart."

THE CONSERVATORY

Dima was wide awake and sprinting for the forward terrace long, long before The Everstar had even dreamt of beginning Her blessed ascent. Today would be the day, he knew. It had to be the day. For this morning, when Her first ray of light crested the distant, thawing horizon, the dawn of the Spring Equinox would be upon them. The dawn of Dyasus would be upon them.

And Dima—he would not miss a moment of it.

For Dyasus was a time of grand celebration at The Conservatory. But it was also a time of great sorrow. For its rise marked the final day a wayward sixth-series might still return from the Twenty-Third Canon alive.

If they did not make it home by last light of this day, their name would be scraped from The Vitoska and written into the stars—into the starstone Ledger of The Fallen, where it would then be read aloud, along with all who were lost, on the dawn to follow.

Each and every spectral and specling within the mighty stone walls—every shihan, every shield, every scribe and scholar, every giver and each sibling that had come—they would all gather as one, convening in the Forbidden Hours of darkness at the brink of The Frozen Fall.

And as The Everstar began Her rise, as the Goddess pulled Herself higher and higher into the sky, as She warmed and woke the slumbering giant at their feet, as She shattered the coverlet of sleeping power, as the azure fall roared to life, the assembly of spectraline would listen.

Through the ferocious, dogged thunder of the massive cascade, they would hear each name as it was read aloud. Arm in arm, The Spectraline of The Conservatory would watch—through spray-sodden eyes—as each and every silvered ash of The Fallen soared back to whence they came.

So far this solar, sixty-seven sixth-series had survived their trial. Sixty-seven sixth-series had endured, returned, and climbed The Alpine Steps. It was more than any solar past. More—but not all. There were still nineteen specling in the wind.

Nineteen.

Nineteen ruthless, relentlessly trained warriors-to-be. Nineteen still lost... or hurt... or stranded... or worse.

Dima recited the names of those missing as he raced up the spiraling staircase at the end of his dormitory's main corridor. He ticked them off one by one until he got to the last. The last that should have been first. He was piecing her face together in his memory when he slammed into something immovable. Into someone immovable.

He staggered back, throwing his arms wide, managing to catch himself before the shadowy prowler sent him tumbling back down the way he had come.

"What—" He blew out an exasperated breath. "—the hell?"

But as the culprit straightened, as he twisted to stare at *who* had ricocheted off him, Dima felt the staircase begin to give way.

His vision began to thrum, the thundering in his chest easing into a cold, killing sort of calm. His hands, shaking with anger, balled into furious fists. His back foot slid left— just a step, just enough to fortify his stance. And as the solars of training overtook even the sense in his body, Dima saw red.

He would end this male.

It did not matter that he had no weapons. It did not matter that this spectral was a Commander of The Shield. Dima would cut him down. He would cut him down and steal his very eternity. Right here. Right now.

But before he did—before he sent the shield straight to the pits of Sempenihil—he had to know. He had to know where she was.

His voice was so edged, so wrathful and callous, that even he did not recognize it when he asked, "What did you do?"

But the male—he—he was panting, swaying on his feet.

Dima did not care. He growled again, "What did you do to her, Decard?"

The male only teetered, staring at nothing.

The fifth-series hesitated and—looked. Really looked at the spectral before him.

He was... he was not in good shape. It was a miracle, Dima thought, that the shield still managed to stand, that he had withstood their crash at all.

The planes of the male's face had been wind-burned so brutally Dima hardly recognized him. The skin along his cheekbones, along his nose and lips, had been split clean open. Deep, black bruises pooled in the space beneath his stony eyes. His neck and arms, his chest—all usually thick with muscle—were worn stick-thin and covered in gashes.

The sleeves of his uniform, and one of his pant legs, had been torn off. High on his bare leg, in the center of his thigh, a large, festering wound rotted the surrounding flesh. And as if that were not foul enough, his entire body—from his sandy hair to his missing boots—was caked in a fine, black filth of some kind. Clenched in his hand, as if a tether to life, was a long dagger stained to the hilt with dried, gray blood.

Dima unfurled his fists.

For Decard Battleson to be this fucked... the young male's pulse quickened. *For the Commander to look this wretched... for him to be this dumbstruck...*

There were but a few living things capable of such a feat. And Nora—*Nora* was one of them.

The fifth-series' legs were already moving, that kernel of hope, as small as it was, propelling him to leap up the stairs four at a time. The thought of her being back, of her being okay—it was nearly more than he could bear.

He cleared the dim stairwell and ran for the archway—for the darkness beyond. Eerie portraits and cracking statues whizzed by on both sides. He pushed his legs harder, faster. The starry threshold grew larger, larger—and then he was through it and under open sky. And when, at last, Dima skidded to a halt on the moonlit terrace, his mighty heart guttered.

For all that hope he had been holding onto so tightly—for all that hope he had carried fortnight upon fortnight—it winked out.

The terrace was desolate. And the silence—the absolute silence—was beyond soul-splitting. Nobody had been here. There was not a soul to be found. Where that beautiful, silvery hope had been, where it had lived within him for so long, an oily, black rage burned hot.

And the male knew exactly who would pay for it first.

Spinning on his boot, he marched right back into Res Ell. Decard was not on the stairs, though. He was not in the corridors or commons either. But Dima... he sensed he was close... he could not not sense it. For the telltale stench of piss-soaked linen lingered low in the air.

The male followed it, trailed it, until—until he was standing outside his own chamber door. His already-blazing temper flared dangerously bright.

That filth-drenched, rotten hide of swine.

And without pausing to level his head, to level his nerves, Dima shoved his door wide open. And there he was—the noble Commander, Decard Battleson—lying sprawled across his floor.

Face-down upon the chamber's gilded-emerald rug, the spectral raised one arm at the fifth-series' approach. He tried to roll himself over, tried to push up off the ground, but his arms—all tattered skin and ailing bones—failed him. With absolutely no taste for his histrionics, Dima crouched low beside the collapsed shield.

"*Where is she, Decard?*"

The spectral tilted his head to speak. But then, he closed his eyes and slumped once more.

"Where. Is. She."

The laboring soldier tried again, twisting toward the voice, struggling to open his mouth. Dima held his breath, waiting for the male to speak—waiting for him to say something, anything, that might lead to Nora Everstar, that might reveal her last whereabouts.

But as he fought to give voice to the words upon his tongue, the Commander's face paled beneath the ruby scars of the wind. And his back—what was left of it—tightened with silent strain.

"Where is Nora, Decard?"

The specling was in his face, in his space, shaking his worthless carcass by the scraps of his uniform. And when he had gone and just about lost it, when he had decided to drag the useless male up the stairs to the edge of the terrace, that was when the bastard finally spoke. That was when Decard

Battleson choked out three words—three Ever-blessed words.

"Warn them all."

Chapter 39

THE CITY

"Why are we here?" the eternal pain-in-her-ass griped from the gravelly rooftop beside her.

"How many times would you like to hear it, Bristol?" She glanced to the prone warrior on her left. "I am looking for someone."

Ever since that first nightfall following the penthouse blast—ever since that nightfall when Everly had tried to walk out her door to locate the mark she'd been hunting for weeks—the Brigadier had taken it upon himself to plant his giant, mindless body directly in her path.

And while his mention of *Korol Qanun* had indeed taken her by surprise, not even the unparalleled peril it promised was enough to sway her to leave with him. To sway her—an Extori, *a forgotten*—to venture into The Black Chasm, into The Crevasse Citadel, into Helavos; the Seat of Reminisce. No. If anything, the dismal prospect only deepened her determination not to go.

So, over the past few weeks, each time the pushy Brigadier insisted on getting in her way, the female had insisted on shoving him over the railing of her penthouse balcony. And when that hadn't solved the problem, she tried knocking the male into oncoming traffic—more than once, just to be sure. But still, none of her efforts proved a deterrent. Not even when she resorted to kicking the warrior in the backs of his knees while they lingered at the edge of the subway platform *as the train rocketed into the station.*

No—the obstinate bastard came out unscathed every single time, which she found particularly vexing. But not as vexing, however, as the smug, preachy declaration he made each time he rose:

You can continue to refuse me, Ev, but make no mistake— in doing so, you are conceding your freedom.

And if the Brigadier was one thing, it was pigheaded. For no matter how she tried to persuade him otherwise, the male refused to let her out of his sights—just as he had vowed he wouldn't.

So, night after night, with the ornery warrior in tow, Everly set out to uphold her oath, to fulfill the onus of her eternity: to protect Lesserkind. For even if she had been ousted from The Shield for the greater part of a thousand solars, that long-forgotten General she'd once been lived still. And that which she'd sworn would never die.

The Swear of The Shield

The might of the sky now sworn at thy behest.
Give to the Ever cause, the eternity within thy chest.
Swear to shield Lesserkind by defending the bounds.
Swear to wield weapon and mind in rending what hounds.
Protect this world from what cannot be sought.
Protect this world from what is Known and what is Not.

That was why they were here, after all—here atop this condemned building beneath its tattered quilt of city-muffled stars. Everly, flat on her belly, fulfilling an oath she had never forgotten. And Bristol, his light-brown hair cloaked beneath a thick, black hood, too stubborn to forget her.

"Looking for who?" the Brigadier demanded, just as he had every night for weeks.

"I will not know," she grumbled through closed teeth, just as she had done every other time he asked. "Not until I see them."

And though the spectraline knew precisely who she was searching for—precisely who she was stalking through the darkest alleys of the chanciest slums to find—she saw little point in telling Bristolwood. But to get the overbearing shield to finally stop hefting her over his shoulder and hauling her back into the safety of her apartment like a sack of soiled linens, she had tossed him a grisly morsel to chew on.

That *morsel* being the conversation she'd overheard between the two policemen in the coffee shop all those weeks prior—the one about The Empire City's evils. And Bristol... he would not let it go.

"Everly," he protested into the night. "If you think to handle this matter as you have your most recent dealings, I will be forced to raise an inquest with The Senate."

"Oh, yeah?" she snorted, not taking her eyes from the canopied entrance across the street. "And what Senate would that be?"

In all truth, the female could not care less that The Spectraline Senate was on the brink of extinction. No, she had long detested The Senate. And The Senate—they had longer detested her. In her eyes, their downfall was far overdue. And Everly... she would not be lifting a finger to protect them. Not. A. Damn. One.

And as far as Bristol and his righteousness were concerned, her recent dealings he was so pissy about—one little street-misted kidnapper and a few human traffickers turned holiday ornaments—both had been by the stone. Just not his stone. For the female had acknowledged long ago that the Brigadier's rigid rectitude impeded his ability to think freely. To think for himself. To truly understand the meaning of the etchings—or, in this case, the amendment to them.

The Swear of The Shield, A.1,17S.S.

If with True Malice in thy heart, a Lesser strikes Ever,
It is due war thou bid start, thy life thou bid sever.

Alas, in the moral shadow of the archaic shroud Bristol wore through the world, there was absolutely no excuse for any member of The Spectraline to bring harm upon a mortal. Doing so was a direct violation of their primary purpose—shielding Lesserkind. But what The Seventeenth Senate, the last just Senate, understood that Bris never would, is that the prodigious evil plaguing Lesserkind does not always hail from borders Known. Sometimes, that evil grows from within.

It is called True Malice, and it is an evil born deep within the weakest chests of humanity—the blight of a fragile soul. And it is a threat to all Lesserkind. A threat that can be dealt with accordingly, as long as it strikes first.

That had been the fun part.

Over the centuries, Everly had all but perfected the ledger of names, insults, and taunts that worked best in every kind of situation. In the cases of big men who preyed on little children, the most effective—and anatomically accurate—slurs often drew attention to their teeny, tiny manhoods.

Those degenerates did not deserve to live. And with how readily they had charged the mouthy tauntress, it was as if they knew as much.

"Everly." The female could feel the weight of the warrior's worried gaze as he surveyed every inch of her body for damage that was not there. "The state of The Senate, Ev, that is exactly why I need to get you out of—"

"Just stop, Bristol," her quiet words edged sharp by hundreds of solars of distrust and disgust. "Just sto—"

But then, down on the poorly lit, trash-riddled street below them, five SUVs screeched to a halt in front of what should have been an uninhabited building. And as she and Bris lay upon their pebbly roof, staring through the small weeps in the parapet wall, the reinforced doors on each of the five vehicles swung open in unison. The bona fide ground force that emerged from behind the heavily tinted windows could only mean one thing.

The mortal evil—the True Malice—that had stolen the lives of so many... she had found it.

"He's in there," she whispered, pushing herself up off the gravelly roof. "Let's go."

Two hours and twenty-one corpses later, Everly and Bristol strolled arm in arm along the swaying, moonlit silhouettes of The City's grandest park. She with three decadent scoops of frozen yogurt. He with a steaming midnight scowl.

"Well," the sulking male finally bit out after ten blissful blocks of silence. "That certainly ought to garner us some unwanted attention."

"Speaking of unwanted attention," she said, ignoring the inane allusion that they had been seen, "did you ever settle on a—what did Mortal Jay call it?"

The goliath cloud of steam at her side blazed hotter.

Whether it was the memory of being thought her cousin... the remembrance of the mortal in general... or the much more specific and rather vivid images of the human man with his hands roaming all over her bare body, Everly couldn't be sure.

"A handle," the warrior growled.

While she had not actually been intimate with the man, that in no way prevented her from painting an entire fucking exhibit of very explicit works for the not-so-rare occasion of Bristol invading the privacy of her mind.

"Right." The long, dark strands of her ponytail bounced with her eager nod. "A handle."

"We do not have time to—"

"Hmm," she thought aloud between licks of melty mocha-mint-cocoa. "What were his instructions again?"

The sweet-faced mortal, when he was not off upholding whatever oaths he had made, continued to materialize at her front door. And Everly would have been more than content leaving him there—except that each time he arrived, he bore a tasty new treat. Beyond even that, though, the female found his special fascination with Bristol to be exceptionally amusing.

"*Your* only instruction is to leave this Ever-forsaken place with—"

"I think it was something about your name... something to tell prospective devotees... or, no, was it disciples?" Everly paused, tending lovingly to her cone. "Yeah... yes, it was something to tell potential disciples a bit about you. A hint of insight as to the kind of male you really are."

The Brigadier's already tense posture had gone fully rigid.

Good. She didn't care. Not in the slightest—not after everything he'd put her through. No, he was here, and miserable, on his own accord. If he didn't enjoy the heat, he was more than welcome to pack up and flee back to his beloved frozen ruins, at any time.

"Something to show what you believe in," the female raised her head to look him dead in the face. "Or something to show what you do not."

Salt tickled her tongue.

"Better yet," Everly sneered, unable to stop herself, "something to show *who* you do no—"

The Brigadier caught her jaw in his palm, the hollow expression dampening his stormy, lazuline eyes absolute anguish. And the female knew—she knew what he was going to say. She knew, and she did not want to hear it.

"Don't—"

Bristol clamped his hand tighter.

"No." And even in the darkness, she could see the color leach from his skin. "You will listen."

In her own chest, what had once, long ago, been a fierce and formidable heart wavered like a torch in the wind.

"I am sorry, Ev." His voice was guttural, shaky. "I am so very sorry for what I did to you."

She tried to protest, tried to work her jaw, but he simply squeezed harder.

"You have to understand, after the—"

Do not go there, Dalon.

"Everly." He tasted her name like the curse that it was. "*Everly*, I did what I did to save you—to protect you—to keep you from ending up like—"

Sticky streams of frozen yogurt seeped into the cracks of the sidewalk as the female gripped his forearm in both hands and hooked a heel around his ankle. The shock of her driving shoulder had the male prostrate upon the pavement before he could finish the uninvited thought.

She pressed her eyes closed, blocking out centuries of unresolved grief. Blocking out the sea of graying, twisted faces. Blocking out the piercing screams and slicing shrieks of the dying. And then, willing her scalding, boiling blood to freeze over once more—demanding that it again flow as ice—she opened her eyes.

"It was *not* your gallantry compelling you, Dalon Bristolwood."

The living, breathing rage that *was* her immortal soul began to temper the moment she made to turn away. And with every inhale of night air, with every hammer of her heart, that rage cooled a fraction more. Finally, when Everly Castile left that worthless, lying male lying there upon the sidewalk like the discarded waste that he was, her fiery rage again burned cold.

"It was *never* your gallantry."

Chapter 40

THE CROSSING

Sticky, rancid air rushed down her barren throat as the raging rivers of forlorn darkness swirled in from every angle, violently gushing in atop her, through each cobwebbed crook, until that small, forsaken tomb in the bowels of The Klekta Mortem began to fill.

She kicked her legs and pumped her arms, trying desperately to swim against the black torrent—but the furious floods were not of dark water. No. The ferocious downpours drowning her in her crypt were cascades of bane. Bane in its purest form.

She knew it when the sensation in her fingers, in her toes, in her limbs faded into nothing. She knew it when the mortal skin began to peel from her very bones. She knew it when the Winds of Hadi began their unnatural whine overhead.

And as her soul, at last, made to break from this cruel world, a chilly voice echoed through the murk.

I know that you, Savallin Prim, are the kind of covenary the world came to fear.

The Keeper's eyes flew wide.

In half a beat, she had lurched from the ground, landed in a low crouch, and readied her fists before her face. Her eyes darted across the tapering desert in front of her, fixating on each and every grain of sunrise sand. She watched it, scanned it, for any movement among the ripples. She focused even deeper, straining her ears for any hint of approaching breaths, any sign of coming footsteps, any—

A snort shattered the stillness.

Savallin spun, her arm lengthening before her—lengthening to hurl the serrated blade in her hand toward the sound—

The covenary did not have time to gasp, to recall the blade, to do anything but gape. For her knife—her steel—was sailing straight for the Special Sentry. Straight for her heart. For Audrian's heart.

Audrian, the stunning everlast warrior, casually reclined back in the sand as if on sabbatical, her long, toned legs crossed at the ankles as she bit into an apple. Audrian, the sure fluke of nature, who, with her free hand, snatched Savallin's spinning dagger clear out of the sky—mid-bite, no less.

As the Keeper's jaw fell slack with disbelief, the Special Sentry only swallowed her mouthful and chuckled. "Wicked dream?"

And the haughty little simper dimpling the spectraline's absurd, immortal face had the covenary unleashing the dagger clutched in her other hand.

But swifter than anyone—swifter than any being—had a right to be, Audrian loosed her own blade. The slender silver stiletto glinted as it flew. Glinted as it sailed insufferably fast, dreadfully straight. Glinted until the moment that finely polished steel struck her clunky, toothed knife—colliding with it and knocking it from the air.

And its thrower? She did not even have the decency to watch it fly. No—the everlast female just took another bite of her breakfast. Savallin steamed.

Clean out of throwing knives and plumb out of patience, she stormed off to inspect the perimeter—to inspect *her* perimeter.

"When you find it within yourself to quit holding back," the female called out from behind her, in between her mouthfuls, "Night knows, maybe then I might have to break my breakfast."

But the Keeper was not having it. Not today. Not now. Not after she had been torn from her sleep, in the dead of night, by the realization that Audrian Adivostov had been toying with her mind. Toying with her, inflating her fear, so that she—a blessed, damned Majlis of Covenarykind—would agree to raise a Skapahni Shasta. Agree to commit high treason.

For a Shasta could not be called through simple trickery alone, not like an Aerie Arras. Because the Earth Song summoned to sew a sand tapestry would eventually be returned back to Her, that rhythm of the barred tune—of Seraphic—was considered borrowed, not stolen, and slightly less destructive. But the Earth Song summoned to alter Her Herself—as a Shasta does—could never be given back. For it was truly stolen, a full-bodied Seraphic rhythm—the Seraphic of The Skapahni. And the extent of charm, of skill, that such a thieving demanded, was immense. Dangerous.

And not one to be outdone, straightaway upon her mid-slumber awakening, the young covenary had pounced upon the sleeping spectral—upon the pitiless immortal. Savallin had shaken her, shaken her shoulders until she roused from her own peaceful resting. And then, and then Audrian had

had the nerve to cast the blame upon her—upon Savallin—before rolling right back over and into dream.

It is but the mildest reminder, Savallin Prim, of what will happen if you insist on leaving that inner shield low.

And if the Keeper had not believed for certain that the warrior would throw her into the next century for it, she might have throttled her. Might have. But instead, as she reluctantly nestled back beneath the warm, feathered coverlet her everlasting menace of an escort had packed along for her, the covenary had mulled over the memory. Mulled over what it had felt like—the exhilaration she had felt surging through her blood—as she had summoned the forbidden tune. As she had commanded Skapahni Seraphic.

It had taken her no less than four attempts to raise the Shasta, to separate and then pull upon those precise notes of power deep within the Earth, deep within Her, deep within herself. The closer she had crept toward their strange sound, the closer she had dared to go, the worse the aching, the pounding in her head became. Her arms, her palms, had bleated and slickened. Within her core, her very center, her stomach had swayed, dipping and twisting, until her knees, at last, hit the dune floor.

But once she had hold of that distinctive, eerie rhythm—once she had latched upon it with the entirety of her body, of her Soul—Savallin began to compose. With each word that spilled over her lips, each prohibited incantation she sang, each breath of the barred tune that flowed from her into the world, the distress tormenting her mortal body dispelled further. She began to glow, to hum. Began to feel... strong.

And when the melding had resonated true—when the song of the covenary and the song of Her had been sung perfectly in tune—the very ground beneath Savallin's feet, the darkening desert floor upon which her slippers rested, melted into fiery red-gold magma before hissing and hardening into an island of earthrock, of purest obsidian, so harmonious, so unyielding, that not even a grain of sand might hope to pass. Even the Special Sentry had whistled.

And the Keeper—she had not been able to help but be proud. Even against the pangs of guilt, even against the dread she knew she was supposed to feel, Savallin had not been able to help but be proud of what she had done.

The memory of her conquest cooled the covenary's boiling temper as she now stood at the edge of that Shasta. As she toed the citrusy-pink sand just past the black rock and... gawked at the cratered basin beyond.

Viciously marring what ordinarily would have been just another pristine, glittering valley wedged between dune crests, a myriad of shallow, spiky mounds—far more of them than Sav cared to count—pocked the desert floor. The jagged, cleaved mounds, and the dark voids at their center, ranged in scale from the slightness of a Wilds Worm to the bursting girth of a Sea Titan.

"I told you your Shasta was sound."

Savallin's goddess-blessed soul vacated her earthly body.

The immortal snickered. "I *also* told you that I do not need a Stellae to creep upon any being."

When her hammering heart, at last, slid back into her chest, the Keeper of Wisdom whipped her head of airy curls up at the spectraline female.

"How many of them did you—" She swallowed her growing shame and tried again. "How many spiraseris did you have to... to kill that first nightfall? The night when I was, uh... when I did not raise the Shasta?"

"Hundreds."

The covenary's brilliant, green eyes threatened to pop clean out of her skull.

But, true to form, Audrian merely shrugged. "I did not have anything else to do."

And it was Savallin who snorted at that—at how wholly indifferent the female was about her feat, her incredible feat. At how vastly unimpressive she thought her might.

Half the morning later, the raven-haired Keeper still shone with that cheery amusement when she and her immortal companion at last rested amidst the cool, yawning shadows of the Rainbow Alps. And truthfully, she had not thought any landscape capable of stealing the light from the wondrous, shimmering sea they had just left behind.

But as Sav craned her head back to peer up into the rising glory of the painted peaks, she decided that this place—this bizarre array of unbelievable color—was not even in the same league as the Auburn Dunes.

Not even in the same world.

As she marveled at the strokes of ruby and sapphire and gold and emerald that rolled atop each of the foothills before flaring wide to soar up even the steepest of crags, a demoralizing awareness struck her low in the gut.

I am going to have to climb these rainbows.

Only if you keep insisting on neglecting your innermost shield.

Savallin's gaze snapped to the spectral leaning against the indigo boulder. The spectral... whose full lips were pursed tight... the spectral whose mouth had not moved at all.

You are quite literally thrumming with power, Savallin. It is a beacon to all other elemental beings—to all other beings created by elemental power.

The everlast's slim arms were crossed calmly over her chest, her eternal face as bored as could be, as she angled that head of moon-pale hair to one side. But the Keeper—she was fixated upon what the female had said.

I am... a beacon? To... to all other... to what other beings?

Closing her eyes of ice and reclining farther, Audrian sighed through her nose.

Your uncut might is astounding, covenary. So much so that it actually chafes my skin.

At that, a whisper of rose blossomed high along the covenary's creamy, caramel cheekbones.

Your veil, your outer shield, is strong. Understandably so, as you have long hidden your physical ability from your sisters. But your inner ability, Covelette—the most fearsome weapon in your arsenal—you leave it totally unguarded. Why?

Because we—because Covenarykind—we have no Lumin. Not like your people. Not like you do. We do not have to hide what cannot be seen.

You know better than that, Savallin Prim. Protecting yourself—every part of yourself—should be second nature to you by now.

I—The color along the Keeper's cheeks reddened.—*It is. I always*—

So, do it. The everlast beauty opened her eyes. *Protect yourself.*

And without warning, the silent warrior *bored* into her soul. Bored into it and ruptured it like glass—blasting it into countless pieces.

All at once, lifetimes of concern and worry and dread speared into Savallin's body. The onslaught seared her skin, the barrage of undying grief twisting her writhing muscles into unending knots. Her breath hitched—and then it stopped completely—as eternity upon eternity of unbridled emotion barreled into her chest, as the unimaginable pain cleaved her rib cage in two.

The Keeper fell to her knees. Then her hands.

No—

She was nearly gagging, choking on the freshest of air.

No more—

Hot tears flooded her eyes and tore at her heart.

"Well?" the tyrant demanded aloud. "What shall it be, Savallin Prim, Keeper of Wisdom?"

But Savallin could not—she would not—endure a moment more. Her very insides were roiling, churning with misery and anguish she had never known.

No, she panted to herself. *No, this is not real. It—*

"This is real. Very real. And only you can put an end to it."

No—she broke. *No.*

Not ever, not in anyone's presence, had she ever felt so small—so hopelessly outmatched. Her crumpled body curled around her trembling knees. And in the shadow of the infinite devastation crushing down upon her soul, in the shadow of the overwhelming heartbreak that would forever live on, in the shadow of the untold legions who lost their mighty eternities—in their shadow—her life... her brief, fleeting, mortal life... it was...

Worthless.

"No. You only pretend it is so. But out here, Savallin, with the closest sahira at least three days away, who is it you still pretend for?"

Blackness began to bloom at the edges of her vision.

"Who is it you still hide from?"

The astounding range of gemstone hues before her dwindled away until it was no more than a quaint sliver, dwindled away until even *that* shred was gone. And only when the world was lost for good—only when Savallin was surrounded by nothing save eternal sorrow and murky darkness—did she realize she was *not* alone.

For in those depthless shadows, staring back at her like twin flares in the night, a pair of eyes shone with light. And the covenary—she knew they did not belong to Audrian. She remembered them, though... those eyes of steel and stardust. She would never forget them, or what they had shown her. Even now, as she tumbled farther into that endless abyss of everlast despair, their first lesson—their first gift—drummed steadily in the farthest reaches of her mind.

You rise now.

The Keeper breathed it in deep.

Or you shall not rise again.

Another sturdy inhale had Audrian's chilly voice slicing in.

Who is it you still pretend for?

A breath in.

Who is it you still hide from?

And then, as she stole yet another mouthful of The Wilds' air, the Special Sentry's voice warmed to that of another.

You rise now, or you shall not rise again.

And with the shift—with that new yet old voice ringing through her mind, her memory, her soul—the Keeper stopped her pretending, at last.

She shoved her palms into the rock floor—shoved her palms through the rock floor. And as colorful dust and painted shards sprayed from where she struck, the covenary shattered through the blistering shame wrenching her spirit.

You rise now, or you shall not rise again.

Biting down harder, she heaved against the ambush of agony. Heaved against the agony that did not belong to her, until she had the momentum. And the moment she won out, Savallin drove that misery backward with everything she had. She drove it backward, and she drove it out.

Through the retreating blackness and sudden invasion of color, she saw it as the warrior—as her attacker—began to straighten. But the heartbeat she was again amongst her thoughts, and her thoughts alone, Savallin threw her walls of obsidian armor high. So high that nothing would breach them. Nothing everlasting, nothing fleeting—nothing at all. And still, she forced them higher, forged them thicker. Just as she had been taught.

She would protect her mind, protect herself, from anything that came for her. And the moment her stone shield locked into place within her mind, the overwhelming assault on her humanity—on her soul—stood no chance. It could not break through. The tremendous pain, the soul-crushing sorrow, subsided like a wave being pulled back to sea.

And as the Keeper of Widsom pushed off the ground and got to her feet, the Special Sentry of The Spectraline was grinning something fierce.

"You are terrifying when you smile, you understand that, right?"

The everlast warrior grinned even wider. "I am terrifying no matter what." And then, Audrian kicked off her indigo perch. "But maybe now you will think twice, Covelette, the next time you wish to greet the dawn by throwing blades at my heart."

Savallin's glowing jade eyes doubled in size. "You did not—"

But before she could finish the thought, the Keeper had flung a chamber-sized chunk of ruby mountain straight at the sentinel. The moment the boulder went airborne, the covenary scrambled—throwing air and raw charm and every forbidden incantation she could think of—to bring it back down to earth. To bring it down before—

The massive, swirled stone exploded into a million splintered pieces, shattering into a massive cloud of pigment against an impenetrable, glittering shield. Against an Everlast Stellae. And the one who effortlessly wielded that Stellae was cackling uproariously at the covenary's Soulful outburst.

"Well, I certainly apologize for the crude tactics, Savallin," the Special Sentry shook off her shield, her eyebrows arching high. "But before I strolled you into Death's Dominion like a lamb to slaughter, I had to be sure you could heft that shield."

As Savallin reeled, the everlast she-devil inclined her head toward the peaks at her back. Then, in her cheeriest tone, she made everything so much worse.

"In the unlikely event it is not yet apparent, if you drop that shield once we set foot into the Alps—if you so much as let it slip—it will not be only your life that is forfeit." Her words had not yet ripened when Audrian snickered again. "For what awaits us, up there"—her frozen gaze skated across the striped swells—"up there, masked by the beauty of the Rainbow... well, it makes *me* seem bland."

And then, as if they were *not* about to traipse into a place called Death's Dominion, the Special Sentry clapped an arm around the Keeper's shoulders.

"Anyhow, with that little chore behind us," the unhinged warrior was all but beaming as she ushered Sav toward one of the smooth rock faces, "now, Savallin Prim, you and I shall have ourselves a bit of fun."

Chapter 41

THE CITY

For the first time in many moons, Everly Castile awoke in a soundless, sun-drenched apartment. Beyond her sealed chamber door, there was no clatter of kitchen pans, no clanking of silver utensils upon ceramic, no savory wafts of frying meat.

Strange, she thought.

Slipping on the pair of wool-lined moccasins waiting beneath her bedside, she padded out of her bedchamber and into the main quarter. After just a few steps, the spectraline found that the wide, marble island in the center of the sunlit kitchen was wholly untouched. And off to the right, the oversized sofa sat undisturbed as well.

Empty.

"Bris?" she called out as she strode for the private chamber at the other end of the corridor. "I was thinking... how do you feel about *BigGluteBris?*"

There was neither a rustle of bed linens nor a huff of displeasure as she neared the oaken door.

"No?" Her knuckles rapped softly against the painted wood. "What about *BigButtBris*? Or... no! How about *BigAssBris*?"

The immortal warrior, though, did *not* take the bait. So she knocked again, louder this time.

"*BrisIsABigAss*?"

Still nothing from behind the door. She must have thoroughly pissed the male off the night before. Good. Perhaps now he would cease with the overprotective, control-hungry nonsense.

Her fist banged against the heavy wood.

"Maybe *BristolLikesGluteStuff* suits your interests better?" she tsked, pressing her ear to the oak. "Or... was it butt stuff?"

Oh, come on.

But even with the exceptional hearing she'd been gifted, Everly didn't pick up so much as the faintest hint of a chest rising and falling.

Fine, she grumbled to herself. *Let's see how you like being violated.*

"I've got it," she sang excitedly, twisting down on the handle. "*BristolMy*..." The door swung free. "...*Biscuit.*"

A familiar tingling sensation prickled up the length of the her spine.

The chamber's large bed was undisturbed—each pillow in its place, the white linens crisp and tucked tight. Clearly unslept in. And aside from that, there were no other signs of the male she had walked away from on that sidewalk.

And suddenly, that vow he had snarled at her, over and over, crept into the corners of her memory.

You can continue to refuse me, Ev, but make no mistake—in doing so, you are conceding your freedom.

For, in all the centuries Everly had known Brigadier Dalon Bristolwood, the male had only ever broken a vow *once*.

No, she breathed. No—their spat, that tiff—it wasn't enough to change his mind. Nothing would change his mind. The brute would never give up and leave so easily. No matter how badly she had wished for it.

But then, before she could settle upon a single course of action, three booming knocks shook the entry door on its hinges. The ancient, unwelcomed strain that had begun tugging on her chest laxed as she whipped on a heel and strode for the foyer. Her heart was nearly beating normally when she gripped the handle and pulled open the door.

"Where have you—"

The demand turned to ash in her throat.

"What?" Having been caught mid-yawn, the mortal ceased rubbing his neck to answer. "Uh... I've been at work? My shift ended not too—"

"Have you seen Bristol?"

Only then did the man in the red ballcap begin to notice the unease limning her delicate features.

"*Oh*. Oh!" With one hand, he spun the hat backwards. "Yeah, no. He crashed on our couch last night."

Everly released the breath she'd been holding.

"Yeah, no—he's all good. He was still there when I got home to shower. I just figured he didn't want to wake the girl curled up beside him."

Her lungs stuttered.

The girl?

The mortal man with the silken tufts of hair peeking from beneath his cap might have said more—might have kept talking about the scene back at his dwelling, might have switched topics altogether—but Everly's mind had gone utterly still as a chalky fog crept across her vision.

Blustery winds atop salt-bleached wharfs sang through her memory like burial bells.

"Everly?"

That name—that name sounded so distant through the thick, blinding mist of times lost.

A clouded sky over a sea pristine with winter blues dissolved in fresh light.

"Everly?"

Her eyes were open, open wide—likely churning as bright as those cliff-bottom tides—but still, she could not see. Vaguely, as if through a wall of warped glass, she recalled that there had once been a mortal standing before her. But still, she could not see.

Flames—flames of the lost, flames she had never herself seen—engulfed her sight.

"Everly?!" Calloused palms, like iron vices, gripped her upper arms. "Ev, can you hear me?"

Ev? her memory echoed cautiously. *Ev.*

"Everly? If you can hear me, it's going to be okay."

The relic in hiding called from the past. Called as a relic of silence.

"Bristol is fine."

Bristol.

"You are going to be fine."

Bris.

"It's only a panic attack—"

Attack.

Everly's battle-honed awareness slammed back into her immortal body as that chalky haze of reflection split in two.

"Are you okay?" The deep, warm brown of the eyes before her guttered in relief as the mortal panted, "Gods, Ev! What was that?"

The female only blinked at the clear daylight. When had they come inside? How had they gotten down... she turned a slow semi-circle. Down here? Here, on the floor, her body pulled high onto his lap. An amber lake of whole milk and spiced chai rippled around them.

"Does that..." The man's chest caved low before refilling. "...happen a lot?"

Does what... She focused up on the mortal's stricken face.

"I..." She tried, but from where her head rested against his rib cage, the rapid beating of his heart was a ferocious war drum in her inner ear. "No... no. It... doesn't."

"Was it... did I say something?"

"No." She sat upright, drawing her long legs in close so the front door could sway fully shut. "No, I just thought..." Her sigh was leaden with guilt. "Last night, I... well, I got irritated and... and I kicked him—Bris—while he was already down."

After the sorry male had been down for an age, no less.

The mortal steadied her hands when they began to tremble. She did not pull them away.

"And then... then he never came home."

His thumbs pressed reassuring circles into the backs of her hands.

"So, naturally, I thought something terrible had happened to him," she swallowed audibly. "I thought something terrible had happened, and that it was my fault."

With an easy tug, Mortal Jay had her back upon his lap.

"But he's fine. Like you said—he is fine. I am fine."

The heaviness of his arms almost felt nice as they wrapped around her. His breath was a caress along the curve of her neck when he spoke again.

"You are fine, all right?" Everly shifted in his hold at the darkening in his tone. "And"—the muscles in his arms stiffened around her—"you are *finally* alone."

All that concern Mortal Jay had worn on his face—all that fear and tenderness—vanished. The sole sentiment left behind, carved into those handsome features, burned in the set of his jaw and the intensity of his stare: hunger. Hunger of the worst sort.

Fucking males, Ever-damned or otherwise.

"Jay." Everly's sharp plea speared like an arrow through the rising tension. "Jay, no."

But that fast, the man's big brown eyes had charred to the darkest cinders of coal.

"Jay," she tried again, harsher. "If I've given you the wrong impression, I—"

"Shut. Up." He growled, shoving his body up off the hardwood in one powerful motion.

"I—I'm sorry, I shouldn't have—"

"I said"—the human yanked backward on the length of her hair until her eyes met his—"*shut up.*"

And the spectral warrior living within her... did. For she could not simply toss the human back through her entry door—back through the very door itself. She could neither choke off his oxygen nor render him unconscious. For her hands were bound by The Oath of Obscurity.

She could do nothing that a mortal woman of like build could not. And resisting him? Resisting that want in his eye? She did not think a mortal woman capable of such.

But as the broad-shouldered man moved toward the barren island at the heart of the lonely kitchen, the spectral snickered to herself. Snickered at the thought of every mortal king who had offered their kingdom for the promise of a night with her—one night.

And these men? These mortal men of today who believed the worth of a woman to be no more than a few cups of coffee? Shameful. Disgraceful.

Oath of Obscurity, my eternal ass.

"Ja—"

But his palm clamped down over her mouth as he set her body on the edge of the marble.

"I promise," his hot whisper sent needle-pricks racing down her core, "I'll be gentle."

The female looked into his face through thick lashes as he slid the lace hem of her thin nightie up her thighs. With just that glance it was plain to see—the mortal was well and wholly lost to that dark, all-consuming fire of longing.

"Unless, of course..." Gripping Everly hard beneath the knee, Jay jerked her forward into his waiting hips. "...you beg me not to."

And then, the force of his need driving her thighs wide, Mortal Jay thrust her down upon that cold, stone countertop. But Everly—she was not a human woman, she was not a woman at all, and she had never once doubted her value.

Not even for a kingdom, Mortal Jay.

Centuries of mindless obedience shattered across the kitchen. She let it go, willed it to fall, let her training, her muscle memory, take over from there. For she had never been anything other than a spectraline warrior, and she could very well resist the likes of him.

Before the mortal could get his greedy, entitled hand around her throat, she wedged the heel of her foot up into his. And wielding his own strength—his own weight—against him, she held him off, held him back, held him at bay.

"I said... *no.*"

Her immortal temper was still shredding through that archaic oath like a ship through stormy seas when Mortal Jay stopped cold—when the man caught in the Maelstrom freed himself at last.

That thick, voracious murk blackening his eyes cleared. Warm, chestnut brown shone once more. She felt his throat bob. Watched his jaw work. Listened as his mouth opened... then closed again.

The man's palms shook as he raised them in submission, as he staggered back a step, and then found her face.

"I don't know what... I don't... I am so—" he tried, but choked on the taste of his own voice. "Ev—Everly," he rasped. "Everly, I am *so* sorry."

Not only did Mortal Jay eagerly mop up the chai lake spreading across the foyer floor, but he also made the trek back downstairs and must have nearly sprinted the two city blocks to fetch Everly another.

The female was just about finished dressing for the day when he knocked upon the entry once more. She did not walk to the door, though. No—the human could wait a few moments. He could wait, out in that chilly elevator lobby, and relive her thorough rejection over and over.

She could feel it in her bones, as she stood before the bathing chamber mirror weaving the cherry-kissed-cocoa strands of her hair into a tight plait, that today was going to be a long one. Tying the braid at her waist, she took one last look at the figure in the pale jeans and dark sweater. Then, stepping into one knee-high boot after the other, she strode for the foyer.

"Pastries," Mortal Jay smiled bright. "To atone."

Everly arched a thick brow but let him pass.

"I didn't know which ones were your favorites," he admitted, placing a muted-pink box on the island. "So, I got them all."

The human pulled the end of the thin twine and the box's simple bow gave way. He propped open the lid. Everly's curiosity—and her undying sweet tooth—would be the end of her. Closing the entry door, she ambled over to Jay's side and peered in.

Her heart quickened just a beat.

"I swear to you, Ev," his hand was on her lower back, "I swear, I did not come over here for... well, for *that*."

Many a gilded kingdom she may be worth, but a pastel box with pastries abounding... an argument could be made.

"You were just so sad. And then, so relieved."

There were three fruit-sprinkled cakes glistening atop sweet pools of cream—peach and raspberry-red.

"And then... in my arms, my lap. In that dress thing. I just..."

Along the back of the box, golden swirls of cloud-soft dough dusted with powdered and crystalline sugar beckoned to her.

"I am truly sorry. Really, I am."

But ultimately, it was the fat, flaky pastry in the center of the assortment that walked away with her hand—that walked away in her hand.

"It's fine, Jay." A mouthful of warm, buttery layers and caramel-glazed almond slivers overlapped the thought. "It happens."

And even with her absolute lack of decorum, it was immense solace that illuminated the brown eyes beside her—immense solace slathered with hints of disbelief as Mortal Jay gaped at her, gaped at how readily she gulped down treat after treat.

"Are you almost..." A quarter of an hour later, when he had found the courage to speak again, his words were worlds lighter than before. "Uh, I don't mean to rush you or anything—take your time—but our ticket slot is in half an hour."

Everly, her cheeks stuffed with vanilla crème and hazelnut dough, paused her chewing long enough to scrunch her forehead.

"Our ticket slot?"

The taxi ride was not pleasant. Sitting on the torn plastic of the car's back bench, every bump and sudden, screeching stop somehow felt infinitely worse than it needed to. And the clear acrylic partition in front of her—even with its plastering of tip notices and safety warnings—did little to block out the barrage of angry horns and obscene gestures from the street beyond.

Mortal Jay, obviously used to this sort of automotive torture, asked quietly, "Did you catch the news this morning?"

The news? On what?

Everly did not have a human television set nor one of their soul-sucking glass handhelds. And besides, he should already know the answer, seeing as how he'd barged in on her still in her nightclothes.

"What news?" she countered, her tone—as per usual—uninterested.

Spears of sunlight glinted off the glass towers that whizzed by on both sides of the avenue. The hordes of people shuffling about, as if their days were not indeed finite, didn't seem to notice the bolts of light ricocheting past.

"Okay, so get this," Mortal Jay said, his subdued speech a bit more animated. "They finally found that guy—you know, the one police suspected of ordering that high-rise fire not too long ago."

Everly pulled her focus off the passing mortals.

"The one across the street from me?"

Lines formed between the man's dark brows—like he did not remember. Like he had somehow forgotten the spectacle entirely.

"Oh. Oh, no." His forehead smoothed once more. "No, it was one farther back. A few months ago."

Perhaps the recall of humanity suffered more, from their fanatic ingestion of microplastics, than she first realized.

"Oh." A half-hearted smile bloomed upon her lips. "Well, that's good, isn't it?"

A series of escalating honks, followed by a volley of colorful swears from the busy crosswalk before them, rattled into her eardrums. Behind the human, the great buildings began to shrink from the sky.

"I mean, hell yeah." But then—maybe after recalling who he was talking to—Mortal Jay bit back on that excitement a bit. "Definitely, yes. It's just that... well, the discovery... it was *really* gruesome. I mean, even by organized crime standards."

Everly grimaced, a half-dozen pastries unexpectedly feeling like stones in her belly.

"Do I even want to know?"

"Hmmm." The mortal hummed aloud, clapping a tanned hand atop her knee. "How do you feel about... roasted, skinless—"

"No, sir." She covered her ears. "Not another word out of that beastly mouth."

Mortal Jay's husky laugh filled the backseat.

"What?" he pleaded, the portrait of innocence. "I was going to say chicken."

The glare she cast his way showed just how deeply she believed that.

On the inside, though, her veins heated at the memory of Bristol's pout as he'd begrudgingly, yet expertly, done her darkest bidding. At the way the male had not once questioned her—not even as she taunted that kingpin with the peeling and preparing of his men for broil. At how the smolder in his sea-blue eyes had put that firelight to shame.

But just then, the taxi driver mashed hard on the brakes. If there had been any pad left, it was surely gone by the time the yellow car came to a squealing halt at the curb.

Everly looked out through the grubby handprints smeared across her window. "You said Bristol recommended this place?"

Mortal Jay's waiting grin spanned from ear to ear.

"He—well, sort of."

The female surveyed the desolate stretch of pavement guarded by a chain-link fence.

"He... more so *misled* me to the idea."

The flimsy, sagging perimeter continued on for what had to be at least a mile in each direction.

"I asked him—Bristol—if there was anything I could do to surprise you, to impress you."

She watched, in the reflection of the glass, as the warmth in Mortal Jay's eyes flickered.

"He snorted. In my face."

Fair, she supposed. *On his part.*

"But then, you know, right when I was heading out to go lay in traffic, he decided to add a dash of insult to injury."

And it was then Everly recognized what this place had once been.

"He said, 'There is *nothing* short of the very sky itself with the power to impress her.'"

The wings were fully extended from the sleek, gunmetal body of the fighter-attack aircraft parked at the end of the old runway. A silver boarding ladder angled up from the ground toward the tandem-seat cockpit. Above the two seats, the overhead glass canopy was locked in the open position.

"You can go first," Mortal Jay sighed as the pilot in the faded jumpsuit waved at them in greeting.

And the smile he got in return—it was genuine.

Everly was up the ladder and harnessed into the rear seat of the fighter jet within minutes. The helmet they'd forced upon her head pressed her cheeks toward her nose, but she did not mind. And when the human in the front seat hit the button to lower the overhead canopy, Everly forgot about the stupid helmet altogether.

"I hope you're ready," the pilot half-yelled into the helmet's radio. "Here comes the exciting part."

Outside the cockpit, at the edge of the sun-bleached tarmac, Jay held onto the brim of his ballcap as the F-18 fired up its twin engines. The mortal was beaming, waving as his hair blew wild in the wind. Everly could not help but smile and wave back at him as the aircraft neared the center of the runway strip.

"Here we go," the pilot shouted.

But the female hardly heard him—because that all-too-familiar thrum began buzzing low in her ears.

Fear.

It was radiating off the pilot. But not only—

Danger.

Everly whirled to where Jay had been standing. She beat her fists upon the glass, willing him to move. To run. But he didn't understand the warning. He couldn't hear anything over the roar of the engines. And the female could do nothing but watch helplessly as a black truck barreled through the chain-link fence at his back.

Her screams died in her throat as six hulking men, all in head-to-toe body armor, leapt from the truck. Streaks of glittering silver rained down the cracks splintering across the glass as that smiling, waving man had a canvas sack thrust over his head. The thrum in her ears rang louder, but still, she could not get to him. She could do nothing to help him—not as the team of men bludgeoned him to his knees—not as his body slumped to the battered pavement, not as they dragged him into the back of that truck.

But then, Everly remembered the pilot.

She ripped off her harness—tore it clean in two—as she lunged for him. But he had been ready. His palm smashed down on the control panel, and a thick, steel partition slammed up from between the seats. Half a beat later, a fine, golden mist began billowing into the cockpit.

Everly knew the taste the moment it touched her lips.

Chapter 42

THE CRYPTS

The promise of hot tears burned the backs of Ava's eyelids as the sound of her mother's name settled somberly upon her chest.

Cadence Carlisle.

It had been years—nearly two full decades—since Ava had whispered the name aloud. It felt wrong to say it, her name, without her being here to hear it.

The stinging in her eyes, the swelling in her throat, the sinking in her stomach—all of it grew worse as the woman seated across from her breathed, "You cannot keep blaming yourself, Ava."

A rasping sound—something caught between a choke and a laugh—scraped free of her chafed windpipe.

She most certainly *could* keep blaming herself, she thought. She most certainly could, and she most certainly would.

"What happened to your mother, Ava—it was not your fault." The earnest expression glowing upon Alice's face was fierce and gentle all at once. "What happened last night at the trampoline park—that was not your fault either."

Bullshit it wasn't, Ava swore to herself. *It was no one's fault, but mine.*

"You could not have stopped it, Ava." Again, that softly lapping tide of tender warmth wet the tendrils of an ever-mounting temper. "Neither event."

And just like that, where a lifetime of self-loathing had lingered—where an insatiable need to suffer had loitered unchallenged—steady waves of serenity swept in.   .

"What is that?" Ava's grumble was muted with fatigue. "What are you doing to me? What kind of counselor are you? Are you... like a hypnotist or something?"

"*I* am not doing anything to you," Alice tsked, her grin positively feline. "That sensation you're experiencing—that is a shattered soul *siphoning* what it needs from a healthy one."

Mother, Ava cursed under her breath. *I am stuck in a room with a woman who thinks she's some kind of fucking psychic.*

And even though the woman might fancy herself a psychic, Ava was fully aware she would remain in this crypt until Alice said otherwise. So, with nothing the hell else to do, she might as well take advantage of the curious opportunity in front of her.

"You spoke my mother's name almost as if you knew her," Ava indulged. "Did you?"

The lineless skin, the fine cosmetics applied with a skilled brush—both made pinpointing Alice's exact age difficult. Like every other woman in this city, Ava reasoned it was highly likely the one before her had paid handsomely for some sort of aftermarket work. But it was possible, she supposed, that Alice could be about her mother's age.

Restraint—a look Ava had not yet seen—tightened the woman's features.

"Yes," Alice admitted after a long, thoughtful pause. "And no."

With that, the last of the light faded from Ava's spirit. Hefting her elbows onto the metallic table, she began massaging the ache in her brow line with trembling fingertips. But then, the woman's voice began again.

"Yes, I did know Cadence. Better than most, in fact." Her fingers eased their kneading, but she did not lift her gaze. "Still, I did not know her in the way, that I believe, you are asking."

Without those holdout rays of hope hiding the path in, weariness crept heavy into Ava's bones. All at once, the buzz of the fluorescents, the creaking of the chairs, the smell of the stale air became too much.

"While I did not know her in this life," Alice continued as Ava scolded herself for humoring the crazy woman in the first place, "I have forever followed her life's work, Ava. I have long practiced her philosophies myself. And because of that— through our shared purpose—I feel as if I did know her."

Her life's work? Ava mocked silently. *Of course. Could there be anything more up a psychic's alley?*

For her mother, she had built her fortune peddling essential oils and other herbal remedies up and down the Eastern Seaboard.

"That is why I have come, Ava. That is why I answered your summons."

My... Ava mashed her eyes closed to keep them from spinning. *Summons?*

"I am here not only on your behalf, but on your mother's before you."

Just then, a medley of Alice's earlier words came spiraling back.

You beckoned me, Ava. So, the question you should be asking is, how long do you plan on keeping us down here?

Ava sat up, straightening in her chair.

"Alice," she asked cautiously, "what is it that you think my mother did for work?"

The challenge lining the woman's uptilted stare chipped away at Ava's confidence.

"What is it that you, Ava, think your mother did for work?"

Bunching her forehead, she opened her mouth to reply—but the only sound left in her mind was the tap, tap, tap of her beating heart.

"What motive might there have been, Ava, for a meek tincture empress to be slain in cold blood?"

"I…" But thought, speech, eluded Ava entirely. And though she still could not picture her mother—not outside those excruciating, unwelcome bursts—she recognized the wrong the moment it flowed from Alice's lips. "She was not meek."

The woman opposite her only brightened. Brightened, if not further admiring Ava's troubled face. And then she made her sentiment known.

"She was not," Alice nodded kindly. "Your mother could not have been meek, not even if she tried."

Something hidden deep within Ava began to warm.

"That is why, when fate came for her, your mother was not afraid."

Murmurs, words—sound of any kind—still tasted wrong upon her tongue, but she desperately wished for the mystic to elaborate. For her to keep folding back that security blanket of oblivion that had long obscured her memories.

And as if reading a letter written upon her face, Alice did just that.

"Cadence," she started, a gleam of pride highlighting her smooth cheekbones, "was many things."

Yes, Ava thought along. *She was strong and funny and smart and smelled of cinnamon and vanilla.*

"First and foremost," Alice's voice was without doubt, "she was a harbinger of peaceful revolution. But more than that, she was an ever-striking reminder to this world of those it had chosen to forget."

Ever-striking. Beautiful. Loving.

"Yet perhaps the title she cherished most—most besides being mother to you, of course—was being the steady, poignant voice of everyone who had been silenced before her."

The voice of... everyone? Of who? Who all had been silenced? Ava shoved against the guilt spreading in her chest. *The mother I knew, the woman I see only in glimpses... was she... if what Alice is preaching holds any truth at all... did I ever even know her? Ever know the true her?*

But the message, the soundless instructions, scribbled upon Ava's skin must have stayed the same, because Alice kept talking—kept describing a woman Ava did not remember.

"She was effective, your mother. Alone and without aid, that unwavering drive of hers, that inexorable energy—the very same energy living within you—brought forth safer working conditions, livable wages, and a more accessible network of care."

She... Ava plunged backward into the past, trying to remember every minute of their happy, too-short life together. *When had she had time to do all of that? To do any of that?*

"In the end, it seems"—the gleam on Alice's face swiftly hardened into something far more dangerous—"Cadence might have been too effective."

Ava could not feel her fingers, nor her toes. Her skin no longer registered the chill in the room. For all she could feel, all she could hear, were the words left unspoken.

"That is why the target she wore upon her back was as vibrant as it was. It had been painted in the essence of a life lit by coveting nothing more than fairness and equality for all."

When Alice leaned forward, reaching for her quivering hands, Ava did not pull away.

"Your mother, Ava—she had a special, unapologetic way of shaking the cocktail of society." The counselor gave her hands an easy, reassuring squeeze before adding, "Her honorable tendencies did not well mix with the fragility of today's patriarchy, nor did they pair with the rapacious appetites of the oligarchs who feed solely upon humanity."

Yeah, Ava sighed sadly. *Yeah, I bet they didn't.*

"And it was the latter—one perverse syndicate in particular—that sponsored the hunt for her head."

"Why?"

The slip of her own voice half-startled her. But across from her, behind those large, purple frames, the glint in the mystic's eyes became near lethal.

"Because she had finally beaten them at their own game. For years, she had worked quietly to get veiled legislation signed into law that would require developers to allot half of all their new builds and renovations to affordable housing." The swipes of severity accentuating her stare blurred a bit as she said, "Cadence dreamed of creating homes—real homes—for everyone still trapped in The Tenements. In the wards."

"It passed?" Ava asked, a new wave of tension seeping into the space between her shoulders. "Her legislation?"

"It passed," Alice smiled. "Right under their pompous, upturned noses."

An air of satisfaction wafted through the room before darkness again spread its shadowy wings.

"But," her counsel went on, "the consortium that developed those towers-to-be would not suffer it—being bested by a woman. So, in their tantrum, in their fit of rage, the syndicate deemed your mother's life a suitable sum for the damage she had dealt their bottom line."

The pressure crawling up Ava's back became full-blown pain. She would find them—those men. She would track down each and every one of them still living, and she would make it otherwise.

"And what happened to..." She began without direction, without first deciding what she most wanted to learn. Collecting herself for a moment, then another, she opened her mouth again. "Who remains of that consortium today?"

For Ava did not truly care what had happened to them after the fact. Whatever the punishment had been, she knew in her heart it had not been enough. Not for what they had done. And she had her own ideas of the justice they were owed.

"Actually, legal fees, illicit vices, and karmic energy relieved the world of most of them," Alice snickered. "*But*"— she sighed disapprovingly—"there is *one* who outlived all the rest. A son. An illegitimate son, born to a reluctant member of the household staff, but a son nonetheless."

"What"—Ava snarled, not at the woman, but at the world—"is his name?"

"I think you mean," Alice amended, sliding a folded slip of paper into Ava's tightly clasped hands, "what *was* his name?"

Chapter 43

THE CONSERVATORY

Commander Decard Battleson stood straight-backed and silent at the center of The Light Hall on the top level of The Conservatory. As he stared up into the three rows of sharp-eyed Senators, the last four filed in and found their seats.

It had taken an act of The Everstar herself to get them here. To get him here.

Two strapping fourth-series had carried him the entire distance from the dormitory to the restricted section of the healing pools in the lowest alcove of the bathing chamber. A team of naturopaths, highly skilled with saving salts and the tonic arts, had attended him while the ultra-potent waters did their work.

After a great expense of their many efforts, as The Everstar rose higher into the sky, only then had Decard been able to stand on his own. And as he tested his strength and stepped from the cerulean waters, a fresh uniform and new boots had been brought in.

While he had been sitting upon his useless ass, restoring, his younger brother, Dima Battleson, had raced to alert the shihan. It had been Shi, he heard, The Shihan of Shields, who had summoned The Crux. The sparsest of Senates, called upon solely in times of extraordinary crises.

And now, as he waited at the heart of the lofty, mountain chamber, as he stood upon the star where the colorful rays of light shining through the enormous, stained-glass clerestory met as one, as he stared into each of the stony faces who had gathered at Shi's request, Decard Battleson swallowed his dread.

The black-haired Senator seated in the middle of the bottom row banged his gavel once. The horror-stricken face and bright red of Jericho Dupree flashed in Decard's mind.

But the Senator, Senator Dnesda, addressed the hall, "Let us get straight to business, then."

Decard listened as the table of scribes at his back began their duty. Senator Dnesda focused his attention upon him.

"Do tell us, then, Commander. Why is it we have been summoned on this, otherwise fine, Spring Equinox?"

The large crowd of spectral and specling amassed in the upper gallery did not make so much as a sound.

Decard did not waste time.

"Senator, you have my deepest gratitude for answering the summons with such haste." His glance swept the three rows. "You all do."

From the top riser to the bottom row, heads of brown, black, silver, and straw dipped as one.

The Commander forged on.

"During the course of her Twenty-Third Canon, while she was still recovering from the brutal effects of"—he selected his words with the utmost discretion—"of the tremendously altered reality she had faced, Eleanora Everstar fell."

Waves of hushed murmurs and outright dismissal rolled through the balconies above.

He had expected that, of course. For they had no reason to believe him. Why would they? Eleanora had never fallen before. No, she was undefeated in her Canons. Had been since the day she arrived from nowhere. In their eyes, she already was, and would be, the Premier of this solar's sixth series. *A Premier to rival them all.*

They, the spectral of The Conservatory, were not prepared for what he must say. They could not yet fathom it. They might never fathom it. But still, with each of their narrowed eyes concentrated upon him, he did not let his heartache, his nerves, win out. He would not. Not after what she had given, what she had given them all.

"As commanded by this Senate, Eleanora's trial was conducted within The Citadel Ruin, atop the tallest Pillar of the Sky."

The gallery went sickly silent, each spectraline holding their breath for what might come.

"She breezed through her test, breezed through it with mastery never before seen," Decard said, glaring at Dnesda. "Even while chained from head to toe, Eleanora Everstar managed to kill five full spectral. Five trained shields."

Raising a thick, unimpressed brow, Dnesda merely quipped, "It seems, Commander, that perhaps your squadron is in need of remedial drills then."

"Perhaps that appraisal is fair, Senator," the Commander nodded his acquiescence, but on the inside, on the inside rage worthy of the goddess fallen, rage hot enough to burn even stars into ash, bellowed to the skies. "Considering she was able to do so even *after* the scheming of this Senate mandated she begin her ordeal with fatigue already weighing heavily upon her bones."

Through the daylit gallery, breaths caught and echoed along the high walls.

"You were the ones to slate the Twenty-Third Canon upon the nightfall of the Twenty-Second," Decard's fury had become a living thing. "A practice never before permitted in The Conservatory's long and storied history."

Not one soul, not a single immortal soul, amongst the crowd gathered in The Light Hall dared move.

"And yet," Decard blazed on, immense pride swelling within his chest, "Eleanora still executed her Canon swiftly, slyly, and with exemplary skill. She freed herself, bestowed upon the survivors a token of her appreciation, and then she began the long trek home."

He steeled himself for what followed. For what he wished, more than he had wished for anything in his eternity, had never happened.

"But, as she descended into the darkness, a terror not even she could think to face rose from the canyon." Glowering straight into Dnesda's beady, black eyes—glowering straight into the Elder who did not look a day past him—Decard dropped his incendiary: "The *ísdreki* fly again."

And every Shihan, every specling, in the mid and upper galleries, every Senator seated upon their polished, stone risers, every last spectraline in the hall collapsed into chaos.

But over the excitement, over the trepidation and disbelief, the Commander calmly reiterated, "The Beasts of Old live anew."

Senator Dnesda, having leapt from his seat, pounded his gavel into the black stone before him. A warrior-sized smear of shimmering charcoal filled Decard's vision.

"Quiet!" The Senator's voice boomed throughout the high chamber. "Quiet in the hall!"

And when the crowd at last settled, when the distraught shrieks and terrified bawls died out, the Senator addressed the Commander directly, "I will not ask you again, Commander, so listen intently. Why is it that we are convened here today?"

Decard Battleson blinked.

He did not understand... he had just finished telling them—telling The Senate, telling damn near everyone in The Conservatory—exactly why they had convened. His confusion must have been apparent because Senator Dnesda continued.

"I understand, Commander, that you were in rather poor condition when you arrived here earlier today."

Decard started, "No, Sena—"

"Do not interrupt me, soldier."

Obedience getting the better of him, the shield begrudgingly bit down on his soaring anger.

"I do understand," the Senator began again, "how taxing these Canons can be. Not only on the specling they are intended to test, but *also* on the spectral who we commission to perform their testing."

Decard seethed, his sights, his sense, beginning to blur.

"While I understand that *you* believe—wholeheartedly, even—in what you saw, I know, for a fact, that the Beasts of Old are just that," the Elder smiled to the hall, "Beasts *of Old*."

The conniving rat gripping the gavel had the upper hand, he knew. For it was impossible, improbable. The beasts should not exist. But he would not, nor would he ever, disclose to this Senate *how* the ísdreki had, in fact, been resurrected. How Eleanora Everstar, bleeding out and nearly mortal, had outwitted them all. How she had wielded their death chains to harness death itself. No, Decard would not out her like that. Never, fallen or otherwise.

So, he took it. The derision. The mockery. The ridicule. He took it all—every insult the Senator threw at him. And when he finally paused, when he at last rested from the attack upon his character, Decard was ready for him.

"I would not, however, be fulfilling my pledge to the Spectraline if I did not do my due diligence and ask you, Commander, what was it that made you think such a beast real?"

"Well, Senator. It was two things." He held his index finger before the risers. "The first being that, after said impossible beast whipped its tail into the Ever Step upon which Jericho Dupree and I clung, all that remained of your nephew was a warrior-shaped splotch of dark-gray starlight."

Gasps rang out through the assembly. The venomous bastard seated before him, though, did not so much as flinch. And Decard, he would not give him the chance to disgrace his friend. So, he lifted a second finger.

"And the final," he indicated towards his thigh, "the final is that before Eleanora Everstar began her descent of the Pillar, she hurtled a hexed dagger into my thigh. And, hard as I tried, the knife would not budge." He closed his eyes. They needed to hear this. They had to hear this. "After the beast struck my Pillar, the entire tower crumbled into pieces and toppled from the sky. Luckily, I was thrown onto an adjacent column face and then able to make the climb down."

His knees weakened at the memory.

"But, as I reached the ground, as my feet again felt the earth beneath them, a scream—the worst sound I have ever heard in this existence—tore through the night."

With his heavy, ruined heart, Decard Battleson looked to his leg. For Nora had known she could not let the ísdreki live. She had known she could not stand by and allow that monster to fly free, to endanger all who crossed its path. She had known, and had used him as bait to take it down.

Fearless, he thought. *She truly had been fearless.*

Through glistening eyes, he focused back upon his leg. For time was not on his side.

"And then," he began again, "then, the knife—*Nora's knife*—fell from my thigh."

There was a commotion from above and—

Stassie Everstar leapt from the uppermost gallery. She leapt, falling eighty paces through nothing but air, and landed not half a step from where Decard stood. She was white with wrath. He swallowed, just once. For he deserved what was to come.

"Coward," she fumed. "You are a coward, Decard Battleson."

Stassie, evidently, knew exactly how hexes worked. She knew that a hex... that it lasted only as long as the hexer.

Fuck, Nora had likely taught her.

"Of course she did." Although a head shorter, the elder Everstar made him feel smaller than he ever had before. "And she would never abandon someone to fight alone."

Decard opened his mouth to—to, well, he did not know what he could offer her, so he only closed it once more. A river of shine welled up in the bottoms of those haunting, silver eyes. *The Everstar eyes.*

He wanted her to know how sorry he was, how absolutely devastated and guilt-riddled he was. He wished for her to understand what immense respect, what love, he felt for her sister. But he did not know how to tell her. He did not know how to ease her pain that was certainly far, far worse than even his own.

And it must have been the grief—the staggering grief of all the spectraline assembled in The Senate chamber—that fogged his mind. For he could not think of one thing to say. Not one. So, instead, he said nothing at all. And the entirety of The Light Hall was mute along with him. Even those that did not fully fathom charm, or its intricacies, sent their hearts to the lone Everstar sister.

And by the time Decard had ousted that haze of regret from his mind, by the time he had recouped the strength to finish his desperate plea, by then, Tabor, Stassie's Parallel, had finally made it down the stairway and across the main floor to carry her away.

He felt her eyes—*their eyes*—boring craters into his soul the whole way out.

And then, scanning the faces of those who were left, Decard's attention snagged upon his own brother. Upon his face. Upon the face that looked... despondent. So, so despondent. Shattered, even. Dima was shattered. As were so many more in the crowd. And he understood then—understood what Eleanora Everstar had meant to all of these spectral.

A female from nowhere, with nothing. No givers, no nobility to her name. Not a day of training. Nothing, and yet, she had walked through those starstone gates and bested them all. Himself included. Time and time again. And she, she had become the very embodiment of power—of near invincible power. So, for her to be beaten, for that kind of power to meet its match, it was an especially sobering sort of blow.

And it was like they already knew what his next words were to be. The next words that he had sprinted hundreds of leagues across plains and rivers and deserts and mountains, without so much as a solitary respite, to speak. And yet, his brother watched him, indescribable despair darkening his fire-forged stare.

It was for him, his little brother, that Decard spoke.

"Assembled Senators, the reason I trust this threat as fact, the undeniable truth as to why it is so imperative that you raise the defenses and alert the outposts this very moment, is that you know as well as I"—he lifted his head to meet each Elder—"that not one beast living upon this earth, not one living amidst this time, not one has ever possessed the overwhelming might it would take *to kill* Eleanora Everstar."

And there was not a strike of Senator Dnesda's gavel loud enough to quell the frenzied roar that erupted from the gathered spectraline.

Chapter 44

THE CITY

The Oath of Obscurity

Protect this world from what cannot be sought.
Protect this world from what is Known and what is Not.
Lesserkind thou shield, they shall be none so wise.
Shroud thy might, shroud thy will, the Ever in thy guise.
For if thou choose fail, thy name shall be lost forever.
For if thou choose fail, time shall reminisce thou never.

A black boot, driven with fury, stomped down onto the spectraline's unbraced abdomen. Her body pitched upward, her eyelids flitting, as a wave of foul, amber-green fluid surged from her belly—from her lungs—and spewed across the floor.

"It's about time you wake up and rejoin the fun, Everly," that godsdamned voice croaked for the umpteenth time.

Her head pounded and her throat burned as she fought to part her eyes. The faces scowling from above her—the murky structure decaying at their backs—all blurred into focus far too slowly.

The sole illumination in the reeking abyss flickered from the rot-covered bottoms of the massive tanks lining the peeling walls. The massive, dormant tanks housing their reserve of putrid, stagnant water.

"Get up!" A steel-toed foot slammed into the softness between her ribs. "You stuck-up whore."

Long, rough fingers scraped into the crown of her sopping braid and yanked high. A muffled groan escaped her lips as the rusted barbed wire binding her lower legs sliced into her skin. Heat bloomed in the bites as trickles of red spilled from where she knelt.

The gangly human—the half-breed hunter—lifted her chin. "I assume you intend on sticking to your story?"

Everly only stared at his face. At his utterly unremarkable, mortal face. For the man—for none of the men—stalking through the crypt possessed even a trace of that ethereal coloring The Israsensore were known for. Not so much as a hint of the fine moonlit features they had borne throughout history.

"Very well, then," the man sighed, dropping her chin once more. "Seeing as how completely unhelpful and forthcoming you have turned out to be, and because I am wise enough to appreciate that even recurring drownings will not kill you"— as if on cue, the uppermost portion of what had at one time been one of the most fearsome predators in all the seas drifted by in the tainted tank nearest them—"not to mention the colossal time constraint we are operating under, well, we are going to try something a little different."

The jagged teeth on the steel cord wrapped around her wrists dug further into her flesh as the man at her back joyously stepped on the slack in the line.

"We know that your... your *colleague* was dispatched to this city with the sole mission of retrieving The Night Heir."

There is not a chance in Sempenihil that—my colleague—told you that.

Because, for his many, many faults, her *colleague*—all brawn and bullheadedness—would not break for anything. There was no form of torture, no flavor of anguish, no want, nor wish capable of compelling the Brigadier to even consider cracking.

Plus, for The Spectraline Senate to task him with that? No. For that mission, it would be folly. A sheer waste of his immortality. The Night Heir was but a legend. A long-whispered-of, longer-felled, bedtime legend. A legend fallen to time.

"So, Everly, I am only going to ask you once more: who ordered you here?"

The female simply hunched forward against her sharp bindings, coughing and racking her chest until the remnants of what had formerly called the now-septic tanks home spilled from her torn airways.

Without warning, a metal pipe smashed into the back of her skull. Her brain bounced. Her vision flashed bright. The overly saturated skin on her wrists and shins split wide.

"Fuck you," she spat, her voice hoarse. "I told you, you fucking jackass, nobody orders *me* anywhere."

"Ah, right. You did say that." The aspirant Captain of the demi-squad clicked his tongue, his pallor glowing with sickliness in the wavering tank lights. "Is that, perhaps, because your *colleague* had you thrown out of The Shield?"

Everly did not move. She did not blink. She did not think. She did not let herself venture anywhere near that demoralizing memory. That silver-painted plain.

"Do you no longer take orders because your very own Brigadier—your second-in-command—had you stripped of your rank and tossed out of time like the soulless traitor he truly is?"

He wouldn't... She rummaged for clarity as her thoughts slowed, as the world slowed. *He would not tell them that... not these clowns.* But then, *then* the ache of doubt, of insecurity, clawed into her chest. *Would he...*

Her face, while black and blue, remained neutral—void of any and all emotion. But her mind, her mind scoured each recent conversation, each book in the library of her memories, every last interaction for the answers it sought. Answers to where Bristol might be now. Answers to what had befallen him.

What would befall him? Is he still alive? Does eternity yet beat in his chest? What else do these hunters know? How do they know it? Who had told—

But at that moment, from the profuse darkness beyond the eerie glow of the tanks, two burly halflings dragged an old wooden chair from the distant corridor.

Mortal Jay.

"If you will not talk for your own sake," the foggy-eyed hunter with the veritable snout barked, "then maybe you will talk for his."

The mortal's proud shoulders were painfully cowed, his considerable form limp and bruised nearly beyond recognition.

Goddess, Everly's throat worked. *What have they done to him? Why have they...* But she took a breath, further slowing the rush of her thoughts. *What do the demi-sensore think he knows? What could they possibly fathom a mortal would know?*

A mortal who... who had, by the looks of him, waged a mighty war. The female did not even *try* to hide the fracture cleaving her immortal chest.

"What is it," she growled so low that the hair on her own arms rose, "that you think I know?"

Her snarled words were aimed at no one and everyone at once. But her cold, dark eyes stayed fixed upon the human man beaten unconscious in the chair.

"What great insight do you believe, in that gods-fucked mind of yours, that *I* can provide to you?"

The metal pipe sang out again, this time crashing into the bones of her lower back with a force no mortal should be able to wield. Her body arched, the strain sundering her flesh anew. The red pool around her knees grew darker, deeper.

"Tell me, Everly, why do you suppose it is"—the soon-to-be-dead squad leader droned—"that we"—with a sweeping gesture, he indicated each of the men spread about the concrete chamber—"are so vigorously pursuing, and killing, your kind?"

"I do not suppose," her focus still ducked the lanky demi-ring leader, "that I give a single blasted fuck—"

The iron pipe belted against her cheekbone, against her nose. Warm blood gushed down her chin. The demi-wit only dipped his finger into the crimson falls spilling over her lips. He raised it to his face, marveled at his work in the dim light.

"It is because we, *Lesserkind,* as you so thoughtfully deemed us, do not need—nor do we want—your kind's pompous sheltering."

A fourth halfling emerged from the black corridor farthest from her.

"No, Lesserkind has nothing to fear. Nothing to fear but *you.* For you, your kind—*you* are the one true evil. The one true evil that plagues us all, that dooms this world."

Everly could not find it within herself to refute the pompous accusation. No, The Spectraline were arrogant by nature. But evil? *No.* And for these whimpering halflings, for these absolute abominations, to dare hurl an allegation like that... an allegation so backward, so utterly baseless—it was blasphemy in its purest form. A dishonor to every shield, every courageous spectraline warrior, who had thanklessly laid their own eternities down for them. Thanklessly given everything for them. *For Lesserkind.*

And besides, she knew—knew deep within her undying heart—that not one of the demi-sensore marching through this subterranean cesspool had ever once laid eyes upon the evil their self-professed leader now preached of. And if they were lucky, if The Spectraline Shield kept holding that line, it would forever stay that way.

"And when we have wiped you and yours from this earth, once and for all, Lesserkind will be the better for it," the halfling's cloudy gaze eddied with excitement. "Lesserkind will revel in it. Because Lesserkind will, for the first time in our history, live freely."

As the leader's sermon ended, the fourth half-mortal, half-filth set the heavy, compact box he had been toting between Mortal Jay's unmoving feet. And then—then every abomination in the chamber turned toward the bleeding female. She tried to block them out, tried to block it all out. All, save the broken man bound to the bowing chair. All, save the kind-eyed human who had shown her nothing but warmth and wanting.

And at last, when the glow of the crypt and the harsh, expectant faces within had all fallen away—when it was only her and him once more—Everly sucked in a breath and snarled, "Heed me when I say, from the very, very bottom of my soul, that I wholeheartedly believe that you are in dire need of professional help."

The muted gingerroot hair of the hunter, hovering much too close to her, shook as he laughed. The sound was a sharp, cruel, grating thing. But across the damp chamber, from the deepest throes of oblivion, Mortal Jay opened his eyes. And for half a heartbeat, for half a breath, those wide, brown eyes shone through the bleakness—truly shone—their defiance scorching the dark. But just as abruptly as they had parted, they closed again.

"No," Everly exhaled as that slightest glimpse of the Maelstrom living within vanished from the mortal's face.

"Oh, hush. I have been more than generous with you." The greenish demi-sensore smirked over his bony shoulder as the fourth of his underlings clamped two metal clips to Mortal Jay's brutalized chest. To his brutalized, exposed chest. "I mean, I have given you what... like twenty-five opportunities so far? Honestly, that seems more than fair."

And with a grin, he signaled to the underling. The underling who flipped the switch on the small box the clips were corded to.

"No!" Everly tugged against her barbed fetters. "Stop!"

"You reap what you sow, I presume," the leader lilted as he called for more juice.

"Stop this!" Her command—her plea—echoed off the thick walls of the stuffy chamber. "Stop it, now!"

Jay's lifeless body thrashed against the unforgiving currents searing through his mortal veins. The chair beneath him creaked and shrieked, threatening to buckle under his weight, under the one-sided tussle. Frothy, white foam began forming at the corners of his mouth. A wet, gurgling noise spilled from his lips.

"Please!" she screamed, the full power of her lungs carrying the broken request. "Please, make it stop."

But with an elated glimmer in his black eyes, the demi-sensore ogre at the controls cranked the power of the battery up a notch. Every muscle, every last tendon and cell in the mortal's body tensed and tore as that white-hot electricity coursed through him. Thick, dark blood ran from his mouth, streaming down his chest.

"I was not ordered here," Everly choked. "I was not ordered to this city." And her hands, still wired behind her back, trembled. "I do not take orders. Not anymore." The sureness of her own chest faltered. "*Never again.*" Her voice, at last, shuddered when the faces of those she had loved—

when the faces of all who had fallen before, all who they had directed to die—raced to the forefront. "Not from them."

Finally, the lanky abomination in charge turned back to peer down at the female. He rolled his thin, cracked lips, considering her, weighing her words. He roved his repulsive, degenerate eyes along every inch of her immortal form as he mulled, as Mortal Jay fought for his fleeting life.

"I swear to you," Everly ground her teeth, biting back both profanities and promises, "I am without allegiance."

And then, as the blood spraying from Mortal Jay's lips darkened to black, the perversion before her lifted his hand. And across the rancid space, his insipid lackey, at last, severed the power.

"Good," the demi-sensore crooned. "Very good."

But Everly—she did not see him. No, the female hardly registered his festering presence, at all. For her gaze was locked upon the unresponsive human so far out of her reach.

"I have a proposition for you, Everly Castile."

Still, she did not meet that galling stare.

"The Israsensore," he said, and the halfling's tone was strangely assured—oddly steady—for someone giving name to the greatest threat this world has yet known. "We rise again."

And after everything they had done to her—after continual drownings, after the constant assaults, after being forced to watch as the mortal all but perished—after all of that, the spectraline found herself truly unable to breathe. Not because the half-breed thought himself a true israsensore, no, but because he truthfully believed in the last words he said.

"Ally yourself with our host, Everly," the scheming abomination began again as she plummeted into an inescapable pit of the past. Of her past. "Join us in ending those who tried to end you. Aid us in eradicating the vermin who dared exile you."

And the demi-sensore lording over her—no longer were his claims entirely off base. No. For The Spectraline Senate, The Shield—they *had* stolen everything from her. Everything and everyone who had ever truly mattered to her.

Whatever look she now wore upon her disfigured face, it must have been plain—must have lain her feelings bare—for the demi underlings at her back began the slow, arduous process of unwinding the barbed wires coiled around her wrists. The rusted barbed wires wedged deep within her flesh. The wires that had been secured to six enormous anchor blocks that ripped her arms from their sockets each time they were dropped into the putrefied tank.

And yet, as the underlings separated the steel from her skin—as her mind, her tunnels of memory, scorched with acidic fury—as her thoughts burned to black—the female could not peel her eyes from the comatose form still tethered to his sagging chair. From the beaten, bloodied, ruined man she could not help. From the beaten, bloodied, ruined man her past had put there. From the most recent, in the long line of losses, owed to The Spectraline Senate.

For the man strapped to that chair—the friend, the normally smiling face—*he* was the Ever-forsaken chambermate of the halfling now standing at her side. The halfling who Everly had seen once before. Had met once before. That first night. The night she had indulged Mortal Jay to avoid Bristol's capture. A decision—a choice—that could not be coincidence.

For it fell upon the very same night, fate would have it, that her listed address was fire-bombed to Sempenihil. The listed address that a faithful soldier of The Shield would have readily given, no questions asked, to The Spectraline Senate. The very same faithful soldier who had deceived her so many times before. The righteous male who *lived* to betray her—to betray those she cared for. The male who had proved it by undermining her time and time again throughout her eternity.

Dalon Bristolwood, she seethed to herself. *The honored, the respected Brigadier of The Spectraline Shield.*

The demi-sensore in charge was still sneering at her when his fumbling thugs, at last, cut the steel line around her shins. The line connected to the overhead crane they had used to drop her—and the blocks—into the Lastisap-soured creature tanks. Lastisap they could only have gotten from *one* place.

Finally, Everly Castile drew her attention from the destroyed figure opposite her and asked, "What is it, Lochlan, that you require of me?"

Chapter 45

THE CROSSING

Savallin Prim had spent a good portion of her life amongst mountains. None of them, though—not a one—had been anything like these.

Where the peaks of her formative years had been either pale-blue and barren or blanketed in powdery, white snow, these alps—the ones she was now hurtling through so fast it drew tears from her eyes—blazed with a vibrancy known only in dream.

From in front of her, the icy-cool female checked back. "I trust you are holding on this time, Keeper of *Wisdom*?"

Savallin craned left, craned around Audrian to see a—

"Audria—"

But her breathless scream was ripped away into nothing.

And the switchback sleigh—the sleek, enchanted sled hewn of colorful rock and darkest nightmares—plummeted over the cliff.

The covenary's stomach shot to her throat, but her hands, they clenched hard upon the smooth, stone scales along the spine of the sleigh as it again slammed down onto the sheer face of the painted mountain. Her feathered curls and torso alike launched backward, but her hold did not budge, not even a fraction, as the sled bounced thrice and gained speed.

There were no words, no thoughts—not as the stone sleigh raced and weaved along the nearly vertical, serpentining path carved into the glittering, emerald band at the heart of the alpine rainbow.

Jagged, warped spears of cobalt, gold, and petrified wood rushed by on both sides as the sleigh fell-flew down the cliff face. Every time one of those beautiful spikes passed too close, an invisible shield of sunlight shattered them into dust. Sav twisted to watch as one of those clouds of blue and yellow and red swirled in their wake. But then, a laugh—wild and wholly unafraid—rang out over the heavy thundering in her chest.

She whipped back around, digging her fingers farther into the sleigh's ruby-golden scales as a renewed sense of horror took over. But Audrian, looking straight into the eyes of Hadi herself, threw her head back to the sky. She would have liked to toss her hands up as well, the Keeper presumed, if only the sleigh did not require every last drop of her immortal might simply to steer. The monstrosity was intended for charm—to be commanded by it and it alone—the Special Sentry had told her. But to cast, to call upon Soul or Seraphic in these alps, it would end in fading.

The sled pitched forward still, and the covenary very nearly choked. For over the spectral's slim shoulder, the feathery coverlet of clouds split wide, giving way to leagues upon leagues of naked air. Leagues upon leagues of naked, open air.

Blessed be the goddess, she whispered. *Blessed be Her.*

Thousands of paces below them, separated only by sure demise, dense groves of evergreens began blurring into focus. At their height, though—at the impossible speed with which their sled screamed down the mountainside—the towering trees might as well have been teeny, tiny blades of grass sprouting from the earth.

Yet, sure demise or otherwise, the paint-streaked beast of legend and stone continued its death plunge. Not only that— not only continued it—but quickened its haste. Winding striations of brilliant, gemstone hues blasted by, faster and faster until they—until the world—blended into one. One tunnel of many colors.

One dark tunnel, she thought. *Of magnificent light.*

And it was then that the Keeper felt it. Felt the broad, unchecked smile stretching like mad across her face. And when Audrian howled her delight to the heavens once more, Savallin found herself raising her own hands into the whir of the air above. And the young covenary—she did not know, not truly, what it was like to ride through the sky atop a shooting star, but this, she thought, was as close as anyone could ever hope to come.

And just as it had while she and her escort had sailed across the Auburn Dunes upon their Aerie Arras, a light wind kissed along her cheekbones and danced through her hair. As harmless as the cool breeze seemed, the covenary sincerely suspected that if not for the unwavering Stellae of the Special Sentry, the might of the alpine wind would most certainly carry her away.

But she did not care. Not now. Not as she and the sentinel rode upon the back of the stone creature who whooshed with ease along the glimmering, switchback mountain pass in between the clouds.

No. Atop this legendary, flying beast, Savallin had a hard time fearing anything. Not even the dark-eaters Audrian had warned her about, over and over, gave her pause now. In fact, not any of the dangers hidden amongst the Rainbow Alps worried her now. And it did not matter to her—not in the slightest—that the gorgeous yet horrifying beast carrying them down the steep and treacherous pass was only doing so thanks to immortal strength and forgotten shame.

The forgotten shame of those sentenced to die.

"Savallin," the everlast female said with an odd sternness. "I need you to trust me."

"Trust you?" Her brow bunched. "What—"

"It is about to get very windy." Audrian half-turned, giving her a wink. "Unless you wish to become airborne, Covelette, you will want to squeeze with your thighs."

The warrior had not gotten through the thick wall protecting her mind. Savallin had made sure of that, checking and rechecking her inner shield constantly. She would not allow herself to be the cause of either of their untimely fadings.

So, what is it she is readying for?

Still staring over her guardian's shoulder, the Keeper did not yet see any real cause for concern. Besides, of course, the insanely sheer drop back down to earth.

"Three," Audrian counted, elbowing the Keeper on the inner thigh, careful not to remove her hands from the helm for even a moment.

The covenary trained her eyes upon the winding path ahead, squinting as hard as she could manage against the rapidly approaching trail. But as she looked—as she focused—she saw... nothing. Nothing, save the splotches of trees far below, the striped peaks rising around them, and the expanse of the sky as it stretched forever on.

"Two," the Special Sentry shouted.

What did the everlast see that she could not? Sav squeezed the spine of the sleigh with her legs as Audrian had instructed, but while doing so, she leaned even farther to get a better glance. And ahead of them—directly below them—

the glinting, emerald path simply curved wide to skirt a mammoth, ruby boulder and then—

Holy Mother Her, she gasped as she saw it. *Holy Hollow.*

For the rocky, green path ahead of them was no more. And they were soaring so swiftly—too swiftly—to even think of stopping in time. But Savallin did not turn away. She could not turn away. No. Instead, the Keeper of Wisdom marveled at what lay just ahead, at what closed in on her and her escort with horrific hurry.

Impossible, she breathed. *It is impossible.*

For it looked as if something massive had crashed into the rugged, rainbow face of the peak before them. And whatever it had been hit so violently that when it fell away, a large chunk of the mountain—*and the switchback*—fell with it.

"One," Audrian yelled the heartbeat before they, and the stone sled, plunged to the earth.

Pressing her legs against the gemstones of the spine with all the might she could muster, she fought to stay atop the scaled beast. She again gripped the arch of its back as it raised up before her. And leaning into her heels as if on horseback, Sav braced for the roaring ferocity of the mountain wind.

And the very instant Audrian willed her Stellae from above to below, it struck—tearing and jerking and whipping long, moonlight tresses and soft, midnight curls through the thin, frozen air.

Fat beads of moisture rained backward, stinging her skin and burning her eyes. But the sleigh—the sleigh did not tumble through the yawning crevasse in the rocky path. The sleigh did not plummet over the exposed edge, either. In fact, the sleigh did not tumble back down to the earth at all.

No. The switchback sled kept on moving—kept on gliding—as if there had been a smooth, stone path beneath it. And even though her racing heart leapt with the thrill of staring down into the absolute nothingness below, Savallin did not dare release a shred of that triumph. In front of her, the muscles of her back glistening with effort, the everlast, too, stayed silent.

For the latter had warned her, somewhat exhaustively, of precisely what would happen if either of them so much as thought too loudly without the Stellae in place—without the light breaker masking their sounds, their scents, and their passing forms from all that prowled nearby.

Sealing her excitement in tight, Sav watched as the winding path reappeared around the approaching bend. She counted the heartbeats until they would be upon it, until she could again breathe. Again laugh.

At the helm, Audrian tilted the great, spiraling horns of the stone beast inwards, toward the cliff face. Her body strained against the momentum of the sleigh, but she remained soundless still. The muscles in her shoulders, of her arms, rippled and shone as she urged the sled away from the fading drop and back onto the carved emerald path to safety.

And finally, after four long heartbeats, the sparkling green stone resumed, and—not one moment later—the brutal gale slowed to a gentle waft as the painted sled began its Hadi-defying climb up the next ridge.

Savallin exhaled graciously. Shaking loose her head of curls, she stretched from her rigid crouch.

"Let us fly again!" she shouted eagerly between her breaths. "I know you are well-aged and all full of ancient secrets and whatnot, but, truly, where did you learn to fly stone giants like that?"

The Keeper was smiling. Beaming, really, as she awaited the dry retort she knew was soon to come.

But the everlast did not appear to have heard. Actually, after steering them to safety, she had hardly moved at all. Which... if Sav was being honest, was not that abnormal. Not since she spent the great majority of her time being unnaturally still. But, her sheen... the sheen soaking her back and loose linen tunic—that was abnormal.

In the short time Savallin had known her, Audrian had not once exerted herself to the point of full sheen. But now... now it was growing heavier still. And her ever-perfect posture—her warrior's posture—began to sway. Sway... until—until her torso fell forward.

Panic, true panic, surged within Savallin's chest.

"Audrian?" she rasped, tugging on the everlast's shoulders.

Audrian did not answer, though. But her shoulder, her body, did.

"Audria—"

But the young covenary's cry was cut short when the undying female sank backward into her lap.

"Audrian," she wept, her voice quivering beyond her control. "*No.*"

Hot, round tears welled up in the bottoms of her eyes. And only then did she see the streaks of glittery charcoal splattered across her own arms, her own chest.

"No. No. No."

For in her lap, protruding from the spectral's still chest like a grave marker, a spear of petrified gray wood stole the life—stole the sunlight—surrounding it. And the smooth dagger—an ashen spike the length of Savallin's arm and every bit as wide as her wrist—appeared to have been... *crafted.*

The force it would take to... to... But her breaths were so wild she could barely think. *To drive a shaft this size... to drive it so far into a chest... into Audrian's chest...*

Hasty, terrible understanding had the Keeper's inhales slowing and her watery vision sharpening into clarity. On instinct, she blocked the everlast's nearly limp body with her own, scanning each passing crag and roving shadow for any hint of movement.

The spear must have struck Audrian the moment she shifted her Stellae. The moment the wind barreled in.

The moment the droplets stung my eyes.

Almost as if... as if... something had been lying in wait. In wait, for the sleigh to appear where the path did not...

Goddess.

But even so—even if it had been a trap, even with that petrified dagger piercing her chest—Audrian had not let them fall. No, she had kept them on course... kept them on the switchback... kept them from fading. Kept her from fading. Just as she was still doing. Still doing despite her very own eternity being leached from her body.

For as the covenary blinked back her hot tears, she found that the spectral's palms, even at the steps of Sempedormir, had refused to part from the helm, refused to part from the sweeping stone horns that steered the sleigh. The stone horns, Savallin was positive, she could have released to block the spear aiming for her heart.

But if she had done so—if she had let go—the covenary was also positive they would have both succumbed. Succumbed to the drop.

But Audrian, without even the briefest hesitation, made her choice. She had refused to let Savallin fall. And the Keeper, she could do no less. Swallowing her sorrow, her sweltering anger, she shoved her hands down around the leaking wound. At the sudden pressure, the everlast's lips parted in shock, but her eyes—her otherworldly eyes—they started to shut. The covenary pushed firmer, silvery-gray blood spreading like shadow across the white tunic.

The spectral tried to move her mouth again, but this time, where her words should have come, a spray of charcoal came instead. Blood began streaming from the corners of her mouth. With the wind still at bay, though, Savallin knew the Special Sentry's Stellae held fast. She knew they were still safe. Still guarded, at least for a little while longer.

While she was not sure how much longer her friend could hold out, she was sure that she would try. Audrian, apparently—willful as she was—would even keep from healing herself if it meant holding that shield in place but a moment more. And the Keeper, she would not waste it.

While Covenarykind could brandish a shield of their own—a Sway—they were not like Stellae. Not in their good or their make. Where a Stellae was capable of *obstructing* the senses, a Sway could only *fool* them. One physical, one perceptual. So, fully aware that her own shield was utterly useless in this kind of situation, Savallin did the only thing she could.

Closing her eyes, she reached deep within herself, reached beyond herself, reached for Her. And then, steadying the breath in her earthly body, the Keeper ruptured her own defense. Ruptured that solid, impenetrable, innermost wall into nothing but splinters. In the same heartbeat, she touched a honey-brown finger to Audrian's temple.

The everlast understood.

Savallin's obsidian wall was still crackling to dust when Audrian's icy voice ricocheted through her mind.

I cannot heal myself, Covelette. And if the covenary had not been holding her body in her arms, she would have only known the Special Sentry trembled with pain by her evasion of a due scolding. *Not until the Relicelm is removed.*

Relicelm, the Keeper cursed herself mercilessly. *How did I miss that?*

Because—Audrian halted to cough up more blood—*without touching it, it is impossible to tell Relicelm from petrified pine.*

That was not the only part that was impossible. No—for the last Relicelm orchard, it had been razed to the ground ages ago. Ages before she—maybe even Audrian—had ever been born.

It is going to hurt, she whispered. *Very much.*

A chilly laugh echoed through her consciousness.

Call it settlement, the warrior murmured slowly. *For before.*

And despite herself, the harsh lines marring the covenary's young face lessened. After ensuring the everlast still had ahold of their heading, and skimming the rushing terrain for danger once more, Savallin latched on to the wooden spear. In the distance, high amongst the dripping caves, she marked three sets of glowing red orbs.

Do not—another wet cough severed the order—*cast.*

But the warning was too late. For Savallin knew—knew with one touch—that she could *never* hope to pry the spear free on her own. Not without elemental assistance.

They will sense you.

But in the span of half a blink, the Keeper had clawed into the mountainside. Clawed into the symphony of elemental power sounding just beneath. And the next instant, those glowing red orbs were gone. Gone, incinerated by burning jade. And the moment after that, she willed her charm to take command of the sleigh. And the everlast sensed it—sensed the shift in the sleigh—her paling hands falling away at last.

If I do not cast, Audrian, you will bleed out before I free this spike. The Earth Song thrummed stronger, tickling her fingertips as it moved through her. *At least this way, we will have a fighting chance.*

And Savallin could feel it—feel it as Audrian willed her immortal body to move, to rise, to get up and put a stop to this nonsense. To her nonsense. But it did no such thing, for it could *not* do such a thing.

Sava—

A huge cobalt boulder blasted against the Stellae. The invisible shield rattled wildly at the impact, gold flecks and blue shooting through the air, but it did not give.

"Mea est tuum!" the Keeper began chanting as the sled slid down its path. "Tuum est meum!"

Audrian's tortured scream flooded her mind. At the sound, the covenary could see nothing but red. Pushing with one hand into the spectral's chest, she heaved up on the spear with the other. The wooden shaft seared her palm, but she kept pulling. Kept chanting. Kept listening to the earthly melody playing through her, to the fading voice inside her head.

"Mea est tuum!" Grinding her teeth, she blocked out the acidic burn and dug deeper, the mountain beneath her quivering with each forbidden word. "Tuum est meum!"

The muscles in her arms and back, her shoulders, strained and ached and cried as she pulled, but still, they obeyed. The creamy, smooth skin of her palm began to scorch, to blister, to peel away. A loud pounding started to dull the desperate screams filling her mind.

"Mea est tuum." And when doubt, at last, began to trickle in—when that inner song quieted and the Keeper of Wisdom started to question her own skill, when the youngest-ever Majlis of Covenarykind began to falter—a pair of bright, ice-blue eyes blazed open. "Tuum est meum."

And it was not her eyes that had Savallin gripping the Relicelm spear with both hands. It was not the slowing of her silvery blood, either. No—it was the faintest quirking of her mouth to one side that had the Keeper roaring that forbidden incantation into the sky.

"Mea est—"

She flew backward, her skull rebounding off the unseen Stellae. But in her hands—melded to her skin—the ashen Relicelm spear still sizzled with Audrian's blood. But that fast, everything went dark. The spear, the blood, the immortal sentry—all disappeared into shadow. And Savallin, flat on her back, unsure whether she was blind or faded, squinted up. Squinted overhead. Overhead... at the—

Another boulder—a larger boulder—sailed hard and fast for the sleigh. And it was so enormous that it blocked out the sun entirely. The breath froze in her lungs. For this impact—this impact would knock the sleigh from its course. It would knock the sleigh off the mountain.

"Sever your power *now*, Savallin."

The covenary started, but the immortal warrior was already back at the helm, already steering the mythic sled onto the straightest, quickest path out of the shadow.

Audria—

"Seal that shield," she barked without so much as turning around.

Wasting not a moment more, she sliced through the earthly tether on her Soul, on her Seraphic, and slammed that obsidian wall into position. Audrian commanded the sleigh to fly faster and faster and faster. And then, then the ruby and cobalt boulder burst into a cloud of richest violet as it collided with the switchback not half a pace behind them.

Savallin lurched up, ripping the slick gray spike from her ruined palms as she bent around Audrian to check for herself.

Blessed be... the covenary pressed her blistered palms onto the everlast's silky, smooth skin... *the goddess.*

But then, as the Special Sentry regarded her with nothing save pure perplexity, an airy laugh escaped Savallin's lips. For there was not a flaw in sight... not even the smallest trace of a scar... no remnant of the catastrophic damage that had been dealt. Just another cream tunic... missing a bit of—

"May I help you find something, Covelette?"

Chapter 46

THE CONSERVATORY

Stassie Everstar was pissed.

It had taken her less than half a beat to shake Tabor from her arm. She had left him reeling, left him in the dust, as she sprinted for The Conservatory battlements.

She would end every last one of them. Every last one. Leisurely. Deliberately. Hideously.

For they had ordered her sister to be bound in chains. They had ordered her baby sister to be bound, from head to toe, in Lastisap chains. And the filthy cowards were so afraid of her, so petrified of what she might do, that they had ordered *him* to do their bidding.

Those gutless, rancid vermin had extorted him. The just, the esteemed, the Ever-blessed Spectraline Senate itself had forced him to do their deed by threatening the eternity of his younger brother. And as if that were not repulsive enough, the swine had taken it one step further—had all but guaranteed the Commander's compliance with the levying of one more. With the endangering of the one eternity that mattered most to the female he held so dear. *Stassie's own eternity.*

That was why he complied. That was why Decard Battleson *always* complied. And that, too, was why she felt so ill. For it was her fault. It was all her fault.

She had only wished to have an edge over her sister. An edge that might level the field of their Twenty-Third Canon. She had wanted to finish first. Just one time. Just once, she wanted to finish ahead of Nora. But she had not known—not when she and Tabor had conspired—that Decard would corner Nora in the bathing chamber. That he would dose her with Seraphease. She had not known.

For if she had, if she had had any inkling that her sister's innermost defenses—that those impenetrable walls of hate-forged steel—were lying in total ruin, if she had known that, she would have never let Tabor or his Thought-Twisting anywhere near Nora's mind.

That simple vision he had planted, the dream meant only to stun for a moment, must have been intensified by the Seraphease in her veins. Because the horror—the pure, undiluted anguish—that had decimated her beautiful, fearless face... it had ripped the shattered heart from Stassie's chest.

But worse still was that sound. The sound that had been rent from Nora's throat as she fell through the canyons. The blood-icing scream that had gutted her where she stood as she had crept through Decard's thoughts. No, Stassie would never forgive herself for the role she played in the mustering of that sound.

For it was her fault. Nora had been drug into her Twenty-Third Canon not simply weary, but heavy. Heavy with senseless heartache. Heavy from the betrayal of the one soul she would never distrust. Stassie had sent her only sister, her only kin in this horrid, never-ending existence, into a battle of survival with a broken will. All for the foolish wish of finishing first.

Shoving cascades of rosemary and low-strung trumpet garlands from her path, the elder Everstar cleared the highest corridor of The Conservatory. And as she ran for the sky stair, warm, Ever-kissed rays of light brushed along her sullen face.

She had been sedated for more than a fortnight upon returning from her Canon. But this dawn, she had awoken into quite the commotion—enough so that she had been able to slip free from her naturopath prison.

As she had weaved her way from the Healing Ell to Res, she had heard what caused the chaos. From the specling draping ropes of bursting yellows and lightrise lilies along the stone archways, to the shihan carefully selecting the perfect stalks of indigo and plum star flowers for the tabletop arrangements, the rumor on everyone's tongue was the same: Commander Decard Battleson had returned, at long last. He had returned *alone.*

The nearer she got to her chamber, the more she had overheard. Beyond simply returning, the once-formidable Commander had reappeared as if chewed up, swallowed, and spit out again.

She had been tugging on a fresh tunic when the news came that said shriveled Commander had not merely returned, but had requested an audience with The Senate. An audience with The Crux.

Stassie had been the first spectraline to reach The Light Hall. And then, from her bench in the front row, she had watched, just like everyone else in the galleries, as the travel-weary Commander squared off against the Minister of The Senate.

Her heart had hammered, and breath—it had seemed—eluded her lungs, and still she had watched. But the moment the Battleson male had spoken of hexwork, *of Lyric,* Stassie had known she needed to see for herself. And so, she had. She had leapt, then stood before the shield, in the center of that high-ceilinged hall. She had stood before him, before them all, and she had bored into his mind.

For she and her sister had *not* been raised by spectraline. They had not been raised by immortal at all. In fact, they had never known their true givers. Before joining The Conservatory, the young specling twins had lived a very different, distant life. And it was thanks to that strange upbringing that both Everstar sisters very well knew their way around tonics and toxins and elementary charm. But no one outside of she and Nora, should have been privy to that.

And as she had rifled through Decard's thoughts, as she had lived out each of those ghastly days within his head, she had discovered *how* he had found out. Discovered that he had witnessed her sister—witnessed Nora—call upon unimaginable, colossal charm from the very core of Earth herself. He had seen her do it, and he had not betrayed her.

Stassie, too, had felt the immense guilt he harbored over his outburst upon the Ever Step, over his outburst that Nora had orchestrated. And when that scream—that terrible, awful, eternity-ending scream—had sounded within the darkness of his mind, Stassie had shared in the shouldering of that agony as well.

That was when her tears had pushed their limits, when those glistening swells, at last, dared to spill upon the stones below. Even as they fell, though, she had stared beyond them, stared into that aching, tortured mess of a mind. And as she had stood there—as she had stood before the male her sister hated so—she could not help but sense the awe, the sheer respect and endless admiration, the *love* for Nora, that Decard Battleson did not know how to voice.

She had seen his truth. She had seen that he was telling the truth. And when Tabor had carried her from The Light Hall, Stassie had felt great sadness for the male standing atop the star in the heart of that mountaintop chamber.

And now—now as she raced up the sky stair and into the clouds—now she was going to make her little sister proud.

Your sacrifice will not be in vain, she panted as she took the steps three at a time. *Your loss will not be in vain.*

Pushing her legs to their brink, she climbed faster, climbed higher, until the only thing she could see within the cloud cover was a lone landing. The lone landing. Swallowing a breath, she counted down from three before vaulting onto the final, flat stone. And then, then she was there. There with her hair blowing wild, there upon the open-air battlement above the cliffside fortress.

In every direction, for as far as her eyes could see, the massive moonstone battlements spread from the stronghold below, gleaming like white serpents of stone as they snaked across the forever-frosted ridgelines of The Vale.

You compelled him to run for us, Nora. Compelled him to warn us all, Stassie whispered to the starry gates of Sempedormir as she made her plan. *I want you to know, little sister, that he did not stop. Not once. Even after your hold had long faded into the night, Decard did not stop.*

And then, her prayer in the wind, she moved. Dashing to where an ancient ballista and its supply of head-high iron bolts sat empty—sat ever aimed into a forgotten era—Stassie lifted the thick leather belt to scramble in when a mammoth hand tore her backward.

"Tell me what you saw, Everstar."

And while his grip was as solid as any smith's vice, it was the quiver in his voice that gave him away.

Dalon.

She did not have time for this.

"Tell me what you saw in his mind!"

No, Stassie did not have the time to tell Dalon Bristolwood that within the Commander's memory, there lived a monster lost to legend. She did not have the time to tell him that that monster was a force of nature so great, so vast, that it itself could be mistaken for the very sky. And she certainly did not have the time, nor the patience, to tell him that that nightmare-come-true—that unholy force that had no right to exist—that it was now barreling down upon *this* alpine fortress.

"Tell me what—"

"Go fuck yourself, Bristolwood."

She did have the time for that. For the elder Everstar had not yet forgotten that it was this male who had stood in her way. This male who had kept her from Nora. This male who had kept her sedated. And the male—he read it upon her face.

"You did not stand even a fool's chance," he bellowed, his features contorting with his wrath. "You would have never ma—"

That fast, Stassie drove her knee into the fool's groin. And then, for good measure—for her pleasure—she fired her fist three times in rapid succession. Groin. Gut. Gullet.

Dalon collapsed like a fresh load of oxenshit. And after rolling his sputtering carcass across the stone skyway, Stassie took her rightful place behind the gargantuan crossbow. Fastening the metal buckle on the archaic belt, she peered out over the winding, thawing mountain pass and into the flowering valley beyond.

To her knowledge, The Conservatory had never before been attacked. For the Qamar Vsadnik, the storied soldiers of the skies, had never been able to locate it—never been able to locate the enemy stronghold hidden beneath their nose.

Slowing her pulse and steeling her spirit, Stassie focused upon the tiny, bleached tower at the farthest edge of the color-speckled valley. It was The Shield's first line of defense, she knew—the large, bronze hearth atop that little white tower. There was one on each of the towers, each of the ancient towers that dotted the back of the white serpent as it crested the stretching peaks. Signal fires, never before lit.

As she surveyed The Vale and the sky above, Stassie could not have cared less that the senators did not believe the Commander's account. Some of them, she supposed, had been alive back when the last Beasts of Old fell from the skies. So, the way she saw it, they had no one to blame save themselves for the scale of horror that was soon to unfold.

No, she did not care. For she would take care of the matter herself. She, alone, would put an end to the beast that ended her sister. Her broken, brave, betrayed sister. She, alone, would steal the life that stole Nora.

This Beast of Old, this monster of myth, this brute of the bygone—it was hers. This ísdreki was hers.

Dalon had just clambered to his feet when that oval hearth far, far in the distance burst into cobalt flame. The sharpness of his inhale might have sliced even the sky, but the female in the ballista—she did not move.

She did not look away, either. Not as hearth upon hearth matched that indigo blaze. Not as the slumbering mountain serpent scorched to life along the snowy ridges. Not even as the Beacon of Beasts lit the Lunaerian blue for the first time in spectraline history. Stassie Everstar did not look away—not even as her tears fell.

Chapter 47

THE CROSSING

Savallin had caught glimpses of fiery red in the dark depths of the passing caves all throughout the day. With each sighting, the ancient, earthly power singing within her blood thrashed riotously. And as the warmth of the sun finally began to wane, as the promise of dusk began dimming the blue from the sky, those eerie flashes of red became far too frequent. The covenary's power shrieked in answer.

A citrusy glow, akin to the sands of the Auburn Dunes, was creeping over the mountain-strewn horizon when Audrian twisted on her perch. A wicked leer kindled her ethereal face.

"Up ahead," she said. "At that star-bleached outcropping just shy of the first peak, the Lunamici will slow." Her look alone told the Keeper precisely what she needed to know before she had ever voiced it. "But it will *not* stop."

They had been sailing the striations of the rainbow all day, rising and swooping and curving with each new alp. And as if she had not just been gruesomely impaled, the Special Sentry had carried right on along—had tapped her spectraline strength to guide their unruly sleigh on its winding way.

"I take it we must"—tilting her head in mock surprise, the covenary crossed her still-weary arms over her chest— "jump?"

"Indeed." The everlast female grinned so wide that her pointed canines sparkled like stars in the dying day. "*We* will jump. But the sleigh, charmed by you, will fly on so that the dark-eaters have something to hunt." Audrian winked. "Something that is not us."

"Charmed by me?" she asked, whipping her attention to the network of caves lining the ridges above. For the simmering red she kept seeing—it was... they were... *The Eyes of The End.* "You almost perished—literally almost perished—because of how adamantly you wished me not to use my charm."

Covenary legends whisper of eyes, eyes the color of polished ruby, eyes that eat darkness.

Following her line of focus, the Special Sentry chirped, "The Orbs of Fire—the last sight of the doomed before being drug into the Realm of Flame."

And the Keeper could only nod. Only nod in agreement, for there was not a soul she knew, living or non, that had faced a dark-eater—faced a chulu shide—and walked away. They were creatures of nightmare, hunched like serpents readying to strike and covered in rotting flesh the shade of night. And worse still, the cave demons, as they have also been known, were said to prey on any and everything senseless enough to get too close.

With the disturbing recollection, the covenary bore into each of the black caverns as they drew by. She, too, thought of the day's journey—the chaos of the day's journey. The wild cornering that sent small rocks and pebbles sailing down the switchbacks. The abrupt, yet constant, shifts in speed. The errant limbs and crooked spires turned to dust.

"You are deranged," she spewed when the pieces finally came together. "Undeniably deranged."

For the everlast—she had been *toying* with them. Audrian, the immortal menace, had been *provoking* the chulu shide! Riling them up the entire time!

"Do not forget, Covelette, my Stellae is worth less than naught once The Everstar falls." And not bothering to refute Savallin's assertion, she added, "After that, it is but you and me." That beautiful, lovely, terrifying smile stretched farther across her face. "You, me, and the legions of cave demons waiting to rip out our innards."

"Oh?" The Keeper's dark brows rose. "Is that all?"

"That is all," she confirmed, turning back toward the ascent. "Well, except for the skeledima, of course."

"The wha—"

"After our dismount, Savallin, we will hike to that ridge, the one there." She pointed with a slender finger. "That one, with the waterfall. We will make our camp just beneath."

What, the covenary frothed, *in Her, Hollow, and Hadi is a skeledima?*

"When the last rays of Bright fade from the sky, *not another sound.*" The Special Sentry's demeanor seemed to darken with the day. "Do you understand, Covelette? Not a single sound, or the night hordes will be upon us before you can even dream of unsheathing that blade."

And ever so softly, Savallin dipped her head.

"So much as scratch an itch and neither one of us will again see the light of day."

The Keeper's black curls swayed as she nodded once more.

And it was unsettling—truly it was—that Audrian could declare something so grisly, so awful as that, with such a lovely grin upon that remarkable face. And as Sav rolled her eyes at the unfair creation that was her immortal escort, one of the female's earlier questions prickled the back of her mind.

Who is it you still pretend for?

For it was an honest question. A reasonable question. Because after all this—after all the two had been through, lived through—who was it, truly, that she was pretending for? Who was it, all the way out here, that she, the Keeper of Wisdom, continued to diminish herself to please?

She was not afraid. Not of the night, not of the creatures lurking in the caves, not really. The young Keeper was more than confident she could take care of herself—more than willing to face any challenge that came prowling.

Plus, she would not be the first covenary to survive the colorless hours of these alps. No, not even close. For lifetimes prior, The Shamed Sisters had fled through this very same rainbow. It was their sleigh, their path, their rising and falling escape route through Death's Dominion, that she and Audrian had ridden all day. And not one of those fleeing Skapahni had endured even a day of the brutal training that she had. Not one. And yet, *they* had survived the night.

Somehow.

As the stone sled scraped up the steep pass, the little Keeper mentally thumbed through her rows and rows of shelves—through her lifetime of knowledge—searching for an incantation, *any* enchantment, that might be of use. But Audrian, marking the pensive look furrowing her face, intervened.

"Besides the sleigh, Covelette, no more casting." Stretching her arms wide and flicking her wrists out for emphasis, she gestured to the colorful crags closing in all around them. "They can taste it. *Taste you.*"

The mighty sled banked around a tight curve. The ascending path narrowed before steepening further. And as Savallin stared over the rocky edge—into the effervescent green and gold swirls of the ravine hundreds of paces below— the great stone beast began its final, furious charge up the incline.

The everlast, though, could not have cared less about the beyond fatal drop less than half a step from the tips of the moon dragon's sapphire belly scales.

"What was that incantation, Savallin? The one you called upon earlier today?"

"Oh." Color matching that of the setting sun stained the covenary's velvety cheeks. She offered a sheepish shrug. "It was a, uh, well..." She gathered her thoughts and tried again. "It is a... *cherished* incantation."

"A *cherished* incantation?" And without needing to turn, the immortal cocked her head of silken white hair in a manner that dared Savallin to go on.

"Yes." She inhaled through her nose. "From a fable. A beloved fable."

The fable, no less, that she had stumbled upon in Coralis' chambers. The forbidden tome, in fact, where the lost Majlis had hidden her warning: *The Listing Isles of Lost*.

The warrior glanced over her shoulder. "A beloved fable?"

"For covelettes, actually," the covenary furthered, taking immense pleasure in the immortal's growing incredulity. "A tale, to help them fall asleep."

"A tale," her eyebrows arched high, "to coax covelettes into their dreams?"

"You always call me that—*Covelette*, I mean. So," she said, "it got me thinking, or, well... conjecturing that if the Listing Isles *are* real—you know, um, the jade ones we are now journeying to—well, then perhaps the incantations, the Seraphic spells written into the story, are not so imaginary either."

And Savallin, goddess help her, could not tell if the spectral was gearing up to pitch her body from the sleigh or devising a plan to make the pain last.

"In *The Listing Isles of Lost*," the covenary blathered on before she could think better of it, "*Mea est tuum* is an incantation that blends the life of two into one. While the

Seraphic is being sung, the might of two bodies forges into one. The weaknesses of both, borne between two."

And when the Keeper paused long enough to suck down a breath, it was the expression upon the everlast's face that kept her from doing so. Because for once, the Special Sentry looked... stunned. Unreservedly stunned.

And then, just when the quiet, the angst, had lingered a beat too long, the warrior whispered, "You needed my strength to free the spear. And I needed yours to withstand the Relicelm."

A wry smile began budding across Savallin's full lips.

From her perch, Audrian let out a slow, high-pitched whistle before snickering, "Nirvana truly is a Seer."

A Seer? The Keeper's smile vanished entirely. *Diadet Nirvana?*

"You," she steamed, "you, with all your immortal wisdom, did not think to tell me that while I wasted away in The Klekta!?"

While she had been a captive in the cells of the prison below The Catacombs, Audrian—disguised as The Lady of the Lair—had divulged all sorts of secrets. Many of which involved the reigning Diadet of Covenarykind. But the most profound of her revelations, by and large, had been that she, Diadet Nirvana, was the first-ever Sovereign Supreme to ascend without even a note of Soul in her blood. That was why, the everlast had claimed, the Diadet sequestered herself like she did. Why she so often refused to hold Council. Why she remained a pale shadow in The Catacombs' scrutinous eye.

"Heavy is the head that wears the fussery crown, Covelette," the immortal snorted. "You were imprisoned for barely two days. I would hardly consider that wasting away."

But this—this freshest of shocks—it meant that, that not only was Nirvana the first Diadet without Soul, but Nirvana was the first Seer to *ever* sit The Obsidian Throne.

"Yes," Audrian moaned, her undying indifference on full display. "Your Diadet sees how history will end. She sees who history will end."

The Yet. The Keeper sat motionless as the words sank in. *Nirvana can see The Yet.*

"Truly, *Keeper of Wisdom*, I thought that to be obvious. She left you a satchel of climbing tools—just prior to, I might add, slipping out unseen the heartbeat before your fellow Majlis came undone."

Still, though, she could not move. For she was adrift, lost within the unending tides of implication.

"Did you not ever wonder, Savallin Prim, acolyte of knowledge, why *you* were ordered to a school of combat?"

At that, the covenary stirred at last, heaving herself back into the present. For no... no, she had not wondered. In truth, she had never thought twice about it. She had always just assumed her fellow Keepers had endured Tutelages of equal difficulty. But as the sky around them eddied between deep rose and blood orange, as the stone sleigh neared the top of its emerald ascent, that dazzling yet chilling grin again adorned Audrian's face.

"Did you not ever wonder, Savallin, why *you* were chosen to be the first-ever being not of spectraline lineage—*the first ever mortal body*—granted admission to The Conservatory?"

The Keeper's mouth dried out. It had all been so abrupt, so hushed, when she, a covelette of just seven years, had been removed from traditional study and packed off under the cover of night. Packed off... the very same night she had ascended.

Nirvana... She murmured to herself in disbelief. *Nirvana had sent me, a covelette, straight to a Malqatil stronghold. Straight to the steps... of The Songbird Slayers.*

"Nirvana," the Special Sentry echoed aloud. "The Seer."

Now it was Savallin who was stunned. For how had she not once—not one time—questioned her circumstance? How had she not once wondered? Not once asked the question? But then, the muscles of the everlast's back shifted as she made to maneuver the fearsome sleigh the short distance to the star-washed stones jutting from the mountain face. And silent as a spirit, the covenary rose into a low crouch atop the wavy, scaled spine of the sled.

When, at last, the blanched overhang was near enough to touch, Savallin leaned forward toward the helm and whispered in a voice dripping with challenge, "Do not make me save your sorry eternity twice in one day."

And before the Special Sentry of the Eastern Reach could whirl on her, the Keeper drove her heels into the back of the mythic beast and sprang for the outcropping.

Chapter 48

THE CITY

Lochlan had instructed his army of demi males to escort the spectral female back to her tower dwelling so that she might bathe and prepare for the night ahead. The ten soldiers had stood guard just outside her splintered bathing chamber door. Everly, on the other hand, had sat upon the black-tiled floor of her shower for what felt like hours.

The scalding water had tickled her scalp as it seared the soured rot and rancid regret from her hair. She had scrubbed a full bottle of orchid lily soap into her skin. But still, she had not felt clean. So, a fresh bottle of lavender peppermint and, then, honeyed-orange turmeric had followed suit.

She had been content to sit there all day, long into the night, to let that running water cleanse her body of all that she had done, but the demi-sensore halflings lurking in her hallway, they had other plans. And so, after pulling on her warmest leisure set, back they all went—back to the ashen scene where the aspirations of the demi-sensore hunters had *almost* come to fruition.

Because the skyscraping tower still did not bear power upon its uppermost levels, Everly climbed the zigzagging stairs into the midnight clouds, one by one. Half of her dedicated militia ascended in the darkness before her, the other on her heels.

The higher they hiked, the stronger the stink of the melted piping and blackened hardwood became. And she was not pleased, nor was she surprised, that the gang of halflings—her new companions—lived up to their name. For their steps were sluggish and their breathing labored by the time the group reached the steel door at the top of the well.

The demi in front had not fully shouldered it open when the dark wind outside howled its fury. Each of the halflings before her, the ones behind her as well, staggered on their feet as the wind roared past. But not her. For it was nothing compared to what she had grown up in, trained in. She was still as ever as she readied herself for what came next—as she prepared her mind, her fool's heart, for what she knew awaited her out on that charred floor beyond the stairwell door.

Shockingly, the hinges didn't creak as the heavy door ripped from the man's hand and blew backward into the concrete wall behind it. And from the middle of their pack, even wedged between some of the most unexceptional soldiers to ever walk this world, the spectraline held her head high as she strode out amongst them.

"Ah," that painfully mortal voice rumbled from the center of the floor, near a large heap of warped appliances.

With her back straight and her shoulders set, she walked toward it.

"You look well," Lochlan murmured into her ear after skimming her body from toe to tip.

The female did not bow in the slightest as she sensed more than fifty other pairs of eyes studying her just as closely.

And then, once more resuming his speaking volume, the pallid halfling announced, "We are thrilled you have joined us, at last."

And as if on cue, the bodies appeared. Stepping out from every burnt corner of what had very recently been a full-floor luxury apartment, the tattered swarm of dreary faces emerged—demi-sensore males in all shapes and sizes.

Everly knew better than to let their glum forms dupe her. For even though they might not look like much on the outside, she recognized that they bore strength that did not belong to them. Speed that did not belong to them.

And as she had suspected, not one of the hunters looked to their leader. No, every last pair of those beady, black eyes was fixed firmly upon her.

But the spectraline—she did not bother with their ilk. No, she only perused the rubble for what she knew—for *who* she knew—had also been brought here.

The overwhelming majority of the level's walls, and all of its windows, had been blown out amidst the penthouse's fiery blast a few weeks back—sprinkled down upon the bustling streets far, far below like a blistering rain of glass. And there, at the farthest edge of the floor, backlit by the tower city twinkling beyond, Mortal Jay had been strung up by his toes.

Everly started, but—

"Purely precautionary," Lochlan groused. "Only for the unlikely event you consider rescinding your word."

But she did not see the demi male speaking to her. No. She saw nothing but the mortal at the far wall. He was battered, and he was awake. He was conscious. These barbarians had threaded him up, hung him over the precipice—all while he was conscious.

"Do not think, Everly, that I did not catch that look upon your face. That wounded expression when we shepherded him from the airfield." She willed her fists not to ball as the abomination dared to goad her further. "I could have even sworn that I glimpsed your blood run *silver*."

And it was then, then that the female met the halfling's watery glare with a steel-edged glower of her own.

Across the floor, suspended over the opposite edge by the thin flesh between his fingers, the *other* captive winced. And just like that, her overpowering urge to toss Lochlan from the top floor of the tower subsided. A slow, soft smirk spread across her lips as she again remembered why she had come.

Fool, she spat into her mind. *Lying, scheming, traitorous fool.*

The spectraline male did not react, did not move again. But she knew—knew—that he had heard her. From the markings upon his body, from what was left of his body, the demi-sensore hunters had been busy. Thorough, even. Meticulous in their handiwork.

For the skin on Bristol's forearms, the golden skin from his fingertips to his elbows, the golden skin where his Valo should have shone, had been peeled off. Peeled off and pulled back—back to the crook in his arm, where it now draped along his shoulder blade.

And Everly—not even she wished to know how much Lastisap the demi force had pumped into him to preserve his body in that sort of flayed despair. He certainly would have made them labor for it, though. That much, she was sure.

And yet, even after enduring every bit of the vibrant torment the demi-sensore had dreamt up for him, somehow, the male's cerulean scowl was just as menacing as it had ever been.

"Don't you worry, Everly," Lochlan assured, noticing her newest fixation and clapping her on the arm. "He is secured. Not a being on this earth could get out of those shackles."

And it took everything the female had—every ounce of self-restraint—not to scoff straight into the hunter's proud, half-human face.

"Is this everyone you are expecting, then?" Everly's voice was cool, unbothered—the picture of the warrior she had once been. "This is the whole..." She hesitated. "What *do* you call yourselves?"

A moist sneer slithered along the halfling's sad excuse for a jawline as he slid an arm around her lower back. And then, he began guiding her through the black ruins to where the immortal warrior swayed in the soaring gusts.

"We call ourselves nothing but what we are, what we do."

She sighed to herself, priming for a vastly underwhelming response.

"We"—he said, turning them in a slow circle—"are the Stayella Zvezdami."

Her sigh hitched in the bridge of her nose.

Well, that, she snorted to no one, *strikes a rather hypocritical chord.*

How would the demi-sensore know The First Tongue? And why—if their sole purpose was to rid the world of The Spectraline—would they wish to use their language?

"Star Hunters?" she mused as she again walked alongside the root-haired hunter.

"Star Hunters," he repeated smugly, coming to a halt at the bank of the blood lake undulating beneath Bristol's feet.

The female paused, blinking at the bank. For she had not realized it from the stairwell door. No. She had not grasped what her eyes—what her mind—was trying to tell her. What they were screaming at her.

"I can only assume you are curious, Everly Castile, as to why we have summoned you here at the height of the Forbidden Hours."

Lochlan extended an upturned hand to the cluster of demi on his left.

Bristol's blood is red.

"Summoned you here, at the very window in time in which The Spectraline are farthest removed from their beloved Everstar."

The shortest of the halflings shuffled forward.

The exposed muscles of his arms, the bare tendons, the flesh—all mortal red.

"At the very window in time that the mighty spectraline are at their weakest."

At the very window in time that if something—say an enormous, broody Spectraline Brigadier—were to go awry, you might yet have an extra second of life.

The compact, mouse-hued hoodlum laid a gleaming, curved dagger upon his maestro's outstretched palm.

"I know that I speak for the entirety of the Stayella Zvezdami"—the star hunter threw a wicked glance over his shoulder, back toward the ogre standing nearest to Mortal Jay, a silent warning—"I know I speak for us all, our entire outfit upon this tower, when I say that we are more than fortunate to be welcoming you, Everly Castile."

But the memory—the memory of that day at the pier, the image of that long-gone golden stare—burned through her thoughts.

"But first, as I am positive you understand," Lochlan said, stepping closer, "we have but one test—one test of loyalty— you must perform."

A new kind of ache fissured deep within her chest. Not at the halfling's words, but at herself. Because she had forgotten. All but forgotten since that very first day. All but forgotten that Dalon Bristolwood had raised a *Sway*—that he had raised a full-form Sway. A feat that would take immense training, decades of training, for a spectraline to master.

"Everly Castile"—the lank-limbed demi extended the finely arched steel toward her—"I present to you this hallowed blade. This blessed blade that has ended many a spectraline eternity."

Bristol commands Sway.

"You are to wield this weapon, this bane-imbued blade"— Lochlan again faced the host amassed at his back—"this Isra Scorcher to steal the eternity of the spectraline who stole yours."

Bristol commands Sway... and he can Thought-Tell.

"Everly Castile, you are to brandish this blade and end the eternity of the male who was sent here to find The Night Heir." Raucous approval boomed into the starless night. "To find the legend who would annihilate us all."

The chaos escalated tenfold when the female accepted the weapon shining atop Lochlan's hand.

Bristol commands Sway and Lumin, the pieces rushed to form the picture for her mind. *There is but one means of harnessing both.*

Everly looked to the blade in her hands. She inspected the edge. Weighed the steel. Flipped it once in the air.

Bristol might have betrayed me, she snarled as the picture became clear. *But what he did, it doesn't hold a candle to what they have done to him.*

The female tossed the weapon a second time, catching it behind her back before taking a few practice slices. With each swing of her arm, the fervor of the demi-sensore strewn about the charred wreckage reached new and astonishing heights.

Unreal, the spectraline blew as she arched an eyebrow. *They are un-fucking-real.*

For Dalon Bristolwood *had* betrayed her, but he *had not* completed The Rite of Parallel.

How long, she growled into his mind as she lifted her callous eyes to meet his, his suspended in the night air above her. *How long have you been dosing yourself with Seraphease?*

Seraphease, the castress healing tonic. The healing tonic that, when given to a healthy being—a healthy Ever being—would not slow time. Would not warp nature. Would not do anything. Anything, save bequeath upon its bearer a sharp, nasty note of Shepherd justice. Justice in the form of *Lyric*. Lyric sent to cleanse the soul.

That, she scolded. *Is one nefarious deed, Brigadier.*

And the agony the cleansing would exact—it would be brutal. Brutal and ceaseless. For as long as an Ever being consumed it, the tonic would sear their soul like a mother. But the male's face remained stone. Unrelenting stone of the cruelest origin. And beside her—truthfully, almost forgotten—the hunter spoke again.

"Everly Castile, with this weapon, you will beckon confession, you will force this male to give voice to his deplorable transgressions, and then—then you will, at last, end his vile existence."

End his vile existence? She huffed. *Why do him the favor?*

For the male, the warrior strung up like an angry wind chime, was already suffering. Likely had been for a very, very long while. Because to dose himself—to dishonor the starlight in his blood with an earthly impurity—Everly could only imagine *one* influence capable of that.

And the female—she wouldn't put it past them, those crones and codgers, to order the most skilled, the most lethal, of the spectraline's warriors to *poison* themselves, *disgrace* themselves, in the sole, futile hope of prolonging their own rule.

No. Everly didn't put it past The Senate, not even for a moment. Not since that day, long ago, when the silver Everstar had fallen from the sky. Not since that day, long ago, when the golden Everstar had ripped into the mind of the Battleson heir and watched as her sister fought for her eternity. Not since that day, almost a millennium ago, when the fall of Eleanora Everstar exposed The Spectraline Senate as the tyrants they truly were.

"Cast light"—from half a step away, the halfling's screech jarred her into reality—"upon the depravities of this male. And then"—the arched blade stilled in her grip—"end him, Everly Castile."

A zealous parade of synchronized stomps started vibrating the thick slab beneath her feet.

"And then," Lochlan's spirited invocation rose over the growing noise, "then, you will finally walk amongst the ranks of the greatest force ever to amass."

Bristol—Everstar save him—sniggered. Actually sniggered at the assertion. But before his jeer had the chance to incite the floor, the two savages on either side of him lashed at his bare torso with whips glinting of razors.

"A force," the halfling barked into the gale as the new wave of fanatic applause crashed across the tarnished story. "*The* force," Lochlan said, leveling his full attention upon the bloodied Brigadier, "that will, once and for all, rid this world of the immortal scum, just like you."

Willing her face into a mask of neutrality, willing her mind to forsake the male bleeding before her, Everly nodded only once and then turned to the crowd at her back. From every distorted corner, every darkest shadow, the din of raunchy cheers quieted. And then, even the stamping, too, dispelled. The female marked each of their faces, the bloodlust clouding their eyes, as she hefted that curved blade high into the night.

Only when she could hear the nervous inhales and exhales of each of the abominations scattered throughout the smelted furnishings and half-standing partitions—only then did she again face her canvas. And with a single step forward, she made to inspect it. The bruised and burned and torn body who, even now, refused to sag before her.

And as she examined him, as she prepared herself to do what was necessary, Everly offered the male one last piece of advice.

Icy be thy mind, Bristol.

That was it. Her sole warning. And then, with a tender hand, she began.

"Brigadier," the female purred. "I have not the slightest desire to be held up in this burnt wasteland all night long. So, let us begin with your offense that *I* find most appalling." Drawing the sharpened edge of her Isra Scorcher along his taut, paling skin, she asked, "Brigadier Bristolwood, do tell us why—why it was—that you *conspired* to have me, *the General Praelior*, forcibly banished and forever barred from serving in The Spectraline Shield?"

Smears of red glistened upon Bristol's teeth as he battled to contain his derision.

"You," his voice was guttural, gravelly, and yet unbroken, "you had yourself banished and barred by *breaching* your oath."

"It is just like your kind," she scoffed. *Our kind.* "To lay blame upon another."

"You," the growl scraped along her inner ears, "you breached The Oath of Obscurity."

"Oh?" And free hand on her hip, she gestured with the other to the mortal hanging upside down over the opposite ledge. "Like *you* very nearly did upon meeting him?"

Him—the human coffee-bringer whose only fault was pursuing her. The human coffee-bringer *she* had doomed.

"No. For you," the Brigadier's lips pulled away from his teeth, "you truly *did* reveal yourself to a lesser being."

There it is, she sighed, rolling her eyes.

"Bristolwood," Everly exhaled, "there is no need to make it dirty."

Bawdy hoots and lewd cackles rang out from far and wide. But Bristol—he stared only at her.

What I did, Bristol, it saved your eternity. It saved everyone's eternity.

The bullish brute above her sent a stream of blood and gore spearing for her face in answer.

"How does it go, that oath?" She tapped her lip with the tip of the blade. "Protect this world from what cannot be sought."

"Protect this world," he groaned, the portrait of loathsome obedience, "from what is Known and what is Not."

When he stopped, Everly slashed her blade up and across his grimace. All around them, the whoops turned to roars. And from much closer by, Lochlan bit, "Go on."

"Lesserkind thou shield," Bris' rough voice was even harder than before. "They shall be none so wise."

Bellowed slurs and hisses of disgust shredded into the darkness at the perceived insult. But even still, the female— she did not miss it, not when Lochlan cast a glance back toward the opposite edge of the flat. *Toward Mortal Jay.*

She stepped it up a notch. Forged on, caressing the Brigadier's cheek with another swipe of her steel. And this time, at the gaping wound she left, even the demi leader shouted his thrill.

Lesserkind, Everly said, keeping her inner voice calm, *it does not simply mean every being not of spectraline lineage.*

She struck again—a solid kick to the gut that sent the male's massive body swinging backward over the edge. Swinging backward into nothing. He did not look down, though. Not as the slab gave way to a fifteen-hundred-foot free fall. No, he never once took his gaze off her.

Lesserkind, she whispered, unwilling to break her own stare, *refers to the beings in need of shielding.* The howls of the demi-sensore had become so brash it was nearly impossible to hear her own thoughts, but still, she went on. *And by now,* she said, *you should know, as I forever have, Dalon, that is not every being upon this earth.*

And in her hand, the Isra Scorcher began to glow. Even she stopped to marvel at it—at the beauty of the blade. And when she flipped it, when she again gripped the hilt and thrust it high into the air, Dalon Bristolwood smiled.

And Everly—she didn't know if it had been the sound of his own name. She didn't know if it had been the ironclad sense in her soundless words. She didn't know how much the male had pieced together in the centuries they were apart. But, nonetheless, she was grateful. Grateful, as she looked upon the broad planes of the Brigadier's face and knew that he finally understood.

Yes, he had done her wrong. Yes, he had stolen everything from her—everything that mattered. But he had done so, she now understood, not out of malevolence. But something else.

You may be a moron, a mindless stooge, a raging Seraphease-fiend, she tsked. *But even that is not worth the trouble of ending your eternity.*

That fast, the mortal red seeping from Bristol's body—the mortal red pooled at his feet—began glimmering into the night until it again shone purest silver.

The bloodthirsty chanting, the ravenous cheer, the roars of the wicked, of the demi-sensore Star Hunters, guttered out as one. Guttered out only to be replaced by an all-too-familiar thrum.

And even though she was outnumbered at least fifty to one—even though those soon to rush her possessed inhuman strength and swiftness—even though her sole ally blew in the breeze like a battered, drugged-up daisy—Everly had not an ounce of worry. Not an ounce. For she was not any ordinary spectral. No, she was something else entirely.

Something else who was more than capable of purging this world from the demi threat gathered upon this ruined dwelling in the midnight sky.

And the belief—or the rising delight—must have been plain upon her face. For the Stayella Zvezdami descended into madness. Panicked orders were snarled. Haphazard defensive positions assumed. Halflings and their quivering weapons alike ushered into formations they could not hold. And as their all-encompassing chaos enveloped the remnants of the torched penthouse, the Brigadier's canines flashed like beacons in the darkness.

But every bit as furiously as it had ensued—the mayhem froze over once more. When Everly, for the first time in over nine-hundred solars, let her own Sway fall. Centuries of mortal dullness, lifetimes of human drear, kindled away from her eternal form—flickering like stardust from her skin, her hair, her vision.

And then, then a galaxy of living stars lit from deep within her soul, sparkling across every inch of her body with the endless radiance of gemstones beneath a crystalline tide. One star for every immortal life she had taken. One star for every Israsensore eternity she had ended. One star for every ancestor she had stolen from this lot.

All around her, the halflings—who had been terrified by her mortal form—were near catatonic. Not one of them rallied to move. Not one of them even braved a glance toward their leader. Not a one, except Bristol. Bristol who, painted in the starry illumination of her Valo, tore himself free of the charred rafters with one swift motion.

Not a being on this earth, my spectraline ass, she snorted. *Somebody, it seems, has been dosing with a bit more than Seraphease.*

But Bristol didn't hear her. For he was already moving. Already moving toward Lochlan, who didn't have a chance in the world. No, the preachy halfling was still gawking at Everly when the warrior reached him. And Bris—he did not need flesh upon his fingers to pluck that puny, conical skull up in one palm and hurl its spindly carcass over the edge of the burnt-out tower.

It happened so swiftly that the hunters, utterly slack-jawed, had not yet fully fathomed it when the halfling's blood-curdling scream faded into the wind. But when they did—when the realization that Lochlan had indeed just plummeted to the earth settled over them at last—it was then that they lost it.

The enraged horde whirled—whirled on her. But as the thrumming in her ears quieted, as the surrounding fear was drowned by fury, the female just made out the wet, burbling gasp from the brink at her back. She spun just in time to watch as one of the demi—the same demi that had manned the battery in the cesspool—sliced his scimitar straight across Mortal Jay's throat.

Mortal Jay. The warm, friendly, kind-eyed human who had only wished to know her. The mortal, the man, who had no kingdom to give her, but had tried gifting her the sky instead.

Everly watched in horror as his gaze—as his sincere, heartfelt gaze—sputtered. She watched as his fleeting life poured from his faltering form. She watched as that beastly ogre of a demi-sensore kicked his dying body off the building's uppermost floor. She watched as the Maelstrom fell away into the wind.

And then, and then flame—flame of searing white—scorched along the female's spine. Scorched down her back, from her shoulders to her arch, as the ivory kiss of Night shimmered free. As great, blinding wings—wings feathered of the brightest, bravest, fiercest of all lights—tore from her very being.

And the spectral—she beamed, a brutal, beautiful thing—as she envisioned the extraordinary pageant of anguish she was about to bestow upon every last halfling perversion assembled atop the ruined tower. For Everly did not just wield the might of The Everstar. No. She, too, commanded the light of the moon.

And with a soft laugh to those stars she forever felt but would never see, Everly Castile palmed that gleaming Isra Scorcher and flung herself at the demi-sensore host who dared hunt them.

Chapter 49

THE CROSSING

The cascades of ivory blossoms spilling from the stone terraces of the Cael Ostium twinkled like waves in the moonlight. And below those streams of glittering white, a large crowd had assembled on near-silent feet.

As the sahira and covelettes huddled together in their bone-washed linen wraps, they looked like a pool of pale flower petals at the yawning mouth of The Catacombs. Each one of the bleary-eyed sisters had been roused from their dreams, swiftly ushered into their Sorrow Stola, and then led through the tunnels to await the Diadet's decree.

From her cushion upon the central veranda, Savallin Prim, Keeper of Wisdom, quietly tracked each of Euclid's Sombers as they crept through the hanging gardens on their patrol of the gate.

On her right, kneeling beside the Keeper of Warriors, Amira Vasser, Lady of Summer, looked out at the faces of the covenary below. But on Savallin's other side, on her left side, both the fourth and the fifth cushion sat empty.

As her gaze traced along the stitching of the vacant Majlis seats, the Keeper's heart twinged at the memories of who last sat there. Young and naïve Phaedra Halla, Keeper of Whispers, felled by trust. And Coralis Carveil, the eccentric and clever Keeper of Wonder, lost to... well, simply lost.

Before she tumbled too deep into her own thoughts, though, the dark-clad figures lurking amongst the florets halted as one. And then, at her back, the line of brass horns along the stained-glass archways cleaved the midnight silence.

As one, the three remaining Keepers rose to their feet.

The horns had just reached their crescendo when the Diadet of Covenarykind stepped out onto the veranda. Her fair tresses had been woven into an intricate blossom at the crown of her head. And resting atop that fair head, a circlet of obsidian.

The Covenary Coronet.

The Diadet's long, silken gown floated like black feathers upon a gentle breeze as she glided to the terrace's stone balustrade. With her head held high, she placed both hands onto the smooth railing as she surveyed the gathered. The trumpets died out as Nirvana turned to Euclid.

The expression upon her face said it all.

Have you lost the entirety of your wits, Keeper?

Displeased at the public reproach, the Himalayan Huntress stormed off to scold her Sombers. Her words must have sailed swift, because below, in the crowd, the Keeper's warriors had already begun escorting the covelettes back inside. And only once they were gone did Diadet Nirvana address the assembled.

"Good, faithful sisters of Covenarykind," she said. "I thank you for coming this night."

Touching two fingers to her forehead, she drew them to her chest with a crescent moon. And when every sahira at the foot of the Cael Ostium had mirrored the gesture, the sovereign spoke again.

"It is with great sorrow, and the heaviest of Soul, that I must tell you now that a traitor has been discovered within the beating heart of our beloved Catacombs."

Oh, goddess, Savallin breathed. *Oh, goddess, no.*

Murmurs wafted up from the torchlit crowd as she whipped her head to the empty cushions.

Phaedra—

The colorful glass doors at the back of the terrace banged open and two of Euclid's Sombers emerged. Strung between them, her bare feet and shins scraping across the stones as they walked, was not Phaedra.

Savallin was already sprinting—already racing toward the two Sombers with her daggers drawn. Her steel would split their throats before either warrior felt its bite. Her feet made quick work of the distance. For the Sombers had not yet reached the center of the veranda when she leapt from the stones.

Neither even had the chance to look up as her blades hit home, as she muscled the daggers in deep, sweeping them from left to right. But the two warriors—even with her perfect kill blows—did not fall, did not falter in the least. No, for it was she who fell. She who clattered to the stones.

She had leapt right *through* them.

But the Keeper was on her feet and charging again as the Sombers paused before the balustrade. And the emaciated sahira suspended between them scarcely had time to look over her ravaged shoulder before Diadet Nirvana read her sentence.

"Coralis Carveil, Keeper of Wonder," the Supreme recited, "the Majlis of Covenarykind deem you *guilty.* Guilty of High

Treason. Guilty of practicing Seraphic. Guilty of *Skapahni* spellcasting."

Savallin hardly heard the words as she willed her legs to move faster, as she urged her breaths deeper, as she focused on that amethyst eye staring back at her.

"Due to the severity of your crimes, you, Coralis Carveil, are hereby sentenced to fade."

A scream tore from Savallin's throat as the two Sombers lifted Cora's broken body above the railing. The scream shattered when she saw the rope wound in their hands. But Cora's voice, it whispered into her mind one final time as the two warriors let go of her body.

The Keeper of Wisdom slammed into the balustrade just in time to see the noose pull taut. Just in time to hear her friend's neck as it snapped in two. Just in time to watch that fiery, waist-length hair fall limp.

A red-hot torrent of pain—pain unlike anything she had felt before—blistered through her veins, blistered through her consciousness, forcing her sodden eyes to fly open at last. And the moment they did, the moment her jade irises woke to meet the true night, the Keeper of Wisdom stopped breathing altogether.

For in the darkness, hovering not a hair's breadth from her face, were a pair of glowing, red eyes. And the rancid breath funneling from the monster's snout—it was so dense with decay it singed her skin.

But the Keeper did not dare blink, not as the stooped creature bared its mouthful of spiny, daggerlike teeth. Not as hot, rotting saliva spewed from its maw and splattered onto her cheeks. Not even when the chulu shide loosed a roar so guttural it shredded through the night around her.

Her bright green eyes stayed fixed upon that glowing red as she slowly eased her hand toward the knife at her thigh. She knew that any moment could be her last. Any movement too noticeable and the monster would strike.

What, she panted, *is it waiting for?*

Why had the beast not ended her already? But there was not a moment to spare in wonder. Not as the tips of her fingers finally grazed that cool, familiar hilt. She opened her hand to pull the knife free—but then, then a tiny pebble went skittering across the rock floor. The monster lunged.

But Audrian Adivostov had been waiting.

Her broadsword glinted in the starlight as she swung it low—just missing the swoop of Savallin's nose—before she angled up, plowing the silver blade through the cave demon's throat. With one slice, the Special Sentry severed the beast's snarling head from its bent body. The gargantuan skull rolled across the damp, painted rocks until it thudded into the still pool at the base of the falls.

And then, Audrian was beside her, hoisting her up by the forearm. "We must go. *Now.*"

The Keeper did not argue. Without so much as a word, she followed the spectral warrior past a second corpse—a second corpse with an impressive, still-smoldering hole burned through the center of its enormous chest. Audrian did not flinch; she simply kept climbing. So Savallin did, too.

Together they ascended the slope out of their makeshift camp, out from behind the mighty waterfall, out—into the horde of chulu shide waiting just beyond.

The rise to the sapphire ridge, to their one chance at escape, was wellnigh glowing red. In the light of the stars, the covenary could barely even make out the hundreds of hunched, leathery forms darkening the mountainside.

"What are they waiting for?" she begged.

Unsheathing a second, thinner longsword from her hidden scabbard, the everlast sentry passed it to the Keeper before answering, "To die."

From the look narrowing the spectraline's eyes, Savallin believed her. Enough, at least, to test the sleek rapier in her small hand. And when she did, she found that it was perfectly balanced, perfectly fit.

Beside her, drawing yet another blade—this one a beautiful, curving thing imbued with some type of shining, living script—Audrian grinned from ear to ear. "If you cannot take the head, Covelette, take the senses."

That was the sole instruction the sentry gave before flipping the curved blade once and charging up the hill into the crawling horde.

Sword in hand, the Keeper darted up the steep terrain after her. But the bloody cries of death and the dying were thick in the air when her short, mortal legs crested the first rise. There was no time to catch her breath, though. For a huge, colorless boulder blotted out the stars as it sailed for her.

The covenary pumped her arms harder, launching herself farther up the incline. But the darkness grew bigger still. Sav managed one more stride up the nearly vertical path before throwing her legs forward and pitching her body board-flat. The spinning projectile all but kissed her face as she slid beneath it—only to pull herself up again and continue running. She was still hurtling up the rise when the impact rattled the mountain behind her.

A wrathful cloud of upended earth and boulder dust swallowed the hillside—swallowed the hillside and Savallin upon it. She did not stop moving, though. No, without her sight to guide her, she focused on sound—on the whine of steel and the gurgles of misstep. She ran for it, shouldering past towering bodies and grotesque extremities with each step. And every stride, every hit, brought her closer, closer, closer until—until she, at last, broke free of that gray haze.

But when she did, when the darkness again enveloped her, the covenary could only watch—watch in utter disbelief, as the Special Sentry, as Audrian, cut her way through the masses of hulking beasts like they were nothing more than wayward stalks of wheat.

She was... gleaming... shining, like a star, in the black.

Swarms of chulu shide rushed at her from every side. And boulders—boulders of all shapes and sizes—rained down upon her from over the ridge. The night monsters, it seemed, were not mindless brutes. They attacked as one—the slashes of their razor-barbed limbs and the aim of their projectiles coordinated. But it was a dance, and she a dancer. For as the beasts sliced and as their rocks struck, the everlast warrior dipped and twirled and leapt out of their clutches.

Her back was turned when three massive figures dove for her at once. There was no heartbeat for Savallin to yell a warning, no heartbeat for her to raise the alarm. But the immortal sentry—she did not need one. No, for her body had already shot into the air, her figure surging up from the ground and tucking into a tight ball as she flipped backward through the dark sky, backward over the charging creatures. Three heads thumped to the dirt before she landed in a soundless crouch.

And then, with a roar so furious it ached the Keeper's chest, the next wave crashed in. But they were no match for the white-haired female with the wicked smile. As she moved, the broadsword, luminous in her right hand, ended every life that it touched, while the scimitar in her left eviscerated each new line of attacker from groin to gullet. Mounds of entrails steamed in the blackness as they spilled from the fallen.

And Audrian—she never stopped advancing. She was swifter than anyone, *than any being*, Savallin had ever beheld.

The Keeper had just kicked off the ground to follow in her companion's gory wake when—when something akin to the force of a landslide sent her flying. Her cheekbone sang as she smashed down into the sharp gravel of the mountainside.

The color leached from her skin as the nightmare with the glowing red eyes snarled over her yet again. She tried to wriggle loose, tried to drive her knee up into the terror's exposed torso, but she—she could not. The creature was impossibly heavy. Unnaturally strong.

Two sets of sharpened claws gouged the flesh of her upper arms as the cave demon reared backward, arched its hooked spine, and bellowed into the night.

A summons, she choked. But then—then she was frozen, unable even to think straight—as she heard the stampede of chulu shide thundering down the mountain, directly for her.

Her thoughts spun wild, coming in crazed jumbles, as she searched for an answer, for a solution—for anything she could use to save herself. But the Keeper came up empty. Found nothing—nothing until that distant voice whispered from her memory:

You rise now, or you shall not rise again.

Her mind stilled, her blood cooled, and then—then her hand turned. She would rise. If it was the last thing she did, she would rise. And when the cave demon lurched for her at last, when its warped spine and protruding chest closed in, she held onto Audrian's rapier with everything she had.

The slender blade disappeared into darkness as the beast impaled itself—wedging its chest farther and farther onto the sword. Its drooling jaw of spiky teeth slowing to a halt just shy of reaching her.

One powerful kick and the thrashing monster toppled to the side. Savallin rolled, regained her footing, and then stalked back toward the downed giant. And as it writhed upon the ground beneath her, as fury contorted its horrific face, the Keeper of Wisdom plunged the everlast's sword straight through each of those glowing red eyes.

"That felt good, did it not?"

The covenary swiveled, her steel held high, ready to spill blood until—

"Easy, slayer," Audrian said, smirking like a sated cat. "Are you about ready to go?"

Savallin started—not at the lip, but at her. At the thick, black blood matting her pale hair, her face, her—but then she saw what lay behind the female. A new mountain had risen. A new mountain of vile, twitching corpses. *The stampede.*

The Keeper blanched. "How... how did you—"

"Immortal," she sang, tossing her scimitar into the air. "Remember?"

Savallin, instantly sorry she had asked, only stared daggers at the everlasting pain-in-her-backside before stomping up the gore-smeared incline.

"More come," Audrian said, catching up to her with a single step. "A lot more. From over the ridge." She wiped the muck from her blade with the linen of her pants. "Worry not, Covelette."

And at that, the covenary paused, trying to anticipate what the spectral would say next. But then, she said it: "The true danger is yet to come."

"The true danger?" The Keeper exhaled through her nose. "What true danger? What is worse than—"

A fresh barrage of boulders poured from the heavens.

"Run," Audrian ordered, again icy-cold, as they sprinted up the rise, hurdling body after body on their final push for the ridgeline.

The boulder rain did not break, but neither did they. And though her lungs burned with effort, the covenary kept moving forward. After several long heartbeats, after a handful of close calls, they were nearly there—there atop the mountain with the ridge looming just before them. But then, a soul-stealing crack boomed through the darkness.

The spectral warrior in front of her skidded to a halt, those eyes of coldest ice blazing bright as she whipped around. She was airborne in an instant—that powerful, deadly body soaring through the night, soaring for—aiming for—*her.*

Audrian's outstretched palms were still pressed into the Keeper's chest, still driving her down into the stone, when the mammoth hunk of mountainside smashed into her body.

A scream—Savallin's scream—split the world in two as the Special Sentry disappeared before her eyes. That head of moon-kissed hair vanished into the pitch blackness, vanished into nothing. And the stars above—even they guttered in the night. For even they knew, knew that the brilliant, blinding immensity of immortal strength coursing through the warrior's body had not been enough to keep Audrian Adivostov from sailing off the sapphire ridge.

The covenary could not breathe. She could not remember how to. Not as the warmth of those hands began to fade. Not as she lay there, flat upon her back where the Special Sentry had left her. Not as she lay in the very spot where Audrian had deemed her own life less valuable than hers. No—Savallin could not breathe, and neither did she wish to.

But behind her, below her, thousands of blood-curdling roars tore through the night—tore through her grief. And the Keeper's sight began to pound, to blur. Then, from deep within the ravine before her, new shrieks—ghastly shrieks, far too many to count—exploded into the sky. The mountain beneath her began to tremble.

The covenary understood then—understood in her heart of hearts—that it was all over. That everything she had done, every bit of earth she—they—had trekked, it was all for nothing. Their journey to the Jade Isles, their desperate crossing to find what had been lost, to find *who* had been lost—finished. The Midnight Message would forever go unanswered.

And yet, even with the inevitable barreling toward her, even with the end in sight, Savallin was not yet ready to let go. No. She would not let go. For there was something hidden within her, some intrinsic part of her being, of her soul, that would never allow it. Perhaps it was the everlast rubbing off on her. She could not be sure.

Whatever it was, though, it had the Keeper shoving herself off that gravelly stone. Her legs shook and her head throbbed, but she rose nonetheless. And in her hand, gripped so tightly her knuckles whitened around it, was the only piece of Audrian she had left. She smiled, then, at the slender blade. Because when the hordes came for her, Savallin would go down fighting.

The chulu shide reached her first, lunging and snarling and hissing as they crested the ridge. The covenary ground her feet into the uneven stones beneath her and swung her sword true. Carcass after carcass fell, gutted and bleeding, upon the sapphire. But the cave demons were strong. And every strike, every slice of her rapier, cost her. And the pack just kept coming, kept charging at her with no signs of slowing.

The Keeper sidestepped springing bodies, ducked below others, even rolled out of the way a time or two. But still, the mountain's edge found her. The heel of her left slipper skidded backward, sliding across the sharp gravel until—until there was nothing left beneath it.

She did not turn around, though. No. She surged forward, driving off her right foot to cleave a leathery torso in half. The two pieces slunk to the ground in a wet heap at the precise moment the skreiching from the ravine overwhelmed Savallin's mortal body.

The cries became all-consuming, wholly unbearable—their sheer volume sending the covenary crashing to her knees. Her rapier bounced across the stones, and she stretched for it, managed to graze it with her fingertips. But then, just as she pushed that little bit farther, a flurry of wings shot from the canyon.

She tucked herself into a tight ball, covering her ears with the bulk of her arms. But she did not close her eyes for even a heartbeat. She watched—watched as the swarm of creatures swelled from the canyon and careened into the chulu shide.

They were horrid. Truly horrid. And even worse, they had spotted her. Pinned to the ridge and unable to get to Audrian's blade through the melee, the Keeper drew the dagger from her thigh. But it was short, and the devil from the depths— the horse-sized monstrosity with the body of a bird and the head of a serpent—had no flesh to pierce. No flesh, at all. For it was skeletal, its entire body, from its fangs to the tip of its bony tail.

Skeledima, she rasped, hurling her dagger for its head. *The true danger.*

Audrian's warning was ringing in her mind as her blade flew wide—as she missed the attacking beast. Yellowing fangs and melted feathers snapped for her face as the steel clattered to the sapphire stone. Savallin freed her last knife. She counted her breaths. And when the monster closed in, when there was nowhere for her to go, she sprang forward. Raising her arms above her head, she thrust that knife into the roof of the beast's mouth.

But the skeledima, it did not so much as notice. No—it only cracked its bony maw impossibly wide before lurching once more. With nothing left save herself, the Keeper willed her body to the side as the devil struck. Its fangs rang out against the stone—the stone she had just been standing atop.

But the moment she dove, the moment she slipped the skeledima's grasp, another nightmare swept for her—a chulu shide that had been lying in wait. The monster's claws ripped into her belly as she rolled into its path. Where they scraped, flesh split. Her vision spotted and her wounds ached, but she made herself small. So small, that when the depth devil screamed by to carry the attacking chulu off the cliff, it did not even notice her.

But her wounds—they were grave. And they were seeping. The blood from her body spilled atop the sapphire rock like a river of ruby. Her strength, too, was spent. And when the fangs of yet another devil rose up above her—when the skeledima was poised to open her throat—the final words of the night's *first* heartbreak settled, at last. The final words of Coralis Carveil, Keeper of Wonder.

And only as the Keeper of Wisdom lay alone, sprawled atop that ridge high in the Rainbow Alps, did she, at last, understand the note that had been hidden within the fable. Only then did she realize what she thought had been a terrible nightmare was, in truth, so much worse. And only then did she fully appreciate the fiery-hot pain that had surged her body from sleep. For it was not pain, but *power*. Cora's power. Cora's very *Soul*.

my strength will soon be yours.

And now, with every last dark eater already privy to her whereabouts, there was no reason not to use it. So, when the skeledima reared back to swipe at her for a second time, Savallin let the Earth Song sound. She listened inward, then listened deeper—listened to the melodies of Her as they flowed beneath her feet. And when she heard the one she wanted, she grabbed hold of it, then she pulled. Pulled on that Seraphic tune until it no longer lived within the ground, but within her own body, her own blood. And then, she erupted.

The Keeper siphoned barred charm from the earth as she bellowed to the stars. Jade light—jade light streaked with ruby—blasted from her body, blasted down the mountainside, blasted into the night itself, incinerating everything in its path.

All across the alp, chulu shide and skeledima turned into steaming piles of ash. Carcasses fell from the sky and toppled from the cliffs as the light—as Her light—consumed them. The roars and shrieks and howls were silenced as one wherever that searing Seraphic struck.

But the ruby-jade light kept flowing—kept burning hotter and brighter and louder. Kept swelling, until the covenary began to sway upon her feet. And not even when the last cave demon and canyon devil had crumbled to the charred earth did that mighty movement of charm cease.

Savallin willed it to stop. She begged it to stop. But none of her commands, none of her pleas, could be heard above the song—above Her song—above the stolen song. No matter how loudly she wished it, no matter how fiercely she rallied her own Soul against it, the Seraphic charm would not stop flowing. For the Keeper had taken too much. Siphoned too much. And now—*now* she had to pay.

And so, she embraced it when her mind pounded against the confines of her skull—when it tried frantically, hopelessly, to escape. She embraced it when her heart, her steady, beating heart, began to boil within her chest. She embraced it, welcomed it, as sizzling pain licked up every bit of her earthly body, as it invaded every facet of her soul. Savallin endured it all—every moment of it. And she was at peace. For she had done all that she could. She had fought to the bitter end and she had taken them all down with her.

The Special Sentry might have even been proud. Might have. And although it was shallow and shattered, the covenary laughed. Then she thought of her sister, of Coralis, who would never believe a word of her tale. And the Keeper laughed again.

And as the world around her again fell silent, as the world within her did the same, as each rise and fall of her chest exacted a steeper toll, the covenary's once-bright eyes dimmed in the darkness. And yet, as the Seraphic scorched her mortal body from the inside out, Savallin Prim, Keeper of Wisdom, youngest-ever Majlis of Covenarykind, wore a smile upon her face.

Chapter 50

THE CESSPOOL

"Ava?" The toe of a boot nudged her side. "Samurai?" Vasquez crooned again. "You still with us?"

When the Sergeant did not move, her partner crouched low. Even with her eyes sealed tight, she could feel it—his stare roving over her. She could feel it as that movie-star grin of his widened upon imagining the damage he might have caused.

"Well," he sighed before jostling her lifeless shoulder. "Clearly, you're even more breakable than you look."

Time, she screamed silently. *I need more time.*

"And that"—he shook her harder—"is really saying something."

But even with his prodding, his violent rattling, the Sergeant still could not move. The sensation in her extremities, the strength in her muscles, her limbs—it had not yet returned.

And at this point, as she lay there slumped upon the ground, utterly helpless in the face of an admitted mass murderer, Sergeant Ava Carlisle wasn't so sure the feeling would ever come back.

Vasquez, aware that time was not on his side either, let his temper get the best of him. He lashed out, his palm stinging against her cheek. And yet, she held completely motionless. Even against the uproar filling her mind, she willed her face, her mouth, not to react.

Time, she repeated. *Time.*

It was her only chance. Her only play. He struck her again, harsher this time. She did nothing—did not so much as exhale.

Why was he trying to wake her anyway? Why didn't he just kill her and get it over with? What was it he wanted to know so badly?

His palm sang against her face for a third time. Her teeth slammed atop one another, drawing blood from the edges of her tongue, but she clamped her lips together and did not open them.

Time, she breathed to herself again. *Buy yourself time.*

And just like that, the truth struck her harder than any of his slaps. For Vasquez—her partner—was doing the very same thing she was. *Buying time.*

He needed to know if she remembered it was him who had knocked her out, if she was truly a loose end in need of tying. A loose end he would have to sacrifice precious time to knot. *To kill.*

And then Vasquez brought that angry hand down for a fourth time. The force was too much, his strike too great. There was nothing she could do to prevent the flutter in her eyelids. And her partner—he had not missed it. Not even in the darkness of the empty trampoline park.

"Ah," his voice was thick and smooth as richest honey. "There you are."

Stall, her wits shrieked. The nervous beat within her chest was slower than it should be. *Whimper and play dumb, if you have to. If you wish to live.*

"Welcome back, *Ava*."

"Sergeant," she rasped shakily, knowing full well that even upon death's doorstep—even facing down the devil himself—she did not have it in her, neither to whimper nor play dumb. "It's Sergeant Carlisle, to you."

When her eyes shot open at last, the only thing they saw were his. The muddy brown ringing his irises, dead as dirt. Dead as she would soon be if she didn't come up with something.

"All righty, then," her partner teased as he brushed away the errant strand of midnight hair that had fallen across her face. That he had knocked across her face.

"For that, *Sergeant Carlisle*," he mocked, sounding out every syllable, "I promise you—"

This should be good.

"I will stage your death to look like the most pitiful, careless, and meaningless of any accident to ever take the life of a law enforcement officer in any line of duty in any city's history."

And as her ogrish partner finished spitting his hatred for her—and her rank—as he knelt there above her half-prone body, the Sergeant's attention snagged upon the thin scar she had spotted earlier. The faint line sketched across his tanned throat.

For it... it was now—now lit by the darkness. Burning. His scar was practically *burning* with silver.

What had happened to him? she wondered. *What kind of weapon leaves a mark like that?*

But he was wholly untroubled by it, it seemed, as he leaned over her to check her belt. To check where her duty weapon should have been. The duty weapon she had dropped in the ball river.

"Dammit, Ava," that happy hatred gave way to mild frustration when he discovered her holster empty. "Well," he exhaled. "From my count, I'd say you pumped about forty-five, forty-six rounds into our perpetrator back there."

Forty-six rounds... all three clips... an entire canister of pepper spray... and it hadn't even fazed him.

"Hmm... I guess that rules out your gun," his weight shifted back onto his heel as he scanned the room around them. "Wherever it is."

The Sergeant begged her legs to kick, pleaded with her arms to push off the ground. It was useless, though. No matter how she asked, no matter how she wished and wanted, her body refused.

"Obviously, I can't just pop off and shoot you with mine," Vasquez snorted, turning his wayward focus back onto her. "Besides," he reassured her, once again brandishing that superstar smile, "where's the fun in that?"

Stall, the Sergeant kept demanding of herself. *Stall.*

She needed both more time and more answers.

"Okay," her partner said, sliding his big forearms beneath her. "Up we go."

What had he and that—that thing—been arguing about? What had it said?

Vasquez rose without effort—hefting her weight—and the added bulk of her weapons belt and vest—as if she were no more than a box of late-night takeout.

What was it that creature had called me? The Sergeant's mind spiraled as her partner strolled toward the EXIT sign casting the farthest corner of the darkened space in gloomy red shadow. *What—or who—was that thing in the first place?*

"*Shit*," Vasquez hissed to himself, slamming his smooth saunter to a shocking halt. His massive chest heaved, only once. And the Sergeant knew it was not exertion, but outrage.

Outrage at what?

"I forgot all about that bitch outside," he groaned.

No. Her fury crackled to life. *No.*

For the girl outside—the young, frightened 911-caller— she was totally innocent, had only picked up the phone to ask for help, to beg for help. She did not deserve to die for it.

"Well, something tells me she'll be joining you rather shortly," he shrugged before resuming his stroll toward the back door.

No. No more innocent lives.

The Sergeant had to make him forget about the girl. She would make him forget about her. At least long enough for backup to arrive.

"How do you know that thing, Vasquez?" Her voice was too high, her speech too fast. "Why are you covering for it?"

Her partner glanced down at her as he shouldered open that heavy door in the corner. And even in the rickety red glow, she had little trouble reading the snarky expression plastered atop the arrogance upon his face. *Whoever do you speak of?*

Fucking piece-of-shit asshole.

"That ugly bastard that attacked me?" she bit. "The very same ugly bastard that attacked *you* first?"

Beyond the EXIT doorway, there was no exit at all. No— just a stale, poorly lit stairwell descending into Mother-knows-where. Vasquez began the climb down.

"He's family," he smirked after a thoughtful pause.

"In what world?"

For Vasquez was built like a dark-headed, one-ton diesel, and that—*that thing*—it was thrown together like a banged-up, electric scooter low on charge.

"He's... well, it's an older sort of relation."

The Sergeant's heart pulsed as a wisp of movement tickled her toes.

"My scent," she gulped, trying to mask her rising excitement. "My scent—you said it was the only reason you didn't kill it... kill your... that thing."

Vasquez's too-white smile shone in the dimness of the stairwell as he turned a landing and continued heading down.

"Why?" the Sergeant asked.

It wasn't until he reached the third flight down that he parroted the question back to her. "Why?"

She said nothing, only nodded and waited for him to go on.

"Why is a good question," he admitted. "Between you and me, I probably should have killed him a long time ago. But, well, his father was kind of a big deal in this city."

And as her partner elaborated, as he strode across the next landing, a wave of sharp prickles washed through her curled fingertips.

"And I thought that another premature death in their household would raise too many unwanted eyebrows."

The sour air grew warmer as they descended farther and farther below the ground floor.

"Again," she growled. "What does any of that have to do with me?"

"Easy, Samurai," Vasquez laughed, taking the steps two at a time. "I was getting there." He shook his head of dark hair. "But basically, long story short, *his* overt failure led me directly to you. Back to you, I mean."

The muscles in her core tightened at the softness of his words.

"You see, that witness I silenced for him—she had the same scent emanating from her body as you do now."

The same scent? The Sergeant crinkled her nose. *Jasmine and cactus flower? Aluminum and cruelty-free?*

"Did you... kill her?"

"Of course not," her partner cackled. "That would've been rookie-level obvious. The *only* living witness in a high-profile arson investigation suddenly dead? *I think not*, Ava."

Vasquez continued bounding down the steps, two and three at once, as if he were simply on another of his twice-daily exercise jaunts. And Sergeant Carlisle, in spite of her current circumstance, found herself breathing a bit easier with every next stride.

"No," he beamed, the pride he had in his inspired plan plain to see. "Even better. I got my hands on her burner and made her a simple promise. If she used her voice in court, mine would be the last heard by every soul in her speed dial."

"Yeah," the Sergeant couldn't help herself, "what a cruel and unusual fucking punishment that would be."

And as she glared up at him, his long legs ate up yet another landing. In the lull, she tested the mobility in her calves, her thighs. And then, a small dimple dented Vasquez's cheek as he crooked his mouth up and to the side.

"Well, I was sort of hoping she'd put up some kind of a fight. You know, so I'd have the opportunity to work some answers out of her," he said, not the slightest bit winded *or* bothered. "I mean, you *are* killers after all."

What... She blinked wide against the blackness. *What in the actual fu—*

"But then, there you were. Placed before me like a teensy-tiny answered prayer."

The bottom of the dark stairwell was finally in sight, but the Sergeant remained still, frozen in her partner's arms, unsure of exactly how to proceed as he closed the distance.

Keep. Your. Cool. she urged herself when he pushed the bar on the steel door with his hip. *Keep stalling. Just a little while longer. Backup will be here any minute.*

"What do you mean, Vas?" she asked, refusing to take her eyes off his. "What do you mean, *you are killers?*"

The laugh that shook his body was not a thing of joy. In fact, he stopped moving altogether. Paused in place as the heavy steel door creaked closed behind him. And then, the moment the rusted hinges quit their screeching, Vasquez glared down at the woman in his arms.

"You and your filthy people," he snarled into her face. "You are nothing more than murderers."

Drugs, she decided. *He has to be on drugs.*

"The Mudamira," he gritted, every word hewn of hate, "they are the slayers, *the executioners,* of my ancestral people."

PCP? That might explain his buddy's resistance to lead... or... or maybe HGH...

"What I wish," Vasquez seethed, squeezing her body ever tighter, "what I wish is to know how they did it. How your people—weak and inferior in every way—defeated mine."

Could it be as simple as too much supplemental testosterone? Her thoughts reeled as she rifled through the options. *Too many supplements in general, perhaps? Is that... a thing?*

"Anyways," her partner exhaled, cheerfulness unexpectedly flooding his voice once again, "that's all I wanted to ask you, Ava. All I wanted to ask her. Alas," he sang, "it appears we just don't have the time."

And then—only then—did Sergeant Ava Carlisle break her stare. Only then did she peel her eyes from her partner and take in her surroundings. Only then did she comprehend how absolutely fucked she truly was.

At the hopeless expression draining the last drops of sunny-sand brown from her skin, Vasquez piped up, "So, you don't know what this place used to be?"

Holy Mother, she breathed to no one. *Holy, Blessed Mother.*

The stale air that had been seeping into the dim stairwell was a thousand times worse in the windowless vault before her. And while it was murky like the building above, this space had a creepy radiance all its own.

Row after row of cylindrical enclosures rose from the rotting floor and stretched toward the sagging ceiling overhead. Within each one, a viscous, snotty, goo-like substance bubbled up and floated atop the static contents of the glass cisterns.

"It was some type of below-board research facility," he stated as if it were the most commonly known fact in the world. "Yeah, I don't know exactly what they were studying here, but I do know it must've been quite dangerous." The fist beneath her knees knocked onto the wall of the nearest enclosure as he added, "Because these puppies—they were built to withstand some rather extraordinary hellions."

In her chest, her heart shook its stupor and began thundering at speed. Every fiber of muscle strung along her frame buzzed and thrummed with nerve. And then—then the rest of her body, every last cell, joined in the willful chorus. The furious melody, an instant reminder of precisely what that gods-forsaken stairwell had returned to her.

Strength. Her strength. In that stairwell, the roles had reversed. For now—now it was her body that begged her to stand. Her body that implored her to hold her ground. Her body that beseeched her to fight back, to kick this miserable motherfucker right in those giant, movie-star teeth of his.

Wait, she breathed, trying to calm herself, her thrashing energy. *Wait. Stall. Buy time.*

For Sergeant Carlisle was dreadfully aware that she would only have one chance—one shot—to strike her much larger partner down. He was strong. Too strong. And she knew she could not outlast him, not in close-quarters, hand-to-hand combat. She would have to be fast—ruthless. And most importantly of all, she would have to choose her moment with the utmost care.

Vasquez meandered through the rows of cloudy vats as he talked, as he scoped each one out, searching for that perfect prison. That perfect coffin.

"The only reason I even know this lab is down here," he admitted, "is because Lochlan's father was the developer who funded the renovation.

Lochlan? She started. *That thing... that creature... its name is fucking Lochlan?*

"This"—Vasquez, still holding the Sergeant to his chest, did a grand spin that ended at a burbling cistern in the center row—"this was his last project before filing for bankruptcy. And when the money did dry up, the contractor tucked tail and just left. Left this festering cesspool down here."

No, her mind roared. *No. No. No.*

For her cheap body cam would never survive the plunge. Not in—whatever that shit was. No. Everything it had recorded—the mangled, drug-fueled man-monster named Lochlan, Vasquez's full fiery confession, this half-assed murder plot—it would all be wiped away.

"Drowning in decay seems fitting, don't you think?" The question—his stupid wink—sliced like a dull spoon. "For a stuck-up, goody-goody whore, like you."

End it or be ended, Ava.

"Any last words?"

Time, she choked. *More time.*

"Suit yourself," he shrugged, tucking her body in closer as he readied to lift her above his head and over the stained lip of the cistern. "Deuces."

She had run out the clock. Run out her clock.

"Why was that—he—so pissed off at you?" she gasped as her sense of self-preservation took over, clawing for anything that might save her. "If you came to his rescue, why did he attack you?"

The reflection of the arcade neons in the pool of his blood twinkled in her memory.

Vasquez stilled, the color in his eyes suddenly enveloped by... by a shade of darkness the Sergeant had never before beheld. He was so rigid, so lost in himself, she didn't think he was going to reply. But then—then that trademark grin spread across his jaw once more.

"Well, you see," he laughed, "ole Loch and I, we fucked around and found ourselves in a bit of a mess last night."

The Sergeant's gaze fell upon his scar as he swallowed.

"And I... well," his chest swelled as he inhaled, "this time, I let him take the fall."

"You expect me to believe," she forced herself to snicker, "that *that* spindly worm got caught, but your giant ass was somehow missed?"

"*I* had an exit strategy." Sheets of triumph fell like rain from each of his words. "A very convincing exit strategy."

And her frantic mind must've gotten a thrill from toying with her, because his scar—it was now blazing.

"The truth," a wet voice driveled from the shadows. "It comes out, at last."

Officer Vasquez whirled toward the broken sound so fast that the Sergeant's head swam.

A vein bulged and slithered up the side of his neck as he scanned the hazy vault around them. His thick lashes lowered and stilled when his eyes narrowed in on what they sought. The haunted gleam of the glass enclosures cast an eerie sheen atop his dark hair as he began creeping past them.

And as the Sergeant watched her partner skulk through that vault, as she felt the nerves mounting within him, not even she could have imagined that there would come a time the slavering voice of that shattered creature would sound like sweetest music to her ears.

This was it, she knew. This was her shot.

"Put me down," she whisper-ordered. "Put me down or we're both fucked."

And the very heartbeat her partner remembered she was there—the very heartbeat he paused his prowling to look at her, the very heartbeat he angled his face toward her—she rammed her forehead into the unguarded bridge of his nose.

His was the stunned inhale that could be heard round the boroughs.

As he staggered backward, closing his eyes and trying to block the surge of pain, his hands faltered. It was enough. With all the strength she could muster, the Sergeant pitched her body into a roll away from his, away and out of his meaty clutches, and then she hit the ground running.

But her escape—daring and clever as it was—was short-lived. For Vasquez had collected himself unthinkably fast and was already hot on her heels. And before her, crouched upon all fours in the red flicker of the EXIT sign, Lochlan blocked the only way out.

She did not stop sprinting, though. No. Reaching into her weapons belt, she ripped her taser from its plastic case and aimed ahead.

Four steps to go and what had once been a man named Lochlan filled her sights. Three steps and she lowered the targeting lasers ever so slightly. Two steps and she threw her legs out to lead the way. One step—one slide—and she pulled the trigger on her last hope.

The taser prongs fired straight up, straight into the creature's undercarriage as the slight Sergeant slid beneath him.

And then, as the thing shrieked and wailed in her wake, she was back on her feet and storming for the heavy door. She was nearly there—just a few more hard breaths between her and freedom.

Faster, she screamed. *Move it or lose it, Ava!*

And then she was there—her shaking hand wrapped around the metal pull bar. Gripping it for dear life, she tore backward but—

But her partner had stolen a play right out of her own book. The *click, click, click* of the firing mechanism struck her eardrums a heartbeat before his shot found its mark. The sharpened prongs of his own taser pierced the soft flesh just below her vest and just above her belt.

It was a perfect aim, a perfect shot. Waves of hottest electricity burned through her veins. Her muscles rioted and cried out as any and all semblance of control was torched from her very being. Her insides convulsed, over and over, as her stubborn body fought on.

But in the end, it was not a battle she was meant to win. Her body blazed through its reserves, racking one final time before locking up for good. The Sergeant crumpled to the floor at the foot of escape. Not far from where she fell, Lochlan's wrecked form lay still, locked by the current.

Vasquez was nearly doubled over with laughter as he stepped over his flunkey and strode to her. Just shy of where she lay, he bent over and snatched the barbed end of a steel wire up off its coil. He was still chuckling as he squatted down before her and wrenched the end of that wire firmly around that same strip between her vest and belt where the taser prongs had embedded.

Then, stretching back toward where he'd found the makeshift binding, he casually slid what had to be a three-hundred-pound concrete anchor over his forearm before again scooping the Sergeant's paralyzed figure off the ground in the other.

No, she wept, every thought an almost unbearable tax. *No. No. No. The body cam.*

The square anchor hit the foul liquid first. And as the greenish-yellow fluid sloshed like snot over the rim, as that block sank below the surface of the cistern, the barbed wire tightened and began slicing into the Sergeant's lower torso.

"For real this time," Vasquez sniggered with the broadest of grins upon his face as he hefted her body upward. "Later, loser."

And that was that. That was all her partner said before letting go and dropping her body into that fusty vat of sludge.

The moment she went under, streams of rot and slime slithered up her nose and burrowed into her ear canals. And still, she sank lower and lower before the anchor, at last, hit the bottom of the tank. All the while, she tried her best to relax, tried her best to ration the little oxygen she held in her mouth, in her lungs.

As she wrestled to overcome the paralysis, to untie the wire weighing her down, Vasquez watched her—giddy fascination spreading across his features with every split of her skin, every gush of her blood that leaked into the toxic goop, every slip of her hand as she raced to undo his bindings.

But then, after either getting his fill or being satisfied with his handiwork, he knocked his knuckles against the thick glass in farewell and turned back toward the door they had come.

"Don't worry, Samurai, I'll be right back," he called over his retreating shoulder. "I'm just gonna grab our little friend real quick."

No, the Sergeant's silent pleas burst into a wild bellow. *No!*

Too far. He had already gone *way* too far. To now threaten a teenager, to harm her—a scared girl who had seen almost nothing? No. In no way, no way in this world, did she deserve to die for being in the wrong place at the wrong time.

But there was not a thing she could do. Not to help her, that young girl. No. She had not even been able to save herself. And as her lungs screamed for oxygen she could not give them, as her inner ears began to ring and skreich, as the flesh tore away from her fingers and palms, she still could not free herself from the anchor holding her under.

A furious, unbridled pressure surged through her. From her toes to her skull, it poured in, flowing swiftly and violently, shoving against every bone of her frame. But even still, the Sergeant couldn't hold out any longer. Nobody could have. For even her level of defiance, it was no match for the mortal body's need for air.

Her mouth gaped wide and her chest shuddered brutally as her very own lungs betrayed her. As her very own lungs compelled her body to swallow. As she did swallow—as she pulled that rancid muck down her own throat.

And as Officer Vasquez swung the door ajar and marched into that stairwell, as he twisted back to wink at his drowning superior one last time, as she pictured the life he was headed to snuff out, as Sergeant Ava Carlisle stopped choking and started dying—that rampant fury building within her forced its way out.

The imposing glass enclosure, the corpse motionless upon the rotten floor, the vile, scheming partner sneering from the stairwell, the entirety of that condemned cesspool—the Sergeant's very world itself—flared from sickliest green to purest jade.

Chapter 51

THE CITY

The streams of light spilling through the bedchamber's sheer curtains were streaked with the dancing shades of afternoon. Far, far below, down at street level, the midnight legion of red and blue had faded with the darkness more than a day ago. The slabs of gore had been shoveled, the splatters of blood sprayed away. And even still, a full sunrise and a half separated from that penthouse, the soft embrace of the feathered mattress beneath her refused to relent—refused to let her go free.

She might have stayed there all afternoon, curled beneath the plush down coverlet. Might have nestled into her pillows late into the new night, even. But as she stretched her legs long, as she arched her spine high, as her sleep-heavy eyes parted at last, something stirring in that shadow-laced air gave Everly Castile new life.

Breakfast.

The intoxicating smell of sizzling pork belly and pan-fried sweetbread had the female rolling out of bed and into her slippers. She was out the door and down the hall in a blink. And waiting for her—simpering at her with a dish towel thrown over his bare shoulder—was the Brigadier.

"The Night Heir?" she prodded a quarter hour later, her cheeks near bursting with syrupy toast. "You told the demi-sensore you were ordered here to find The Night Heir?"

"I had to tell them something," he sighed, scooping another powdered-sugar-cinnamon slice onto her heaped plate. "Those little bastards kept cutting out my tongue."

The warm slice did not survive its new home for more than a few heartbeats.

"A bedtime legend," the female laughed. "You saved your miserable hide with a bedtime legend."

The miserable warrior slapped her hand with his spatula when she reached for another piece of the maple-and-brown-sugar-crusted pork.

"No," he grinned. "The promise of a spectraline warrior, a warrior so mighty that only they might once again align the sun and the moon, saved my miserable hide."

Everly snorted. "Folly."

"Is it?"

"Yes."

"Well," Bristol popped a forkful of spiced peach into his mouth, "your demi-sensore brethren certainly didn't think so."

Her eyes couldn't have spun harder if she commanded it.

"First of all, Bristol, they were demi-brained." A fat chunk of cocoa-almond banana loaf shot for his face. "And second of all, how many times am I going to have to drill it into your thick skull that I only pretended to go along with their delusions to save us some godsdamned time?"

A basic strategy Everly knew her counterpart had been employing as well. For the male—the male that had just forked the hurtling bread straight out of the air—could have ripped free of his shackles any time he wished. But enticing the hunters, giving them a reason to gather, was, simply, as efficient as could be.

The Brigadier, though—he just adored being an ass.

"I don't know, Ev. That scowl on your face," he replaced the moist chunk she had launched, "you could've fooled me."

"A fecal-furred swine could've fooled you." She stabbed the prongs of her fork into a link of peppered meat. "I was not going to kill you. That would've been a bland waste of my prodigious talent."

Bristol, arching his brows to sarcastic heights, turned for the fridge.

"I mean, would I have enjoyed causing you a little more distress? *Absolutely.* But would I have ended your eternity to prove a point?"

The male set a frosted carafe of citrusy-pink nectar upon the counter.

"Actually... maybe."

"I tried to tell you, you know. Right here, in this very Ever-forsaken kitchen. I tried to tell you that I had not, that I did not complete The Rite." He poured two frosted glasses to the brim. "And wouldn't you know it, you bit my fucking head off before I could even begin to explain."

Everly made a pouty face. That did not sound anything like her. Didn't ring any bells, either.

"And whose fault is that?" she exhaled. "Seems like, to me, you didn't try very hard."

At that, the warrior snatched the second glass of juice out of her reach.

"Your mortal interrupted us."

My mortal? Oh, please.

"Speaking of," Bris paused, "why didn't you fly for him?"

It was a fair question. Why hadn't she flown for the man with the kind face? The man with the soft eyes and the warm smile. She could've made it, to where he hung, before that ogre keeping guard had even remembered the blade clutched in his fat, sweaty hand.

In the absolute chaos that had overtaken that charred penthouse, Everly and Bristol had not had a chance to hash everything out. No, they had both been far too preoccupied with seeing which one of them could rid The Empire City of the most halfling scum.

It had been a total farce, of course. Everly had won the bout by a mountainslide, dispelling thrice as many Star Hunters as the larger, lumbering Brigadier.

"It was too late for him," the female admitted, taking the tangy, blush juice by force. "His was a soul not even I could hope to save."

She thought of him then, as Bristol's brow furrowed. She thought of Mortal Jay—of how helpless and hurt he had looked as he disappeared over that edge. Of how he, a human, had almost knocked her to the ground the first time they met. Of how he, a man of the modern era, had an ancient phone hidden amidst his closet. Of how he, a man with an innocent presence, had lied to her with unnatural ease.

For he had never spotted Everly walk into the atrium of this tower. He had never pried her name from the cobalt-crowned barista at the corner café. Nor had he ever given it to the building concierge and been sent to her floor. No. For this apartment, her barista—neither of them had ever heard mention of an Everly Castile.

"Plus," she hummed pensively, "I don't think it was my inaction that did him in."

For there had been no thrum. No thrum in her ears—*not from him, at least*—as the masked men beat and kidnapped him from the airfield. Nor when he had been electrocuted in that morbid aquarium. Not even when his electrocutioner had raised the blade to his throat at the tower's edge.

There had, also, been a handful of other tells. Like, for instance, the way that gingered demi leader had kept glancing toward *him* for approval. And the way his mortal body sometimes had trouble containing the Maelstrom living within.

"He told me you stayed over that night, you know," she shrugged, scenting the bittersweet juice. "That night after our barbeque."

"Is that so?"

"Yes, he told me not to worry for you because you had spent the night on his couch." The female sipped the nectar. "Spent the night, and awoken next to a girl."

"Oh?" The spectraline cocked his head to the side in wonder. "What did this girl look like?"

"Too mortal for your liking."

Bristol chuckled, nearly drenching the marble island in a mist of rosy spittle.

"That's when you knew, then?" The brute had the gall to look offended. "That I'd been *taken*."

And regardless of the finger quotes still airborne on either side of his face, the claim had raised her eyebrows—raised the alarm. Because throughout the solars she had known him, throughout even the centuries they had been apart, Dalon Bristolwood had only ever bothered with one female.

The magnetism had been so strong, so woven into the starlight in his veins, that he had gutted himself to protect it. To protect her. He had piled his honor atop her memory and buried them both. He had willingly betrayed her, knowing that in doing so, he was losing her forever. Losing her for all eternity. All so that she might live on.

"Well, *that*"—Everly said, blinking the enormity of that heartbreak away before extending her empty mug toward the male who had so long borne it—"*and* the prick put Lastisap in every coffee he brought me."

Bristol stopped mid-pour. "And you still guzzled them?"

"Eh," she shrugged. "I didn't hate it. It gave them a bit of a... of a nostalgic zest."

Making a face that showed just how poorly he thought her tastes to be, the male filled her ceramic mug halfway, then topped it off with ice-cold milk and three cubes of sugar.

"Okay. Question, then. Two, actually," he said, sliding the cooling, milky brew into her eagerly awaiting palms. "If Mortal Jay was in on it, if he was a demi-sensore, how did he get your information? Truthfully, I mean."

The smooth ceramic warmed her skin as the Brigadier considered.

"Even if your perverse pastimes were luring the hunters out of their sewers, you would never be so casual as to let that ilk trail you home. And that mortal—he did not see you walk into this building."

The female offered him a knowing smile over the lip of her raised mug.

"So why, if they had your address the whole time, would the demi-sensore fire-bomb the wrong tower?"

Fire-bomb the wrong tower they had, all right, she seethed. *Just not that night.*

But in all honesty, she had been pondering the first question since that day the mortal had appeared in her elevator lobby—since the day after *she* had blown up her own penthouse to see what the hunters would do. The hunters she had not yet had a name for, but had sensed following her. And it had not been until she was trailing Lochlan across that burnt-out apartment floor that the last part of the riddle was laid bare.

She grinned wide, beyond pleased that the shield had not yet pieced it all together. "It's all in the name."

With an exasperated breath out, the warrior leaned down, resting his elbows upon the counter, and then waited for Everly to elaborate.

"Tell me, Brigadier," the female whispered, spinning the coffee cup in her hands, "do you speak The First Tongue?"

The steady rise of Bristol's chest stilled. His relaxed posture stiffened. And then, when he again straightened, the realization hit him like a catapult to the forehead.

"Stayella Zvezdami."

"Stayella Zvezdami," Everly echoed, an unmistakable grimness washing across her newly bright features. "Amongst the Isra, even the slightest slip of The First Tongue, Bris, it was a—"

"A death knell."

And after taking a deep, sweetened drag of milky goodness, she nodded along. "And where, since the..." Her mouth dried out.

Bristol, seeing her light gutter, saved her the heartache.

"There is but a sole stronghold still standing where one might learn The First Tongue."

One stronghold.

"Helavos."

One spectraline stronghold. The very same one, in fact, where what's left of the scum who had ordered Bristol to poison himself—to torture himself—with Seraphease were now holed up.

"More will be coming, then," he breathed, his Brigadier's mind already working up a plan. "Many more."

But then, sparing her the climb into that crevasse of nightmares, the timer on the oven began chirping with the fury of a canyon devil. Bris whirled, donned the hot pads, and reached into the lowered door with a feline-like swiftness.

And when he faced her again, a pan of perfectly golden blueberry cake shone atop his oven mitts. She stared, wide-eyed. She might have drooled. She might have been mouth-breathing. But then, as Bris flipped the cake onto a plate and slathered the still-searing top in a healthy coat of butter, Everly found her composure once more.

He cut a thick slice, dusting it with finest sugar before passing it over to her. It was her favorite. It had forever been her favorite. She gazed at the gorgeous cake—at the piece of art laying upon her plate—and for a moment, all her worries slipped away.

She fisted her fork. But then, right as she was about to shove that entire Sempedormir-sent cake into her mouth, a knock sounded at the entry door.

As one, the two spectral glanced from each other to the door, and then back. The rapping grew louder, the tranquil sea in Bristol's eyes beginning to rock and pitch. The warm, golden, buttery blueberry cake suddenly laughing in her face. And as the knocking continued, the female sighed through her nose.

"Don't you go anywhere," Everly purred to her beautiful blueberry cake. "I will be right back."

And then, Everly Castile rose from the barstool and padded toward the front door.

Chapter 52

THE CITY

"That color truly suits you, Ava. Just as they all have," Alice had said as she waved her through the door of The Crypts. "That cross look, though—it does not."

And Ava was still a bit puzzled by the odd exchange as she climbed the front steps of the address written upon her little slip of paper. But still, she walked inside, where the well-dressed man stationed behind the tall marble desk took one especially hard look at her badge before pointing her toward the correct bank of elevators.

She thanked him with a quick nod before turning on her heel to make her way through the sprawling, urban rainforest that was the building's atrium. The elevator bank she needed was the farthest one to the left.

"Go straight past the pink dogwoods and don't turn until just after the palest azaleas," the concierge had instructed.

It took her less than a minute to locate and walk the proper path. Her calls didn't typically bring her to establishments like this—not to sparkling skyscrapers that could double as indoor parks. Winding herself to the leftmost bank, she pressed the call button and waited. The ding of the arriving car beckoned her to the end of the waiting area. She reached it just as the elevator's two steel doors slid open.

It wasn't until she had walked onto that mirrored car, until she had hit the glowing number to initiate its rapid ascent, until she had watched those shiny doors close her in, that Ava realized Alice had not told her what to ask.

No, the somewhat eccentric psychiatrist-mystic had only given her the folded slip, promising her that the answers she needed most would be found there—there being the address she had penned for her upon the paper. And then? Then Alice had reassured her that she would handle all matters at the police station before unceremoniously escorting her out.

Classic, Ava sighed. *Classic crazy.*

If she hadn't been counting the numbers as they ticked upward on the car's large monitor, she might not have believed the elevator was moving at all. The ride was so smooth—so unnaturally smooth—it was slightly off-putting, if she were being honest. But then, the number stopped climbing and the doors parted once more.

Ava slipped the creased paper back into her pocket before striding out into the foyer. A cursory scan indicated to her that this particular floor held but a single unit. And at the foot of its entry door, a rolled-up newspaper waited to be read.

Who the hell still gets a paper? she wondered as she stooped to pluck it up. *Oh, for fuck's sake.*

For as she raised her arm to begin knocking upon that front door, she skimmed the headline printed in bold font across the top of the first page.

Bros will cover for bros, it seems.

She knocked again, this time her frustration giving each rap a little more umph than the previous.

Even in death.

But then, just as her knocking escalated into a full-blown frenzy, the lofty door swung open. And Ava—she forgot every manner she had ever been taught. For the woman standing on the other side of that threshold was staring down at her with eyes too bright to be of this world.

And as the young Sergeant turned to stone upon that doorstep, as she blinked and stumbled over words, the woman crafted of light itself lifted two polished fingers to her brow before drawing them to her chest in a crescent-moon motion.

"You look well," her voice was as sultry as it was sure. "Different, but well." And then, then the slyest of smiles bloomed across that staggering face as she added, "Worlds better than the last time I saw you, *Diadet.*"

And if Ava Carlisle thought she had been startled before the woman spoke, then she was flat-out thunderstruck now. While her senses waged war on her sanity—while they battled to rationalize what was happening, what and who she had just waltzed into—her traitorous mouth, for once, remained soundless.

She didn't know what to say, how to respond to this strange woman—this strange, shimmering woman who seemed to know exactly who she was. So... Ava did the only thing she could think of in the moment. Without a word, she extended the rolled-up newspaper white-knuckled in her hand.

And thankfully, the lady of smirks and secrets accepted her mute offering, glancing gracefully at the front page—at the two portraits plastered upon it in black ink. Then she went still—impossibly still. So still, in fact, that the half-dressed gladiator, who must've been eavesdropping from the kitchen, stalked from his post to peer over her slim shoulder.

And right as Ava was seriously contemplating making a mad dash for the elevator at her back, the woman with eyes of living silver shocked her yet again when she whipped that head of star-kissed hair around and laughed, "Told you, Bris, it *wasn't* my inaction."

BREAKIN

OBLITERATED IN THE LINE OF DUTY

HEROIC ECPD OFFICER JAY VASQUEZ VAPORIZED DURING DARING RESCUE OF DISGRACED REAL-ESTATE BARON'S ONLY HEIR

THE END.

ARCHIVE
OF APPENDICES

Appendix II

THE LINE

THE ERAS

THE DAWN

With the dawn of day came the rise of The Samaritan. Three mighty, everlasting Saviors given to this world to defend its people, The Fleeting, from the darkness that would come to claim them. For millennia, The Sword, The Shield, and The Shepherd did just that, working as one to fend off the darkness. Until came the day they became the darkness.

The eras that followed are named for the war that defined them: The Great, The Good, The Gone.

THE GREAT

The Great War was the longest-spanning conflict in history. For centuries, Savior battled Savior for dominion over Jidana. After tremendous loss on both sides, The Shield prevailed. This is known as the war that felled Beasts.

THE GOOD

The Good War though much shorter in span was far worse in casualty. For when the vanquished rose, they did so with a strength The Shield was not prepared to face. By its bloody end, two of the three Saviors had fallen. This is known as the war that felled Saviors.

THE GONE

As the darkness faded from Jidana, so did the surviving Savior. Their deeds, their victories, and their sacrifices became nothing more than myth whispered into the night as the reign of The Fleeting began.

Appendix III

THE LEXICON

THE PEOPLES

Note: *Commonly used slang variations are written in parenthesis.*

THE SPECTRALINE (SPECTRAL)

The last Savior of The Samaritan. Immortal beings crafted from the might of The Everstar herself; The Shield; The Everlast in other tongues.

THE ISRASENSORE (ISRA)

The Savior who wasn't. Immortal beings crafted of light who fell into darkness; The Sword.

COVENARYKIND (COVENARY)

The mortal Savior. Contrary to their counterparts, the sisters of the covenary are mortal. And yet, they were given a gift the others can only dream of—magic; The Shepherd; Earth Casters in other tongues.

LESSERKIND

The entirety of beings, fleeting in make, that The Samaritan was forged to protect. The most populous among them is Mortalkind.

THE PLACES

THE CONSERVATORY

(Good Era) A fortress-like battle academy built where the earth meets the stars. This mountaintop stronghold in the Lunaerian Vale is where spectraline young train to join the ranks of The Shield.

THE CATACOMBS

(Good Era) A sprawling cave system spilling from the heart of Jidana herself. This intricate, winding subterranean citadel is home to the sahira of Covenarykind.

THE CITADEL

(Great Era) A long-abandoned spectraline stronghold nestled between the banks of the South Caspia and Artera rivers. Within its ruined bounds lie the star-scraping columns known as The Pillars of the Sky.

THE CROSSING

(Great Era) Not so much a place as it is a path, The Crossing is not kind to those who dare enter.

THE EMPIRE CITY (THE CITY)

(Gone Era) A shimmering metropolis of glass and steel, known informally as The Mortal City, situated upon the shore of the former Mortal Coast. It is but one of the many mortal citadels that flourished in the wake of the Good Era.

THE PARTICULARS

Note: Commonly used slang variations are written in parenthesis.

━━━━━━━━━━━━━━⟡•⟡━━━━━━━━━━━━━━

Aerie Arras: a flying tapestry woven of sand; *magic carpet* in other tongues.

Beacon of Beasts: an archaic early-warning system built into the mountaintops of the Lunaerian Vale.

Beast of Old: a fearsome and long-extinct giant of the sky; true name, ísdreki; also known, informally, as devil of the night, the forgotten; *Lunamici* in other tongues.

Brightbreak: a shield of light that can be raised as a form of camouflage; *Stellae* in other tongues.

Cael Ostium: the main entrance into The Catacombs.

charm: the innate power of Covenarykind; presents in one of two tunes; *magic* in other tongues.

chulu shide: a dark, hulking creature that lurks in the blackest caves of the Rainbow Alps; also known, informally, as dark-eater and cave demon.

covelette: a young covenary.

covenary: a member of Covenarykind; can be of either sahira or skapahni descent; of or relating to Covenarykind; *castress, earth wielder,* and *witch* in other tongues.

Death's Dominion: the colloquial name of the Rainbow Alps.

demi-sensore: the offspring of a mortal-israsensore pairing.

Diadet:	the supreme ruler of Covenarykind; also known as Sovereign Supreme; *Queen* in other tongues.
Dyasus:	the last day a sixth-series may return from the Twenty-Third Canon; *Spring Equinox* in other tongues.
Earth Song:	the song of the goddess Her; the well of power used to summon Seraphic.
earthstone:	stone of the earth that is black in color; *obsidian* in other tongues.
Eternity's Eye:	the black sands at the bottom of Widow's Finger; the name comes from the whisper that the sand is not black at all, but rather a mirror into a dark past.
Ever Step:	the sacrificial dais built atop The Pillars of the Sky; an altar among the stars; also known, informally, as a Sky Step.
Extori:	a spectraline oath-breaker forgotten by time; an ousted.
General Praelior:	The Spectraline Shield's highest rank, General of Generals.
giver:	a spectraline who brings forth offspring; *parent* in other tongues.
Hadi:	the third deity of Covenarykind, the goddess of death.
Helavos:	the spectraline stronghold home to the Seat of Reminisce; also known, informally, as The Crevasse Citadel.

Her:	the first deity of Covenarykind, the goddess of life; also known, informally, as The Mother.
Hollow:	the second deity of Covenarykind, the goddess of the gap.
Illicit Offering:	the archaic and banned spectraline practice of sacrificing mortals to summon unholy power.
israsensore (isra):	a member of The Israsensore; of or relating to The Israsensore.
Keeper Tutelage (Tutelage):	the secretive schooling a Majlis must complete to earn the title of Keeper.
Keeper:	the title bestowed upon a Majlis who has completed her Tutelage; *Mage* in other tongues.
Known and Not:	the two classifications of realms; those known, or seen, by The Everstar and those that are not.
Korol Qanun:	a directive given by The Spectraline Senate that, in the event of their downfall, the Kings shall again be raised.
Lastisap:	the sole toxin capable of rendering an immortal mortal; produced from the sap of the orchards that grow atop only the bloodiest of killing fields.
Lesserkind:	all beings without immortality; including, but not limited to, Mortalkind; *The Fleeting* in other tongues.

Lumin:	the gift of clairvoyance bestowed by The Everstar upon The Spectraline; its bearer becomes either a Thought-Teller or Thought-Twister; *Cosma* in other tongues.
Lunae:	wings woven of pure moonlight that a spectraline can only claim by stealing the life of the beasts who bear them; *The Night's Wings* in other tongues.
Majlis:	a covenary selected for Keeper Tutelage.
Mudamira:	the apostates; *Shatteress of Sword* in other tongues.
Night:	the deity of The Israsensore.
Parallel:	one half of a spectraline pair vowed, for all eternity, to share the burden of Lumin.
Premier:	the specling who has accrued the most Scars and is ranked highest in their series at The Conservatory.
Priyatel:	a spectraline promised to complete The Rite of Parallel.
Qamar Vsadnik:	one of the few and famed vsadnik lethal enough to fly as part of The Israsensore Iclara; *Moon Rider* in other tongues.
Raise:	the act of elevating a covenary to the position of Majlis and then, upon completion of her Tutelage, to Keeper.
Relicelm:	a type of tree, similar to petrified pine in appearance, that is toxic to The Spectraline.
Sahira Sway (Sway):	a shield of charm that can be raised to alter appearance; *glamour* in other tongues.

sahira: a covenary with the ability to wield Soul.

Scars: the points awarded to a specling based on their performance in The Canons.

Seat of Reminisce: the cathedra of The Sempiterne Scholars.

Seer: a being capable of seeing The Yet.

Sempedormir: the Heaven realm in spectraline faith.

Sempenihil: the Hell realm in spectraline faith; *The Realm of Flame* in other tongues.

Seraphease: a tonic, originally created by Covenary-kind, to aid in the healing of mortal; when abused, however, its side effects are unnaturally sinister.

Seraphic: the unnatural tune of charm; *Lyric* in other tongues.

series: an academic year at The Conservatory; *class* in other tongues.

shield: a warrior of the The Spectraline Shield; of or relating to The Shield.

shihan: an instructor of The Conservatory; *teacher* in other tongues.

skapahni: a covenary with the ability to wield Soul and Seraphic.

skeledima: a monstrous, winged creature that prowls the darkest depths of the Rainbow Alps; also known, informally, as canyon devil and depth devil.

solar: the period of time required for Earth to circle The Everstar; *year* in other tongues.

Somber:	a covenary guard under the command of the Keeper of Warriors.
Sorrow Stola:	a bone-washed linen wrap customarily worn by the covenary during periods of mourning.
Sorrow:	the deep, lilac waters at the center of Widow's Finger; named for the countless lives lost to its depths.
Soul:	the natural tune of charm; *Lull* in other tongues.
specling (spec):	a spectraline who has not yet graduated from The Conservatory.
spectraline (spectral):	a member of The Spectraline; of or relating to The Spectraline.
spiraseris:	a spiral-mawed creature that swims the sands of the Auburn Dunes hunting for charm; also known, informally, as dune dweller and sound serpent.
Stayella Zvezdami:	a militia of demi-sensore; *Star Hunters* in other tongues.
Stellae:	a shield of light that can be raised as a form of armor; *Brightbreak* in other tongues.
Taiso:	a specling who remains undefeated through all twenty-four Canons of The Conservatory.
Tellings:	foretellings gifted by the covenary goddess, Her; *Prophecy* in other tongues.
The Canons of The Conservatory (Canons):	twenty-four brutal tests, administered over the course of six series, designed solely for assessing competency in combat.
The Chasm of Rozvaline:	the crevasse in which Helavos is located; also known, informally, as The Black Chasm.

The Covenary Coronet:	a circlet of peaked earthstone worn by the Diadet of Covenarykind; *crown* in other tongues.
The Cry of Illicit Offering:	the tolling of an ancient gong that accompanies The Night Song.
The Ever Language:	the language of The Everlast; *The First Tongue* in other tongues.
The Everstar (Ever):	the deity of The Spectraline; *Bright* in other tongues.
The Eyes of The End:	eyes, like burning rubies, rumored to see the darkness within; *The Orbs of Fire* in other tongues.
The Fallen:	the honored dead of The Spectraline.
The Five Majlis (The Five):	the council of five Keepers who serve as advisors to the Diadet.
The Fleeting:	the covenary term for a being that is not long-lived.
The Forbidden Hours:	the darkest hours of the night, those that fall when The Everstar is farthest from the sky.
The Immortal Tear:	a large, pearlescent, tear-shaped jewel that has long rested atop Eternity's Eye, at the bottom of Widow's Finger.
The Infinite Spring:	the prophetic stream that flows from the heart of the goddess Her.
The Israsensore Iclara (Iclara):	the most savage and storied legion of The Israsensore's aerial force; also known, informally, as The Screaming Sky Legion.
The Klekta Mortem (The Klekta):	the deadly, abandoned prison beneath The Catacombs; *The Death Promise* in other tongues.

The Living:	a covenary expression referring to all beings of The Surface.
The Malqatil:	those who sentenced the Shamed Sisters to death; also known, informally, as the Songbird Slayers.
The Night Heir:	a warrior of myth and legend whispered to wield the celestial might required to once again align Bright with Her Night.
The Night Song:	the song sung to summon a Beast of Old.
The Oath of Obscurity (The Oath):	the vow a shield takes to uphold their eternal duty from the shadows.
The Obsidian Throne:	the covenary seat of power.
The Orbs of Fire:	the last sight of the doomed; *The Eyes of the End* in other tongues.
The Pillars of the Sky (Pillars):	a collection of earthstone spires, located within the Citadel ruins, that are so jagged and lofty as to scrape the stars themselves.
The Realm of Flame:	the volcanic realm of eternal punishment; *Sempenihil* in other tongues.
The Rite of Parallel (The Rite):	the ceremony that forges two lives into one and seals the Parallel bond for all eternity.
The Samaritan:	the three saviors crafted to shelter the spinning of time; The Sword, The Shield, The Shepherd.
The Sempiterne Scholars:	the sect of The Spectraline tasked with preserving the secrets of time; *The Lasting Scribes* in other tongues.

The Skapahni:	the last covenary of skapahni descent; also known, informally, as The Shamed Sisters of Covenarykind and The Shamed Sisters.
The Spectraline Senate (The Senate):	the governing body of The Spectraline.
The Spectraline Shield (The Shield):	the lethal force of spectraline warriors sworn to protect Lesserkind.
The Surface:	the above-ground realm; the home of The Living.
The Swear of The Shield (The Swear):	the vow of eternity a warrior must make to be granted entry into The Spectraline Shield.
The Vitoska:	the prominent black stone where the rankings of each series' specling are etched.
The Yet:	that which is still to come; *Kismet* in other tongues.
True Malice:	an often-overlooked darkness that plagues Lesserkind from within.
tune:	the classification of charm; can be either Soul or Seraphic
Valo Markings (Valo):	a star-like marking seared into the flesh of The Spectraline that only becomes visible during The Forbidden Hours; the penalty for stealing an eternity.
vsadnik:	a warrior in The Israsensore's aerial force; *rider* in other tongues.
Widow's Finger:	a tall, earthstone chimney, resemebling an old, yearning finger, that hides both secrets and a hollow, water-filled center.
Winds of Hadi:	the last song of the goddess Hadi; the song that carries Covenarykind into the afterlife; also known, informally, as the Hail of Hadi.

PRONUNCIATION GUIDE

Aerie Arras	Air-ee Uh-ross
Amira Vasser	Uh-meer-uh Vass-er
Cael Ostium	Kay-ul Ah-stee-um
Chasm of Rozvaline	Chasm of Rahz-vuh-leen
chulu shide	chu-loo she-day
Coralis Carveil	Cor-al-is Car-vale
Cosma	Cause-muh
Dalon	Da-len
Decard	Deh-kerd
demi-sensore	dih-mee-sen-sore-ee
Diadet	Die-uh-det
Dima	Dee-muh
Dyasus	Die-a-sus
Euclid Istra	You-clid Ee-struh
Extori	Ex-tore-ee
General Praelior	General Pray-lee-or
Hadi	Hay-dee
Helavos	Heh-luh-vose
isdreki	ees-dreh-kee
Israsensore	Ees-ruh-sen-sore-ee
Iclara	ee-clair-uh

Jidana	Jih-dahn-na
Korol Qanun	Ker-ole Kuh-nun
Lunae	Loo-nay
Lunaerian	Loo-nay-ree-un
Lunamici	Loo-nuh-mee-chi
Majlis	Madge-lee
Malqatil	Mal-kuh-teel
mea est tuum	may-uh est toom
Mudamira	Moo-duh-meer-uh
Phaedra Halla	Fay-druh How-luh
Priyatel	Pree-uh-tell
Qamar Vsadnik	Kuh-mar Vuh-zahd-nick
Relicelm	Reh-lih-kelm
sahira	suh-heer-uh
Savallin Prim	Suh-va-lin Prim
Sempedormir	Sem-pay-dor-meer
Sempenihil	Sem-pay-nih-hil
Sempiterne	Sem-pee-tare-nay
Senator Dnesda	Senator Dih-nez-duh
Seraphease	Sair-uh-feez
Seraphic	Suh-ra-fick
shihan	she-hahn
Shihan Halor	She-hahn How-ler

Skapahni	Skuh-paw-nee
skeledima	skel-ih-dee-muh
Soledad Adaleya	Sul-ih-dad Add-ih-lay-uh
Spectraline	Speck-truh-leen
spiraseris	speer-uh-sair-is
Stayella Zvezdami	Steh-lay-uh Zivez-dah-mee
Stellae	steh-lay
Taiso	Tie-so
tuum est Meum	toom est may-um
Valo	Vay-low
Vitoska	Vih-toss-kuh
vsadnik	vuh-zahd-nik

MEET THE AUTHOR

Luz Evan Kanin is a lifelong reader and lover of fictional worlds. After growing up in Texas, she packed her things and moved across the country to live along the waves of the Atlantic.

These days she can usually be found pounding blueberry cake donuts, munching on chips and queso, slurping ramen, or taking cold brew to the dome.

On the rare occasion she's not stuffing her face, hot girl walk-ing under the sun, or being an embarrassment on social media, Luz busies herself crafting the worlds only reachable through ink and dreams.

ALL TITLES BY LUZ

Mindless Among Us

all the shops in charlotte are closed
all the airports in atlanta are closed
all the motels in memphis are closed

Heir of Ever

Kingdom of Time
Realm of Ruin (Dec 2026)
Chasm of Chaos (Dec 2027)

Kitchen of Time

Let's Get   Shop
Social   Now